STARSTRIKE

STARSTRIKE

BOOK TWO IN THE MOONSTORM TRILOGY

YOON HA LEE

DELACORTE PRESS

Delacorte Press
An imprint of Random House Children's Books
A division of Penguin Random House LLC
1745 Broadway, New York, NY 10019
penguinrandomhouse.com
GetUnderlined.com

Text copyright © 2025 by Yoon Ha Lee
Cover art copyright © 2025 by Priscilla Kim
Map illustration copyright © 2024 by Daniel-Andre Sorensen

Penguin Random House values and supports copyright. Copyright fuels creativity, encourages diverse voices, promotes free speech, and creates a vibrant culture. Thank you for buying an authorized edition of this book and for complying with copyright laws by not reproducing, scanning, or distributing any part of it in any form without permission. You are supporting writers and allowing Penguin Random House to continue to publish books for every reader. Please note that no part of this book may be used or reproduced in any manner for the purpose of training artificial intelligence technologies or systems.

Delacorte Press is a registered trademark and the colophon is a trademark
of Penguin Random House LLC.

Editor: Hannah Hill
Cover Designer: Liz Dresner
Interior Designer: Michelle Canoni
Production Editor: Colleen Fellingham
Managing Editor: Tamar Schwartz
Production Manager: Tim Terhune

Library of Congress Cataloging-in-Publication Data is available upon request.
ISBN 978-0-593-48837-9 (hardcover) — ISBN 978-0-593-48839-3 (ebook)

The text of this book is set in 11-point Adobe Caslon Pro.

Manufactured in the United States of America
1st Printing

The authorized representative in the EU for product safety and compliance
is Penguin Random House Ireland, Morrison Chambers, 32 Nassau Street,
Dublin D02 YH68, Ireland, https://eu-contact.penguin.ie.

Random House Children's Books supports the First Amendment
and celebrates the right to read.

For Ursula Whitcher—mathematician, writer, poet, game designer, scholar, and all-around inspiration

ALL CLEAR   DEPLOY

SERPENTINE

TOPAZ

NACRE

Abalone Gravitational
Observatory

SPINEL

CORE WORLDS   PERIPHERY WORLDS

CROWNWORLD

CITRINE

AC281-51B1-06-55

THE MOONSTORM

CARNELIAN

THE EMPIRE OF NEW JOSEON

PREVIOUSLY, IN *MOONSTORM*

In the Empire of New Joseon, gravity can't just be manipulated; conformity and ritual *cause* gravity. The Empire constantly seeks to expand its borders and enforce its own traditions using the deadly mecha known as lancers. This brings it into bitter conflict with the clanners who live in the wilds of the Moonstorm.

Hwa Young was ten years old when her clanner moon disintegrated during an Imperial attack and a lancer pilot rescued her. Six years later, she's a ward of the state, determined to become a pilot herself. She gets her wish the hard way: during a clanner attack on her new homeworld, she and her classmates are recruited by New Joseon's Eleventh Fleet.

Hwa Young bonds with the lancer *Winter's Axiom* and joins the squad. To her dismay, so does her nemesis from school, queen bee Bae, and class clown Seong Su. Hwa Young's best friend Geum is rejected by the lancers and instead becomes a technician.

Hwa Young's old rivalry with Bae evaporates after Seong Su dies in action. But their newfound camaraderie is jeopardized when Hwa Young learns that her clone-mother Aera didn't actually perish when her clanner moon home was destroyed, and Hwa Young's rebel heritage is exposed. Even worse? Aera claims that the Empire is preparing to deploy a monstrous weapon, a singularity bomb powered by amplified faith in the Empress that sacrifices people to create a ravenous black hole.

Aera is right. The Empire's First Fleet unleashes the singularity bomb to destroy a clanner base. Faced with a harrowing choice, Hwa Young and her fellow pilots narrowly prevent the tragedy by destroying the bomb's power source—the designated human sacrifices. This is high treason. They are forced to seek refuge with the clanners.

HWA YOUNG

Hwa Young, pilot of the lancer *Winter's Axiom*, hated navigating by the stars. She'd learned the techniques and calculations as an orphan in the Empire, a ward of the state—and she'd excelled at them. But she'd been born a clanner on the border, one of the denizens of the unruly Moonstorm, and clanners grew up knowing that *their* territory featured wandering stars and itinerant moons.

Stars are meant to wander free, Mother Aera whispered to Hwa Young in her earliest memories. *Stars are meant to fly. Not stay chained like jewels in the collars the Empress provides her pets.*

As a clanner child on the world of Carnelian, Hwa Young had navigated by means other than the stars: familiar trees and boulders, land formations and the give of the ground underfoot, a subtle awareness of characteristic smells and air currents. How the clanners navigated in *space*, where there was a paucity of trees and boulders and land formations, she didn't know. But the clanner fleet that she and her lancer squad had defected to, *they knew the way.* That had to be enough, she thought as they flew toward their current objective—New Joseon's Jasper Research Station, located on the largest outpost moon of the world Jasper.

This mission—this one mattered more than usual.

If the intel she'd retrieved from her friend Geum proved reliable, and if they extracted a critical codebase on lancer-pilot neural interfaces from Jasper Research Station, Commander Aera—Hwa Young's long-lost heart-mother—might *finally* allow her to enact her plan to retrieve Geum. Her best friend, a skilled technician, was stuck on the Imperial flagship, where they'd been forced to leave zir behind when Hwa Young and her lancer squad turned against the Empire—a memory that still crushed Hwa Young. Even worse was the fact that Geum remained imprisoned after helping Hwa Young escape.

Though they'd been covertly communicating ever since, Geum had proven reticent about giving the clanners a lead on real intel, as opposed to what Aera uncharitably termed "random distractions," code for intel that didn't advance the clanners' military aims. Hwa Young told herself that Geum was trapped with the enemy and had good reason to exercise caution. Getting caught collaborating with the clanners was a sure death sentence. But even Aera (*commander,* not *heart-mother;* one of the many adjustments Hwa Young was still making) conceded that the promised codebase would represent a breakthrough in the clanners' attempts to replicate Imperial lancer technology. It was the one thing they wanted above all else—the very tech Hwa Young and her fellow lancer pilots possessed—and the crucial missing piece was the intimate mental link that lancers shared with their pilots.

This hunt has too many hunters, Winter's Axiom remarked, right on cue. Its voice was drier than usual, like a cold night after the obliteration of ice.

We have our orders, Hwa Young reminded it, trying not to be perturbed by the odd echoes in her skull, as though the lancer spoke with a multitude of voices and not one. It wasn't the first time she'd experienced peculiar sensory effects through the link. Some of them, like the way it shared its scan data like a map inside her head, were useful. Others—well. She was still adapting.

At least *Commander* Aera had done her homework based on the clanners' dossier on Jasper. Awkward as Hwa Young's interactions with her heart-mother had been since their unexpected reunion, she appreciated the woman's fundamental competence.

"Jasper wasn't originally Imperial territory, decades ago," Commander Aera had said during the briefing. She'd met with the lancer pilots in a designated conference room. The crisp holographic maps detailing friendly clanner strongholds and known vs. projected Imperial movements had contrasted sharply with the absurd riot of purple-green vines and potted flowers growing up the bulkheads, the effervescent fragrance of starblooms and pungent smell of damp earth reminding Hwa Young vaguely of her old clanner moon home. "We didn't notice we'd lost the world until . . . well. There was a political complication. Border territory has always gone back and forth; it's one reason border moons often have Hangeul-speaking communities.

"We've intercepted a distress signal regarding raiders, so we'll offer emergency assistance while our agents secure the codebase. You'll deal with the raiders, and Falcon Fleet"—the clanner fleet they belonged to—"will evacuate Jasper's personnel to safety. It's similar to our previous rescue-and-goodwill missions, but you'll be operating within sensor range this time, rather than securing the perimeter. The codebase is our primary goal, rather than rescue and evacuation."

The other missions they'd executed during the past few weeks had involved border communities with ambivalent loyalties, some of which included people of both clanner and Imperial descent. Falcon Fleet lacked enough supplies to care for that many civilians. They'd made stopovers time and again, transferring their human freight to other clanner fleets that would convey them to resettlement in safe locations: Ekphora Fleet, Canopic Fleet, Stupa Fleet, and others with foreign names she had difficulty pronouncing.

"Commander, aren't you worried we'll cause panics?" Hwa Young said, remembering just in time to address Aera with the proper honorifics and formality levels. At times, she felt like a child all over again; had intense flashbacks to *But, Heart-Mother, could I have another cookie?* She wouldn't embarrass them both by regressing.

Out of the corner of her eye, she caught Eun side-eyeing her because of her unusual diffidence. She rarely criticized missions, not when so much was at stake—for the clanners, for her squad . . . for her relationship with Commander Aera.

Aera's expression didn't alter. "Explain, Pilot."

Hwa Young's heart sank at Aera's dispassionate tone. Why was Aera making her spell this out? "A lot of clanners only know of lancers as weapons that can take down a starship. As *Imperial* weapons. They might not have heard that we're friendlies—or they may panic anyway. I just . . . I wanted to be sure there was a plan to deal with any panic so that people don't get hurt."

"We have liaisons in Communications dealing with that," Aera said after a moment. "You needn't worry."

Besides, if the mission failed, it would blow Geum's opportunity to rejoin her. Aera had said time and again that she'd authorize a rescue of Geum once she was able to present evidence of Geum's usefulness and reliability. Hwa Young hoped a success *this* time would do the trick.

"So we're framing this as a goodwill mission, although the primary objective is intel," Commander Ye Jun said, smoothing over the moment of tension between Hwa Young and Aera. Ye Jun led the lancer squad and was Hwa Young's immediate superior in the field. Aera, as second-in-command for all of Falcon Fleet, outranked zir, but the two addressed each other as equals. Hwa Young kept trying to figure out whether the guarded quality to the interactions between her heart-mother and Ye Jun was due to mutual caution or genuine courtesy, or she was imagining it entirely.

To say Hwa Young felt ambivalent about the chain of command was an understatement. Her first week with Falcon Fleet, she'd answered an order with *Yes, Mother* rather than *Yes, sir*. She was determined to track down every witness who'd guffawed and drown them or, alternately, offer them her lunch money for the rest of her life not to talk about it.

Commander Aera nodded. "We want to present ourselves as a friendly presence. It will make the agents' job easier. Jasper's people will be grateful for the intervention, and we'll have negotiators on standby to keep matters calm. You don't need to worry about that. We'll follow up with our auxiliary supply ships, which is standard operating procedure, but we want you to make the initial contact this time."

"It doubles as cover for the intel-gathering too," Ye Jun noted, and Aera didn't deny it.

Hwa Young rolled her shoulders, fruitlessly attempting to bleed off her tension. The protective charm in her pocket, a carved wooden starbloom given to her as a welcome gift by a clanner ensign, made her feel off balance, even with its slight weight. So far it hadn't done much for her luck one way or the other.

There was a dark aching gap at the back of her mind. The squad numbered four, where there should have been five. She did not want to think of the fifth pilot or his death.

Yet an unwanted moment persisted: the taste of the chicken and rice porridge Seong Su had gotten for her, a mediocre prepackaged meal, yet all the more delicious when she was a refugee crammed into a starship's storage bay. It flooded her mouth. She wasn't sure whether the gnawing in her stomach was hunger or nausea or the acid residue of grief.

"Research station has entered long-range visual," Bae reported now over their comms. She piloted *Farseer One*, the recon unit. Hwa Young noted the characteristic grace and precision of *Farseer*'s flying, her eyes lingering a moment longer than necessary over the way it swerved past a stray micrometeorite.

"Understood," responded Eun, the fourth member of the squad with *Hellion*. He'd served as a pilot longer than Hwa Young or Bae, as Ye Jun's second-in-command. Here, he sounded bored, with none of his usual acerbic growl. Hwa Young, who had been trained by him, wasn't fooled.

From a distance, the research station resembled a crumpled piece of chiaroscuro circuitry spread incongruously over the moon's rugged, dull green surface. Bae, piloting sleek, swift *Farseer*, hovered just out of the base's estimated scan range, making sure not to silhouette herself against Jasper's sun. *Farseer*'s advanced sensor suite transmitted an updated close-up view to all the pilots. It would also alert them when the raiders showed up.

Through her neural link to *Winter's Axiom*, Hwa Young could see the station and its machinery in her mind's eye: everything from gun mounts, consisting of simpler pedestal designs with a limited range of motion, to supercooled quantum computer cores; from the pumps and filters of life support to the pulsing glow of the base's power generators. While the lancer's cockpit provided displays monitoring everything from navigation to threat analysis, the link was faster and more intuitive.

"We've got twelve incoming starships below the plane of the ecliptic," Bae said over the comms, enunciating with exaggerated clarity.

"Do you have ID?" That was Commander Ye Jun from *Bastard*.

"Not yet," Bae said, sounding vexed. "I can't get IFF"—Identification Friend or Foe—"on the units at all. Which argues in favor of raiders rather than Imperial forces."

"What the hell kind of raiders fly in formation?" demanded Eun. Like Hwa Young and Ye Jun, he hung far back. His lancer, *Hellion*, specialized in artillery. While *Hellion* had heavier armor than the other three, he did his best work from a distance.

"I imagine any raiders who *don't* coordinate their attacks don't survive," Ye Jun said dryly.

Hwa Young, whose lancer was the sniper unit, took up a position to the rear, tenuously sheltered by one of the smaller moonlets. More of a glorified asteroid, to the extent that the distinction mattered in the Moonstorm. Her pulse thrummed with mixed eagerness and anxiety. *She* was safe from immediate danger, and so were Eun and Ye Jun.

But Bae with her scout was vulnerable, which bothered Hwa

Young more and more, and the squad no longer had a heavily armored brawler unit to join her up front and protect her from ambush.

Don't think about Seong Su. He'd been dead for two months. She had to accept that.

It was your fault he died.

Hwa Young's hands convulsed on the controls, although they were locked since she was piloting through the link and not in manual mode. Still, *Winter's Axiom* shuddered and veered off course.

Ye Jun's voice, sharp as a flensing knife, cracked over the comms: "Steady there, Axe."

The callsign almost threw her, despite two months of acclimation. They all had new callsigns to go with their new allegiance. In the Empire, she'd gone by Winter. Now, among the clanners, she was Axiom—Axe.

What would Seong Su's new callsign have been?

She couldn't linger over that thought. Not here, not now.

"I'm fine, sir," Hwa Young flung back, determined to do better. To *be* better.

Especially since she was doing this for Geum too.

From a human standpoint, lancers were massive war engines: they resembled armored warriors but stood a good three stories tall and wielded weapons like Hwa Young's super-sized sniper rifle or Eun's ship-destroying missiles. Their control of gravitational technology allowed them to soar through space on their levitators. In her dreams, Hwa Young envisioned them blotting out the sky. She'd once imagined that having her own lancer would make her invincible.

We're here to help, Hwa Young thought, willing the people of Jasper to understand. In her heart of hearts, she added, *Please don't screw it up for Geum and me.*

"Time to make an appearance," Ye Jun said. "With any luck, we can resolve this without violence. Fly to the marked coordinates." The waypoint showed up on the map of the system, flare-bright.

"Sir, that's going to take us within scan range of Jasper Research Station." Eun's tone was carefully neutral.

"There's no point in coming here to be seen doing good if we're not *seen,*" Ye Jun pointed out.

"Understood." Eun's voice was half growl this time.

After all the drills they'd undergone and two months of fighting together after defecting to the clanners, the act of flight itself went smoothly. Bae took point, despite the risk, with Eun and Hwa Young ready to fire on anything that threatened her. Hwa Young was stingingly aware of the distances involved, despite the feeling of close-knit camaraderie: that any bullet she fired, any artillery barrage Eun released, might reach any hostiles too late to save Bae in case of ambush.

We can take on twelve ships, Hwa Young thought. Not very large ships, at that, although the readings were fuzzy at this range. Their approximate size, heading, speed, and rate of deceleration were the only things that Bae could ascertain.

"This is Commander Ye Jun of the lancer *Bastard,*" the commander said, broadcasting in the clear. "We are here to offer our assistance to Jasper Research Station. Incoming starships, please identify yourselves."

Hwa Young sucked in her breath, startled, when the comms returned fizzing static, then an answer in a deep, suave voice.

"Commander, it's a relief to see you. This is Strike Leader Jong of Ninth Fleet. Here I was thinking we wouldn't have lancer support for this mission. I didn't realize that Eleventh Fleet had also been tasked with securing the base here!"

Hwa Young's stomach sank. She didn't want to fight Imperials if she could help it. An untenable position, given who and what she was, yet she kept hoping anyway.

"Commander!" Bae said sharply over the lancers-only channel, her voice sharp with alarm. "Incoming missile barrage from the station!"

Hwa Young saw them twofold. Primarily in her mind's eye, as with all the other lancers' recon data, through her link with *Winter's Axiom* and its systems: swift-footed wolves speeding toward each one of them. For redundancy's sake, this information also appeared on her lancer's tactical display, with sterile icons representing each lancer, the station, the missiles, everyone's vectors.

Unfortunately, *Winter's Axiom* was glitching *again:* all the station's missiles, as well as the newly arrived Imperial strike force, appeared in the starry blue that indicated *allies.* Someone at the station must not have gotten the memo that the lancer squad was here to help. She should have known the mission would go awry from the start.

Cut that out! she told the lancer sharply. How many times was she going to have to deal with this? Fighting with the interface while in combat was going to get her killed one of these days.

Winter's Axiom responded with sullen unease, then changed the blue to the ugly gray that indicated enemies.

The missiles hadn't launched from the strike leader and their twelve ships—but from the station Hwa Young and her comrades had been tasked with aiding.

What if they caught the clanner agents and the station no longer trusts us as a result? There was a chance the mission was blown. Bad for the clanners, who'd counted on getting that data.

Bad for Hwa Young and Geum's hopes of reunion.

Back when they'd fought the clanners, the squad had relied on Bae's jamming capability to make it more difficult for weapons to achieve target lock. The Imperials' superior armaments had worked in their favor.

Now they faced a station of hostile former Imperials, ones with reason to protect critical research.

"The strike force said the *one thing* that would fox this mission," Ye Jun said, grim. "Jasper must have overheard. We came in claiming to work with the clanners, except the task force addresses us as Imperials. I have reason to believe Jasper doesn't trust Ninth Fleet, and now they think *we're* trouble too, because there's a discrepancy in our story. All units evade at will." Zir unit, *Bastard*, retreated until it was barely within communications range.

It wasn't cowardice. Hwa Young, too, did her best work from a distance. There was a lot of that going around. Unlike *Winter's Axiom*, *Bastard* possessed few conventional weapons or defenses, a consequence of an earlier battle that had left it and its pilot permanently scarred. *Bastard* acted strictly as a C2 unit—command and control—coordinating the squad's actions.

If Seong Su were here—Seong Su, with the brawler *Avalanche*. But Seong Su *wasn't*.

Winter's Axiom spoke, its chilly voice reverberating all the way down to marrow: *It's high time for the hunt to begin. It's never too late to start a skull collection.*

Hwa Young almost shot back a retort—*Was that necessary?*—but she had more immediate concerns.

The leading missile zoomed toward her. With a burst from the levitators, Hwa Young whirled and dodged behind a tumbling asteroid just in time. Thwarted, the missile sped past—and toward the strike force.

She hadn't been its target after all.

It was easy for them to retreat beyond the effective range of the base's defenses. But what had Jong said about "securing the base"? Did Jong suspect the *base's* loyalties?

Sure enough, the strike force released its own barrage of missiles—toward the base.

"Sorry to make the first strike," Jong said easily, as if the attack were a joke, or a bet, "but someone's got to do it."

Jong thought the lancers were on their side. Apparently they hadn't heard the news about Eleventh Fleet's turncoats: an example of how unreliable communications were in the Moonstorm.

Commander Aera had led them to expect raiders. Lowlife pirates. Not a strike force from New Joseon's highly regarded Ninth Fleet. A fault in Aera's intel? Had the Imperials uncovered Aera's sources and fed them misinformation?

"Orders, sir," Eun hissed. "Do we hightail it out of here and leave them to it? Defend the station that just *attacked* us?"

"We defend the station until we hear otherwise," Ye Jun said, as calm as Eun was agitated. "Falcon Fleet may still be in the process of exfiltrating its agents."

"Whatever your plan is," Bae said, apparently unfazed by the thought of fighting her former people, "make it fast. The base will be ready to launch a second salvo of missiles in approximately thirty seconds. We may be here to 'save' them, but they don't seem impressed."

Ye Jun addressed the strike leader: "I'm sorry, but we have

orders to preserve this base." Zie hadn't, Hwa Young noticed, mentioned *whose* orders.

"*I'm* sorry," Jong said, almost sincere, "but Ninth Fleet operations take priority over Eleventh Fleet's. As you know."

"Axe to Vagrant," Hwa Young said. Her new callsign, and Ye Jun's. That initial fungal bloom of missiles had given her an idea. "We don't have any chaff to confuse the next round of missiles." Two missions ago, they'd run out of the reflective particles, which confused sensors. The clanners' chaff wasn't compatible with lancer delivery systems, and attempts to manufacture a stopgap had failed. "But we do have these rocks. Maybe we could *make* chaff."

Confusing the missiles would buy them time to talk down the station's chief, whoever they were, as well as Strike Leader Jong, and come to a peaceful resolution.

She heard the grin in Commander Ye Jun's voice. "It's a good idea, Axe."

"Is it that simple?" Bae asked. *Farseer* danced through the wilds of space. "They're showing up as Stinger Twelve missiles on my scan suite. That trick's not going to fool smart missiles."

Memory swept Hwa Young back to the cramped classroom on the Imperial flagship where Eun had lectured her and the other pilot trainees on different missile types, their ranges, their capabilities. Eun hadn't gone into much detail, because lancers employed specially designed, smaller missiles compared to the ones wielded by starships or silos, and the computer system regurgitated any statistics they needed to refer to. Hwa Young did remember that the modern Stinger series contained their own scan suites and computer guidance systems, which enabled them to track their quarry. They wouldn't be fooled by debris.

A pang started up in her gut as she considered the most important reason they hadn't spent much time on those details: they hadn't expected to fight fellow Imperials.

Commander Ye Jun said, "I can jinx the missiles' brains. Leave that to me. Silence"—Eun's callsign, given to him by way of irony—"you see the rock that Winter's shadowing? Blow it to pieces. Axe, haul ass out of there so you're not caught in the radius of effect."

With a lancer, thought became motion. *Winter's Axiom* sped out from behind the asteroid's cover, jinking this way and that to evade enemy fire, before Hwa Young consciously made the decision to do so. At times the lancer's responsiveness frightened her and made her wonder who was really in charge. Right now, that immediacy of action made her more effective.

Eun's *Hellion* was out of visual range—not difficult, given the vastness of space. Hwa Young thanked the stars and ancestors for the luminous map in her head, which detailed the positions of Jasper's dimming red sun, the ocean-tempest world of Jasper itself, the primary moon with its troublesome forward base. She saw the other lancers clearly in that orrery of orbits and strikes: the regal gold and green of Commander Ye Jun's *Bastard* lurking almost out of sight; Bae's streamlined violet-and-silver *Farseer*, its grace only hinted at in the schematic; Eun's orange *Hellion*, flare-bright; and herself always at the center of the view in *Winter's Axiom*, white accented with chilly blue and silver.

From Hellion erupted a fusillade of missiles. A warning chime sounded in Hwa Young's cockpit, reinforced by a jarring haptic sensation in her bones: *INCOMING MISSILES*. Spheres of overlapping hectic light in different colors indicated the projected point of impact, the trajectory of the asteroid Hwa Young had just vacated, the projected radius of effect.

Radius of effect, Hwa Young thought as she urged her lancer to greater accelerations so they could reach safety. What a bloodless way to describe a firestorm that could vaporize you before you drew breath to scream.

Unwanted memories battered her. She was no longer in Jasper's system but hovering outside the shattered ruins of the gravitational observatory they had visited shortly before they defected from the Empire. The ruins where they'd been ambushed by clanners—specifically, clanners from Falcon Fleet.

Back then, another deluge of light had blotted out everything in every direction, propagating spherically. Fire beyond fire, obliterating their fifth pilot, good-natured Seong Su, and his lancer *Avalanche.* Nothing had remained of him: not ash, not bone, not a scar on the integument of space-time.

We're working for the people who killed Seong Su.

"Axiom!"

She landed back in her body. Details reached her in disordered flashes, all of them clamoring for her attention although they weren't equally important. Her vision was blurry. Only afterward did she flinch from the hot tears seeping down her cheeks. Red lights swept through the cockpit in an on-off tide, picking out highlights on the console in a gore of radiance. The entire lancer thrummed subliminally. Its vibrations transmitted themselves through the seat to her tailbone and tensed legs despite its suspension.

Bae's voice cracked like stressed ice, roughened, and dropped a half octave before resuming its usual upper-class cadences. "Axiom,

I'll give you the vector. Burn in that direction with everything you've got."

Was Bae *worried* about her? Hwa Young's heart stuttered with an embarrassing surge of warmth she didn't know what to do with, and which was going to get her killed in battle if she didn't pull her focus back where it belonged.

What about the commander? Hwa Young wondered. Was Bae intervening because Commander Ye Jun was preoccupied dealing with the strike force? She tried to refocus on her part of the battle.

I can't let the others down.

Her connection with *Winter's Axiom* snapped, leaving her spinning and vulnerable. She reached out to the lancer, questing for its predatory intent, the icy calm that she had learned to rely on, even the surprising macabre sense of humor. It could tell as many tasteless jokes about corpses as it wanted if it would answer her.

Nothing. Pain scythed her temples, like a headache twisted ninety degrees.

Hands trembling, Hwa Young gripped the lancer's joysticks. They should have conformed to her hands, one of the lancer's many customizations. Instead they were too cold, and newly grown protrusions bit into her palms.

That left manual control. Eun had drilled her and the other pilot candidates in the procedure. Hwa Young had (if she was honest with herself) filed them in the back of her head alongside other useless factoids like the composition of the liquid fertilizer they used in hydroponics, trigonometric identities, and Bae's shoe size (smaller than hers, despite Bae's height).

Her life depended on information she'd been cocksure she'd never need.

Her foot quested for the pedals beneath her seat, found them. "Here goes nothing," Hwa Young muttered, although she couldn't hear herself over the clamor of the proximity alerts. She yanked the joysticks back and floored the accelerator.

With the mental connection severed, she didn't *feel* the acceleration as a glorious surge, as though she herself soared through the vast and dangerous wilds. In battles past, she *was Winter's Axiom*.

Now, no longer anesthetized by its presence, Hwa Young became aware of ordinary sensations. The acceleration smashed her back against her seat, forcing breath out of her lungs despite the cushioning. Her eyes watered; the edges of her vision guttered black.

"Axiom, watch your nine. What did that asteroid ever do to you?"

Alerted by Bae, Hwa Young dodged the asteroid. It hardly merited the name. Her sensors told her it was mostly ice laced with salts and minerals, interstellar grime. Still, a small object could kill her if it hit her hard enough—or the other way around.

As she maneuvered, she heard Commander Ye Jun's voice. "Missile brains hacked. They'd believe I was their mother if I told them so. Axe, you'd better clear the danger zone in the next ten seconds if this is to work."

"What about Jong—" Hwa Young started to say.

"Leave Jong to me."

The timer ticked down in Hwa Young's head, courtesy of the neural implant. Like all Imperials, she had one that allowed her to interface with their tech, including the lancer.

She moved because she had no choice. In the cold-hot savagery of battle, movement was life and stillness was death.

In the back of her head, she heard *Winter's Axiom* resuming its connection with her, exultant: *The enemy will eat death. We will feast on their desolation and collect their skulls.*

Five seconds.

Geum, I'm sorry this went sideways. I'll figure out something else. Try something different.

Her eyes teared up again. The acceleration was getting to her. She must be doing eight or nine gees as measured against Imperial standard gravity.

The water obscuring her vision had nothing to do with grief, or the comrade she'd lost, or the friend she'd left behind with Eleventh Fleet. She wondered sometimes if Seong Su would have turned coat with the squad, as easygoing as ever, or if some obscure reservoir of Imperial patriotism would have caused him to break ranks. If she'd narrowly escaped a future in which she faced off against Seong Su. They'd never find out.

Zero—

Ten seconds had elapsed. The commander was nothing if not precise.

The enemy missiles scattered like a flock of birds fleeing the report of a shotgun. Each one veered toward a different asteroid. How had Commander Ye Jun accomplished that?—actually, that wasn't her problem. Her problem was getting out of the way before the missiles took her with them.

The missiles exploded like fireworks for the Empress's birthday, a comparison Hwa Young regretted as soon as her mind offered it. Asteroid upon asteroid shattered. Fragments of ice and rock and dirt scattered toward the base and, with any luck, screwed over their sensors.

"Vagrant to Axe. Fire on the target I've marked for you."

She looked at the target Ye Jun indicated, lit up in red. Balked. "Sir, that's one of the strike force's ships." Specifically, its engine. A critical hit would take out all twelve.

An engine going critical was how Seong Su had died.

"If Ninth Fleet doesn't know of our status, that may afford us an operational advantage. We need to eliminate the strike force so they can't report back." Commander Ye Jun's voice was crisp, impersonal.

It's happening again, Hwa Young thought numbly. She was going to fire on Imperials.

"Axe, do you copy?"

"I copy," she said hollowly.

We are clear to hunt, her lancer said, its exultation unmistakable.

She should have shared its joy. Instead, revulsion seeped into her heart.

If you dislike skulls, it added, with the air of one granting a grand concession in the face of unreasonable recalcitrance, *metacarpals are also acceptable.*

Then a new voice, or an old one, said over the comms: "You've lost control of your sniper, Commander Ye Jun."

Hwa Young shuddered. It was Seong Su's voice, down to the slow and easy cadences, and it came from the station. But that was impossible. *I'm stressed. Hallucinating. It's someone else.*

And: *I can't afford to freeze* again *during combat.*

"Why don't we talk this over—" Seong Su's voice began.

Mercifully, Commander Ye Jun interrupted. "We're not here to negotiate."

The voice went on. "I see. In that case, the rumors about your ambitions toward the *throne* are—"

Hwa Young pulled the trigger.

The bullet flew.

She'd always associated bullets with flying, and her lancer too.

It was one thing to fly, and another to fall. Freedom from gravity's hand as opposed to being its prisoner.

She was its prisoner now.

Critical hit. The engine blew. The conflagration blossomed outward, a sphere of light and devastation, swallowing whatever Jong had wanted to say.

Hwa Young had always wanted to have ice for a heart. To fight without sentiment. This wasn't the first time she'd failed to achieve that ideal.

"That's it," Eun said, his voice strained to the snapping point. Hwa Young heard his next words through the roaring in her ears: "We've killed Imperials in cold blood."

HWA YOUNG

The flight back to the clanner fleet took only two hours. Falcon Fleet was outfitted with the stealth technology controlled by the more powerful clans and had spent the operation lurking out of sight. On the way, the lancer squad passed clanner auxiliary ships moving in to offer humanitarian aid and evacuate the station's personnel before passing them on to the rescue fleets, so Hwa Young assumed negotiations had gone well. The auxiliaries, like most clanner ships, sported spikes and angular protrusions and vinelike embellishments, in contrast to the smooth, flowing lines of Imperial ships.

On any other occasion, Hwa Young would have taken an interest in the logistics. The briefing they'd received hadn't disclosed the number of auxiliaries involved, since the lancers didn't have any involvement with that side of operations. The lancers' job had solely been to secure the base for the agents' benefit; mopping up and negotiations afterward were someone else's domain.

She should have been strategizing. Thinking about how best to approach Commander Aera about retrieving Geum. Aera could be hard to read, and aggravatingly stubborn. In her more honest moments, Hwa Young admitted that was a trait she shared with her heart-mother. With any luck, the agents had gotten out in time. Had retrieved the data that Geum had promised was there, the last in a long line of hoops to jump through.

Instead, Hwa Young replayed Seong Su's voice in her head, like the world's most unwanted earworm. What were the odds that someone else would have *his* voice, the characteristic slow cadences, the easy manner? *You're imagining things,* Hwa Young told herself. She needed to find out if she was hallucinating under stress. But how could she do this without Commander Ye Jun finding out? She didn't want zir to think she was unreliable and leave her out of missions—or worse, sever her from her lancer and give it to someone else.

Only the missions held her together these days, and her determination to excel so that Aera would no longer have any reason to keep her from rescuing Geum.

I got the job done. I'll keep getting the job done.

A new voice broke in, with a lightly sibilant accent: "This is Falcon Command. Axe, you're drifting toward *Bellflower*'s lane. Please watch where you're going."

Falcon Actual was the flagship, their current destination. It took its name from Admiral Mae: *mae* meant *falcon* in Hangeul. The admiral came from one of the border communities, according to Aera. As a courtesy to zir, Falcon Fleet used Hangeul as its common language.

"Correcting course," Hwa Young responded. Sometimes she

missed her original callsign, Winter. But she reminded herself she'd left New Joseon and its callsigns behind.

She was a better pilot than this. Unfortunately, the link between herself and her lancer meant any distraction could result in her going off course. The invocation of Seong Su had dredged up old memories and new fears.

I'm with my heart-mother's fleet. This is where I should be. She couldn't bear the thought of disappointing Mother—Commander—Aera *and* the other pilots.

Winter's Axiom provided a panoramic view of the fleet's fighting vessels, almost a hundred strong, as well as the large, ungainly auxiliaries, used to transport supplies or offer manufacturing or medical support. The fleet's movements possessed a ponderous grace, like the choreographed dances that commemorated the New Year back in New Joseon.

While the lancer squad had been part of Falcon Fleet for the past two months, they'd never before witnessed an operation on this scale. Hwa Young had supposed, to the extent that she considered the matter, that this was because the clanners *couldn't* cooperate for large-scale logistics. She'd been wrong.

A strange unease tickled her thoughts, a welcome distraction from her worries: *When did the clanners become so coordinated?*

It was a truism among the clanners that the Imperials enforced a stifling conformity in their worship of the Empress. That very conformity, coupled with Imperial rituals, created reliable gravity in the Empire. It was equally axiomatic among Imperials that the freewheeling clanners lacked discipline, resulting in unreliable gravity throughout the Moonstorm. What Hwa Young saw here didn't suggest an inability to work together; quite the contrary.

She returned her focus to piloting, a simpler task. It was a problem she could solve. She had a dearth of those in her life right now.

Her fellow pilots, born and raised in New Joseon, distrusted the mercurial skies of the Moonstorm and the navigational difficulties they posed. Hwa Young found the mutability of the stars and moons, familiar from childhood, reassuring, an anthem of untamed exuberance. The Moonstorm, with its unstable gravity and unchancy wandering objects, was vast and variable. Most clanners considered the thought of regulating it completely to be offensive.

Hwa Young entertained fantasies of disappearing into the starry drifts, borne away by dust and dreams, aether and ice, an adventurer guided by the lodestar of her heart. She could find a new star, a new name; she could pass into the realm of whispers and wonder.

But that would mean leaving the other pilots behind and giving up on Geum, and this she would never do. Seong Su's death, and the dreadful shared knowledge of the Empire's singularity bomb, powerful enough to destroy an entire world, bound them together.

Besides, there was the matter of her heart-mother Commander Aera.

In the white-and-blue glow that illuminated her cockpit, Hwa Young imagined the conversation the other three pilots were having about her.

Hwa Young's cracked like thin ice, Eun might say. *You've got to replace her before she gets us killed.*

She didn't like that, even in her imagination. Had the others heard the familiar voice as well, or if it had been an artifact of strung-out nerves? How could she find out without asking them outright?

And Bae—Hwa Young didn't know how Bae would react to Eun's hypothetical pronouncement. Defend Hwa Young? Say something derisive? It could go either way.

They'd been enemies once, long ago and far away. Bae, her tormentor, effortlessly beautiful with her long, silken hair, the school's queen who had everything but a crown. If gossip was to be believed, it would only have been a matter of time before Bae's mother secured that as well, by arranging a marriage for Bae with someone in the royal family.

Long ago and far away had been less than a year ago. Hwa Young thought about that sometimes. They'd been *students* vying over the stupidest possible stakes: who got the nicest seats in the cafeteria, who scored highest in applied geomancy, who flaunted the hottest hairstyle without falling afoul of school regulations.

Now the things that mattered involved life and death, death and life, patterns intertwined like the black and white stones of a game of baduk.

They reached the clanner fleet before Hwa Young decided which side Bae would come down on. She hadn't considered the question of what Commander Ye Jun would say either. The commander thought three moves ahead, on a game board that the rest of them couldn't conceive of. A survival skill for an Imperial bastard, she imagined.

Ye Jun rarely spoke of zir mother, the Empress. Hwa Young couldn't tell whether that reflected the awkwardness of switching sides or natural discretion. Maybe the Empress was an embarrassing *mom*, what a thought.

Hwa Young returned her attention to piloting before she

could incur another reprimand by drifting again. Once was bad enough. She wouldn't allow it to happen a second time in the same approach.

From sufficient distance, clanner and Imperial ships looked the same: specks that resembled stars when observed with the naked eye, especially in the Moonstorm, where *moving* specks could be moons, or stars, or ships. Their sensors told the true story. Stars emitted characteristic spectra based on the elements burning in their cores; the same was true for the surfaces of the moons that reflected that light.

Ships were another story *if* their engines were burning. The emissions from a ship's maneuvering thrusters or main drive told the observer whether they were Imperial or clanner or other, and sometimes the class of ship as well. However, a ship drifting in the aether currents, without using its thrusters or drive, could camouflage itself amid the flotsam of lights.

Closer and closer the squad flew to *Falcon Actual*. The most powerful starships resolved into jagged individual shapes with thorny protrusions, freckled by patterned running lights. The squad assumed a tight formation, one that an Imperial officer would have been hard-pressed to criticize.

"Vagrant to Falcon Command," Commander Ye Jun said over the comms. "Falcon Command, lancer squad requesting clearance for docking."

Zie didn't have to specify which lancer squad, since there was only one. Something that clanner leadership was eager to rectify.

"Falcon Command to Vagrant." This time Hwa Young knew the voice all too well. It sounded almost identical to her own, except harder, with an air of authority she desperately wished she could project as easily: Commander Aera, her heart-mother, the admiral's second-in-command. "Moon's own blessing. You're cleared to land in Magnolia Docking Bay."

That was another difference, one that Eun harped on. The Imperials labeled their ships' rooms, bays, and corridors with numbers and letters, following tidy linear logic. The clanners named everything after flowers and foliage, evoking absent gardens, nowhere landscapes. They didn't put up signs, either, in case they were boarded by hostiles.

The clanners cultivated starblooms and other plants everywhere on the ships, even on the flagship's bridge, in the docking bays, a devotion to horticulture that Hwa Young found inexplicable. Eun, who had discovered brand-new allergies, complained about this too. Regular crew had shifts for pruning and plant care, overseen by an ensign *dedicated* to the role.

Hwa Young had grown up on a clanner moon rather than a shipboard community or fleet. Perhaps there was some spiritual or religious reason. She chickened out of asking in case *that* would prove she wasn't a true clanner.

Besides, the one time Hwa Young had lingered over a planter, Commander Aera intuited the question and claimed the logic was so simple a child could deduce it. Hwa Young hadn't figured out if this was an insult. She was trying to give her heart-mother the benefit of the doubt, but it was hard.

The physical act of docking wasn't too different than with an Imperial ship. Still, Hwa Young remained vigilant. A moment's carelessness could result in a collision or worse. She couldn't bear the thought of hurting her comrades, or the soldiers and technicians who worked in the docking bay.

Green-and-gold *Bastard* glided in first, neatly landing in its designated spot. Someone had color-coded the reflective tape, green and gold, like the decorative tape that Hwa Young's friend Geum was so fond of.

Geum, Hwa Young thought with a pang, remembering zir bright smile, the way zie had left her a care package full of snacks and confetti. Highly inconvenient confetti, but still. *Geum, I'll find a way to change Aera's mind.*

Flamboyant *Hellion* landed next, equally precise. While the artillery unit was the least agile of the four lancers, Eun made up for it with the ease of long practice.

Third came *Farseer,* eerie violet and silver, the most maneuverable. Its thin armor meant it relied on evasion to protect itself. *Farseer*'s pilot, Bae, prided herself on mastery of anything she did, whether that meant high fashion or hand-to-hand combat. Perhaps Bae saw them as two facets of the same jewel.

That left Hwa Young and *Winter's Axiom.* They decelerated smoothly, making contact with the deck so lightly it might have been a snowflake's kiss. Hwa Young listened for the lancer's chilly voice, wondering if her lancer would graduate to jokes about intestines or go back to blander commentary.

Her mind's eye encased her in a snowy landscape. A slender silhouette drifted toward her, blade-straight, its dark, disarrayed hair so long that it faded into an infinity of mist. It left no footsteps, and she couldn't see its face, if it had one. Then the vision faded.

Was that you? she asked the lancer. But it didn't answer. Besides, she associated the lancer with predatory intent. The silhouette hadn't carried that same sense of barely leashed violence. All the same, Hwa Young didn't think it was precisely friendly. A ghost out of the horror stories Geum liked so much, maybe, with ambivalent intent.

It better be the lancer, and not another stress hallucination.

Four lancers, four for death, Hwa Young thought, an Imperial superstition: the words for *four* and *death* sounded similar in Hangeul.

Seong Su had piloted *Avalanche Four*. At the time, she'd dismissed any intimation of bad luck as an artifact of the stressful circumstances under which they'd become pilots. Now, she wondered if the bad luck would follow them throughout their mission.

Hwa Young disembarked using the lancer's built-in lift. The others were already on the deck below. Commander Ye Jun waved her over, and she joined the other three pilots.

Ye Jun's eyes shone green-gold, Eun's hot orange, Bae's violet and silver, visible marks of connection to their lancers. Hwa Young's own eyes, although she couldn't see them, were arctic blue and silver. They'd had to ditch their original outfits because wearing the Imperial uniforms was untenable. Nevertheless, Ye Jun had arranged for clothing of similar cut, except in the rougher fabrics favored by the clanners.

Unlike the rest of them, Eun had experimented with clanner styles, from hanbok-inspired wear that would have been outmoded in New Joseon, to severely tailored brocade vests and slacks, to belted robes (a bad idea from a safety standpoint; he ditched those quickly). Every few days he tried something different, dissatisfied with the sheer variety of options. To everyone's relief, suits rated for aether used double-layer zippers with a pressure seal, same as the ones in the Empire.

Hwa Young had her suspicions about the reason for Eun's explorations in attire. Like the time she'd caught him talking to that researcher, so close they were practically breathing each other's nose hairs. Eun's acceptance of life with the clanners should have gratified her, yet it rang false. It was hard not to fret about it, to wonder what Eun *really* felt.

Hwa Young glanced around, both reassured and perturbed by the activities in the docking bay. Technicians swarmed around several fighters in various stages of disassembly, addressing themselves to landing gear, thrusters, engines. None of them was Geum.

Geum would love first crack at all this tech.

"We're to debrief with Commander Aera," Ye Jun said crisply.

Long practice following orders caused Hwa Young to snap to and follow, even as her less-practiced mouth opened: "All of us, sir?"

Commander Ye Jun glanced back over zir shoulder without breaking stride, while Eun's broad shoulders tensed. "All of us."

Hwa Young didn't know what to make of that; was afraid her hesitation in battle would be called out. Especially in front of her heart-mother. She couldn't be sidelined and forced to sit uselessly on the ship—a ship full of people she didn't understand how to get along with, even though they were supposed to be *her people*—while the others continued to fly missions.

Couldn't lose her chance to get Geum out.

Couldn't bear the thought of her heart-mother looking at her, lips pursed, and saying *Bringing you home was the wrong decision.* For six years she'd thought herself an orphan, her family wiped out by the Imperials' attack on Carnelian. Now that she had a mother again—her *heart-mother*—she would do anything to avoid screwing that up.

"Wish we could shower first," Bae said with a sniff.

"Yeah, you smell ripe," Eun agreed. "We have a sensitive op in this sector but everyone has to wait while you try out the latest designer shampoo."

Once upon a time, Bae would have taken offense to a jab like that. Instead, she smirked. "Yes, luxury goods are something we have a surplus of in this fleet."

Hwa Young had never experienced designer anything, in the Empire *or* the Moonstorm. Still, the fact that Eun and Bae were capable of joking about something so trivial provoked unjustified rage. Here she was with a hole in her heart, and they were smiling at each other, even if their smiles had edges like knives.

She reached out for the icy shell of her lancer's mental presence and took refuge in it, numbing her worry and grief and outrage. When she connected with *Winter's Axiom,* she became greater than herself. She had the endurance and vastness of glaciers. She didn't have to *feel.*

"You're awfully quiet," Eun remarked to Hwa Young.

She returned a tight smile, not trusting herself to speak.

"Maybe she's trying to avoid inhaling your stench," Bae said. "Doesn't that boyfriend of yours tell you to put on some cologne?"

Eun squirmed, uncharacteristically avoidant, and changed the subject, saying to Hwa Young, "I will say you're doing a better job of picking up the local accent than the rest of us. But then, you have a home court advantage, huh?"

Hwa Young stilled her face with an effort. She hadn't shifted her speech patterns consciously. It was as though the childhood dialect she'd worked so hard to eradicate while she lived in New Joseon was seeping out now that she interacted with clanners on a daily basis again. She should be happy about fitting in—so why did Eun's remark sting?

"Pilots, please," Commander Ye Jun said, mildly enough. "We can discuss personal hygiene another time."

Hwa Young was grateful for the intervention, even if she didn't notice the stink of sweat and scored metal anymore. Her own lancer's cockpit possessed an efficient air filtration system. Only if something went wrong did she smell anything beyond the faintest whiff of chemicals. On occasion, she imagined the sweet fragrance of starblooms ghosting through the air.

Falcon Actual possessed an organic miasma of accumulated dirt and decaying leaves, in contrast to the Imperial flagship *Maehwa* of Eleventh Fleet, where she'd served previously. The hallways of *Falcon Actual* were narrower that the *Maehwa*'s, but better lit. Paradoxically, this made them feel more claustrophobic. Hwa Young, accustomed to the open spaces of a moon or planet, forced herself to breathe normally, which wasn't normal at all. Bae, damn her, showed no sign of discomfort.

Yet *Falcon Actual*'s gravity had a steadiness that reassured Hwa Young. An artifact of discipline on the flagship? Or was gravity this reliable throughout Falcon Fleet?

As they approached the last turn, Hwa Young heard the percussion of footsteps. An ensign careered around the corner. She and Bae tried to step aside, but the ensign collided with Hwa Young anyway. The breath whooshed out of her.

"Watch where you're going, boy!" the ensign snarled, and was off again.

"Not again," Hwa Young muttered.

In Falcon Clan and its territories, men had short hair, women had long hair, and people who were neither wore different combinations of braids, depending on the flavor of "neither." Hwa

Young should have grown her hair out after being forced to cut it, thanks to the latest trend direct from the Imperial crownworld. Instead, she'd kept it trimmed short, conforming with Ye Jun, Eun, and Bae. Commander Aera disapproved: Hwa Young's short hair, along with the wide white streak she'd gained when she bonded with *Winter's Axiom*, obscured her resemblance to Aera and confused the crew.

Hwa Young expected Bae to make some snippy remark about the ridiculousness of clanner conventions. Instead, Bae looked . . . smug? What was that all about?

All too soon they arrived at the designated conference room, Three Wisterias. "Commander Ye Jun with the lancer squad," zie said to the door.

The door, unlike the plaque, was polished to a sheen like still water. In it, Hwa Young scried their faces like ghosts from uninstantiated futures: the commander's angular, sardonic face, like a battle-tarnished version of the Empress with her radiant beauty; Eun's habitual scowl and muscular frame; herself and Bae, who resembled gangly teenage boys with their visages blurred in the metal.

Hwa Young was struck all over again by Bae's beauty, more pronounced than it had been when they were both children. *The rest of us mortals have pimples,* she thought. Bae's fine features had grown sharper, her build leaner, in a way that only accentuated the architecture of her bones and made Hwa Young's pulse accelerate for reasons she didn't want to examine while going into a debriefing.

The door opened. Light spilled over their toes, tinted red and blue. Someone had a tactical display running, a holographic orrery of moon trajectories, base locations, and fleet movements, all the icons color-coded and labeled. A distressing amount of space showed up in the sickly gray that meant *contested territory.*

Mother Aera—*Commander Aera,* Hwa Young reminded herself—stood at the head of the room, fingers flickering as she rearranged ship icons as though they were children's jacks. She didn't wear a uniform, or more accurately, the clanners didn't have a standard one. Some wore armbands or sported tattoos indicating allegiance to specific subclans, which Hwa Young wished she understood better. Commander Aera herself affected a practical dun jacket and tunic above pants with a staggering array of pockets and buckles. Her hairstyle, too, probably had some meaning, loops and braids held in place by vicious steel hairpins.

Hwa Young suppressed the familiar stab of unreality as she studied her heart-mother. They should have been identical. But Mother Aera stood a full handspan taller and had a lighter build. Hwa Young had spent her adolescence on an Imperial world with stronger gravity, which meant she'd never achieved the spindly height of a typical clanner. Each time Hwa Young saw the ways they'd diverged, it hit her like a knife slash to the eye.

Does she feel that too when she looks at me? Hwa Young wondered. Was that, rather than matters of rank and propriety, why Aera remained frosty toward her?

Commander Ye Jun faced Aera and saluted, Imperial-style. The rest of them had given up the practice, a bone of contention between Ye Jun and Eun, although they didn't argue about it this time.

"Your report, Commander Ye Jun," Aera said. Her gaze flickered to Hwa Young, then away. Hwa Young's heart seized in response.

Ye Jun delivered the after-action report briskly, adding at the end, "I've taken the liberty of transmitting the combat data to Falcon Command"—what *Falcon Actual* called its Combat Information Center, locus of the flagship's decision-making.

"We need a better system," Aera said flatly. "Reformatting the data so we can use it takes days of computer cluster time."

Commander Ye Jun had explained it to them: the lancers ran on a proprietary operating system developed on a different chip architecture from clanner standard. Past efforts to automate data translation had failed. Software, not hardware, was the most difficult part of reverse engineering a lancer so the clanners could build their own.

Geum had promised them access to that software, an immediate side benefit to the codebase they'd just attempted to obtain. Speaking of which . . .

"Did you secure the codebase?" Hwa Young asked. "Do you have the information you need?"

"It's no good," Aera said flatly. "The data's scrambled. It may take months to recover anything useful."

Hwa Young deflated. *Not again.* Her eyes burned. One setback after another.

Without lancers, the clanners had no chance of resisting New Joseon's attacks.

Without the codebase—

"I'm open to suggestions," Ye Jun said.

"If you'd allow us to disassemble—" Aera began.

"No disassembly." Ye Jun's voice was sharp.

Hwa Young shivered, and Eun's scowl grooved deep lines around his down-turned mouth. Only Bae looked bored with the argument, which had been going on for the past two months.

Hwa Young didn't know what happened to a pilot who was disconnected from their lancer in such a fashion, but she eyed Ye Jun's disabled arm. Zie had lost the use of it in the same attack that had damaged *Bastard:* the link between pilot and machine meant that injury to one sometimes caused injury to the other.

Aera paused, regrouped. "One of our scholars, Zeng, has come up with an alternative that he thinks will work."

This time Hwa Young glanced at Eun, who redirected his grimace to the floor. Zeng, the researcher he'd been making out with. Did Eun know something?

Ye Jun cocked zir head and waited.

"Zeng has designed a device—he calls them scribers—that can be installed into your lancers. They'll record system data in a format we can read. It's the least invasive solution."

A tense pause. Then: "It's worth a try," Ye Jun said.

"I'll authorize their manufacture and installation, then."

Aera asked some rapid-fire questions pertaining to the strike force as well as Ye Jun's observations of the region. Hwa Young was getting twitchy. While she didn't want to interrupt them, she didn't want to miss an opportunity to press Aera on a rescue mission either.

After this, she wanted a fresh new battle to wash the taste of the previous one out of her brain, or a shower. Even if the "shower" was a sonic one, rather than the water she'd enjoyed on the *Maehwa*. The *plants* rated more water than she did.

"One more thing," Commander Ye Jun said. "I'm not sure that strike force had a human crew, as opposed to a programmed response. Unfortunately, it's unlikely any evidence survived the critical hit to the engine. But if it did have human crew, they were feeding comms through a vocal synthesis program."

This possibility hadn't occurred to Hwa Young, even though her lancer was a machine and there certainly wasn't a human locked up in it to generate the voice. "You mean all that 'Why don't we talk this over' was a computer?" she blurted out.

Commander Aera ignored the outburst, her dark eyes intent on Ye Jun's face. "Either they knew you were coming, or word has gotten out that there's a renegade lancer squad operating in this sector and they were trying to demoralize you with your comrade's voice."

Zie shrugged expressively. "That, or someone thinks fast on their feet."

The next few minutes might as well have occurred in the next galaxy over as far as Hwa Young was concerned. She hadn't imagined it. She'd heard Seong Su's voice.

Commander Ye Jun's words, spoken softly but pitched in her direction, jolted her back into awareness of the room—and the conversation that had been going on. "Voice synthesis techniques date back to Old Earth," zie said. "Still, imitating a specific nonfamous person . . . someone must have obtained and distributed the voiceprint for the purpose."

Hwa Young didn't care about the technical details. Neither did Eun, who said, "Well, whoever it was, they're dead now, and good riddance."

Bae said, "I'd be more concerned about figuring out whether someone leaked our mission and knew we'd be there."

"I will investigate," Aera said, with a distinct chill at the suggestion that there was a mole in *her* fleet.

Hwa Young knew she should be worried about the possibility too. Right now, though, anger and shame threatened to choke her.

The Imperials had used Seong Su's voice deliberately. To hurt her. To hurt all of them. She wasn't the only one mourning him. And she'd fallen for it. It had *worked.*

"If nothing else," Aera said dryly, "this is the first time in *months* that an Imperial ploy has made sense." She eyed Ye Jun, an eyebrow cocked, inviting explanation.

Ye Jun didn't fall for the bait. "Absent identification of the admirals involved," zie said, "I have no insights to offer."

Hwa Young believed Ye Jun, but she wasn't the one zie had to persuade. While Aera had questioned them separately, Hwa Young had caught snatches of Ye Jun's observations ever since: one admiral had a weakness for calligraphy stones, another was sleeping with her aide, a dismaying amount of dirt about people she had, however abstractly, once looked up to.

More than the sordid gossip, Hwa Young worried about New Joseon's strategy. They all did—because they couldn't puzzle out what was going on. Attacks here and there at random. Fleet movements that didn't suggest any reasonable targets, some of them near New Joseon's core worlds, removed from the Moonstorm border or any threat of clanner attack. Signs of simple incompetence, or an ingenious way to hide their true objective, whatever it was?

"Anything else to report?" Commander Aera added.

This was Hwa Young's opportunity to come clean. To admit she'd frozen in battle.

I know it was a faked voice, Hwa Young thought. She wouldn't freeze again. The next battle would be fine.

"Commander." Hwa Young squared her shoulders and reminded herself not to look into her heart-mother's eyes the way she had as a child too young for manners. "I wanted to broach the possibility of retrieving Technician An Geum." She kept her tone formal, deferential. "Geum has passed on reliable intelligence more than once." Even if they hadn't gotten the big immediate payoff they'd hoped for.

Commander Aera's expression, which had warmed when Hwa Young opened her mouth, smoothed back into a dispassionate mask.

Hwa Young's heart sank. She'd chosen the wrong approach *again*. She should have worn some prominent piece of clanner jewelry, or leaned on their blood connection, instead of speaking soldier to superior.

Should have talked to her mother as *her mother*, despite the breach of protocol.

It wasn't too late. Hwa Young lifted her chin and looked directly at Aera, willing Aera to *see* her. "Heart-mother," she said, "please. Geum was—Geum looked out for me all those years I was trapped in the Empire. I owe zir."

Aera gave her a tiny nod, her eyes warming, but before she spoke, Hwa Young knew the answer. "I'm so sorry, Pilot. I've discussed it with Admiral Mae, but zie feels this isn't the right time. We appreciate the technician's contributions, however, and will certainly take them into consideration as we decide on the right time for an exfiltration."

Hwa Young cast her gaze down before Aera could see the humiliation and disappointment warring on her face. At the same time, she was conscious of the other pilots' stares. *Trapped in the Empire,* she'd said—alienating her comrades, and to what gain?

"All right," Commander Aera said, although Hwa Young barely heard her through the roaring in her ears. "Dismissed."

3

GEUM

Geum, the most datable and brilliant hacker on the Imperial flagship *Maehwa* of Eleventh Fleet, had a long list of regrets and a large amount of blackmail, neither of which did zir any good locked up in the brig. None of the guards had proved susceptible to flirting. The cell lacked any access to the ship's computer systems, and the authorities had confiscated zir slate.

Fortunately, Geum also had *plans*. And a friend on the outside, where "outside" meant "outside the Empire."

Zie had considered blackmail, except the guards didn't look like the type to care that Admiral Chin had a collection of dog photos. Who knew she liked them dressed up in adorable little sweaters? They wouldn't care about the admiral's stash of slasher novels either.

Besides, considering how much trouble Geum was in, zie

didn't want to do anything that would make zir situation worse before Hwa Young rode to the rescue.

Like any number of life decisions, it had seemed like a great idea at the time. Eleventh Fleet had been mired in battle around the clanner moon of Carnelian. Geum couldn't think of any sane reason for Hwa Young, one of the fleet's *lancer pilots,* to cool her heels in the brig during the heat of battle. It had to be a misunderstanding. The fact that Hwa Young was Geum's best friend didn't have any bearing on the matter. *Of course* Geum had released her...

... only for Hwa Young to turn around and join the clanners. And take the entire lancer squad with her.

She had good reason, Geum thought over and over, holding on to the fraying threads of zir conviction. A different Imperial fleet had threatened to destroy everyone with a singularity bomb. Geum's life plans did not include being sucked into a black hole. But deserting like that was *technically* treason.

Which left Geum to take the fall.

She had good reason, Geum repeated to zirself. Hwa Young would come back for zir at the earliest opportunity, and they'd escape together. She had promised.

Have I really been here for two months? If Geum had remembered to bring a tube of glitter lipstick, zie would have tracked time with marks on the wall. The time stamps on Hwa Young's communiqués were no help, given unpredictable travel times through the Moonstorm.

The *Maehwa*'s computers kept track. Geum had figured out how to finesse access and retrieve the answers to some queries. But the guards' presence, and the limitations of zir improvised interface, meant zie had to be circumspect.

Geum had set up a haptic interface, which relied on the ship's computers tracking the movements of zir fingers when triggered by a specific gesture, in the absence of a slate. Zie had adapted the movements from New Joseon's military sign language, which had oodles of words for different types of grenades and only one for food/edibles. Funny how something zie'd half-assedly coded—for a hacking challenge issued by someone doing physical therapy after an accident messed up his hands—had other applications.

(It had occurred to Geum that losing fingers would make this tricky. Zie had modified the interface accordingly. If zie lost both arms, well, zie would deal with that when it happened.)

Everyone assumed that Geum liked to fidget. Okay, Geum did fidget. In reality, most of the time zie was up to things. Giving input was easy and zie could do it almost anywhere, including this brig cell.

Getting *answers* out of the computers—that was harder.

Geum had spent three weeks in the brig learning that debugging *sucked* when one couldn't check the results or error codes by the usual methods. At one point zie had shorted out the lights in hydroponics by accident, fortunately attributed to "this ship must have ghosts and we should pour them an offering of wine." Eventually zie hit on the janky solution of asking the ship to communicate output via knocking noises generated by its maintenance robots. It was time-consuming and infuriating and risked attracting the suspicion of some conscientious technician, not least because Geum had learned the old-time radio code from the ship's archives, which meant someone might recognize it.

So far, Admiral Chin had come by three times, asking the same sodden questions, receiving the same sodden answers. Each time, Admiral Chin glowered at Geum's offered "It must have been a terrible misunderstanding."

Geum's stomach rumbled. Zie had stopped being picky about the food. It was the same food that they served in the mess, rice gruel with vat-grown "fish" protein, fiddleheads and spinach from hydroponics, a cursory few pieces of gimchi. In the brig, though, it was served with weak-ass recyclable chopsticks and a spoon that disintegrated partway into the meal. It would take a superhuman assassin to employ these utensils as weapons.

How long until the next meal, anyway? zie wondered, scratching zir chin. No razors here, either, and with zir luck, the geniuses who supplied the brig would invent blunt razors. Perhaps zie should check to see if word had arrived from Hwa Young?

A voice drifted from the guard station: ". . . talk for ten minutes, not like it does any harm. But you can't bring that stuff in here."

Normally guard chatter was a great time to check in with the computers to see if Hwa Young had made contact. But it sounded like someone else had arrived? Any break in the routine might be good—or bad.

"Talk"? Geum wondered, squinting through the bars. The weird angles of the twisty little passages down here made it geometrically impossible to catch a glimpse of the visitor. Geum considered zirself an exceptional individual, but seeing around corners wasn't one of zir abilities.

Geum's spirits lifted when the visitor spoke again, this time loudly enough for zir to identify her voice: Hyo Su, a technician like Geum, only a few years older than zie was. What was she doing here? And what was "that stuff"? A rocket launcher? A raccoon? A rocket-launched raccoon?

"Fine," the same guard said, sounding more enthusiastic, presumably in response to some silent offer. "But if I catch you in here again, you'll need to bring me the next chapter, okay? And high resolution, none of this neolithic low-res crap."

Hyo Su sauntered in with a . . . toolbox? A dented, lidless toolbox pressed into service as a lunch container. Geum refrained from drooling over the tantalizing smell of sweet bean pastries and smiled at Hyo Su, suddenly aware that zie couldn't remember the last time zie had combed zir hair, shaved, or moisturized. Moisturizer was rarer than iridium on a battleship, even for people who weren't in the brig.

Hyo Su herself looked the same as ever, broad, tawny face and mussed hair over round eyes, stocky and strong-boned. Deprived of friendly company as Geum had been all this time, zie found that Hyo Su looked even tastier than the food. Hyo Su had dexterous fingers, which Geum daydreamed about sometimes; she'd hoped to become a musician specializing in the gayageum, a traditional zither, before she was drafted. One of the "get to know you" factoids they'd exchanged a few months ago, when Geum failed to become a lancer pilot and was first assigned as a technician instead.

"Geum," Hyo Su said, voice cracking in relief. "You're okay."

"They haven't spaced me yet," Geum said, and regretted the joke when Hyo Su's face crumpled.

"Geum, do you know how much trouble you're in?"

"Yes," zie said, serious for once. Serious—and warmed by Hyo Su's distress. Guilt twisted in Geum's heart. It was one thing to screw around and play practical jokes, another to upset a friend. Especially a friend who cared enough to sneak in on zir behalf, despite the risk.

The kind of friend Geum had endeavored to be to Hwa

Young—and look where it had gotten zir. Geum was determined to do better, even if Hwa Young had good reason. To *be* better.

"Well," Hyo Su said, glancing over her shoulder at the guard post, "let's get some decent food into you. I don't know how much time that guard is going to give me."

"What *did* you bribe them with?"

"I have the complete translation of this weird manhwa from some foreign country beyond the Moonstorm. Not even clanners, straight-up foreigners. I can't pronounce their names and the computer system blocks me when I try to look them up. It's boring unless you're into competitive baking, cute character designs, and fancy hats."

Geum had only the vaguest idea about nations beyond New Joseon. Imperial instructors didn't encourage students to think about that. They'd scarcely discussed the Moonstorm and its clanners except for propaganda: undisciplined, unwilling to accept the Empress's beneficence, unwashed.

Hwa Young was a clanner. She'd been *incredibly* diligent about showering for someone who never dated. So what other "facts" about clanners weren't true?

They've welcomed us, Hwa Young had said in her last message. Short on details, but this was because *Geum* had cautioned her about the limitations of zir information-receiving methods. Geum's resentment about Hwa Young's failure to chat or wax sentimental was partly unreasonable . . . and wholly unavoidable.

"You know," Hyo Su added, "if this was your gambit to get out of dealing with space gunk"—what she called glues, sealants, and what passed for brown noodle sauce—"it's kind of overkill."

Geum's mouth quirked in a reluctant smile. "Anyone else miss me?" zie demanded.

Hyo Su chewed her lower lip. Under any other circumstances, the mannerism would have struck Geum as adorable. "Work-wise? We've missed the extra pair of hands," she said, and they shared an eyeroll. "Admiral Chin keeps complaining about how shorthanded we are and how her chief of staff has to reassign people every time something breaks. She likes everything nice and tidy, down to the style guides for after-action reports."

Geum wasn't happy about this, exactly, but it was good to hear the news from a friend. To see a face that didn't belong to a guard. Zir days had devolved into a dreary quagmire of staring at the walls, waiting for the latest request from Hwa Young (or more accurately, her asshole clanner superiors, who offered endless excuses for delaying Geum's rescue), and the humiliation of sponge baths, because the alternative was stinking up the place.

"Yo, Geum." Hyo Su waved a sweet bean pastry in front of Geum. "I didn't hit the black market for real sweet beans to have you space out."

Last Geum had checked, the mess's "sweet bean pastries" were made from fungal protein and possessed an icky clay aftertaste. Trust military recipes to ruin dessert. "Thank you," zie said fervently. Zie would have to brainstorm for a suitably extravagant thank-you gesture before zie left with Hwa Young. "I owe you one. I owe you *ten*." Geum reached out for the pastry.

"Hey," the guard called, "you better get out of here. Admiral Chin's on her way."

"Shit! She's off schedule!" Hyo Su startled like a rabbit, down to the twitching nose. "Gotta go. You take care. I'll be back when I can." She dropped the pastry and scuttled off, leaving the disconcerting mixed smells of gun mount oil and wisteria perfume in her wake.

Geum stared in dismay at the pastry, now splatted on the deck with its filling oozing out. Zie could smell the red bean paste more strongly than ever. The pang that started up in zir stomach was one part hunger to nine parts atavistic frustration.

When are Hwa Young's commanders going to let her come for me?
Geum fixed zir gaze on the opposite cell and its bars. No one occupied it. Geum was torn between the desire for company more scintillating than the guards and the grime, Hwa Young or Hyo Su for preference, and the sneaking feeling that a nice person shouldn't *want* someone else to be in jail.

What has being "nice" gotten me so far?

The sweet bean pastry gave evidence that Geum had enjoyed the company of a visitor. Geum didn't want to land Hyo Su in trouble. Hyo Su had done nothing wrong, even if the military in general and Admiral Chin in particular were tight-asses about pointless regulations.

The tight-asses took a very dim view of people who didn't share their high regard for protocol. Alas, the tight-asses controlled shipboard life. The least zie could do was spare Hyo Su any unpleasantness.

Like everyone on the *Maehwa*, Geum recognized the cadence of Admiral Chin's walk. Some soldiers took assertive strides, while others oozed or performed a peculiar shuffle. A far cry from the polished marches on the propaganda holos.

The admiral had a quiet tread, as though she walked in silk slippers. Admiral Chin had originated on a less privileged station that suffered from weak, unreliable gravity, resulting in the attendant unusual height and spindly build. Less privileged meant *less loyal,* but no one said it to the admiral's face. It made her resemble a clanner. No one remarked on it in her hearing either.

Admiral Chin came into view.

Geum became aware of zir general grubby state again. Zie itched from shoulder to toe. The admiral didn't look much better. Her navy blue uniform was crisp, and the metal buttons gleamed, but her face was shadowed, and the wrinkles around her eyes and mouth had grown deeper. She shared the reek of exhaustion and sweat, the faint chemical odor that seeped into the water.

Geum had never thought of the admiral as a person so much as an ambulatory phenomenon, like a storm cell. Zie had previously figured that the chance of encountering rogue weather on the *Maehwa* was higher than personal contact with the fleet's admiral. This, alas, only applied to people who avoided aiding and abetting the escape of so-called traitors.

Hwa Young stopped First Fleet from massacring people with the singularity bomb. It had absolutely been the right thing to do.

But Hwa Young and her bravery were far away, and Geum had to face the admiral with no shield but zir own faltering convictions.

The admiral looked pissed off, like someone had used up all the hot water. Geum wished zie had quizzed Hyo Su about the state of the *Maehwa*, or Eleventh Fleet. Surely zie would have noticed a battle going on? A fleet could run into all kinds of problems that didn't involve out-and-out combat.

This time the admiral had not brought her goons with her. Geum's hackles rose. There wasn't any *good* reason for a deviation from routine, especially for someone who worshiped order almost as much as the Empress herself.

That's it. She's going to shoot me through the bars, or slit my throat, and it will be all over.

If only Hwa Young had arrived earlier. If only Geum had asked Hyo Su out *before* the Battle of Carnelian. If only—

As the admiral loomed closer—looming must be part of officer training—Geum's pulse sped up. Would it be better to leave a tragically beautiful corpse, like in the dramas, or a grittily realistic one, to make people mourn losing zir? Contemplating the morbid dilemma prevented Geum from spiraling into anxiety about the prospect of death or exile.

I'm sorry, zie thought at zir two fathers back on Carnelian, who would be spared the knowledge of zir disgrace *and* the upsetting sight of zir tragically beautiful corpse.

"Technician An Geum." Admiral Chin stood a precisely judged distance back from the cell. Geum was positive she knew to the millimeter how far her prisoner could reach through the bars.

Geum rose and saluted, tottering thanks to a sudden wave of hunger. Zie tried to prevent zir eyes from darting toward the luckless fallen pastry, which rested less than a centimeter from the admiral's left boot. *Don't notice don't notice don't notice—*

The admiral laughed dryly. It sounded like she was hacking up half a lung, always reassuring. "Technician," she said, her eyes crinkling in a simulation of amusement, "do you think I am so unaware of my surroundings as to have missed the lump of perfectly good pastry on an otherwise spotless deck?"

Geum was a good liar when it involved talking to fellow technicians or students. An admiral with the power of life and death, not so much. Zie remained silent because zie couldn't think of a better way to cover for Hyo Su.

"Loyalty to your friends is your greatest virtue," Admiral Chin went on, "and your greatest fault."

"Sir," Geum said, and came up blank. What rebuttal did zie have?

Geum did zir best to channel Hwa Young's *I am serious business* vibes as opposed to zir preferred whimsy, on the grounds that Admiral Chin showed limited signs of having a sense of humor. "Sir, if I'd known anything, I would have told you the first time you asked."

"That can't be true," the admiral said very dryly. She looked Geum up and down the way warriors in the dramas examined cavalry horses, if cavalry horses were suspected of having gimchi stuck between their teeth. (Did horses eat gimchi?) "You failed to mention your forays into my files."

Geum's hands fisted at zir sides. Some people stayed calm and collected when faced with angry authority figures. Geum had always admired that about Hwa Young—her ability to take decisive action, even if it led to more trouble.

Geum's talent? The gift of gab. Useful when one was fast-talking one's way past bored security, not so useful here. Geum *babbled* instead of keeping cool.

"It was part of a game challenge." The words came out in a rush. "You see, we're randomly assigned tasks and we score points and it's all gamified and—"

The admiral's mouth quirked. The slightest of expressions, but Geum was not so anxious that zie didn't notice. The world narrowed to the admiral's face, which resembled a moon of colossal consequence.

Geum took the hint and closed zir mouth with a snap so hard zir jaw ached.

Admiral Chin continued to stare, as though she'd installed one of those rumored eye implants that allowed her to see past the skull and its sutures into the crenellations of someone's soul. Alternately, Geum's hair was bad? What a dreadful thought.

Because the pressure was getting to zir, Geum blurted out, "Why haven't you had me executed?"

Geum had not devoted a huge amount of time to studying the military justice code. Senior Warrant Officer Eun, who'd instructed the pilot wannabes, had hit the high points: "Seditious talk about the Empress will get you thrown out the airlock, so don't do it" and "Do not touch my energy drinks on pain of death." Eun had cared more about training people to check their oxygen gauges and making sure they knew what to do if their IFF failed and they were in danger of being shot down as hostiles because they weren't transmitting the right identification codes.

One thing Geum did remember: an officer could carry out a summary execution for a grave offense. One didn't get much more "officer" than an admiral. Geum had always dismissed this as theoretical. Especially since "summary execution" sounded like what happened when one flunked a high-stakes essay test.

The admiral's breath huffed out. Now she resembled a cat who had just grown thumbs *and* discovered a stash of extremely stinky wet food. Geum disliked this image intensely, not least because zie was the stinky wet food in this analogy.

"You finally think to ask the question," Admiral Chin said. "There might be hope for you."

Geum knew that licking zir lips nervously was contraindicated, yet did it anyway. The admiral's tone had warmed to a purr. Geum did not mistake this for affection. More like that special aggro purr that cats made while staring into one's eyes, claws out, when they expected one to dish out the good fish *or else*.

The chief of the technicians had nicknamed Geum *Spider*, on account of zir nimble fingers. As zie stared into the admiral's slitted eyes, zie felt trapped in a web spun from whispers and cruel calculations.

"Hwa Young was extremely fond of you," Admiral Chin said. "You were her only friend. What if we took advantage of that?"

Oh no, Geum thought, face freezing. *I'm being used as bait.*

Geum was more useful alive than dead. Did the admiral also know zie was in contact with Hwa Young? That was what Geum had to ascertain. Zie might be able to warn Hwa Young of any traps.

The question remained, though: Why now? Why not earlier? Admiral Chin wasn't so stupid that the possibility hadn't occurred to her earlier. What had changed for Eleventh Fleet?

"Do we even know if she's alive—" Geum began to say, to buy time.

The admiral's badge chirruped. "Excuse me, sir," said a staticky voice. "Urgent call for you."

Geum was distracted by the side issue of the static. The comms *within* the ship hadn't been this bad in the past. If the admiral would let zir out, zie could troubleshoot. (Zie hoped it wasn't a bug from zir code.) Surely it wasn't a bandwidth issue. Wouldn't they prioritize bandwidth for the *admiral*?

The admiral tapped the badge. "I'm *busy*," she ground out. Geum bet her molars could have reduced granite to smears of ignominious igneous dust. "I gave orders I wasn't to be disturbed for a reason."

Geum heard a distinct gulp from whoever it was. "Sir," they said, "it's the Empress."

HWA YOUNG

Hwa Young liked routines, which her friend Geum had found endearing. ("You're a weirdo, but you're *my* weirdo.") One controlled the world through routines. This was true both in New Joseon and in the Moonstorm. In New Joseon, prayers to the Empress ensured that everyone conformed to her will, and this stabilized the force of gravity. The clanners had their own, competing rituals for the same purpose. Having survived a catastrophic gravity failure that had destroyed a *moon*, Hwa Young had strong feelings about this.

She'd established a new routine. The clanners seemed bemused by her regimen of exercise, reviewing safety procedures, and poring over the layout maps that were available to her, alongside the time she spent training with the other lancer pilots. Still, they didn't stop her either.

Right now, her routine called for her to visit the rec room. Hwa Young wasn't sure why she bothered. "Fun" was the last thing she felt like having. After Aera had turned down her request regarding Geum—*again*—she wanted to hole up in her quarters and brood.

On the other hand, Aera might ask other clanners for their observations. She needed to make an attempt to fit in, like Eun (however grumpily), as opposed to staying aloof like Ye Jun or Bae. Unlike Eun, she didn't have an *excuse* for her failed efforts.

Several clanners looked up when she entered the rec room. Like every other room on the ship, it featured starblooms in a planter, perfuming the air with a fragrance reminiscent of lilacs.

A dark-skinned ensign knelt next to the planter, stroking the petals with squared-off, steady fingers: Rose-Merline, who worked in cryptobotany, whatever that meant. She straightened and waved at Hwa Young; the prisms braided into her curly hair danced and flung jagged rainbows across the room. Hwa Young smiled back, more out of habit than genuine feeling. It wasn't Rose-Merline's fault she'd had a terrible day.

Rose-Merline had been overtly friendly from the beginning, unlike some of the other clanners, going so far as to leave a small "Welcome to the ship!" box containing the protective charm that Hwa Young had unbent enough to wear, a jigsaw puzzle she still hadn't solved, and, most pragmatically and most appreciated, handwritten notes on where to go for the *good* coffee. Hwa Young assumed Rose-Merline was hitting on her in the nicest, lowest-pressure way imaginable. Every time she thought about exploring that, though, she wondered what Bae would think, and her interest cooled. This time, like the others, Hwa Young looked away. Rose-Merline didn't press further, although she bit her lip in obvious disappointment.

"Pilot Hwajin, Moon Archer's blessing," another clanner said with a polite nod: Zeng, the scientist Eun had been hanging out with, and the most attractive man on the ship for those who liked a strong jawline paired with long-lashed eyes. (This did not describe Hwa Young.) His glossy hair hung almost to the floor, in defiance of Falcon Fleet's conventions, which was allegedly part of his appeal. While his hands were free of rings or bracelets, his gray silk jacket featured embroidery in geometric motifs.

Rumor had it that, beyond the good looks, the colognes that Zeng favored were brewed in his laboratory to *enhance* the dating experience. Hwa Young vacillated between asking Eun if this was true and realizing that quizzing a higher-ranked pilot about his love life would get her punched in the nose. Any curiosity about what the colognes would smell like on Bae remained in the realm of idle speculation, with no further significance.

"Moon Archer's blessing, Zeng," Hwa Young said. Not the greeting her family had used back on Carnelian. She recited it now in an attempt to fit in, but her stiffness spoiled the effect.

In her peripheral vision, she spotted Zeng's heart-brother Tora watching their exchange with a smile that never went away. The two were clones, like herself and Commander Aera, but born with a gap of a mere two years. Tora, the elder, bore little resemblance to his brother, not just because of his preference for clothes in glossy black star-serpent leather or his shaved head. His expression gave him the appearance of a malevolent bodhisattva.

Tora sported a tattoo on the inside of his right wrist, a roaring tiger, which he flashed at every opportunity. It commemorated a moon-tiger he'd brought down. As a fellow hunter, Hwa Young should have been interested. Instead, she ignored him. The way he stared at her creeped her out.

The clanners called Hwa Young by her childhood name,

Hwajin. The one she'd gone by as a clanner child. Commander Aera had instructed them to do so her first day in Falcon Fleet, without asking Hwa Young what *she* wanted. It was a stupid thing to care about, yet she couldn't let it go.

A whiff of cologne, spice and aromatic woods, brought her attention back to Zeng and his heart-brother. Hwa Young was convinced that Zeng had mastered the trick of waving his sleeves *just so* and exploiting the air currents to stink up the target; if so, she'd never noticed any ill effects. "Join us for Tarocchi?" Zeng asked, dimpling at her.

She hesitated for a moment. "Sure." She'd learned the card game three weeks ago and sucked at it. But the point wasn't to prove her awesomeness, it was to be seen socializing.

Hwa Young took a seat at their table. Like many furniture items on *Falcon Actual*, it looked as though someone had carved the motifs of falcon and flower by hand. The chisel marks in the dark-stained wood had not been sanded into oblivion but left there for aesthetic reasons. A far cry from fixtures on Imperial ships, all of identical manufacture, all smooth.

"Now all we need is a fourth player," Zeng said, looking around the room appealingly.

Rose-Merline fidgeted with a stray curl of her hair. She wasn't looking at Hwa Young, but she wasn't *not* looking, either.

She's been nothing but friendly, Hwa Young thought. *I should give her a chance.* Hadn't Commander Ye Jun hinted that they should maintain good relations with people on *Falcon Actual*? Hwa Young wondered if Eun's pursuit of Zeng had a basis in intelligence-gathering, or if that was a pretext for advanced tongue gymnastics.

Hwa Young glanced sidelong at Tora, whose smile remained

malevolently unrevealing. Was he staring at her again? If so, he was getting better at plausible deniability. "We could find a friendly ghost," she said, wishing for an excuse to bail.

Zeng laughed. "Let me message Eun. I bet he's free."

For you, *yeah.* Hwa Young distracted herself from Zeng's annoying goofy grin by studying the Tarocchi cards. They featured animals, people clad in baffling fashions, and detailed filigree borders. She wondered if she could purchase her own deck. The delicate pastels and realistic, three-dimensional style of the artwork, unlike anything she'd seen in New Joseon, appealed to her.

A few minutes later, Eun and Bae strolled in together. "Hwa Young," Eun called out. "So you need a fourth player?" Today's outfit involved a bright orange scarf. He resembled an escaped safety cone.

Bae drifted after him, her expression as haughty as ever. She achieved an enviable offhand elegance despite clothes of startlingly severe cut, which emphasized and flattered her lean build. There was little of curves or softness to her anymore, and Hwa Young caught herself admiring Bae's shoulders, broader than she remembered them. Come to think of that, Bae had previously worn loose, flowy tunics for some time.

Hwa Young liked the change, despite her sudden uncertainty about what, if anything, it signified. She wasn't the only one looking, either: Rose-Merline had stopped pretending to fuss over the plants and was admiring Bae openly. The ensign caught Hwa Young's eye and shot her an absurdly endearing conspiratorial grin, as if to say *You too, huh?*

Don't be ridiculous, Hwa Young told the fluttering of her heart. She wasn't dating Bae, and she'd tacitly turned Rose-Merline down. If anything was going on between the two of them, it was none of her business.

Besides . . . she wasn't sure the emotion that gripped her was *jealousy*. For a wild moment, she imagined herself in both their arms, complete with advanced tongue gymnastics. She didn't know what to make of that; wished she could blame Zeng's cologne. Some of the clanners practiced group partnerships, but it was uncommon among New Joseon's nobles, who emphasized one-on-one marriage alliances.

Tora finally deigned to speak. "Nice of you to join us." He had a huskier voice than his heart-brother. His intonations always sounded faintly sarcastic.

Eun gazed at Zeng, who smiled back as though everything else in the universe had dissolved into accelerated heartbeats and adrenaline static.

Tora watched them both, his lips turning down at the corners, his eyes hot with—distaste? Envy?

Eun can take care of himself, Hwa Young thought, despite her own queasiness. She had trouble reconciling the way Eun had thrown himself into the relationship with his unsubtle awkwardness with clanner culture. Was it the way of life that bothered him, or the fact that the squad had turned coat?

I should ask him. But not here, not in front of an audience.

"I'll be Hwa Young's partner," Eun said. At least he didn't seem like he minded: partners sat across from each other. He pulled up a seat around the corner from Zeng. Bae remained standing, like a watchful peregrine.

Zeng dealt out the cards, and they began to play.

Two of the women in the rec room paused in playing darts to exchange knowing glances. During the first trick of the Tarocchi round, their jeers were loud enough to be overheard, and it couldn't be accidental. *Suck-up* was the least insulting word they used while critiquing his latest (failed) attempts at clanner fashion, with bonus snide comments about the scarf and what it implied about Eun's *preferred position* in—

Hwa Young slapped down her cards and rose. Glared. "Excuse me," she said to the women, who wore matching knotwork bracelets: lovers. "You have something to say?"

Eun growled under his breath. "Hwa Young, let it go."

She didn't turn her head. "If you want to share your opinion, do it to our faces."

Threat, Winter's Axiom whispered. And: *Substandard skulls, but it's a start.* Hwa Young didn't know whether to be dismayed or elated by its eagerness, like the star-stab of knives turned outward.

A vision flashed in her mind, superimposed over the two women in her field of vision: in place of their heads, pale skulls stripped of flesh, pierced from top to bottom with icicle spikes, the eye sockets frozen over. *That* was new. Yet no matter how macabre the vision, the violent conviction gave Hwa Young a strength of clarity she exulted in.

The larger woman laughed harshly and said something in a language Hwa Young didn't recognize, and then: "We couldn't possibly criticize Commander Aera's treasured heart-son." She scooped up one of the darts and flourished it as though to fling it at the pilots.

It was a taunt, not a serious threat, yet Hwa Young launched herself at the woman. Her body moved automatically, exactly what she had honed it for; exactly what she was primed for after combat training and endless missions.

The blade-like edge of her hand struck the woman's arm at a pressure point. The dart went flying. Bae snatched it out of the air, displaying enviable reflexes, before it could hurt a bystander.

Hwa Young clasped the woman in a vicious armlock. The heat of her struck Hwa Young like a blow, more devastating than any counterstrike the woman could have devised. She hadn't *touched* someone in so long, with precious little time these days for sparring. If only this were an embrace—if only it were Bae, or—

"What in the name of all the moons is wrong with you?" the woman snapped, struggling, exactly the wrong reaction. Hwa Young instinctively tightened her grip. The woman's breath hitched in a sob.

Eun's shadow scythed over them both. One by one he pried Hwa Young's fingers loose. She resisted; she didn't want to be deprived of her prey. Hwa Young was strong for her size, but Eun's bulk consisted of muscle and aggression. "Let it go, Axe." And again: "*Axe.*"

Hwa Young recoiled from the growl in his voice. He was using her callsign, usually reserved for missions. She went limp in his grasp. It had been so long since she'd been the target of his anger—or worse, disappointment.

It was for you, she wanted to protest. The way everyone stared at her pierced her like rusted needles. Rose-Merline, her eyes round with shock. Bae with the familiar scornful twist to her mouth. Eun's boyfriend Zeng, his averted gaze suggesting genteel dismay. The only one who *wasn't* transfixed by the tableau was Tora, who was cheating at Tarocchi by switching cards while everyone was distracted.

Hwa Young's attention returned to the trouble she was in when the clanner woman spat something that could only be a curse word.

She then added, in perfect Imperial-accented Hangeul, "I wouldn't dream of interfering in *Imperial* matters."

Eun's fingernails dug into Hwa Young's forearm, preventing her from lunging. Bae slid forward to block her view of the clanner.

"We'll finish the game another time," Eun called to Zeng and Tora as he hustled Hwa Young out of the rec room.

A day later, Hwa Young cooled her heels in the nicest detention room imaginable, complete with an adjoining washroom and a meditation chamber lit by lanterns of phosphorescent fungus. She imagined hosting tea here, if not for the fact that most of the clanners scorned it in favor of coffee. A tea party no one wanted to come to: an apt summary of her life.

Back in New Joseon, in Forsythia City, she'd passed by the boarding school's detention room more than once. A large window made it easy for passersby to gawk. Every time she glimpsed the unlucky students within, reduced to regurgitating essays on the importance of orderly behavior, she vowed that she'd never join them.

Hwa Young tried not to think about what had become of her school: blown up by the fleet she was now part of.

School had been a means to an end. She'd gladly left it behind in exchange for her goal: mastery of a lancer. No one had warned her that being a pilot would land her in a *detention room* like the one she'd avoided as a student.

Hwa Young had snuck off an update to Geum. Instead of sending it from *Falcon Actual*, which would have attracted Admiral

Mae's attention, or worse, Mother Aera's, she'd linked with her lancer to do it. She hoped Geum received it soon.

Eun had marched her here and left her with orders not to budge. Hwa Young attempted to burn a hole into the wall with her stare, certain the clanner women had gotten off without a reprimand. Eun's parting words still stung: *We can't afford to pick fights, Axe. You of all people should know better.*

When did you turn into a coward? Hwa Young had thought. *Is it the boyfriend?* Saying that out loud would have gotten her knocked into the next star system, so she refrained. She was learning the rudiments of tact too late to benefit from them.

At least Bae still cared about her. Bae had lingered a few minutes after Eun stomped off. "I'll talk him down, Winter," Bae said, her voice unaccountably rough. She was the only one who continued to address Hwa Young by the old callsign in private, an intimacy that unsettled Hwa Young, not in a bad way. "Give him a few hours to cool off." Then Bae was gone too.

I blew it, she thought. Word would get back to Aera. How was she going to explain to Geum that the long-planned rescue was delayed once more—on account of a stupid fight? *Her stupid fight?*

How was she going to explain herself to Aera?

When she'd first rejoined the clanners, Hwa Young had envisioned smiles and an easy adjustment. The world had turned right side up after her home crumbled into debris six years ago. Her heart-mother *and* her comrades, the desires of her heart. Once she rescued Geum, everything would be perfect.

Perfection had gone sour from the start. She couldn't figure out where she'd gone wrong.

The room's décor was so beautiful it depressed her. Living

tapestries of vines and pink flowers obscured the bulkheads, alongside the familiar silvery starblooms. The table, bolted to the deck, was a lovely example of foreign marquetry. She suspected Falcon Fleet had plundered its furnishings and decorations from raids past, which would explain why the crew never gave a straight answer when she asked about them.

That wasn't what unnerved her. It was the steady gravity, without even the small fluctuations she had come to take for granted on the *Maehwa*.

You're paranoid. Calm, rational argument was the way to defuse her nerves. *You're so distracted you wouldn't recognize a real gravity fluctuation until it—*

She suffocated beneath the weight of memory: the moon of Carnelian shattering around her, the maelstrom that had swallowed her family. Her first sight of a lancer squadron. Blue-and-red *Paradox* in the lead, piloted by Captain of the Guard Ga Ram, one of the Empress's oldest children.

Did the captain know what the Empress was capable of? Her willingness to sacrifice her own citizens to power a singularity bomb? How could someone in zir position *not* know?

It didn't matter. She was unlikely to ever meet zir again, let alone pose the question.

Several minutes later, if the clock on the wall was reliable, the door swung open: hinged, unlike the sliding doors on Imperial ships. The jostling of the nearby vines released yet more pollen. Hwa Young wasn't allergic, but the yellow specks clung to her sleeves in an unsightly manner.

"Commander—" she began, then swallowed what she'd been about to say.

It wasn't Ye Jun, but Commander Aera.

Great. I'm in for it now. Aera, the one person she wanted to avoid. Aera wasn't here to pat her on the head and tell her she'd done a good job. Aera hadn't been the type to mince words when Hwa Young was a small child. No one could fault her sternness as a commander.

Yet Hwa Young wished Aera would soften just a little, relent just a little, where no one else could see the two of them.

Oddly, Aera carried a lumpy satchel. Hwa Young eyed it, trying to determine what it contained. The head of an enemy, as a demonstration of what Hwa Young had to fear if she slipped again? The head of a friend? A moldy head of *cabbage*?

"I received a report of yesterday's incident from Eun," Aera said briskly.

"Excuse me," Hwa Young blurted out. "Where's Commander Ye Jun?" She should have been conciliatory, but her nerves got the better of her. Every time she spoke to Aera, it was as though she reverted back to an awkward ten-year-old.

Neither Ye Jun nor Eun would have tolerated the mulish edge to her tone. Aera only nodded as though this were a reasonable challenge to her authority. Hwa Young was torn between irritation and respect.

"Zie agreed to let me speak to you, Hwajin." She gestured at the table. "Have a seat."

What could she do? Refuse? Especially since Aera had her over a barrel and knew it? Hwa Young lowered her eyes and did as instructed. Still, she added, almost in a stammer, "I go by Hwa Young now."

Great. Now Aera was going to think she was weak. That was worse than defiance.

"Yes, that was one of the things I wanted to talk to you about."

Hwa Young recognized Aera's smile. It was the one Hwa Young saw in the mirror when she was preparing to have an unpleasant conversation and had a clever but doomed plan for handling the situation.

Is that what I am now? An unpleasant conversation?

"It would help with integration of your unit—"

"Excuse me," Hwa Young cut in, her heart seizing at *your unit*. It was Ye Jun's unit. "I'm not in charge of—"

"Let me finish."

Hwa Young subsided.

"*Your* unit is how the other clanners see it. You're the one who turned on the Imperials first. You're one of us. People resent the fact that all of you cling to your Imperial customs." Aera made a moue. "Well, except Eun, we can all see how hard he's trying, but . . ."

So much for Eun's efforts.

"But?" Hwa Young prompted when Commander Aera lapsed into a fretful silence.

"It would mean a great deal *symbolically*," Aera said, "if you tried harder to fit in." After a subtle pause, she added softly, with a vulnerability Hwa Young would never have suspected in her, "It would mean a lot to *me*."

Hwa Young's heart ached. "What can I do?" she asked, because she needed to hear the specifics. To make her heart-mother say it out loud.

If it helps my comrades—if it helps Geum—

If this meant Aera would look at her as a heart-daughter again, and not one of a thousand soldiers under her command—

"Your name, for a start."

Aera had gone back to attempting to play it cool. Hwa Young

wasn't fooled. Aera's voice had flexed on the word *name*. She cared about this, more than she wanted to let on.

My heart-mother.

The part of her that was braided with winter winds and ice storms, her lancer's unceasing taste for violence, noted: *I could use that against her.* She couldn't tell whether it was her thought, or that of *Winter's Axiom,* or if there was any difference.

Hwa Young hated herself for it. Knew she had to let go of her reflexive defensiveness. They were on the same side, even if Aera's attempts to reestablish their relationship usually fizzled into mutual awkwardness.

Hwa Young didn't know how to explain her resistance in terms that Aera would accept. It wasn't that she hated being Hwajin, exactly . . . but the other pilots knew her as Hwa Young. *Geum* knew her as Hwa Young. She didn't want to surrender that.

"My name," she said slowly. "I could . . . I could talk to the other pilots about that. Although I think it'd take them time to make the adjustment."

She'd chickened out and she knew it. Ye Jun, Eun, and Bae were sharp. They hadn't slipped once when adopting their new callsigns. She hadn't either. She was proud of that. The barrier was her own reluctance.

Despite Hwa Young's equivocation, Aera's answering smile made her entire face radiant. Hwa Young was forcibly reminded that she hadn't seen her heart-mother *happy* since . . . since they'd been torn apart. Shame wormed in her belly at the reminder that Aera had also lost family; had, perhaps, thrown herself into fighting New Joseon in revenge. How did she feel about the fact that the only other survivor, her heart-daughter, had dwelled with the enemy for *six years*?

Hwa Young almost blurted out an apology, then thought better of it. Instead, she attempted a hesitant return smile.

She could ask about Geum now . . . but best not to ruin the moment. Build up goodwill, cooperate with Aera, wait for the right time.

Aera's eyes crinkled as she settled the satchel before Hwa Young. "Oh, a small gift . . . I hope I'm not overstepping."

Hwa Young blinked in bemusement. Aera, concerned about being pushy? What was she about to pull out of the bag? A baby dragon to babysit? A plushie, as though she were still a kid? A baby dragon plushie?

She yelped and rose, drawing her gun, when Aera drew out a *hair thing* that her hindbrain interpreted as a disheveled vicious animal.

Aera burst into laughter as she pushed Hwa Young's hand down so the gun pointed harmlessly at the deck. Hwa Young had switched to carrying a clanner semiautomatic pistol, which fired kinetic bullets, rather than her Imperial Mark 25 flare pistol, which fired plasma bolts. The battery packs for the Mark 25 had run out of charge long ago; she kept the Mark 25 in her cabin as a memento.

Hwa Young flushed, still wary. "What *is* that?"

Aera didn't answer until Hwa Young had holstered her gun. "It's a wig." She lifted it up and fussed with the strands until it looked less like a vicious attack mop.

It was, in fact, a wig, with rippling dark locks that would, when donned, extend down to her waist. Hwa Young found this ridiculous. For reasons of practicality she'd have to pin it up. Why not make it in that style to begin with? Or keep her hair trimmed short, like it was now?

Did it disturb Aera that much that clanners kept addressing Hwa Young as a boy? Even if it didn't matter to Hwa Young herself? She couldn't articulate why she'd continued to trim her hair short. Sometimes she thought it wasn't all bad to keep people guessing, or to defer the question. If the clanners couldn't handle it, that was their problem.

It didn't help that the wig was hideous.

Only for you, Geum. Only for you.

If making nice with Mother Aera meant wearing a wig until her hair grew out, so be it. She didn't imagine that her smile looked genuine, but Aera's eyes lit up. Maybe Aera couldn't tell the difference.

Hwa Young struggled with the wig cap before settling it atop her hair. Aera helped her do it up, which was good because Hwa Young had always relied on Geum for help with any complex hairstyles.

Aera beamed as she produced a mirror. Hwa Young goggled at her reflection. The wig obscured the white streak in her hair. She and Aera looked like twins.

Because Hwa Young had grown up with clanner customs, the long hair that now framed her face felt like it accentuated her femininity. The Imperials wouldn't understand; they didn't have the same rules around fashion. But Hwa Young had never unlearned those responses. She'd *cried* when she was forced to cut her hair all those months ago.

Why did she hate being given back long hair? Did having short hair like the other pilots mean that much to her? Or was it something else—a hint that, deep down, she didn't see herself as a young woman, but something else?

Aera and I look the same, and that's the point, Hwa Young recited over and over in her head. *This is right. It makes Aera happy.* Seeing Aera happy made *her* happy.

"I see the Rose-Merline has taken a liking to you," Aera added, as though discussion of someone flirting with Hwa Young was a segue guaranteed to distract Hwa Young from the *itching*. Her smile took on a secretive amusement.

"The" Rose-Merline? Hwa Young wondered. Was Aera so self-conscious that she was making errors? Had she run afoul of some weird clanner grammar convention? Or had Hwa Young misunderstood that Rose-Merline was a name, when it was actually a foreign title?

Before Hwa Young could inquire further, Aera offered, "Snack?" She pulled a packaged cookie out of one of her many pockets, then held it out as though Hwa Young were a wild animal to be tamed.

Hwa Young had planned on accepting the cookie like a civilized person. Instead, she met Aera's eyes—an open challenge—and blurted out, "If you were keeping track of me for *six years,* why didn't you come for me earlier? Why did you let New Joseon have me?"

Before, she would never have dared say this out loud, despite thinking it often during the past two months. She wouldn't have risked losing Aera's cooperation—for Geum's sake. Now, however—she couldn't let the question drive them apart while both of them avoided bringing it up. This was the best chance Hwa Young would ever have, with Aera in a good mood.

Aera's hand froze: so like Hwa Young's, except the faint tracks of scars and burn marks from cooking, evidence of a separate life.

Her face remained smooth, calm, as unrevealing as a veiled mirror. Then her fingers tightened. Inside the wrapper, the cookie went *crunch*.

Oh no, Hwa Young thought, shoulders tensing. *I misjudged the moment.*

Hwa Young considered disintegration herself. She hadn't meant to upset Aera that much. Especially when her heart-mother had made a longed-for overture.

What she should do was lower her eyes. Offer an apology in the formal clanner way, as she'd learned in childhood. Take the jagged words back, even if they expressed the way she felt—the messy turmoil she'd been trying to deny since they joined Falcon Fleet.

Aera said, with a quiet wretchedness that hurt Hwa Young more than a fist to the face, "I wondered if you were happier with the Imperials than you were with me. If you had a new family to love you. A new mother who didn't fail you."

Geum would have known what to say. Hwa Young scooped up a napkin and heard herself murmuring, "I'll clean that up, Mother-mine."

Aera's eyes brimmed. She set her hand down as carefully as though it were a wounded nestling, and the cookie with it. Only then did Hwa Young realize she'd used a child's form of address to a heart-mother, rather than Aera's rank or the more formal address appropriate once one entered puberty. The term had slipped out. Unlike the earlier fumbles, however, this one strengthened their connection rather than snipping at it, gaffe by awful gaffe.

Aera sat in silence for several moments. Everything about her spoke of calm consideration, from the stilled face to the careful softness of the hands—everything but the glimmer of tears unshed.

Hwa Young started to panic at Aera's lack of response. *Breathe. It'll be all right. Breathe.*

She could have reached for *Winter's Axiom*, seeking solace in its heart of ice. When she'd newly bonded with the lancer, she wouldn't have hesitated to do so. She admitted to herself now that, at times, she'd sought excuses to cocoon herself in the welcome chilly numbness.

Instead, Hwa Young reached across the table and pressed Aera's hand in hers. She'd been so focused on how *she* felt about their forced separation that she'd never wondered about *Aera's* feelings.

"It must have been hard on you too," Hwa Young said, hating the stilted quality of her words.

"Everything is harder than you think," Aera said, almost to herself, with a brittleness that Hwa Young had never associated with her. Wasn't Aera the one who always knew what to do?

Hwa Young released Aera's hand. She knew how to ease that frozen, masklike expression from her heart-mother's face. It would require giving up something that had brought her comfort for years, the one memento of her childhood—but it hadn't belonged to her, not really.

She reached for her belt, found the sheath there, leather lined with a tough, oily wood that wouldn't absorb moisture. It was Mother Aera's voting knife, the one Hwa Young had saved when the Imperials destroyed their home. While she assumed Aera had obtained a new one, Hwa Young hadn't caught sight of it.

After all, debating and *voting* on orders made little sense in a military context.

"Your knife," Hwa Young said. She didn't resent how the roughness of her voice revealed her vulnerability. The *point* was vulnerability. "I—I saved it. I should have given it back earlier."

Hwa Young held it out to Aera, with the sheathed blade pointing toward her heart-mother. In clanner tradition, if the blade had belonged to Hwa Young, this would have signaled an expression of loyalty: *My blade is ready for you to guide.* While she prided herself on her steadiness, this once she didn't mind too much that her hands shook.

Aera's eyes widened as she sucked in her breath, so immediate her surprise had to be real. "I knew you had it," she whispered. "But I didn't want—didn't want to ask what you'd done with it, after."

How could she not know? Hwa Young had attacked her with it back on Carnelian, before realizing who she was. Had Aera thought Hwa Young had discarded it in a fit of pique? Dropped it in a vat of acid?

"It's yours," Hwa Young said inadequately. For years it had served as the one thread knotting her to the clanner past she'd cast away . . . the family she'd lost, the heart-mother who'd died.

But Aera wasn't dead after all, and they had a chance to try again. To braid themselves back into a family, even if it was only the two of them.

Aera accepted the blade, her lips slightly parted, her expression avid to the point of ecstasy. "You're mine and I'm yours," Aera said reverently. Then Aera offered the blade *back* to Hwa Young. "You should have received your own when you turned sixteen. I'm giving this to you now."

Aera's thumb shifted to reveal the character for *heart* carved into the hilt.

Hwa Young's heart lifted as a weight she hadn't known she was carrying dissolved. "You're mine and I'm yours," she repeated, receiving the blade in turn. Maybe—just maybe—her wish for a real family, a real *mother*, was coming true after all.

5

GEUM

After the Empress called, Admiral Chin left Geum rotting in the brig. Geum wished this weren't such a familiar sensation. Zie was dying for an update, or a replacement sweet bean pastry.

The guards had forgotten about zir too. They made no effort to keep their voices down. Geum caught fragments, maddeningly garbled thanks to the acoustics: ". . . really? Only two?" or "Like that's gonna help the supply situation" or ". . . 8–1 on the betting . . ."

Geum dismissed the comment on supplies as griping. The food was plentiful, but it tasted dismal no matter how often zie had flattered the cook. Zie had a policy of not offending the people preparing the meals, which was difficult to do from here.

An indeterminate amount of time later, Geum's stomach lurched. After several minutes of fighting back the urge to puke, zie connected the dots: ship's gravity had shifted. Even on Carnelian, the downward pull hadn't been this assertive, this *overwhelming*.

"Excuse me," Geum called out, wishing the guards would drift back into visual range. A superpower of killer dimples did no good if no one was watching. "Did we wander into the path of a feral black hole or something?"

I can't be the only one who remembers the singularity bomb. Getting sucked past a black hole's event horizon, its point of no return, and being stretched like overheated taffy for a time-warped eternity sounded like a shitty way to die. Hwa Young might have confronted the threat fearlessly. Geum knew too much about physics to contemplate the weapon without shuddering.

This time the guards consulted each other in hushed voices.

So much for eavesdropping. Geum sighed, closed zir eyes, and stretched out on the pallet that passed for a bed. "Fine," zie muttered, "be that way."

Idly, zie queried the computer. Had Hwa Young sent any updates on her latest operation? Metal-on-metal taps and clangs gave zir the answer: *Not yet. Miss you. Together forever.*

No signature, but *together forever* was how the two of them always closed. Additional clangs indicated that the message dated back two weeks. Still, why not think positive? Perhaps something had changed and *not yet* was about to become *right now*.

A clue as to the source of the new improved gravity appeared with Geum's next meal. Zie had spent the interim ogling the stale and now-gross red bean pastry, which nobody had removed from the deck. Appallingly, Geum started salivating whenever an air current wafted its smell in zir direction.

Geum heard the footsteps first. *Hwa Young?* zie wondered,

except the tread was off, and it made no logistical sense. The same self-assured quality, but sharper, louder. Hwa Young had the soft footfalls of someone for whom ambush and camouflage were a way of life.

The newcomer came into view a moment later. She would have stood out anywhere in Eleventh Fleet, not just because she was a stranger: a compact, flat-chested woman in her late twenties, half muscle and all vigor, imposing despite being short. No one on the *Maehwa* affected her hairstyle, a crown of blond braids. And her eyes—she had the eyes of a lancer pilot, blazing with unnatural colors, hot amber with leaf-green flecks. The eyes of most pilots only changed color when they were actively linked to their lancers. Geum had heard that, for those who achieved deeper levels of connection, the change became permanent. Hers matched the name of her lancer, *Summer Thorn*.

Geum recognized the woman; who didn't? Mi Cha, lieutenant to Captain of the Royal Guard Ga Ram, second most powerful lancer pilot in New Joseon. Not the kind of person an ordinary citizen, let alone one in the brig, expected to pay a call.

Behind her, eyes downcast, was another woman, pretty enough, but cursed with an unflattering haircut. Geum almost didn't notice her due to her unassuming, servantlike demeanor. Then zie marked her insignia: Mi Cha's copilot. Geum struggled to remember the woman's name.

I bet she makes a great spy and that she works *at fading into the background.*

"Pilot," Geum said shakily. Zie rose to salute, remembering that the second-in-command of the Empress's own guard was no ordinary officer. She probably ate lesser officers for a snack.

Mi Cha studied Geum's insignia. "Your name, Technician?"

She used the bluntest language imaginable, just short of insult even allowing for the difference in their ranks.

"Geum of the An Clan." Zie lowered zir eyes in a proper show of respect.

"Lieutenant Mi Cha." She had a low voice, one that carried. Mi Cha didn't reveal her family name, as was proper. Pilots gave those up when they bonded with a lancer. As elite fighters, their devotion to the Empress superseded any family ties.

Nor did she introduce her copilot, who stood diffidently a step behind Mi Cha, apparently uninterested in the proceedings. Geum wasn't fooled.

Hwa Young, as a ward of the state, hadn't possessed a family name. At least, not an *Imperial* one. Geum still didn't know anything about Hwa Young's birth family. The realization made zir feel terrible. What was more important than family or friends? Something zie would remedy when they saw each other again.

Mi Cha bared her teeth. "So you're the best friend of the traitor Hwa Young."

Geum swallowed a protest. Admiral Chin must have briefed Mi Cha. Was she here to carry out the beatings or torture that the admiral had refrained from? Or was she that desperate for a spoiled sweet bean pastry?

"I know what you're thinking," Mi Cha went on. "Feeling sorry for yourself because you're about to be punched full of holes until you confess the way that thug Chin wanted you to."

Hearing the admiral referred to with such naked disrespect shocked Geum into silence. Not because zie had any love for Admiral Chin, but because zie had grown a sense of self-preservation.

"Chin," Mi Cha said, "allowed her anger to cloud her judgment.

I can't blame her." Her voice turned sweetly sarcastic. "It must be embarrassing beyond belief that her own lancer squad—her *lancer squad!*—would rather fight alongside a bunch of grubby clanners than stay one more second in her fleet. I would have paid cold hard cash to be a moth on the wall when she was sweating blood over her report to the Empress." Mi Cha's eyes sparkled with malicious amusement.

Geum found that zie was leaning forward, drinking in every word. Mi Cha had a nasty sense of humor, but she wasn't wrong. Still—what did she *want*? And what was her unnamed copilot listening for?

Mi Cha's smile hit Geum like a crescent moon crossed with an uppercut. "You're wondering what I want, Technician."

"Yes, sir," Geum said. There was no point denying it. What was she doing aboard the *Maehwa*? Did that mean the rest of the Imperial Guard had accompanied her here? Was Eleventh Fleet about to be sucked into battle?

"It's the wrong question."

Geum blinked. "Yes, sir." The words spilled out automatically; a flush heated zir face.

Mi Cha began to pace in front of Geum's cell, like a predator strutting down a fashion runway. She couldn't be unaware of the effect, especially with the way she paused every time she passed in front of Geum.

Meanwhile, her copilot stood silent, faking boredom. *How is it that I don't know her name?* Geum fretted. Captain Ga Ram's copilot was Shi Woo, some Imperial cousin twice removed, mentioned on the news once in a while. But *Mi Cha's* copilot? Not one word, nowhere in the records that Geum recalled. Why?

"The real question," Mi Cha said, "is what the *Empress* wants."

Her entire face glowed with the exaltation of a true believer, a status Geum had never claimed.

Geum wondered what it was like to have that kind of guiding star in one's life. What would it be like to *believe* in the rituals that glued the Empire together, as opposed to mouthing them by rote? Ironically, the one person zie knew who possessed that focused faith was Hwa Young.

"Sir," Geum said, increasingly uncomfortable, "Admiral Chin must have told you everything I've reported. I had no idea that Hwa Young was going to join the other side. I don't know what she's up to now." The lies slid easily off zir tongue this time.

"Chin's convinced that you're covering up some deep secret." Mi Cha leaned in and grinned, like a shark menacing a minnow. "Here's what doesn't make sense. Why in the name of Heaven and Earth would you make your friendship with Hwa Young visible from outer space, leave your tracks all over the system while helping her escape at that battle, and then *stay behind?*"

I didn't plan to stay behind! Geum thought, struggling to keep the defensive anger from zir face. *I didn't think of escaping until it was too late.* Hwa Young hadn't *planned* to turn coat. She'd told Geum the story in one of her messages. Zie believed her . . . even if it meant swallowing zir resentment. It wasn't the first time Geum had bailed Hwa Young out of a tight spot and taken the fall as a result.

It would have been better if zie had insisted on riding along in *Winter's Axiom*. Neither Geum nor Hwa Young would be stuck in this fix.

Think positive. Geum studied the amber flecks in Mi Cha's eyes as though zie could map the topographies of her soul, her strengths and soft spots. *Let her think you're listening. Let her think she's figured you out.*

Never mind that Geum *was* listening, and Mi Cha did, in fact, have zir figured out. Those were negligible details.

Mi Cha's flaw wasn't the gilt-and-porcelain arrogance of Bae, born to wealth and a high station, saturated with suppurating conceit, a big fish in a small pond. Everyone in New Joseon had heard Mi Cha's story, inspiration if one was feeling generous and a sop to the lower classes otherwise. Her meteoric rise despite parents who were sewage workers.

Geum had assumed that Mi Cha's social climbing involved a talent for sucking up to powerful people. Having met her, zie couldn't imagine this woman sucking up to *anyone*. Nothing in their interactions suggested that Mi Cha had a small ego; quite the contrary. Zie could make use of that.

Geum lowered zir eyelashes in embarrassment that was only partly simulated. Allowed zirself to stumble over words as though zie was being graded on a presentation for a class zie hadn't prepared for. (Too easy to channel *that* feeling.) "Like I said. I had n-no idea she was a clanner. That she was going to go over to the other side. You're—you're the first person who's listened to me."

Geum clung to the truth that burned in zir heart, the lodestar certainty that Hwa Young would come for her. With any luck, Hwa Young would ditch Bae in the process too.

"Must be difficult," Mi Cha agreed. Her eyes slitted.

Don't overdo it. This wasn't a drama, where battles stopped dead so people could give ten-minute speeches, or they canted their heads so the moonlight reflected enchantingly off one perfectly framed perfect tear. Any acting had to look naturalistic.

"I knew the moment Chin mentioned that she had you locked up that I needed to talk to you for myself." Mi Cha smirked. "I can't imagine you stayed out of gratitude to *her*. Her own lancer squad deserted. Doesn't speak highly of her ability to inspire loyalty, does it?"

Geum didn't have a glib, nontreasonous response to this, so zie settled for looking attentive. *Don't forget you're being watched by two people, not just one.* That copilot had a positive gift for invisibility.

"It must have been very tempting to leave—this." Mi Cha's expansive gesture encompassed not just the brig but the entire situation. The hardscrabble existence of Eleventh Fleet. "Why didn't you?"

"Is this a discussion we want to have here?" Geum asked, trying not to squeak. Mi Cha might not care what the guards overheard, but zie did.

"Ah," she purred. Her eyes lit up like hard radiation.

"Let's . . ." Sweat crawled, antlike, down Geum's spine. *Damage control. Think of this as a mechanical problem: break down the big issue into small steps.* "There might be implications for shipboard security. Sir."

Would it work? Would this convince Mi Cha to open the cell?

"You know what I do to people who waste my time, Technician?"

At last the copilot showed a reaction other than apathy. Her eyes gleamed, brightly avid. Geum was starting to think that the copilot might be the scarier one. Mi Cha had a loud roar, but the copilot's subtle attentiveness suggested the deadliness and cunning of a scorpion.

"Yes, sir," Geum lied. Zie imagined it involved rocket launchers, novel uses of gardening shears, or the copilot's unknown talents. Good thing zie had no intention of engaging Mi Cha or the copilot in hand to hand. *Step one. Regain freedom of action.*

After that—I'll figure out what to do once I understand what in the Empress's name is going on.

Mi Cha shouted back to the guard station, "Hey you! Open the cell."

One of the guards poked his head around the corner, mouth working before he said, "Sir, that's Admiral Chin's personal prisoner."

What, like I'm a pet?

Mi Cha had turned toward the guard, so Geum couldn't see her expression, but the line of her back and shoulders radiated displeasure.

"Right away, sir."

If only I could make things happen like that. Geum had never had any luck with blunt force, as opposed to soft words and smiles. The way of bullet and hammer was Hwa Young's style: one reason they made such a great team.

The cell door opened with so little fuss that Geum almost didn't notice it. If it had happened in the middle of sleep shift, zie would have continued drowsing, missing a chance at freedom. Never mind that any liberty would have been short-lived, given surveillance on the *Maehwa*.

"Come on out," Mi Cha said, impatient, and Geum did.

Maybe I'll finally learn what's going on.

Geum didn't see a signal, but the copilot slipped off on her own as Mi Cha and Geum exited the brig together. Mi Cha *still* didn't mention the copilot's name, or acknowledge that she existed. A good sign, or a bad one?

At first, Geum thought the lieutenant was lost and didn't want to admit it. Then zir mood darkened: Mi Cha knew exactly where she was going. Maybe asking for privacy hadn't been such a good idea. In the brig, zie had gotten food and access to sanitary facilities. Where they were going, on the other hand—

They wound up in a supply closet. The place was filled with pipes, beakers, and a stinging chemical reek zie associated with the color neon green, and which was probably teratogenic.

A lopsided chair rested amid the clutter, bolted to the deck. Instead of seating herself, Mi Cha pointed imperiously at it. Geum sat. Not only was the chair wicked uncomfortable, this redressed the height difference between them, a fact lost on neither of them.

Geum finally identified the smell: "Is this a *distillery?*"

"You shouldn't drink while on duty," Mi Cha said dismissively. "Also, I fed some to a bug and it died, so the quality control has some issues."

She'd been here long enough to source bootleg . . . whatever? Geum wasn't wild about bugs, but the casual way she talked about killing one as a test subject disturbed zir.

"You were Hwa Young's advocate from the moment she showed up at that boarding school."

Alarm bells went off in Geum's head. This was much more of a background check than Admiral Chin had conducted. "Everyone needs a friend." Zie tried not to sound defensive, and failed.

It was true, though. At that time, Bae had already secured her position as the resident rich bitch. As one of the rare people who didn't kiss up to her, Geum had few friends . . . until Hwa Young showed up and, predictably, pissed off Bae. Geum had immediately seized the opportunity. Hwa Young had never figured out that Geum needed her as much as she needed Geum.

"Of course." Mi Cha clasped her hands behind her back. She would have made an excellent statue if one wanted to impress the viewers with their inferiority. Anyone taller couldn't have managed it in the confined space. "*Nobody* on this damned ship thought about what the *Empress* would want."

Above my pay grade did not seem to be the desired answer. Besides, it wasn't above *Admiral Chin's* pay grade. "We've been out of touch for so long . . ." Geum trailed off as zie realized what a pathetic argument this was. Besides, zie had ignored the opening; time to remedy that. "What *does* the Empress want?"

Mi Cha's smile hit Geum with the force of a fermented supernova. "She wants Ye Jun to come home."

Geum gaped, then clamped zir mouth shut. This wasn't where zie had thought the conversation would go. "Excuse me?"

"The Empress is preoccupied with matters of policy and grand strategy," Mi Cha said. "Now that the clanners have access to turncoat lancers, they can reverse engineer Imperial technology and become a *real* threat. It's imperative that she destroy that lancer squad *before* the clanners figure out enough to build lancers of their own. So far they've made little progress, but it's only a matter of time. She needs to extract Ye Jun and crush the others."

Geum's blood temperature plunged. Hwa Young was one of "the others."

Besides—how did Mi Cha know that the clanners were stymied in their reverse engineering attempts? Spies? Was *Ye Jun* still loyal and feeding information to New Joseon by means unknown?

"I don't see how I fit into this," Geum said.

"You have an opportunity to prove yourself a loyal Imperial citizen. All you have to do is bring your friend back home where she belongs." Mi Cha's voice softened, but it was the softness of poisoned petals. "She won't come to harm."

She hadn't said what would happen to Commander Ye Jun, or

Eun, or Bae. Not that Geum would cry if Bae got screwed over. And Seong Su was already dead.

"I suppose the Empress wants to make an example of Ye Jun," Geum said, remembering at the last moment that zie shouldn't refer to Ye Jun by rank.

Mi Cha neither confirmed nor denied this. Instead, she said, "The Empress would be a fool to ignore the potential of a pilot who bonded with *Winter's Axiom*." She spoke its name with a mixture of reverence and resentment. "You know the story, I assume."

Geum had supposed that Eleventh Fleet had received lancer units no one else wanted. Its lancer squad hadn't been feted the way Geum and Hwa Young had expected. They only found out about *Winter's Axiom*'s lethality when it killed Ha Yoon, Bae's loyal minion. Needles of dread pierced zir nerves when zie thought about the way it could have claimed zir, or Hwa Young, during the test to determine who would become pilots.

"I don't," Geum was about to say, because zie had never had the self-control to resist a juicy grain of gossip. What information did Mi Cha possess that Ye Jun *hadn't* shared with them—or hadn't known about either?

Before Mi Cha could spill any secrets, the door crashed open, notable since the distillery was one of the few places that had a hinged door. Which suggested, when Geum reflected on the oddity later, that this was a later addition, with the specific goal of escaping the notice of higher authorities. A mechanical door, unlike the powered sliding doors in the rest of the ship, did not involve any betraying power draw each time it was used. Either one would already have to know of its existence, or track someone to the location.

Geum had a scant moment to think *My voice isn't that loud, is it?* at the cacophony. A sudden new pull—a gravitational pull—overwhelmed zir.

"There you are, Lieutenant," said a sardonic alto, not the one Geum had expected. "You thought you could sneak away?"

Mi Cha glowered at Captain Ga Ram, the Empress's thirdborn and pilot of the lancer *Paradox*. "I have this handled. How long were you listening at the door?"

"Long enough," Captain Ga Ram said. Zie stood framed by the doorway, zir shadow cutting toward Geum. Zir face resembled the Empress's in its oval, fine-boned perfection, and zir eyes flashed, one red and one blue. "She's waiting for you to wrap this up."

"The Empress *is* here, sir?" Geum asked cautiously. It didn't take much brainpower to figure out that if gravity had righted itself and members of the Imperial Guard were swanning around on the *Maehwa*, the Empress couldn't be far behind.

"Of course," Mi Cha said, as self-satisfied as a cat who had purloined a swordfish steak.

Geum tried, and failed, to think of a good reason for the Empress to visit Eleventh Fleet, as opposed to enjoying a banquet of roast peacock and candied jujubes, or contemplating a collection of teacups carved from fossilized dragons, or ordering a moon to be moved so she could enjoy a full moon for a scheduled poetry contest.

"You see," Mi Cha added, before the captain could stop her, "Ye Jun sent word that zie's going to sabotage the clanners from within. The Empress has come to capitalize on this opportunity—with *your* help."

6

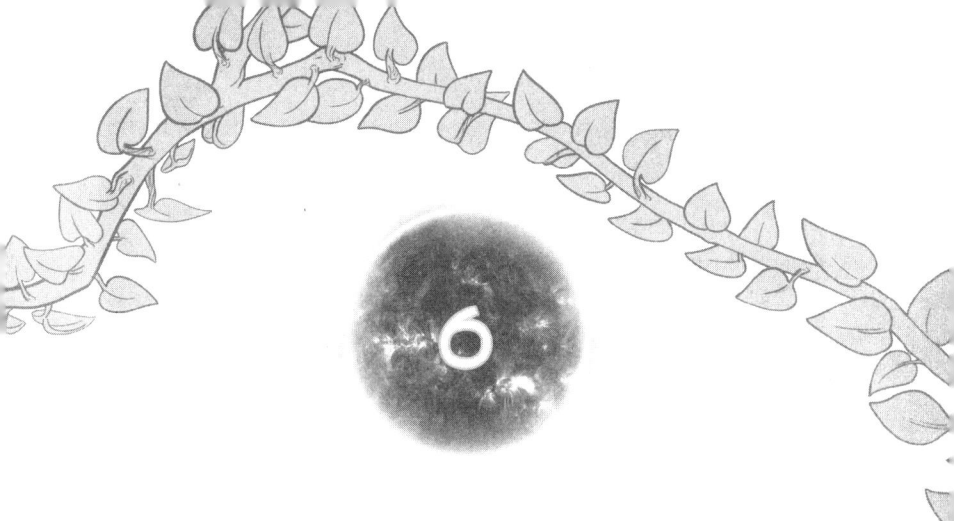

HWA YOUNG

My name is Hwajin.
  My name is Hwajin.
  My name is Hwajin.
My name is Hwajin.

She should have stopped writing the sentence after the third time. The Imperials and some clanners considered *four* to be bad luck, because the number sounded like the word for *death* in Hangeul. It struck her as appropriate, though: she was shedding her identity as an Imperial.

Four lines on a repurposed candy wrapper wasn't enough to scrub those years away. Besides, she'd run out of space, despite writing as small as she could. How could she surrender that part of herself when she piloted an Imperial lancer?

You are always yourself, the lancer said, untroubled, *skull and all.*

"Looks like you're trying to convince yourself," Eun commented from over her shoulder.

Hwa Young stared at the desk because she didn't want to meet his eyes. "Don't make this any harder."

Earlier today, she'd wondered why Eun was uncharacteristically late for a session of sparring at the gym, and traipsed around the ship to find him. She found him at Zeng's lab, the doors ajar, the two of them with their hands all over each other. His love life wasn't her concern, but her cheeks heated whenever she remembered the way his head had tipped back, his eyelids fluttering shut, mouth open on a noise she was trying not to think about.

Hwa Young had attempted to slip away unnoticed. Unfortunately for her, Eun's situational awareness was as good as ever. He snapped to, spotted her, and grinned with an unabashed delight she'd never seen before on a face accustomed to scowls.

"Don't tell me *you've* never dated," Eun drawled.

Hwa Young fixed her gaze on a table, as opposed to the scarred and muscled expanse of chest revealed by his open shirt, among other open things. It was pretty clear that they were doing more than just *dating*. "Excuse me," she'd muttered. "I was leaving."

To her surprise, *Zeng* had been blushing too. Hwa Young thought, *If you didn't want an audience, maybe close the door first?*

"Hey." Eun's expression fell into sober lines, not unfriendly but concerned. "Seriously. I can, uh, deal with this later. Was there something you needed to talk about?"

Hwa Young and Zeng exchanged a wry look of perfect mutual understanding: *No, Eun! Don't put your foot in it by dissing your date right in the middle of making out!*

"No, no," Hwa Young said. "Find me later when you want your ass kicked."

"Anytime," he shot back as she waved and turned, too hastily, so she wouldn't have to see what the couple did next.

Hwa Young squirmed, wishing she could stuff that memory into a box rather than have it play out in her mind's eye while Eun himself was looming over her here and now. If she found him carving his and Zeng's initials into the side of the table she was sitting at, she was going to die of secondhand embarrassment.

Would anyone ever touch *her* like that? She hadn't entertained the idea before, despite Geum's friendly teasing. She'd been so focused on training to secure a lancer that relationships seemed petty and irrelevant. Now that she had a lancer, though . . .

Is Bae seeing anyone? Everyone had been scarce of late. Ye Jun spent hours closeted with the officers on *Falcon Actual,* attempting to solve the riddle of the Imperials' disjointed strategy. Eun— well. It warmed her that he'd interrupt a hot date to check in on her. He would have made a great older brother, or what she imagined a great older brother to be like. She sometimes wondered what family he'd left behind, but he never spoke of them.

Bae, on the other hand—Bae vanished without a word to anyone, except maybe Commander Ye Jun. Hwa Young had no idea where Bae spent off-duty time, whether that involved a quest for bootleg facial masks, advanced combat training from an underground fighting ring, or . . . a mystery date of her own?

Hwa Young hated the thought, hated herself for caring. It was none of her business how Bae spent her free time. Still, they were a *squad.* The point of the squad was that they had each other's backs.

Their accommodations aboard *Falcon Actual* consisted of a suite larger than the one they'd had on the *Maehwa.* It boasted a table, one end of which Hwa Young currently claimed. Alcoves in the bulkheads held wire sculptures of trees. There was a fragrance dispenser next to the door, which none of them used. (The fragrance made Eun sneeze, like many clanner perfumes. The previous one had given him hives. It would be a great way to poison them, with or without anaphylactic shock.)

Commander Ye Jun shared their living quarters, which Hwa Young had almost adjusted to. At the moment, zie sat at the other end of the table, politely ignoring Hwa Young and Eun, zir head bent over a notebook filled with logistical calculations and diagrams.

Hwa Young finally gave in to curiosity. "Say," she said to Ye Jun, "where's Bae, anyway?"

"Personal business," Ye Jun said without looking up.

Hwa Young deflated. The commander's tone had been level rather than reprimanding, but she could take a hint.

"You know," Ye Jun added with a casualness that didn't fool her anymore, "if you're going to pursue anyone, you might as well cultivate the cryptobotanist."

As far as Hwa Young knew, that meant Rose-Merline. Or *the* Rose-Merline, whatever that signified. There didn't seem to be anyone else in cryptobotany.

Hwa Young bristled at having her love life dictated. But maybe this was normal to Ye Jun, as a member, however illegitimate, of the royal family. Royals and nobles rarely got to choose partners for romantic reasons, as opposed to political ones.

"She's nice enough, sir," Hwa Young said, keeping her tone bland. Better than nice, to be honest. She'd caught herself wondering what it would be like to kiss Rose-Merline, run her hands along those strong arms, cup the curvature of her hips. They worked in different departments; it wouldn't break clanner regs against fraternization.

"New Joseon has been aware of the clanner preoccupation with horticulture for some time," Ye Jun said. "No one has ever uncovered an explanation other than 'spiritual practices' or 'some founding colonist adored container gardening and inflicted it on everyone.' Maybe the ensign knows something."

This only made Hwa Young want to shrivel up and hide. Her tentative curiosity about Rose-Merline was one thing; hitting on her for the purpose of gathering intel made her feel grimy. Especially intel about *gardening*, of all things. Ye Jun couldn't be unaware of her reaction. "I'll think about it."

Ye Jun shrugged. "Just keep an ear out, if you would."

Hwa Young wondered what zie *wasn't* saying. She knew better than to assume that they enjoyed true privacy even in their quarters. Did zie suspect that there was something more sinister behind all the plants? Did zie have a secret burning desire to enter a flower-arranging contest? "All right," she said reluctantly.

Meanwhile, Eun peered more closely at Hwa Young's self-imposed journaling: "I don't know what's weirder, the new wig or the fact that you're using candy wrappers to write on."

"They were available," Hwa Young said grouchily, choosing to address the less fraught topic of candy wrappers. She had a small stash of Imperial snacks stowed in her lancer: the remnants of the care package Geum had bestowed on her. She'd consolidated the original box for space but retained the items.

"This wig itches," Hwa Young added, feeling like a child for mentioning it. She hadn't asked Aera if there was some way to ameliorate the sensation on the grounds that Aera might take it the wrong way. Since she'd been unable to replicate Aera's hairstyle after some of the loops came loose, she experimented with other styles. One of them had, according to a note from Aera flagged as *URGENT,* been actively offensive. Something about . . . puppet theater? Eun wasn't the only one making fashion gaffes.

Naturally, Bae was admired throughout the ship for her good taste and style. Maybe she should ask Bae for wig help, if she was ever around.

"I bet," Eun said, sympathy from an unexpected source. "My aunt lost all her hair after a radiation accident. At least you *have* hair. She said the wigs itched worse against her bald scalp, no matter how many wig caps she went through."

His voice had wavered on *aunt.* Hwa Young was forcibly reminded that the rest of them had families, as unquiet ghosts or unreachable shadows. It must have taken a lot for Eun to share this, when he was normally reticent about his relatives. She had the dubious advantage that Aera had turned up alive.

Ye Jun's badge chimed. "We're to meet Commander Aera at the docking bay," zie said.

"What about Bae?" Hwa Young asked, attempting to settle her wig so the bangs didn't obscure her vision.

Ye Jun relented. "Bae has business in Medical and will meet us at the docking bay."

Medical? Oh no, is Bae sick? Hwa Young regretted all her snippy thoughts about Bae's absences.

Ye Jun slanted her a long, thoughtful look. "I want you on your best behavior, Hwajin."

Indignation flared in her heart every time someone addressed her by that name, no matter how much she tried to reconcile herself to it. But she had promised Aera she would try. If that meant suppressing her grimace, so be it. "Of course, sir."

We'll joke about it when you get here, Geum. She didn't expect *Geum* to switch the name zie called her by; wouldn't want zir to.

Ten minutes later, they crowded around their lancers, still an incongruous sight in the docking bay. The machines were never *not* going to look like Imperial technology, whether powered up or in their neutral gray state.

Commander Ye Jun's *Bastard* and Eun's *Hellion* had emblems painted on their chest armor: an upside-down antler crown for the former, a stylized flame for the latter. Hwa Young and Bae had never done likewise; there'd never been a good time for it. Sometimes she thought about requisitioning paint and giving it a try, although art wasn't one of her better skills. Yet Hwa Young could have identified *Winter's Axiom* in the darkness, navigated unerringly to it by its wintry presence echoing through her soul. She could just as easily identify the other lancers, although their minds remained closed to her.

Winter's Axiom was home, not the clanners. Hwa Young shoved away the thought the moment it came to her.

Of the lancers, only *Winter's Axiom* talked to her, currently a watchful murmuration without any mention of bony anatomy. The other lancers repelled her, strongly or subtly. She could no more have piloted *Bastard* or *Hellion* or *Farseer* (she avoided thinking about Seong Su's *Avalanche*) than she could have manifested gills and transformed into a shark.

Commander Aera hadn't shown up, but Zeng was already here. He and Eun didn't use the opportunity to flirt. She approved of their professional demeanor: a casual observer might have mistaken them for cordial strangers. She ducked her head, flushing, flashing back to the image of the two half undressed.

Hwa Young was more intrigued by Zeng's toolbox. Exquisite

work, all gleaming lacquer and vine-curve abalone or mother-of-pearl inlay, the kind of item that should hold heirloom jewelry.

A clanner technician and her team were hard at work on lancer maintenance, an ongoing bone of contention. The lead technician went by Flute, on account of her high-pitched voice, bamboo-slender build, and swaying walk. Hwa Young had a hard time following the way she half spoke, half chanted in lilting syllables. A number of clanners spoke languages with tones or pitch accents. Maybe Hwa Young's own speech sounded disrespectfully monotone to Flute. She'd have to ask sometime.

Eun leaned over the edge of his lancer's lift, about one story up if the lancer had been a house. Hwa Young hoped he didn't fall and break his neck. "This missile rack isn't retracting properly after it fires."

Flute shared the lift with him, her pinched expression and nervous, darting glances at the deck suggesting she shared Hwa Young's concerns about safety. "Hellion," she said, "I don't think the issue is with the rack, but with the control software."

Occasionally Eun surprised Hwa Young by employing tact, not a trait he wasted on most people. "I can't run diagnostics on that, Technician. Do you have tricks that might help?"

Flute launched into a discussion of control interfaces and purloined firmware updates, which Hwa Young listened to with half an ear. She attended to her own maintenance, remotely guiding the clanners' robot assistants in cleaning out her lancer's massive rifle. The buildup of chemical residue could prove dangerous, and she didn't want to risk a misfire or worse.

When they'd belonged to Eleventh Fleet, they'd depended on a team of technicians who specialized in lancers. During training,

Eun had only covered the basics, the emergency how-to of "if your lancer breaks down during combat and you need to jury-rig some fixes until you can return to base for a proper repair."

As pilots, they had more direct experience with the lancer units, especially the neural link, than any of the clanners. Even Zeng, who claimed it as one of his areas of research.

If only we had Geum. Geum had trained under Chief and learned fast. Surely Aera understood that zie would be an asset to the fleet?

Bae swept in partway through Flute's lecture. Hwa Young was too preoccupied to do more than glance her way. *Her* hair remained short: she clipped it assiduously.

Not long after that, Commander Aera showed up. "Sorry I'm late," she said, breathless, face flushed, as she ducked beneath a vine and jogged toward the lancers. She gave no further explanation of what she'd been doing despite being the one to call the meeting. "I have a proposal for you."

She addressed herself to Ye Jun, but Hwa Young joined them. Eun and Bae followed suit.

Commander Aera squared her shoulders. "Admiral Mae has requested a combat capability drill."

"What," Eun said, "our combat data isn't good enough?"

"This will be different," Zeng said at a nod from Aera. He gesticulated as he spoke, wafting cologne everywhere. "We want your lancers' flight computers hooked up to our scribers while we run you through a standardized set of exercises. An obstacle course of sorts. Just so we can get a baseline on the neural link and its haptic encoding."

"So they're like flight recorders?" Hwa Young said, frowning.

"You've overcome the operating system issues?" Hwa Young's knowledge of computers was confined to what she'd osmosed from hanging out with Geum and zir hacker adventures or trying to adapt ancient games to run on modern hardware. The clanners didn't just run incompatible software; their chip architecture was completely different.

"Mostly, yes," Zeng said, speaking more rapidly as he warmed to his subject. "It's a new design. We're hoping that, by correlating the scribers' observations of the neural interface with the raw telemetry data, we'll be able to reverse engineer the lancers' brains—*without* vivisecting one for parts."

Hwa Young shuddered at the word choice, as did the others. The lancers might not be human, but like any pilot, she felt damage done to her own. Couldn't imagine what such a procedure would do to the living *pilot*.

I am not a skeleton to be taken apart for trophies, Winter's Axiom agreed.

"No downside, huh?" Eun said with forced cheer. He cocked an eyebrow in Ye Jun's direction. Ye Jun ignored him.

"The 'brains' are what you care about?" Hwa Young asked. "Not the gravitic technology?"

Aera was the one who answered. "The basis of *gravitic* technology is easy enough to figure out, Hwajin."

Hwa Young's cheeks heated.

The clanners possessed sophisticated biotechnology, hard-won from adapting their own people to the harsher living conditions in the Moonstorm. New Joseon had more advanced control of gravity and terraforming thanks to its citizens' trained conformity and worship of the Empress. This permitted the establishment of sizable worlds with stable orbits, as opposed to the Moonstorm's wandering celestial bodies. The technology extended to artificial gravity aboard starships and bases, levitators for vehicles, and the gravity lances from which the lancer mecha took their name.

The Imperials had taken this to its logical endpoint by inventing the singularity bomb: the artificial generation of a black hole from which nothing could escape once it passed the event horizon. A brilliant and devastating weapon, if one disregarded the human cost. The black hole's creation required the sacrifice of Imperial subjects brainwashed into single-minded prayer; and then there were the casualties, and the aftereffects. Hwa Young had never heard that one could get rid of a black hole once it existed. Even decay radiation couldn't cause a sufficiently large black hole to evaporate within a human lifetime, or an empire's.

"Besides," Aera added, "we've captured scraps of Imperial tech before. We have been working on singularity lances of our own." She might have been referring to fancy food processors or next-generation nose hair trimmers, as opposed to military hardware. "The opportunity to study state-of-the-art, top-secret tech like the lancers themselves and their control systems, though—that's new. We need your cooperation."

Hwa Young willed Ye Jun to say yes. To keep Aera in a good mood. This sounded better than *vivisection.*

"It needs to be done," Commander Ye Jun said.

Hwa Young caught herself exhaling in relief.

Eun grunted his assent.

Hwa Young looked at the others. *Four for death,* whispered an omen in her head. Maybe *Winter's Axiom,* invoking the old superstition.

Seong Su's death permeated the shadows, intensifying their darkness so it seemed impossible that no one else saw the way the docking bay had transformed into a dungeon of portents. Everywhere she looked, his silhouette stretched toward her, reproachful: *Why didn't you save me?*

She wasn't the only one who carried death at her heel like an untamed hound. The others had haunts of their own. Commander Ye Jun and Eun were the only survivors of Eleventh Fleet's previous lancer squad, before she and Bae and Seong Su were recruited.

"And you, Bae?" Aera asked.

Bae coughed. "I'm amenable." Her voice cracked.

Hwa Young looked at Bae, *really* looked. She had spent most of her school years scrutinizing Bae, trying to figure out how to defend herself from the next put-down or prank. Bae's hair had been freshly trimmed, shorter yet, in a new style that accentuated the finely sculpted face, the high cheekbones, the newly prominent angles. Hwa Young had seen less beautiful actors. The clothes, which looked drab and utilitarian on everyone else, achieved a grunge chic on Bae.

Why didn't Aera provide Bae with a wig too?

Hwa Young finally put two and two together. Bae wasn't a girl—might never have been one. "*That's* why you've been at Medical," she blurted out. The moment after the words galloped out of her mouth, she wanted to plummet through the deck. She hadn't meant to put Bae on the spot like that.

The corner of Bae's mouth twitched. "I was waiting for a better time to tell you. When—when things were further along." This time Bae's speech emerged in a smoky baritone.

"We'll talk more later?" Hwa Young said, hating the way her own voice squeaked.

Bae gave a quick nod, with a sardonic smile that let Hwa Young know that he wasn't *completely* pissed at her for missing the obvious. How ironic that she'd been fooled by inertia, by the way Bae had always possessed a slender build. Hwa Young had been going by *Imperial* social cues, not the clanner ones.

Commander Ye Jun resumed the conversation, discussing technical details with Zeng: ". . . assume you'll be receiving data from the recorders over a dedicated comms channel. Or are you going to rely on physical retrieval and readout?"

Zeng nodded. "Dedicated channel. It'd be too inefficient to monkey with a screwdriver just to get at the data. Not like anyone else is going to be able to glean anything from the transmission anyway. You can shut it off as needed to avoid giving away your position."

All they wanted the pilots to do was open up the cockpits so the technicians could gain access. This was simple enough. While the technicians performed the installation, Hwa Young tried to figure out what, if anything, she wanted to say to Bae.

"Your hair looks great," she offered, wishing she had Geum's talent for flattery. Even if Geum and Bae had never gotten along. Surely that was safe enough to say?

She was desperate to talk to Bae about it, find out *why now* and not when they'd both lived on Serpentine. Bae might or might not be willing to talk about it later. The docking bay, in front of a bunch of technicians doing delicate work, was *definitely* not the right time or place.

Bae tossed his head and flashed a smile, this time with a genuine affection she'd never expected to be directed at her. "*That* goes without saying," he remarked, and they both laughed.

What *were* the technicians doing up there? Manufacturing silicon from scratch by seeding stellar formation in the nearest nebula? Occasional exclamations of "What is *that*?" and "I think you put it in upside down? Or maybe backward" did not reassure Hwa Young.

Commander Ye Jun had similar reservations. "Researcher," zie said, "how much longer will the installation take?"

Zeng fidgeted, releasing a whiff of a completely different cologne. How many different ones was he wearing at the same time? "At a guess—"

He was interrupted by the shrilling of high alert.

"Admiral Mae of *Falcon Actual* to all units" came the voice, deep and harsh with urgency. "We have contact with hostiles. Repeat, we have contact with hostiles. We've ID'd them as Imperials. All units prepare for immediate combat."

Ye Jun cursed. "No time to uninstall all this. We're needed *now*. All pilots suit up and prepare for launch."

7
GEUM

After Mi Cha rescued Geum from the brig, she allowed zir to return to zir quarters. The first thing Geum did was check for messages through a slate, a luxury zie would never take for granted again. A new missive had arrived.

CO says wait. I'm working on it. Together forever.

Geum's eyes misted despite the tightness in zir chest at yet another delay in a litany of delays. *I won't give up,* zie promised Hwa Young, absent though she was. Zie whispered, "Together forever." The words tasted like summer honey over soured fruit.

The second thing Geum did was to check the duty roster: no assigned tasks. Zie was touched that the task log included friendly notes from Hyo Su: *I used Spider's technique of cycling the components,* or *I thought about how Spider would isolate the positive feedback we've been getting in the optics.* She had never forgotten about Geum.

I'll make it up to you, Geum promised as zie committed Hyo

Su's schedule to memory. What would make a good gift? Something musical? Or would that stir up too many painful memories? Zie would have to think about it some more.

Then zie took an overdue shower. Zie stood in the stall after the water ration cut off, until zie started to shiver in the last remnants of steam, luxuriating in the experience. This was so much better than the sponge baths. Zie could even *shave.*

Next, Geum had the dubious pleasure of preparing for the Empress's reception.

Like every Imperial citizen, Geum had grown up familiar with the Empress's visage. She appeared on the news, on statues, on commemorative postage stamps and physical currency, although the stamps and coins were aimed at wealthy and/or suck-up collectors. Her bastard Ye Jun, formerly of Eleventh Fleet, had a pronounced resemblance to her.

Geum, as a junior technician, didn't expect to interact with the Empress. Nevertheless, the Empress had scheduled a reception. Everyone in Eleventh Fleet except a minimum of essential personnel would be halting their duties to attend, even if "attendance" meant fake-smiling at a holo.

This meant wearing a formal dress uniform for the occasion. Geum had been issued one ages ago and had never tried it on. Zie hadn't wanted to get grease stains on it.

It pained Geum that the dress uniform had sleeves too long and zie couldn't locate any safety pins. Even if no one was going to see zir—

Someone rapped enthusiastically on the door. "Geum!"

Zie instructed the door to open, and grinned in greeting when zie saw the visitor. *Finally someone who's excited to see me!*

Hyo Su's face radiated joy. "How did you get out? Did you tell the admiral what she wanted to know?"

Geum's smile faltered. *She didn't mean anything by it.* Even if Hyo Su thought zie had been holding something back, what did it matter? She'd stopped by with that ill-fated sweet bean pastry when everyone else had been content to forget about zir existence. When *Hwa Young's* messages were intermittent. "Something like that."

Hyo Su had already donned her dress uniform. "The sleeves are too long, huh?"

"You too?" Geum asked, weirdly gratified to discover zie wasn't the only one.

Wordlessly, Hyo Su produced safety pins and began fixing Geum's sleeves.

Geum's eyes stung at this simple, straightforward expression of care. "You're the best," Geum said, dimpling at her in an attempt to mask the outpouring of emotion with flirtation. "How much time do we have left, anyway?"

Hyo Su's eyes flickered as she consulted her neural implant—something Geum should have been able to do for zirself, except the guards had disabled some of its functions as a security precaution. Zie needed to see someone about getting them restored. "Twenty minutes. C'mon, you're supposed to be with the rest of the crew for the Empress's speech."

Geum appreciated the matter-of-fact way Hyo Su said *the rest of the crew*. Zie had a place among the technicians again. It was almost enough to wash away the memory of Mi Cha's words, the idea that zie was being used as bait to lure Hwa Young into a trap.

Still, that might give Hwa Young an excuse to approach Eleventh Fleet. Then Geum could reach *Winter's Axiom* and make good zir escape. Zie smiled at the prospect, despite an undercurrent of hesitation: Was it all that bad here?

Hyo Su elbowed zir. "What's the joke?"

"Just imagining the Empress dressed in safety pins," Geum lied.

Hyo Su snickered. "If you linked a bunch of them together, they'd make the world's worst chain armor? Set a trend back on the crownworld."

"Say," Geum said, sensing a good moment to ask the question that had been bothering zir, "did the Empress arrive with the entire Imperial Guard in tow or what? Maybe Second Fleet as well?"

Traditionally, First Fleet defended the Empress's own person as well as the crownworld. But First Fleet had perished at Carnelian two months ago after deploying the singularity bomb. Geum assumed its admiral had been acting on the Empress's orders.

Junior technicians did not ordinarily concern themselves with grand strategy. Geum, however, was a junior technician with a connection to a renegade lancer pilot. Zie needed to understand the Empress's plans, and Mi Cha's involvement, so zie could protect zirself and Hwa Young.

Hyo Su gnawed on her lower lip. "That's the funny thing. I bet Second Fleet and Third Fleet are lurking behind space rocks somewhere, but . . ."

"But what?"

Hyo Su's eyes darted from side to side before she answered. "As far as I know, the Empress arrived in her personal yacht and an escort of two lancers."

"I'm sure there's some top-secret reason for this," Geum said, bewildered. One *yacht*? Two lancers, when the Imperial Guard was supposed to consist of a full complement of twenty-five? Where was Second Fleet? And the rest of the Imperial Guard?

What if the missing lancers and ships were out hunting Hwa Young and the clanners?

Calm down. There could be another explanation. Maybe the Empress had decided that traveling with the expected huge entourage would endanger her by making her easier to track.

Worry gnawed at the pit of Geum's stomach and would not stop.

They reached the technicians' workshop. Geum surveyed it with fresh appreciation. No amount of scrubbing or decorations could gussy it up. The utility shelves, toolboxes, and matter printers, while neatly stacked and labeled, sported dents, unmentionable stains, and treasonous graffiti.

The very familiarity of the mess made Geum feel at home. A spotless workshop was an *unused* workshop. Zie had spent zir share of time here sharpening knives, sorting wrenches, machining parts that the matter printers couldn't handle.

Someone had made a good-faith effort at decoration. Braided banners displayed New Joseon's five colors: red, blue, green, yellow, and black. Its flag, the Starry Taegeuk with its red-and-blue yin-yang symbol, adorned the far wall. The air stank of rancid perfume oil. Geum kept from gagging with an effort. Zie preferred the honest reek of rust and sweat.

Chief stopped fussing with a lamp and straightened to greet them. "Spider," he said. "Took your sweet time getting here."

This was Chief's version of affection, which Geum accepted as zir due.

The past two months hadn't treated him well, nor any of the other technicians. Geum looked sidelong at Hyo Su. How had zie missed it before? Everyone had sunken cheeks, bloodshot eyes, an air of desperation. Zie had missed it earlier in the tidewash of relief at escaping the cell.

Geum had avoided examining zir reflection too closely after the shower. Zie didn't imagine zir appearance was better. The polite thing to do was to pretend not to notice.

"Sir, might I have my accesses restored? And a backup slate?"

Chief grunted assent. He looked grateful for a mundane request, as opposed to ceremonial matters that required him to shave. (He'd nicked his chin. What the hell had he used, a sharpened screwdriver?) Chief pointed a thumb at the chairs. "Take a seat."

Geum did so.

"It'll be fine," Hyo Su whispered from the next seat over. She squeezed zir hand beneath the table.

Geum was torn between *Do that again* and *Did anyone see us?* No one here cared, but a guilty pang started up in zir chest. It *felt* like betraying Hwa Young, and never mind that Geum and Hwa Young had never aspired to anything beyond friendship. Geum compromised by crinkling zir eyes at Hyo Su.

Chief led the prayer to the Empress that signaled the beginning of the ceremony. Geum had long practice at going through the motions.

Trust the Empress. Move at her will. Act as her hands.

Words that every Imperial citizen engraved on their hearts, at least in theory.

The broadcast began. The Empress appeared in full court regalia. Even in holo, the contrast between her embroidered silk finery and the hastily decorated room was ludicrous. Geum inventoried the number of ways her jewelry violated safety code. Rings, necklaces, bracelets, and hair ornaments, all begging to get tangled up with a drill press, resulting in mutilation.

Everyone else was either entranced by the Empress's glory or better at faking it. Geum settled in to do something highly treasonous: diving into the *Maehwa*'s communication logs to ascertain whether Commander Ye Jun had sent the *Hey, I'm pretending to be a traitor* message as Mi Cha claimed.

It would have been nice for Ye Jun to clue the *admiral* in so that Geum didn't get caught in the crossfire. But Geum was willing to forgive and forget, especially if that meant Hwa Young, too, was cleared of charges, unlikely as it was.

Geum loaded a custom haptic slate template, one that gave feedback via coded vibrations and textures: a standard feature, intended both for blind users and for use during disasters in space when the lights went out. After enforced practice with zir own variant back in the brig, the feedback made giving input and receiving output easier. Geum had memorized the interface, and working by touch enabled zir to screw around under the table without looking at the screen.

Either the message didn't exist in the records, or—aha. A trail in the computer, with hidden files dating to the time of interest. No one hid files unless they had something *to* hide.

Geum was so absorbed in zir surreptitious investigations that zie didn't notice when Lieutenant Mi Cha stomped in. Geum squawked when her hand closed on zir shoulder.

"Am I interrupting something?" Mi Cha said, mock-solicitous.

Chief's face grayed. In the holo, the Empress was making a proclamation, or a threat, coupled with a literary allusion—

something about *the footfalls of destiny*—Geum recognized it because zie had flunked the question on an essay exam.

"I'm here for An Geum. Important business," Mi Cha announced to the room at large. "The rest of you carry on."

Geum hastily blanked the slate's display and rose.

The mysterious copilot wasn't present this time. "Your copilot?" zie asked.

"She's running an errand," Mi Cha said, the way one might mention a servant sent to fetch the *good* tea cookies.

Mi Cha unceremoniously dragged Geum out of the room. Zie lost zir grip on the slate. It clattered to the floor—no, *deck*.

"You won't need that," Mi Cha said when Geum bent to scoop it back up. She dragged Geum down the hall as zir fingers closed on empty air. "*I* don't care if you spend state ceremonies playing xiangqi or betting on slime mold racing or shoe shopping, but you shouldn't be doing it in the Empress's physical presence."

Geum wanted to protest, but zie knew better. Instead, zie grimaced as though zie had in fact been engaged in one of the mundane activities she had named. "Where are we going, sir?"

"You'll see soon enough."

Geum couldn't glance over zir shoulder at the abandoned slate. Mi Cha's fingers dug in like a hypertrophied grappling hook. Zie hoped zie would have an opportunity to retrieve the slate later.

No one could have missed the Empress's presence, even before they reached her yacht. Gravity grew more definite, more assertive, in its vicinity. A balm after weeks of minor fluctuations that revealed ruptures in Eleventh Fleet's faith.

The Empress's yacht occupied an entire docking bay by itself, although it only took up half the space. Geum couldn't tell whether this was a consequence of the Empress's status, or the fact that docking bay three had stood empty the entire time Geum had served with Eleventh Fleet. Zie had visited it once to retrieve a specialty wrench some idiot had left behind. At the time, the bay had contained only a few skewed crates and archaeological evidence of a war between graffiti artists and the unlucky privates assigned to scrub the bulkheads.

"Beautiful," Geum breathed as zie beheld the yacht's graceful form. It resembled a queen among gulls, with dartlike wings that could handle atmospheric flight as well as aether. Judging from the jointed segments, the wings employed variable geometry, enabling them to change configuration based on the type of flying its pilot wanted to do.

The yacht also sported gun turrets and missile racks, a disproportionate amount of weapons for its size. Geum had seen specifications for less heavily armed battleships. The designer had embellished the weapons with symbols of good fortune and longevity. This did nothing to diminish the threat.

"Only the best for the Empress," Mi Cha said, clearly pleased by Geum's reaction.

The boarding ramp lowered at their approach.

"Up you go," Mi Cha said.

Geum was torn between gawking and keeping zir head bowed in deference. It wouldn't do to turn a corner and look the Empress in the eye. Zie didn't *think* she would order an execution for an accidental breach of etiquette, but why take chances?

The yacht's interior was indistinguishable from a palace's. Carpets, tapestries, ink paintings of bygone cities and arcologies upon scrolls of shimmering silk. It took unparalleled hubris to decorate a *starship* with priceless celadon vases, their pale green glaze so luminous that one could imagine they were living jade.

It came as a crashing disappointment to enter the receiving room (cabin?) and find the Empress curled up in a chair with her hair imperfectly pinned up, wearing a simple beige blouse and slacks like an office worker, if office workers went barefoot. She'd discarded her socks inside out on the deck. A single table held snacks: shrimp crackers and choco pies rather than court cuisine.

"The presentation?" Geum blurted out, too shocked for tact.

"Oh, that," the Empress said. She sounded . . . normal? Like a regular woman?

A regular woman wouldn't exude this all-encompassing centripetal pull. It struck Geum as absurd that someone lounging in bare feet could be the center of the known universe, as though every machination of heart's desire and Heaven's fires revolved around stinky toes.

"I prerecorded that," the Empress added nonchalantly, "and the AI marionette can handle basic questions if anything comes up."

Geum wondered why zie had assumed that the Empress did everything in person as opposed to taking advantage of modern automation techniques. Part of her public image? Imperial propaganda didn't discourage the impression that the Empress spent all her time on ceremony.

Belatedly, Geum sank to zir knees.

The Empress waited the bare minimum called for by protocol, then said, "Have a seat, Geum."

Geum flinched. Zie hadn't expected the *Empress* to know zir name, or remember it. Mi Cha must have briefed her. After a moment, zie sat across from the Empress, aware that Mi Cha was leaning against the chair's back, so close that zie felt her heat like a blow to the spinal column. "Your Majesty," zie whispered.

The Empress smiled, which emphasized the tired lines around her eyes. It wasn't the polished, perfect smile that appeared in the news broadcasts and proclamations. *Those* reminded zir of Bae, as though Bae's primary crime was aiming above her station.

"I have a favor to ask of you," the Empress said, clasping her hands and leaning forward. "I could command, but I'm going to ask. It's important to me that you do this because *you* want to, because *you* believe in what I'm doing here."

"Of course, Majesty," Geum said, torn between being awestruck and wondering *Why does* my *opinion matter to her?*

"What you're going to do for me," the Empress said, "is send Pilot Hwa Young a message once we engage the clanner fleet. Tell her to come in out of the cold. That's not so bad, is it?"

"Of course," Geum said. It was what zie wanted . . . just not the *only* thing. Things were looking better and better. Zie could communicate *openly* with Hwa Young, while explaining the situation to her. The two of them knew each other so well that Geum had every confidence that they'd be able to set up their escape without anyone else catching on. But— "Majesty, why ask me in person?"

Why hadn't the Empress simply given zir an order? Wasn't that how things worked in the military? Or an empire?

The Empress munched on a shrimp cracker before answering. "One could be forgiven for harboring mutinous thoughts after being held in the brig for two months."

Geum unpacked this, then thought about the least incriminating way to respond. "I should have checked the regs *before*

I broke Hwa Young out that one time, Majesty." Confessing sucked, but the Empress already knew. Everyone did.

The Empress chuckled ruefully. "Well, now you have a chance to make it up to me."

Geum's eyes widened when zie realized the Empress was teasing zir.

The Empress pushed the bowl of shrimp crackers toward Geum. "Have some? It's so easy to get out of touch in the palaces, doing nothing but paperwork and administrivia for hours."

Declining wasn't an option. Geum ate a cracker, wondering what the catch was. The Empress's casual geniality contrasted so much with her public persona that zie didn't know what to make of it. After zir recent run of bad luck, zie didn't dare let down zir guard.

Yet the Empress's friendliness seemed genuine. *Maybe sometimes a shrimp cracker is just a shrimp cracker. It'd be nice to have someone powerful on my side for once.*

HWA YOUNG

Hwa Young hated it when someone interfered with her routines. Going into battle with an untested, *half-installed* recording device? Not on her bucket list.

This time there was no question of *Will I reach my lancer in time?* or *Will the flagship be disabled before we can launch?* scenarios that kept her up at night. These days she flew fully suited, including her helmet, in case her lancer was breached. She'd learned *that* lesson the hard way.

Falcon Fleet had been heading toward Dragon Mountain, an alliance of space stations at the edge of the Moonstorm, in the hopes of resupplying and securing their support against New Joseon. As far as Hwa Young knew, the alliance controlled no dragons (if only!) or territory more substantial than an asteroid field, but their banner showed a dragon coiled regally around a mountain.

"'Only' an asteroid field?" Aera had said wryly during the last briefing. She eyed Hwa Young with bemusement. "You think fleets are forged from wishes and lint? It's crucial that we secure the raw materials in those asteroids, especially the metals and ice, before the Imperials do. New Joseon might be vast, but when their fleets operate in the Moonstorm, they need *local* supplies as badly as we do."

Negotiations wouldn't mean anything if the fleet didn't reach Dragon Mountain. Which was where she and the squad came in.

For the past two months, Falcon Fleet and Eleventh Fleet had dodged each other like boxers, each aware that a knockout blow from the other might be fatal. They'd participated in nothing more than raids and skirmishes. Aera and Ye Jun were still baffled by New Joseon's strategy. Sometimes the smaller Imperial task forces, who were supposed to patrol the border, failed to show up, as though they'd been recalled. At other times, Falcon Fleet spotted, and raided, convoys taking nonstandard routes.

Falcon Fleet's strategy made more sense, although Hwa Young had to piece together parts of it for herself thanks to Commander Aera's reticence. Opportunistic raids against New Joseon's military forces, weakening them through attrition while looking for the right time to move in for the kill. Chewing pieces out of New Joseon's borders. Last but not least, goodwill missions evacuating civilians from border communities so they wouldn't be left in harm's way.

One thing Hwa Young still didn't know, and which Commander Ye Jun kept trying to find out, was how ships navigated in the Moonstorm. "If you leave for five years and you come back and everyone's different, how do you know it's the same moon?" Eun had demanded during an earlier layover at a clanner station. He'd never received a satisfactory answer. New Joseon had reliable beacons and networks *within* its territory, but the aether currents made comms dicier for Imperial ships venturing into the Moonstorm.

The clanners clearly possessed *some* technology that enabled them to locate moons and stations. As long as the lancer squad was part of Falcon Fleet, they didn't have to worry about dealing with navigation. This state of affairs made Ye Jun edgy. It bothered Hwa Young, too, but she assumed that the commander had matters well in hand. She couldn't face the thought of coming all this way and rejoining the heart-mother she'd thought lost to her, then leaving all over again.

The cockpit lit up around her, glacial whites and blues and silvers. Hwa Young's awareness detached from her body and re-settled within *Winter's Axiom.* She celebrated becoming part of something larger and deadlier.

A map of the area unfurled in her mind's eye. This time there was a distracting overlay: a winter storm, winds driving snow before them like portents of fury and famine. Hwa Young thought she heard whispers at the edge of her hearing, words she couldn't discern, voices she almost recognized. She was distantly aware that her hands had clenched, and she relaxed each finger one by one as she strove to bring the map into clear focus.

Within the flagship's womb, they had access to its sensor data, which included information from a network of far-flung scouts. The clanners had stealth technology and took every advantage of it. Even *Farseer* couldn't pierce the veil. The question was, had the Empire developed a way to detect stealthed ships—hence the attack?

Once the lancers launched, they would be cut off from communications with *Falcon Actual* unless it dropped stealth. *Falcon*

Actual would likewise be unable to view the situation clearly. An active area of research, Aera had assured them.

"Bastard to Falcon Command," Commander Ye Jun said as Hwa Young examined the surrounding area. "Falcon Command, requesting clearance to launch."

The fighters launched ahead of them, swift darts: going, going, gone. Hwa Young longed to be out there too. Longed to *fly*.

"Falcon Command to Lancer Squad One. Hold for the moment, I say, hold. There's a situation."

What situation? Hwa Young *reached* for *Winter's Axiom*'s sensors. One disadvantage of fighting alongside the clanners: the lancer pilots didn't enjoy automatic integration with the clanner fleet's datasphere the way they had with Eleventh Fleet's. Incompatible data standards meant that Commander Ye Jun had to coordinate with *Falcon Actual* the hard way.

Hwa Young suspected that Admiral Mae was freezing them out because zie didn't trust them yet, even if Aera vouched for them. When Hwa Young broached the possibility to Eun, his expression turned grim. *It's only been two months,* he'd said. *Give it time.* The meaningful look he gave her, which she took to heart, suggested that he didn't want her causing trouble by talking about it.

Hwa Young had to rely on her lancer for information about the engagement to come, as well as anything that Bae's *Farseer* shared with the squad. She'd learned how *Winter's Axiom* conceptualized its surroundings: itself at the center, with allies marked in starry blue and hostiles in clots of gray, like mold.

Commander Ye Jun and Falcon Command exchanged comments, none of which illuminated the situation to her satisfaction.

Falcon Fleet had found trouble near a binary system, one bright star and one dim, with chancy aether currents. *How do people go between stars when the stars don't have fixed positions?* Hwa Young had asked Mother Aera as a child, after Eldest Paik told the household a story about star-riders hunting stray suns and roping them to light their moon so the crops could grow. If Aera had answered, Hwa Young didn't remember.

To her annoyance, *Winter's Axiom* currently labeled clanner units, from individual fighters to the flagship, as hostiles in that clotted gray.

Not again, Hwa Young thought in exasperation. *Fix the colors.*

They are not ours, Winter's Axiom retorted. *They have souls of storm and tempest. We have souls of gravity law.*

They're our allies now, Hwa Young said. She'd hoped they'd gotten beyond this, but apparently not. *I need to be able to tell them apart from our* real *enemies! Fix the colors* now.

Winter's Axiom gave her a reluctant compromise: marking all clanner units in attenuated red. This allowed Hwa Young to differentiate them from the actual hostiles, a fluctuating constellation of mottled gray triangles decelerating as they approached the clanner fleet.

"Mirror to Vagrant," Bae's clipped voice came over the commlink. "I've ID'd the leading elements as Imperials."

"I'll pass that on to Falcon Command, thanks."

"Mirror, which Imperials?" Hwa Young said.

Asking was a mistake. Better to fight the battle without the heart-puncture knowledge of who was on the other side. Better for the enemy to be an abstract, a target she could lock on to without conscience.

What if Geum's in that fleet?

Bae, who was privy to none of these thoughts, answered. "I have eyes on an Imperial fleet. Under strength if the numbers are anything to go by."

The mention of numbers sparked alarm in Hwa Young. She told herself not to jump to conclusions. Eleventh Fleet couldn't be the only one fighting at partial strength. Eun said it was common for Imperial units to have a paper strength at odds with the actual soldiers and ships in the field, given attrition and recruiting challenges.

"Falcon Command to Lancer Squad One," a different voice responded, lightly accented. "You have clearance to launch. Watch your backs. Moon's own blessing out there."

Like there's more than just us, Hwa Young thought, grimly amused. Still, she appreciated the optimism. There wasn't a lot of that these days.

"On my mark," Ye Jun said, "launch." And, several agonizing moments later: "Mark."

The docking bay opened like a vomiting leviathan. Bae's *Farseer* jetted out first, followed by Eun's *Hellion,* Hwa Young herself in *Winter's Axiom,* and finally the commander in *Bastard.*

Hwa Young reveled in the acceleration, which pushed her back against her cushioned seat. The skies opened before her, the dance of aether currents greeting her in a caress of lavender-and-blue light that she felt as though against her skin, not just the lancer's armor. The sweeping sensation of flying elated her. Nothing stood between her and the symphony of stars. This aspect of being a lancer pilot was *better* than her childhood imaginings.

Her exultation lasted four seconds.

Bae cursed. "Mirror to Falcon Command. Two lancers incoming!"

"*Which fleet?*" Commander Ye Jun demanded. "Which fleet are they from?"

"We see them," Falcon Command responded over Ye Jun's query, laconic. "We trust you have the situation in hand." Then, unhelpfully, the flagship blinked out: stealthed, therefore no longer available to assist or advise.

Other lancers? Hwa Young thought. She sucked in slow, measured breaths to counteract her nausea. The heat of memory rocketed through her: Seong Su's death, except this time it was as though *she'd* blown him up. *We're going to be fighting lancers?*

She was being ridiculous. Used a cruel, chisel-edged logic against herself: *Seong Su's already dead. It's not like you can get him killed again.*

Hwa Young beheld the unfamiliar lancers through *Winter's Axiom*'s senses. Wondered how she could have missed them. It painted them an astonishing amber, not a color it had used before.

The hostile lancers were close enough to show up with exact locations and vectors, rather than hazy probability clouds of *I could be anywhere in this radius.*

"All units on me," Ye Jun said. Zir voice, normally so steady, shook. "We don't want to engage yet. Not until we know who we're facing."

"Lancers," Eun breathed. In contrast to Ye Jun, his voice roughened in—anger? Self-recrimination? "Eleventh Fleet can't have trained *competent* pilots in two months. Not without you or me to do the training, Vagrant. Which means . . ."

What if Eleventh Fleet had detoured to pick up pilots, or people capable of training pilots?

Caution, her lancer said abruptly.

Hwa Young returned her attention to the battlefield. The sky opened up around her. The pale gleams of distant stars were almost drowned out by the brilliance of the local binary system, with its large red sun and dimmer white dwarf companion. She wondered how stars achieved coalescence, a topic neither her clanner family nor her Imperial teachers had addressed. Perhaps it raised too many uncomfortable questions.

The Moonstorm's aether currents buffeted her lancer with unusual force. Hwa Young angled *Winter's Axiom* to reduce the drag. She'd trained for this, but she hadn't experienced such strong forces before.

Hwa Young squinted at the void through the cockpit window. The ever-shifting shimmer of dust occluded her view. She could have been moon-bound, planet-bound, yoked to the vicissitudes of dirt and storm. The particulates' dance and their iridescent half glow invited a painter's tribute; but she was no painter, and she had a battle to fight.

The clanner ships receded behind her. Hwa Young didn't have them on visual, but she could see them in the expansive vision that her link with *Winter's Axiom* granted her, a map unfurling in all directions, with her and her lancer at the center, and on the backup tactical display, which she glanced at to confirm that they matched.

For a moment she allowed herself not to worry about the enemy lancers, and to exult in how rapidly they left the clanner fleet behind, in the squad's role as rapid response.

"Hostile lancers altering course to intercept us," Bae reported. His voice tightened on *hostile*. "They seem to see us fine."

We're fighting other lancers. We're fighting lancers. Hwa Young strove to overcome her disbelief. Why had she thought the status quo, their lancers against vulnerable ships, would endure forever?

"Stay at range," Ye Jun said. "Do not let them draw you in."

More than ever, Hwa Young missed Seong Su, whose *Avalanche* had served as the squad's heavily armored brawler. They'd depended on him to be their front-liner and shield. Without him, they were vulnerable at close range and unable to execute tactics that relied on someone to fix the enemy's attention up close while the ranged units pummeled targets from a distance.

No, she didn't miss Seong Su for his *combat utility*, as important as that was. She missed *him*. When they'd been students together, she'd dismissed him as a useless goofball who drifted from one school assignment to the next without putting in much effort, secure in the knowledge that his family would provide for him.

The useless goofball had made her smile with his jokes, brought a much-needed easygoing stability to the squad.

The useless goofball was dead because of a battle *she'd* dragged the squad into.

You were already vulnerable, the lancer noted, its interruption both welcome and unwelcome. *One pilot away from a dangerously imbalanced squad.*

She allowed herself a moment's hope that the data they were recording would lead to more lancers, more pilots. Useful in some imagined future, although not right now.

"Silence here." Eun's voice crackled over the comms, a low growl. "If there's something *specific* you know about those units, Vagrant—"

"I'm waiting on a definite ID," Ye Jun snapped in an unusual display of temper. "Stay out of range until we've provoked a response."

What do they know that I don't? Hwa Young fretted. They were speaking around something that both of them knew but the rest of them didn't. Operational security, so the enemy wouldn't overhear . . . or a personal matter neither wanted to admit to?

Suddenly, the squad, which Hwa Young had come to think of as a bulwark, no longer felt safe or steady. Childish as it was, she hated that the strange lancers had shown up and messed up her sense that she could rely on her comrades.

Ye Jun and Eun knew something they weren't telling her or Bae. How many other secrets were they holding back?

The worst part was she couldn't demand answers. Not in the midst of combat. Not when Falcon Command might be listening in.

At least Geum was unlikely to be involved with enemy lancers. She held on to that thought, painfully aware that she was distracting herself from the source of her distress.

Avoiding contact was easier said than done. Enemy lancers One and Two were intent on closing the distance.

Hwa Young's heart constricted: the hostiles were fast. Faster than any of *their* lancers. These must be experienced pilots. Beyond experience, they might enjoy the benefit of stronger bonds with their lancers, which reputedly unlocked advanced configurations that rookie pilots weren't able to access.

She remembered to use her new callsign. "Axiom here. They're on my ass. Do we scatter or stay together?"

"Scatter," Ye Jun hissed.

Hwa Young startled at the commander's vehemence—and

that alarming blade-edge of fear. She'd already counted on an engagement; had to reverse her vector instead. She hadn't expected *that* answer.

"Get away *now*. Do not engage, I repeat, do not engage. I'll explain lat—"

"The hell?" Hwa Young demanded when static choked the comms dead. "Vagrant, this is Axe! Vagrant, come in. There's two of them and four of us, we can take them!"

Then the first attack came.

Hwa Young almost didn't register it as one. Her lancer drifted off course, so subtly that she mistook it for the buffeting effect of the aether winds that had affected her flight earlier—except the vectors were wrong.

Her heart banged painfully against her chest as she fought the pull. At the Battle of Carnelian, she'd been terrified of being sucked into an all-devouring black hole. Whatever passed its event horizon would never return to the known universe.

This was different. With a normal gravity well, like that of a star or planet or moon, one could hope for rescue.

But this wasn't gravity—was it?

"Axiom to Mirror." Her breath came in hard gasps. One part panic, two parts connection to her lancer, itself struggling against the mysterious pull. "Axiom to Silence, do you read? Something's drawing me in. It's . . . it's not another black hole, is it?"

Was anyone listening?

She hadn't been sure she'd be able to say it out loud. *Black hole.* A bizarre astronomical phenomenon when she'd learned about them in physics class. They hadn't given her nightmares then. She'd learned them for her exams, forgotten about them afterward. But that was before she saw Admiral Hong of First Fleet try to use one to destroy a moon and the people who lived on it.

Maybe he acted against the Empress's orders. Something she wondered about. But hadn't the Empress raised Hong to his rank? In New Joseon, which regulated everything from fashion to the language of flowers, how could any battle plan come to fruition without the Empress's approval?

More static scraped against her nerves. No one was answering.

Hwa Young leaned into her bond with *Winter's Axiom*. She reached for its presence, the mordant comfort of its remarks. This once she would even have welcomed its creepy comments about bones.

At first, all she heard was the subliminal whine of the levitators redoubling their efforts, resisting whatever was yanking them off course.

Pain slammed into her like fire and thunder. A scream burst from between her teeth. The entire cockpit dimmed, flashing red and blue. Not the familiar pale blue of a winter sky, but a deep royal blue, alien and threatening.

"*Winter's Axiom*," Hwa Young croaked, not caring that she tasted blood in her mouth, that her tongue throbbed where she'd bitten it. "Answer me!"

It stood silent now.

Had the scriber caused this? Or the attacking lancers? It would suck to die because her lancer was disabled by *her own side's* tech.

Her lancer floated helplessly toward the hostiles. She was on manual now, staring at the tactical display. Not that she trusted it, but what else did she have?

The map in her head had evaporated like birdsong during a storm. The tactical display malfunctioned, too, smeared into jittering pixels.

Hwa Young grabbed the joysticks and worked the pedals in an effort to make the lancer respond. It did, more sluggishly than with a direct neural link. She shoved down both fear and hope—she couldn't afford distractions—and focused on breaking free of the mystery force.

Pain spiked in her head again. Trying to concentrate was like doing calligraphy while someone knifed her liver, one torment even her boarding school hadn't subjected her to. But she'd powered through pain before. She could do it now.

She'd forgotten that propulsion wasn't her only difficulty. Without the ability to direct her lancer's movements, as opposed to drifting aimlessly in space, she was easy meat for the enemy. The first shot hit her shoulder, a bolt of gold and green that sizzled in her nerves, sudden as summer lightning. The second grazed her side.

Unfairly, despite the fact that the scriber had trashed her connection to the lancer, it did nothing to mitigate the *pain* flooding her like fast venom. Every hit to *Winter's Axiom* felt like a hit to *her*.

Hwa Young tried to move her hand. To push the joystick, an action she normally took for granted. Against her will, her fingers spasmed. She yelped. She failed to snatch her hand back. Her eyes burned with pain and humiliation.

She tried again. Had better luck this time, but the status panel confirmed her fears. The attack had disabled her sniper rifle. Her longest-range weapon, and her best hope of returning fire.

Whatever the enemy might think, however, she wasn't out

of the fight. That green-gold bolt had come in straight. Tracing back its vector suggested her attacker's location, a probability cloud based on its likely movements afterward. She returned fire with the weaker gravity lance, which dispersed over distance. Had she aimed true?

Unlikely. Not at this distance, and not with the delay due to her reaction to the pain.

Then she heard it, a voice whose absence she'd suffered for two months. "Winter, this is Spider, do you read? Winter, this is Spider. *Don't respond.* Just listen."

Hwa Young's eyes flooded, and she choked back a sob. *Winter.* Her old callsign. Teardrops splattered against the base of her helmet, pooled against her neck. *Geum? Is that you?*

Was it a trick, like the Imperials imitating Seong Su's voice? Was she going to be haunted by everyone she'd lost or left behind?

Hwa Young longed to open a channel. To answer—to ask questions. But she knew the risk of doing so. Instead, she listened as instructed, scarcely breathing in case she missed it when Geum spoke again. The voice had been exactly how Geum sounded when zie was worried about her—and trying not to reveal it. No one could fake that, right?

Zie called her Winter, not Axiom. It felt right. Felt like *home*.

"I know you're out there, Winter," Geum's voice continued. "Follow the indicated path. It'll get you out of this fix, at least for now. And Winter—be careful. They're—they're setting a trap for you at Dragon Mountain."

Then the voice cut off, leaving Hwa Young alone in the darkness.

9

GEUM

Geum had a great overview of the battle with the clanners for someone who wasn't participating. Zie had originally planned to spend the engagement doing what zie normally did: accompanying the other technicians in the docking bay, on call for emergency repairs.

Unlike the lancer pilots who'd deserted, or the here-and-now starfighter pilots, Geum's group of technicians spent the grind of battle with their lives on hold. *Others* kept busy during the engagement. Some made sure the guns didn't jam or the lasers didn't fry themselves. Some teams handled damage control, ready to put out fires, repair shorted-out wiring, or most terrifying of all, seal hull breaches—the worst nightmare of anyone who lived in space. Automated repair systems provided a first line of defense against that last, but one never knew when a human touch might be required.

Geum was a member of Technician Group Six (to match the number of their assigned docking bay). They specialized in the maintenance and repair of the *Maehwa*'s lancers and starfighters, as well as any upgrades. Their group couldn't help lancers *or* fighters while the latter two groups did loop-de-loops in space. Technicians were busiest before and after battle . . . when the battles were ordinary.

During most battles, Geum didn't send clandestine messages to the enemy. Even if the "enemy" was Hwa Young, and zie had done it with the Empress's authorization. Zie wasn't sure why the Empress couldn't have clued in Chief so that Geum didn't get in trouble. The Empress had said that she wanted it to look as genuine as possible, as though Hwa Young were in a position to rummage through the ship's records.

Geum had a fine needle to thread: making it *look* like zie was complying with the Empress's orders while dropping enough hints that Hwa Young would come in prepared, yet also not making the situation sound so alarming that Hwa Young bailed . . . and left Geum behind *again*. It sucked thinking of Hwa Young in those terms, especially since she'd always been the responsible one. A lot had changed since the clanners destroyed their home.

Would Hwa Young understand the warning? Zie hadn't closed with *Together forever* on purpose, to clue her in that something was wrong. Surely she'd take it from there.

Group Six hung around the back of the docking bay, sitting on crates because Empress forbid they have folding chairs. Chief had explained that this prevented safety issues in case of uncontrolled landings. No one had pointed out that the *crates* could pose a problem if the magnetic locks decoupled.

The rest of the battle had started in an ordinary way. Preflight checks and yelling. Then the launches and the technicians sharing snacks. Hyo Su had a monopoly on the best ones. "I saved a whole box of shrimp crackers for you," she confided to Geum when she thought the others weren't paying attention.

Geum beamed at her, then asked her permission to pass a few around, in case either of them needed to ask for a favor in the future. Hyo Su agreed to this with a quirk of her mouth, as though this wasn't what she'd hoped for. Belatedly, it occurred to Geum that zie had misunderstood her overture.

The older techs drank, although they weren't supposed to. Same for the betting. Chief looked the other way. Morale was bad enough as it was, Geum overheard him telling some indignant officer.

"You think anyone's going to call for tech support this time?" Hyo Su asked through a mouthful of *her* favorite snack, chocolate-dipped biscuits that resembled edible chopsticks.

One of the senior technicians, who went by Spade, looked up from his slate. He'd been watching one of the propaganda broadcasts. Geum overheard a tinny voice saying *The Empress's benevolent dictate* but not the dictate itself.

"Hardly no one radios for tech support these days," Spade said in his nasal voice. "It's either a before-battle rant to the tune of 'Why can't you overclock the engines even though it's against regs and Chief will have our heads if he catches us,' or BOOM! They're already dead."

Geum listened with half an ear, trying not to obsess about the message and failing. Had Hwa Young received it? It sucked that she hadn't acknowledged it. Granted, per the Empress's instructions, Geum had *asked* her not to respond. The silence gnawed at Geum's nerves anyway, like a parasitic infection.

What if Hwa Young shoots Mi Cha? Or Ga Ram? Geum didn't think the Empress would forgive that.

Think positive. She'll swoop in and take me away from this messy situation.

Even if zie would miss people on the *Maehwa,* now that zie was no longer in the brig.

Despite their tense encounters, Mi Cha's aggression actually appealed to Geum. It was a trait zie had despised in Bae. The thing was, Bae had been born into a high-ranking family, trained to think of herself as superior. (Geum shrugged off the fact that zir clan had been almost as prominent. No one in Eleventh Fleet knew or cared.) Mi Cha had *worked* for her position.

Mi Cha reminded Geum of Hwa Young, high-handedness and all, fast-forwarded ten years into the future.

Or Hyo Su, benevolent provider of snacks, who gave every indication that she might say yes if Geum asked—

Hyo Su opened another pack of biscuits. "Geum, you want more?"

"No thanks," Geum said reluctantly. Not when zie was so tense that the prospect of food aroused nausea. At Hyo Su's crestfallen expression, Geum added, "After the battle, maybe?"

Geum was rewarded by Hyo Su's smile, unexpectedly shy.

The battle played out on a feed of CIC's tactical map, except with notations stripped out to reduce the clutter. Chief's idea: mere techs didn't need all the tactical details.

Mere techs did, however, have *opinions.*

Spade leaned forward. "What in Heaven and Earth is Wing One doing?"

"I wasn't sure you were paying attention," Geum quipped.

Real battles, unlike videogames, existed in a peculiar time

warp. They alternated between slow boring periods where nothing happened and fast ones where everything happened at once. Only the CIC analysis after the fact could unriddle what had gone right or wrong, and sometimes not even then.

Geum hadn't been tracking Wing One, the elite starfighter squad. Zie reserved zir focus for the four-pointed stars that denoted the Empress's lancer pilots. One appeared in alternating red and blue: Ga Ram's *Paradox*. The other, venomous yellow-green: Mi Cha's *Summer Thorn*.

Zie wasn't looking for the Imperial Guard, as much as zie hoped that Mi Cha would share stories of her exploits afterward. Zie was keeping an eye out for the deserters, especially *Winter's Axiom*.

The deserters materialized between one blink and the next. It took Geum a moment to register their presence. IFF correctly marked them in enemy gray, which zie wasn't accustomed to. In the past, they'd appeared in their lancers' colors: jade green for *Bastard*, fiery orange for *Hellion*, eerie violet for *Farseer*, copper-brown for *Avalanche*, and pale blue-white for *Winter's Axiom*.

I'm a dumbass, Geum thought. Zie chewed on a fingernail, which was gross. That was a great way to ruin sparkly nail polish, a rare commodity on the ship. Besides, technicians always had grime and lubricant beneath their nails.

Hyo Su's attention was elsewhere. "That's the spirit!" she crowed as *Summer Thorn*'s icon flared and another, unfamiliar icon sparked into existence.

"What happened?" The only way to remedy zir ignorance was to ask. Geum had spent zir childhood collecting lancer figures, constructing scale lancer models, and (ahem) counterfeiting lancer trading cards to profit off the gullible until Hwa Young made zir stop. Yet Geum had no idea what the elite lancers did in terms of special powers or weaponry, because the details were classified.

On the other hand, surely the Empress didn't expect techs to work on zero information?

Geum didn't realize zie had said this out loud until Spade laughed. "You think the Empress"—he made a reverential circle gesture, a superstition peculiar to his homeworld—"is going to entrust her best and brightest to the likes of Group Six?"

Hyo Su bristled. Geum had known she would. Another technician laughed indulgently as Hyo Su exclaimed, "We didn't do anything wrong! We keep the maintenance schedule! It didn't have anything to do with—" She clammed up, eyes darting toward Geum.

Geum forced zirself to smile. The two of them felt differently about Hwa Young, but Hyo Su had stopped before saying something unforgivable. Her effort to consider Geum's feelings mattered, however awkward the moment.

Besides—*Where* are *the Imperial Guard's technicians?* Geum didn't expect them to hang out with lesser beings, but . . . there was no record of them in the computers, and zie had looked. No one had caught sight of them. They hadn't requisitioned tools or supplies or food, although perhaps they'd brought their own.

Why ask Group Six to provide support to the Imperial Guard, unless their own technicians no longer existed?

Geum's thoughts regarding this mystery dissolved when one of the turncoat lancer icons flew in an astonishing straight line *toward* blue-red *Paradox*.

The turncoat was *Winter's Axiom*. It had originally taken the path that Geum had indicated in zir message. Geum had assumed that Hwa Young could be relied on to follow instructions, which zie recognized as pure naïveté. When had Hwa Young *ever* followed instructions, especially if Geum was around to bail her out? Now Hwa Young's lancer was grossly off course.

She's playing a deep game, Geum thought, hands clenching and unclenching. *She wouldn't fire on the Imperial Guard. She wouldn't really attack us.*

She wouldn't really attack me.

Unless this was the prelude to a rescue?

Chief fiddled with the tablet. Suddenly they heard staticky comms chatter from CIC.

"Confirmed," someone was saying, low and tense. "It's the traitor Winter."

"Why's she on a collision course?" Geum asked in a thready voice. Was she going to be able to decelerate in time? How could they resume their friendship and be *together forever* if she died in a fireball?

Chief's face expressed a complicated discomfort as he scowled at Geum. "I know Winter was your friend, but . . . you'd figure it out anyway. *Paradox*'s special ability is large-scale telekinesis. It can grab a target and push or pull it in any direction. Looks like that's what it's doing to that friend of yours—launching it at the nearest moon or into the next star over."

"She's not my friend," Geum said automatically, because that was the safe, politic thing to say. Zie felt like a cad, as though Hwa Young could overhear zir.

Hyo Su's eyes went round. "Telekinesis. Wow."

"As for *Summer Thorn*," Chief continued, "it flies like a bee and stings like one too. ECM—electronic countermeasures. It *disables* spacecraft and their subsystems."

Hwa Young had flown into this, as Geum had told her to, and she was going to die. Geum had warned Hwa Young that this was a trap, but zie had been too subtle.

This can't be happening.

Geum watched in horror as *Paradox* flung its victim toward the smaller of the two local suns. "That lancer's gonna die," zie said thinly.

"Yeah," Spade said, misinterpreting Geum's emotion. "The pilot will eject if she has the sense the Empress gave a rice seedling, but we're gonna lose the lancer. Crying shame, given the manufacturing crisis."

"That's for real?" Hyo Su said with sudden interest.

Chief harrumphed. "Hasn't been an issue because the bigger problem has been finding suitable pilots. That Ha Yoon girl isn't the first candidate we've lost, although they hush it up real good."

They all fell silent. Geum remembered Bae's doomed friend. Resented being reminded of the dead girl, and felt guilty for zir resentment. The two of them had never gotten along. Still, Geum hadn't wished for Ha Yoon to die.

"Technician Group Six, you people asleep back there?" CIC said over the intercom.

Chief snapped to. Geum stood up so abruptly that zie would have knocked over the seat had it been an ordinary chair instead of a crate full of—actually, zie had no idea what it contained and zie preferred it that way. Hyo Su crammed one last cookie into her mouth, causing her cheeks to puff out adorably like a squirrel's, and picked up her toolbox. Grateful for the reminder of what to do, Geum grabbed zir own as well.

CIC again. "Patching you through to—"

"Oh, that's not good," Hyo Su muttered, spraying crumbs. "Someone out there needs tech support after all?"

"That smooth-tongued hacker of yours." Mi Cha's voice this time. "Put zir on."

Glad you noticed my charm? Geum squared zir shoulders. "What's the situation, sir?"

"I need you to hack *Winter's Axiom*. It's urgent."

"To save her?" Geum couldn't think of any other reason. It wasn't as though a lancer on the way to a fatal clinch with a dwarf star needed anything else.

Time slowed. Geum beheld the gyring of the starfighters, the deadly trajectories of projectiles and flotsam. An unshielded collision could, at high enough velocities, puncture a ship with enough energy to destroy it. The battle cruisers, ponderous whales in comparison to the falcon-and-gull movements of the fighters, with deadly armaments. The arcs of missiles soaring toward their targets, scenting the clanners with the guidance of specialized processors modeled after predators' brains.

Before Mi Cha could respond and give details, the *Maehwa*'s alarms bellowed. A terse voice blared from the PA: "All hands, we have had a shield malfunction. I repeat, shields are down. Brace for impact."

"*COLLISION ALERT,*" the computer said at the same time. "*COLLISION ALERT.*"

A shudder thundered through the *Maehwa*, then another. Geum's hearing was overwhelmed by the catastrophe roar of atmosphere venting. Hull breach. Red lights, flashing on and off, staining everything in sight.

All Geum could think about, for a horrible frozen moment,

was whether the shop vacuum could cope with the quantity of crumbs that Hyo Su had left in the docking bay.

Geum was used to sound effects in videogames. One could turn down the volume or edit out anything that prevented one from hearing useful feedback like *hostiles on your six,* filter out the problem frequencies that kept one from discerning a favorite lyric in the boss fight song. As a child, Geum had enjoyed tinkering with games for zirself and zir cousins, and later Hwa Young, to customize the experience.

The assault evoked nothing of customization or convenience or control. The concussion of the attack roared like a chaos tiger. Coolant fluid gushed from one of the inert lancers zie had stopped noticing. No pilot to yank it out of the way, a sitting duck. That wasn't from the projectile itself, but secondary damage from a ricocheting fragment of hull armor, something Geum learned much later.

Geum dived behind a crate and huddled with zir hands clasped over zir head.

Geum would forever remember the label on the crate, smashed up against zir face hard enough to leave contusions, and the typo in it, visible even through the kaleidoscope-hell of afterimages: *THIS SIDE UPP.* (The crate was upside-down.)

Then an unsecured tool clipped zir in the side of the head and everything went dark.

10

HWA YOUNG

Hwa Young considered the message from Geum. *Together forever.* That couldn't be fake. It really was Geum.

She had to choose a course of action soon. Lancer combat didn't favor measured two-hour decisions. If she'd been able, she would have consulted Commander Ye Jun, but she didn't have that option.

Still—just as the Imperials knew she'd been close to Seong Su, everyone on the *Maehwa* knew she'd been Geum's friend. Maybe someone was using Geum to feed her disinformation. She didn't believe Geum would do that knowingly, but zie could have been tricked.

If she sprang the trap, two could play at that game.

Do you think you're cleverer than the Empress's finest? a snide voice asked inside her head. It sounded like Bae or one of Bae's cronies from their boarding school days.

Shush, Hwa Young responded, wishing that *Winter's Axiom* would talk to her instead.

Geum's path offered a narrow route away from the grapnel force that gripped her lancer. With an effort that she perceived as a strain in her joints and muscles, she guided her lancer away.

And then the path ended. The enemy was waiting for her.

It had been a trap after all.

Hwa Young swallowed her rage. It settled like cold lead in her belly. She could deal with her inconvenient emotions later.

Time to fight. Even if she was forced to pilot on manual, rather than the fluid, intuitive bond where moving *Winter's Axiom* was as easy as thought.

The enemy lancer filled her field of vision as it drew her closer, too close. Hwa Young's heart sank. She recognized it: how could she not?

It was larger than *Winter's Axiom* in every dimension, the plates of its armor shifting in dizzying whorls from red to blue and back again as light hit it from the nearby white dwarf. The lancer's head, which contained its cockpit, featured a visor that was red on the left, blue on the right, then vice versa. Twin cannons jutted from its shoulders.

Paradox. Piloted by the Empress's third-born, Captain of the Guard Ga Ram. The one who'd led the attack on her childhood home, then rescued her from the wreckage, offering kindness and comfort when she was ten years old.

Once again Hwa Young was a child clutching the reeds so she wouldn't float away into the void, choking on bile and terror. In her memories she stared up into Ga Ram's eyes as zie gave her a hawthorn candy and a chance at a new life. She had not expected to run into zir again, not like this.

She couldn't let the past paralyze her. Hwa Young jerked the joysticks sideways and up. Hit the trigger to activate her gravity lance.

The lance speared outward. Hwa Young monitored its path on the tactical display, since visual was no good. Funny how gravity was *invisible,* despite its importance.

Her reflexes were good. Ga Ram's were better. *Paradox* soared away, as agile as a swallow, as majestic as a swan. It returned fire.

Unlike *Winter's Axiom, Paradox* wasn't disabled by whatever that yellow-green attack had been. An electromagnetic pulse? Eun had warned her about them, but an EMP should have knocked her computers offline completely, rather than acting on them selectively.

While Hwa Young's mind raced, she maneuvered, seeking a clear shot. She didn't like being this close. Didn't like the fact that she and the captain were circling each other, that she kept spiraling toward *Paradox* as though it were the jewel at the involute heart of a labyrinth.

As a ten-year-old, Hwa Young hadn't thought about *Paradox*'s armaments or fighting style. She had known only that it represented power—power she wanted to claim for herself, so she could never be helpless again.

Paradox's colors were red and blue. Right now the former as it drew her toward itself. The blue mode must represent repulsion.

How can I trigger that?

Commander Ye Jun would have engaged in cyberwarfare, hacking into the other lancer for a command override. Hwa Young didn't have that ability. So instead—

Ga Ram had *met* her, but zie had never *fought* her. Whatever zie knew about her fighting style was in *Maehwa*'s records. Hwa

Young was betting the captain of the Imperial Guard didn't keep zir position, or stay alive, by ignoring intel or neglecting to do zir homework.

Which meant Ga Ram knew her as a sniper, someone who hid behind asteroids and fired from cover.

Hwa Young stomped down on the pedal to activate the levitators at full power and *charged* straight at *Paradox*.

Her instincts guided her true. She surprised her adversary. *Paradox* flashed from red to blue, the tidal blue of deep ocean that Hwa Young had only seen in pictures. A repelling force slammed into *Winter's Axiom,* sending her flying like an importunate comet.

Hwa Young adjusted her attitude and fired a parting shot opposite her movement vector, reflexively using the sniper rifle. Pain sizzled down her nerves, but it worked. *It worked.*

Whatever had disabled her lancer had worn off. It wasn't permanent. The slug streaked out of her rifle.

Hwa Young squeezed the trigger again. A warning tone sounded, indicating that the next round of ammunition was still loading. *The hell?*

The earlier attack must have triggered manual cycling mode, which she'd never used before. It had already cost her precious seconds.

She switched the lancer back to automatic reloading. By the time the system acknowledged, unfortunately, she'd lost a chance at a clear shot.

But her sensors showed that she'd inflicted serious damage on *Paradox*. Her slug had blown out some of the chest armor, exposing its main engine and damaging its levitators. As a result, it was falling into the white dwarf's gravity well.

Paradox flashed red. It was dragging *Winter's Axiom* with it. Should she fight her way out and put some distance between herself and *Paradox,* or do the unthinkable and *eject*—

Eject, only to live the drifting half-life of a pilot whose lancer had been destroyed.

"Call incoming," the computer reported, its voice bland, without the predator's edge that Hwa Young associated with her lancer.

Hwa Young punched the button. "Hwajin of *Winter's Axiom,*" she said. "Say your piece."

"This is Ga Ram of *Paradox,*" came the reply.

Her hackles rose. Not because of the voice and its familiar smooth cadences, but the simplicity of the introduction. Zie had given no rank, military or otherwise, but an unadorned name, as though they were equals—the one thing they could never be.

"I doubt either of us longs to burn up in the corona of a star," Ga Ram said. "I wish to speak to you."

Where's the trap?

"You will have to decide quickly. This binary system has a captive planetoid. Unstable orbit, but at the moment local conditions are such that people can survive on its surface for short periods of time. I'm transmitting a proposed landing site."

Hwa Young hacked up an incredulous laugh. "You want a parley."

"That's correct, Hwajin."

She'd prepared for a fight to the death. Had briefly contemplated ejection, if only to dismiss the idea out of hand.

Hwa Young had not considered the possibility that *Paradox* had isolated her and drawn her out here, with or without Geum's help, to *talk.*

Secret talks, with a "mutual crash" as a cover story. It would be incriminating on her end to have a chat with New Joseon's captain of the guard. It would be more incriminating for the captain to talk to *her*, unless this was another layer of deceit.

Did Geum arrange for this?

She could come ask. But if Geum *wasn't* involved, or had been tricked into luring her here, she might put zir in more danger by doing so. That she couldn't abide.

"I cannot make you talk to me," Ga Ram said. "But I can ask. And I would not ask for anything less than a matter of vital importance. Decide soon. The longer you wait, the riskier this becomes."

Ga Ram *still* addressed her as an equal, through zir choice of verb forms and formality levels in the language they shared. That, above anything else, decided her. Zie hadn't answered her question, but zir statement was true as far as it went.

"Fine," she said.

Hwa Young did not trust planetoids, or asteroids, or flying chunks of rock. This one was dappled gray with faint speckles of green and violet. A miner's assay might have revealed deposits of jade, fluorite, or other valuable minerals. Instead, Hwa Young studied the asteroid with a pilot's eye, searching for cover, fault lines, and indications of dangerous terrain.

She did not have much practice with manual landings. The asteroid shuddered as *Winter's Axiom* touched down. Her heart almost stopped: was it going to split and crumble, leaving her adrift amid earthquake scars?

Paradox touched down not two meters from her, with the neatness of a heron.

Show-off, Hwa Young thought. Her heart lifted: zie hadn't

blasted her into oblivion. But the deadliest attacks didn't reveal themselves immediately.

Time to take the initiative. She opened a channel to *Paradox*. "Before we proceed, I need to know why you're talking to me and not someone else."

Ga Ram was on full video. She followed suit, as a courtesy. Zie already knew who she was, so why hide?

Six years had aged Ga Ram's face surprisingly little. *Imperial moisturizer?* Hwa Young thought. Zie shared Ye Jun's oval face and good looks, but there was a heaviness in zir red-and-blue eyes.

"Two reasons," came the response. "First, because you're the heart-daughter of Commander Aera. She is second to none but Admiral Mae, isn't that correct? She may be willing to listen to you where she wouldn't listen to someone else."

Hwa Young didn't reply, although *I can neither confirm nor deny* ran through her head like an inane chant. Ga Ram vastly overestimated her ability to talk Aera into anything but fashion consultations, or Hwa Young would have reunited with Geum weeks ago.

Instead, she stared out the cockpit window at the surface of the asteroid, pitted by the unending fall of dust and micrometeorites. She wished she could lose herself in the way her lancer's shadow knifed across the surface, and *Paradox*'s as well, with a starkness uncommon on inhabited worlds with their buffering atmospheres.

"Second, because I *can't* talk to the leader of your squad. The blood relationship complicates matters."

Commander Ye Jun rarely spoke about being an Imperial bastard, or why zie had left a comfortable existence on the crownworld. Zie had wanted to be a lancer pilot; everyone with a pulse understood that. But there were holes in the story, unanswered questions, and she hadn't considered it proper to pry. Pissing off someone who could *take over* her lancer seemed like a bad tactical decision.

"Commander Ye Jun is an excellent leader," Hwa Young heard herself say frostily.

"Of that I have no doubt," Ga Ram said dryly. "I was the one who trained zir."

Oh.

"Nevertheless, Ye Jun sees me as our mother's creature. The animus is not entirely unearned." A soft pause. "I am here because the Empress is here. She fled a coup on the crownworld. She's trying to regain her throne, whatever the cost may be, with the forces she has left: myself, my lieutenant, Eleventh Fleet. Anyone who can be strong-armed into obeying her."

Hwa Young struggled to take this in. Did clanner leadership know? Assuming the information could be trusted. But they'd verify any development of this magnitude.

This might explain why Imperial forces have been thrashing around like a dragon with its head cut off. Because they are *a dragon with its head cut off.*

Despite the fact that she had joined the *other side,* this explanation, for all its logic, inspired immediate dismay. The years she had spent as a citizen of New Joseon marked her yet. She didn't know how to reconcile this with her current loyalties; she resented the roiling guilt that assailed her.

"How long ago?" she asked.

"Three weeks ago."

"The singularity bomb?"

"She has another, as well as the plans to build more," Ga Ram said. "Eleventh Fleet has it now. Ninth Fleet may or may not be willing to offer her succor—for a price. The situation is very fluid right now."

"I can't take your word for any of this." Hwa Young winced as she said this. She reminded herself that she was no longer part of New Joseon. There was no need to defer to royalty.

Geum could verify the intel. But she wasn't going to rat zir out like this. She'd have to find a different source.

"Why are you doing this?" Hwa Young asked.

Once she would have considered this a positive event. A chance for peace or détente.

Two months gone and she was no longer young.

A muscle jumped along the side of Ga Ram's jaw. After an agonized pause, zie said, "I was raised to believe that it is the crown's duty to provide for its citizens, and not the other way around. I am oath-sworn to serve the Empress. But my duty is to New Joseon's *people,* who are being sacrificed. That takes precedence. If my honor is compromised in the process, so be it."

It was a compelling story. Ga Ram sounded so reasonable. So anguished. She *wanted* to trust zir. Zie might be counting on that.

The Empress might be counting on that.

"I have a token that should be persuasive. But you will have to open your cockpit to receive it."

Hwa Young doubted that Ga Ram was offering her a care package loaded up with confetti and glitter, like the one Geum had once surprised her with.

Paradox walked two meters until its cockpit was pressed up against her own, and she let it.

It was a good life while it lasted.

Hwa Young opened her cockpit, grateful for her helmet and her oxygen supply, because small comforts mattered during hair-raising moments like this.

Ga Ram rose to greet her. Zie was holding a . . . cake box? It couldn't be a cake box. Except it said *STAR BAKERY* and *OUT OF THIS WORLD CAKES*.

She couldn't hear Ga Ram, but she read zir lips. *It's heavy,* zie was saying.

Hwa Young stood, teetered, and accepted the cake box. Staggered at its weight. After a moment's thought, she secured it in the copilot's seat. She didn't want that coming loose and clocking her during high-gee maneuvers.

They returned to their seats. Closed the cockpits.

Over the comms channel again: "Take a look," Ga Ram said.

Hwa Young lifted the lid. Her eyes were dazzled by antlers of gold, themselves embellished by a ransom's worth of comma-shaped jades. A crown in the style of the ancient Silla kingdom, back on Old Earth.

Her mouth dropped open. "You stole the *Empress's crown*? Isn't she going to notice?"

For the first time, Ga Ram chuckled. "You've noticed how heavy that monstrosity is. It's solid gold, and the sheer quantity of jade is no joke either. You could give someone migraines with it. The Empress never wears it if she can help it. For broadcasts she has someone edit in a virtual model. Or she wears a fake. She only takes out the real thing as a last resort."

"Why?" she asked.

"As an earnest of my sincerity," Ga Ram said, humor dropping away. "There is no one else with the access to have taken this. There is no one else who would have dared. If clanner leadership wishes to reject my overture, they have only to leak word to Eleventh Fleet. At that point the Empress will discover the theft, and my own life will be forfeit. I am, as you would say, *all in*." And, quietly: "Carnelian wasn't the first time the singularity bomb was used, as you must realize. My fiancé was a casualty of the first successful test."

If *this* declaration was an act, Hwa Young would eat her own liver; who needed a gumiho? "I'll convey the information," she said, shaken.

She rechecked the planetoid's trajectory at the same time that Ga Ram said, "It's time to get out of here. Back to our respective fleets."

Hwa Young hoped that the value of her intel would justify the excursion. "Of course."

Paradox launched first, stirring up a cloud of violet-green dust.

Hwa Young shot off a single brief message to Geum when *Paradox* was no longer visible. Then she launched as well, heading for her own fleet.

11

GEUM

Geum previously conceived of timekeeping in terms of days or classes. Eight days to study for a calligraphy exam; fourteen to prepare a presentation on the philosophy of right-minded governance. Zie didn't track minutes or hours, because the neural implant took care of that. Zie didn't factor in scheduled prayers to the Empress, either; they were so ingrained as to be axiomatic.

Now every hour mattered. Every *minute* mattered. The passage of time reverberated through Geum's entire body with each heartbeat.

Twenty-three hours and forty-six minutes had elapsed since the *Maehwa*'s shields malfunctioned midbattle. The ship suffered hull breaches from random flotsam and stray projectiles that slammed into it before CIC and the hardworking, underappreciated technicians restored the shields.

In an ideal world, Geum would take it easy in sick bay. Hunker down behind a pillow fort and sleep for a month.

Instead, a medic had given Geum some hinky stimulant/analgesic shot to jolt zir out of the concussion. "You'll pay for it later," she had said, "but we need you now." Zie had just taken a third dose of stimulants because zie had a job to do. Everyone did.

Geum hadn't had any chance to shower. The only hygiene care zie had received was getting hosed down with a five-second blast to remove the worst crud. Not as a concession to propriety but utility: fine motor control was worthless if one introduced contaminants into circuitry or equipment while doing repairs.

Currently Geum was assisting with repairs to life support two levels above docking bay six, away from the technicians' ordinary stomping grounds. Gruesome work, which required them to climb up into passages tenuously designed for human comfort. Geum's lower back and shoulders hurt from hunching over for hours. Zie wondered if Hyo Su would agree to an exchange of massages when they got off shift. If *anyone* ever got off shift.

The leakage of unmentionable fluids, and the attendant smells, penetrated the filtration masks. Geum monitored invisible microorganisms through a primitive handheld environmental probe: their unchecked growth might crash life support.

Chief and most of the senior techs were preoccupied with the trickier task of temporary repairs to the hull breach itself. The *Maehwa* needed to put in at some friendly shipyard for real repairs—assuming they were physically able to make the trip.

Geum wondered how the engines were; hadn't dared to ask. Zie wasn't sure zie wanted to find out.

Prioritize, Chief liked to say. *Always assess the damage and prioritize before you do anything.*

It sounded so neat. So simple and self-evident.

But how did one prioritize between *life support* and *hull breach* and *engines?*

Not my problem, Geum thought. It wasn't heartlessness. Zie could only do zir small part. This involved reconnecting pipes and reprogramming the master regulators for the environmental filters. Ordinarily this required a team of four people, not two, one of whom, however brilliant, had never done this before.

"It shouldn't be possible," Spade said over and over again. "A shield failure of that magnitude? Midbattle? Our computers are shitty, but not *that* shitty."

Twelve hours ago, Geum had wished that Spade would shut up about this, and not because he was disrupting zir concentration. Geum's thoughts kept circling back to Hwa Young. When they did, a tumultuous mixture of emotions threatened to overwhelm zir.

Is she okay? Did she die in the heart of a white dwarf before I could even say goodbye?

Had Hwa Young died because of a trap Geum had helped set for her?

Geum and Hyo Su had exchanged a brief hug before going to their respective assignments. "We should hold a dance party after this is over," Geum had said, and Hyo Su had nodded into zir shoulder. It hadn't been clear who was comforting whom.

Now Spade's shocked mumblings faded into the background. Geum tuned it out like zie had once tuned out history lectures. Zie was impressed by the steadiness of zir hands as zie applied sealant to the two reconnected pipes, which fed into a condenser and from there into waste treatment to recycle chemicals, and to filter and reclaim water. Someone would have to weld them properly later, as opposed to the temporary measure of glorified fast-drying space goop, as Hyo Su called the glue. No one had time for *properly*, only *good enough*.

A light turned from red to blue. What percentage of reclaimed life support did that represent? One percent? Less?

"Next thing on the list?" Geum croaked.

"What? Oh." Spade squinted at his slate, then held up the checklist.

Geum nodded wearily. Another pipe. Of course.

"It doesn't make sense," Spade repeated, as though something had snapped inside him. He returned to his own task, which involved biochemical analysis that Geum wasn't yet rated for.

Geum had done a lot of things in the past twenty-four hours that zie wasn't rated for. But it was nice to pretend that everyday procedures still applied.

Something snapped inside Geum, too. Zie gave Spade's words serious consideration for the first time while punching controls to divert flow from *here* to *there*. This was partly so the glue wouldn't be washed away, partly so Geum wouldn't get splashed with effluvia.

Spade was right. That early in the engagement, the *Maehwa*'s shields should have prevented a direct hit. Why had they failed?

People had died. Zie had walked past the bodies on the way to this assignment. Hadn't had the stomach to look at them, or think about the fact that everyone was too busy to clear the dead, give them some dignity. But the smell—the smell clung to the inside of zir nostrils.

Don't think about the dead. Just keep working.

⊙⊙

Eighty-seven hours passed, or eighty-six, before Geum was relieved of duty and told to catch what sleep zie could. Numbers ceased to mean anything. Zie was out of stims. The hallucinations had set in. Geum started seeing kaleidoscope-whirl butterflies cavorting through the ship's passages.

Geum woke in zir cabin an indeterminate period later, to an urgent buzzing. *Funeral address in two hours,* the message said. *The Empress herself will lead the service. It is a great honor.*

It took Geum four attempts to close the notification so zie didn't have to stare at the words *great honor,* which seemed to glow with a radiance like exploding suns.

Is Hwa Young on the list?

Hyo Su had passed out too. She was snoring in the other bunk. Geum welcomed the noise as evidence that she was alive and not . . . well.

Geum checked for messages.

A sob escaped when zie found one sent late in the battle, if the time stamp was to be believed: *Together forever.* That was all.

Hwa Young had survived.

Hwa Young had survived. Hadn't fallen for the trap. Was still talking to Geum. Didn't—probably didn't—blame zir for the ambush.

The shower cut off after two minutes instead of the usual ten, wholly inadequate. Water rationing must be in effect. Geum ended up scooping up what shower water hadn't already swirled down the drain and destroying two towels scrubbing zir skin clean. Zie emerged blinking back tears, and applied lethal amounts of deodorant and cheap perfume to blast away the remnants of the stench.

Geum shook Hyo Su's shoulder. She rolled over and redoubled her snoring. Geum grinned in spite of zirself.

I should let her sleep in. Not like anyone's going to be taking attendance. Was Hyo Su the type who would care about missing a funeral service?

Geum tried one more time to wake her up, then gave up. If she was that far gone, she needed the rest more, anyway.

Geum showed up for the funeral service on time, the first miracle, and without bursting into a fresh round of confused tears, the second miracle. The other technicians made space for zir with only a slow murmuration of reassurances. Zie couldn't explain that zir messy feelings were about Hwa Young. Even if they were *happy* feelings, having to keep them secret was its own kind of awful.

One technician was absent—Geum tried, and failed, to remember her name. Not dead, but in sick bay. She'd recover. A small relief.

Spade, concern on his seamed face, rested a hand on Geum's shoulder, gave it a squeeze. Geum's vision blurred at this wordless gesture. Couldn't say anything, thanks or otherwise, just a small choked noise. No response seemed to be expected, anyway.

"I've seen a lot of folk come and go," Spade said in an gentle undertone, "a lot of hurt. It's always hard."

The *Maehwa* was so depleted of personnel that docking bay three sufficed to hold the mourners, everyone but a skeleton crew. The space was soberly bedecked with white azaleas, white banners of death and mourning. It pained Geum—Geum, who had never cared about tradition, whose previous funeral attendances had been for grandparents and one aunt zie had not been close to—that so many of the mourners, including zirself, wore uniforms that were patched, stained, hastily mended.

There were musicians, playing traditional music projected to the furthest corners of the docking bay: a piri wind instrument with its keening overtones; a gayageum, a zither in the ancient style rather than the modern variants, whose player embellished the plucked notes with expressive vibratos. Geum had not expected live music. Recalled a mention, in passing, that a few of the crew doubled as musicians. They'd been nowhere in sight during New Year's, perhaps some quirk of Admiral Chin's, now overruled by the Empress herself.

Hyo Su might have liked this. She'd mentioned once that she couldn't bring her gayageum because it exceeded her personal allowance in both weight and dimensions, and no one had yet invented a folding zither. Then Geum winced: was *funeral music* something one enjoyed?

A single casket stood at the front, representing the massed dead, another compromise. The bodies would have been given what little dignity was available, cremated, the ashes loaded into canisters so they could be fired into the nearest suitable star.

The murmuring stilled when the Empress entered, flanked by Captain Ga Ram and Lieutenant Mi Cha, and behind Mi Cha, the unnamed copilot. Based on their one meeting, Geum had expected the Empress to glide in on bare feet, wrapped in a bathrobe.

(Why didn't Ga Ram have a copilot? Another mystery.)

The Empress did not insult them with impropriety. The massive gold-and-jade antler crown of New Joseon gleamed from her brow; Geum expected it to cause instant migraines. She'd sheathed herself in layers of silk hanbok stiff with embroidery in iridescent threads spun from harvested butterfly scales. Geum wouldn't have been surprised to learn that the robes doubled as body armor. At least, the Empress would wear body armor beneath the finery, in case of attack.

The *Maehwa*'s crew bowed in the deepest possible obeisance, although Ga Ram, Mi Cha, and Mi Cha's copilot only went to their knees; Geum couldn't resist peeking. Eleventh Fleet had suffered fissure and fragmentation in months past, blows to its loyalty and its ships and its crew. None was evident now.

As one, they recited the Empire's motto: *Trust the Empress. Move at her will. Act as her hands.*

Geum clung to the earth-solid presence of the Empire's gravitational center, rooted zirself in it like a codependent tree.

"Honor to Eleventh Fleet," the Empress said, in a voice that reverberated down to marrow. "Rise," she added, and they did.

She flung a hand outward. The extremes of the docking bay lit up, holographic displays but no less stunning for their artificiality: behind her, a wild expanse of ocean, blue with an intensity that seared the eyes; to the left, a pine-furred mountain guarded by a prowling tiger, flame-bright and ferocious; to the right, another mountain, this one guarded by a coiled dragon, a pearl shining from its forehead; and behind them, although Geum dared not turn to look, there would be a third mountain, with its wise black tortoise.

Geum could swear zie smelled the salt-winds of the sea, the invigorating sharpness of pine. Imagination, or artifice—fragrances pumped into the air vents—zie didn't care. It was right and proper.

On a planet, the funeral would have been planned in consultation with a geomancer. They would have aligned the site with the local topography and ley lines, finding a way to calm the spirits of the dead and bring fortune to the survivors. Out in space, where there was no *north*, other conventions prevailed.

The Empress inclined her head to them, her expression grave

but not forbidding. She radiated a frank sympathy that even Geum found convincing. Geum's breath caught, and zie choked back a sob, surprised by the force of zir reaction. *This* must be why the Empress inspired such devotion in those who encountered her in person.

"Honor to those who gave their lives," the Empress said. Either her voice caught in an unrehearsed manner, or she was a superlative actress. She carried the ritual bowls: three each of rice, vegetables, soup; three coins, exaggerated in size so as to be easily visible; three pairs of shoes, likewise.

Huh, Geum thought, startled out of the trance-state of solemnity. *The pilots are helping her with all the paraphernalia. Where are her servants?* All the broadcasted ceremonies had featured servants.

That question fled when the Empress resumed. "Eleventh Fleet fights hard," she said, "and fights well, and will continue to fight."

The rest dissolved in a static of cheers, shouts, stamping feet.

The Empress lifted her hands, lowered them; ducked her head with a startled smile that made her appear surprisingly young.

The screens shifted, showing, in all directions, the canisters with their freight of ashes being fired toward the waiting star.

Eleventh Fleet fights hard, and fights well, and will continue to fight.

It was the Empress's use of the present-and/or-future tense that caught Geum's attention: the nuance of her choice.

Eleventh Fleet will continue to fight, Geum repeated to zirself. *Hwa Young, please hurry.*

12

HWA YOUNG

Hwa Young docked last, wondering all the while how the others fared. Falcon Command had been too preoccupied with damage control (said the autoresponder) to give her a status update when she requested one. No matter how much Hwa Young told herself this was a reasonable response, her heart thumped with dread as she imagined the worst.

I would have felt it if someone had died. An irrational conviction, yet one she couldn't shake. She waited for *Winter's Axiom* to reassure her with an inappropriate quip about skeletons, then fretted when it refrained.

Hwa Young had strayed farthest from Falcon Fleet. The signal that guided her in, from a single unstealthed scout, had come as a relief. No one liked to contemplate being abandoned in space. Her body thrummed with anxiety as the lift conveyed her from the cockpit down to the deck.

Her heart clenched painfully at the sights that awaited her.

Commander Ye Jun was in a stretcher. For a moment Hwa Young couldn't breathe. The commander was arguing with a medic, so at least zie was conscious—and alive. Hwa Young side-eyed the medic's belt of bone-colored knives, which looked like they'd been ripped out of tigers' mouths.

What happened while I was separated from the rest of the squad? Eun stood to the side, making no interjections. *That* anomaly caused her heartbeat to race all over again. And Bae—

She didn't recognize Bae at first. The entire side of his head had swollen up, an ugly mottled purple. It was the first time Hwa Young had seen him with an injury to his face.

I should have fought dirtier when we were enemies, Hwa Young thought, because that was better than panicking about how everyone was hurt. Then she cringed. What if the bruises hid worse injuries?

Hwa Young strode toward the others, her meeting with Ga Ram, even the precious box in her arms, momentarily forgotten. "Are you all right? What happened out there?"

Bae's eyes were shadowed with an odd ambivalence. "Word is *Maehwa* had a shield failure. *That* was why Eleventh Fleet turned tail. *Maehwa* was in bad shape, last we saw it. It took Admiral Mae by surprise, so we're guessing it wasn't zir cunning plan."

Hwa Young's mind blanked. She was aware of something falling, a heavy *thunk*. All she saw for moments, or perhaps hours, was a snowfall of regrets.

Imperial starship shields could be battered down with enough firepower, but a *failure*? An unexplained one?

Unless someone on the inside had sabotaged them.

Someone like the Captain of the Guard.

One of the first things she'd learned about space combat was the application of physics: *an object in motion remains in motion.* Anything fired into space kept going until it spiraled into some gravity well, was swept up by aetheric currents, or collided into something else. Space contained a lot of emptiness—but space near *two fleets in battle* was another matter.

No wonder Eleventh Fleet had retreated.

Geum's on that ship.

"The *Maehwa*," Hwa Young croaked. Her vision grayed around the edges, as though hazed by smoke. "Did it—did it survive?"

Did Geum survive?

"Like I said, we're not sure." That was Bae. "We had to withdraw too, due to heavy losses."

Heavy losses that she and the other pilots were supposed to prevent.

Hwa Young swayed, gripped by the reality she'd avoided facing during the past months of border missions. Always targeting outposts or research bases so they could steal data and the auxiliary ships could evacuate people in dangerous territory, resettle them somewhere safer; chasing off scouts from rival clanner fleets, once in a while.

She'd known intellectually that she'd switched sides. But she hadn't grappled with the fact that this meant shooting at people she'd trained with. Had known, in Geum's case, since childhood.

Geum could be dead. She'd been in talks with the person who was the most likely culprit.

Bae gripped her shoulder with an unaccustomed fierce strength. "Steady there," he said. Their eyes met. His sheened violet and silver, eerie and familiar both. He mouthed, *Geum?*

Hwa Young nodded wordlessly.

Once she would never have imagined herself receiving comfort from Bae, who'd tormented her from the moment she'd shown up at the boarding school in Forsythia City. Nor would she have envisioned Bae caring about Geum's existence. After everything they'd endured together, however, from Ha Yoon's death to Seong Su's, none of that mattered anymore. The surge of gratitude that warmed her was both confusing and comforting.

The other pilots needed her, not just Bae. They were bound together by shared decisions, shared responsibilities, the unique connection between pilot and lancer. She owed them the best of her efforts.

Hwa Young shook, a delayed stress reaction. Her skeleton was about to shudder apart. She remained upright thanks to Bae's steadying arm, her own force of will.

"Listen." Commander Ye Jun spoke from zir stretcher. Bitterness shaded zir voice like subtle poison. "We always knew this was a possibility. We have to trust that they got out in time."

Had Ga Ram intended to destroy the Empress while conveniently absent? Did zie hope to seize the throne? *If* zie had told the truth, *if* the Empress was in fact on the *Maehwa*—

But if Ga Ram's goal was to usurp the throne, why tell her as much as zie had? And why hand over the *crown*?

Abruptly Hwa Young remembered the crown. Wondered why her arms were empty. Looked down, where the box sat on the deck. Star Bakery must use extraordinarily sturdy boxes. She was lucky she hadn't dropped it on her *foot* or it'd be broken.

Commander Ye Jun was looking at the box too. "Explain," zie said coolly. "I assume your jaunt wasn't a snack run, even if that bakery makes the best sponge cream cakes in the capital."

"Commander," the medic hissed, "for the sake of moon and stars and little fishes, lie down, you're going to aggravate the damage to your spinal column. Unless you want to zap *more* body parts out of commission." She jabbed zir nonfunctional arm.

Ye Jun ignored the medic, eyes boring into Hwa Young.

Showing up with an unexplained cake box did invite questions. Too bad the cake was a lie. "I agreed to speak to the Captain of the Guard. Zie requested parley."

Ye Jun's lips compressed, although zir voice remained level. "The 'crash landing.' I wondered if that was what was going on."

Hwa Young's face heated.

Geum. Geum, are you out there? Are you okay?

Commander Ye Jun was waiting for her report. She had to pull herself together.

Hwa Young recounted what had passed between them, shaky at first, then with increasing steadiness. She'd rehearsed the account, although they'd been temporarily driven out of her head when she learned about the *Maehwa*.

"Eun." Ye Jun's voice was deadly soft. "Pick up the box and bring it to me."

The medic was swearing under her breath, an ongoing rush of disgruntlement. No one paid her any heed.

Eun did as Ye Jun asked. He swore too, surprised by the box's weight. "Open it, sir?"

Ye Jun's eyelids flickered in assent.

Hwa Young was awed all over again as Eun lifted the lid, revealing the crown in its antiquated glory. *A crown in the style of the ancient kingdom of Silla,* she recalled from her lessons. *Chosen as New Joseon's emblem in honor of our heritage back on Old Earth.*

Ye Jun stared at it, eyes filling with shadow. "Closer."

Eun brought it to zir. Hwa Young and Bae kept their distance, scarcely daring to breathe.

Ye Jun reached out and pried free a single comma-shaped jade with a fingernail. Hwa Young stifled a gasp. The empty socket stared like a skull's.

Ye Jun's smile lacked humor. "The Empress never did get that loose stone fixed by a jeweler, and no one else knew about it. This is real. The Empress has taken the field. We have here the crown of New Joseon. Eun, secure this in *Hellion*'s cockpit. Do not release it to anyone without my direct order. Tell Commander Aera I will discuss this development with Admiral Mae at zir earliest convenience."

⊚

Hwa Young distracted herself the best way she knew how: by taking a shower. The clanner ship's sonic shower wasn't as viscerally satisfying as the water ration she'd had on the *Maehwa*. She took a mordant solace in the annoying subliminal humming, lingering as she scrubbed at imaginary grime.

As a child, she would have run to Mother Aera and demanded attention: one of Aera's rare hugs, a story of star-dancers and aether-sailors, a snack. If Hwa Young did that now, Aera would look at her in disappointment. Hwa Young didn't want that.

Why didn't parents come with instruction manuals, like rice cookers and lancers? The six years of separation had kneecapped her ability to say hello to her heart-mother without feeling as though she'd done something wrong. Left a shoelace untied, maybe.

Besides, the real grime stained her soul. Hwa Young laughed dryly at her own melodrama the moment the thought occurred to her. What was she, a dirty bedsheet? A flush heated her cheeks at the metaphor.

The next thing she knew, someone was rapping impatiently on the door. Hwa Young startled awake. She'd been so exhausted she had slumped asleep in the shower. All her hair felt like it was standing up on end and vibrating, although the shower had automatically shut off.

"*Hwa Young.* Do I need to grab a welding tool and cut off the hinges? Are you alive in there?"

"All right, all right, I'm alive," Hwa Young snapped, wondering who it was. Muzzy-headed as she was, she didn't recognize the low, husky voice. Wouldn't have recognized her *own* voice, for that matter.

She realized a second too late that she'd forgotten to grab her robe or a towel. In principle, one could take a sonic shower while fully clothed. Rose-Merline had mentioned that in passing their first week aboard *Falcon Actual,* another reminder that the *plants,* cosseted with triple-filtered water, rated higher than *people.*

Hwa Young had never lost the habit of disrobing to shower, nor had Eun. They'd all become blasé about en passant nudity, living in close quarters the way they did. (She was grateful that Eun took his *needs* elsewhere, rather than inviting his boyfriend over.) After facing death together, after surviving massacres and contested moons together, what did a little skin matter?

All the same, she was standing naked in front of Bae. The last time she'd suffered such total embarrassment, she'd been a five-year-old getting chewed out because she ruined Elder Paik's *good* scissors, reserved for fabric, by cutting paper dolls out of what she now recognized as a book of erotic paintings.

Bae, on the other hand, had all his clothes on; stood with his accustomed haughty bearing despite the bandages plastered to the side of his head.

She looked at him, really looked. Stared, because discretion and decorum lived in another galaxy, perhaps the one where shoes spoke prophecy and choco pies grew on vines. Still annoyingly pretty; still essentially Bae, complete with that annoying air of "my insoles are better bred than you are."

Better bred, with manifestly better manners: Bae's gaze remained fixed on Hwa Young's face, rather than the rest of her body. She would have believed that he had somehow neglected to notice her lack of clothing. A downward glance on her part confirmed, however, that he was not unaffected by the sight, which answered a question even Hwa Young wasn't so crass as to ask out loud.

"So your voice finally broke" was what popped out as she lunged for a towel.

Bae hacked out a laugh, still not looking. "Does it bother you?"

Maybe it was better that they were having this conversation while drunk on the ebb tide of a postcombat adrenaline crash. Hwa Young didn't think she could have gone through with it otherwise. She could wrestle with her obscure sense of disappointment another time. "It's not any harder to get used to than the mean-girl act."

To her surprise, Bae broke eye contact: direct hit. "It wasn't an act."

The closest Bae had ever come to apologizing to her, or anyone else. A year ago, Hwa Young would have scented blood, struck when Bae was vulnerable. Today—"Whatever," she said, rolling her hand palm up, then down, in an ambivalent gesture of acceptance. "But why now? Why didn't you do this years ago? Or whenever you felt like it? Your family could have bribed a genetic sculptor to give you anything from mandibles to a marsupial pouch if you wanted a cutting-edge illegal body modification."

"Shows what you know," Bae said bitterly. "My mother wanted the perfect daughter, the perfect doll. *She'd* failed to catch the eye of a royal, so it was up to me. And that meant I had to play the part or she'd—" Bae broke off, resumed as though they were discussing nothing of more consequence than seasonal trends in earring designs. "You're very lucky. Your mother cares about you. I've seen how she looks at you."

Hwa Young wasn't fooled by the measured dispassion of his voice. It might *be* a different voice now that it had emerged as a low tenor, but she'd grown up orienting toward Bae's whims and words as though they constituted a warped compass north. She didn't know what to say to Bae's statement; didn't want to pour salt into the wound she'd unintentionally opened.

"And you?" Hwa Young demanded, although she wasn't sure where she was going with this line of inquiry. "Do *you* like what you see?"

Too late to take the words back. Rather than play-acting at modesty, which was a lost cause anyway, Hwa Young raised her chin, stood tall. Dared him to look, now that she had the towel in place.

Bae didn't take her up on it, but the pulse in his neck accelerated. For the next several seconds, it was the center of Hwa Young's world. She could see nothing else, think of nothing else.

Bae's hand moved infinitesimally, then dropped back to his

side. When he spoke at last, his voice was soft as ash, soft as dawn deferred. "You don't need to prove your worth to *me*, Winter. I watched you every moment of those six years. I know exactly how hard you work. You were the reason I could never slip up, never make a mistake, never coast. At least now we're on the same side."

With that, Bae spun on his heel and exited, leaving Hwa Young aswirl with insights that she didn't know what to do with.

13

HWA YOUNG

Commander Ye Jun was absent from the squad's next meeting. Instead, Commander Aera summoned them to a conference room. With her came Zeng, his handsome face taut.

Reminded of the recent fiasco, Hwa Young had trouble focusing. *Geum.* The thought ran through her head over and over. *Geum.*

She reached for the frigid numbness that *Winter's Axiom* had offered her in the past. No luck. Not a snapped connection, but a muted one. She sensed it distantly, as though it was too preoccupied to answer her or help her focus.

Her very fixation on Geum distressed her: shouldn't she be more worried about Commander Ye Jun? Yet she knew why her thoughts kept turning to Geum instead. They'd exchanged messages across the aether without laying eyes on each other for two months. A lot could happen in two months.

Geum was alive. She had to believe that.

They sat. She had little awareness of that, either. The table, the chairs, the ubiquitous starblooms in their planter: all of these faded into uninteresting abstractions.

Aera addressed Eun. "I would ordinarily not broach this to you," she said. "But your commander has reservations about some of the medical technologies available here, which have no Imperial equivalent. It's too late to do anything about zir arm, something we could have treated at the time of injury. But the current injury to zir spine—*that* we have the power to heal."

Eun shrugged. "Commander Ye Jun doesn't need an arm to be deadly," he remarked, "when it's all in zir brains. But yes, you have a point. I'll talk to zir."

Aera started to speak, but Eun interrupted her. "My turn. The scribers compromised our combat effectiveness. *Especially* in the face of *Summer Thorn*'s special attack, which disrupts the link between pilot and lancer. We can't go into another battle like that."

Hwa Young looked from Eun to Zeng, and back again. Belatedly, she registered the tension between them, like an overstressed wire. The way neither looked directly at the other.

Zeng bowed, tight-lipped. "You have my apologies, Pilot." He wouldn't meet Eun's eyes. "The emergency override in case of situations like this—failed. I'm working on a fix."

Eun's lip curled. "Hwa—Hwajin. Tell the researcher about your experience out there."

Hwa Young blinked, surprised by Eun's adamant growl. Just in time, she realized he'd involved her in the conversation on purpose to shake her out of her daze. Eun meant it as a kindness. His way of looking after her, however brusque, the way he had throughout her training.

For once, what she felt wasn't gratitude but resentment. She hated that he'd put her on the spot. She could back the squad—led, in Ye Jun's absence, by Eun—or she could throw her support to Aera. Not both.

Don't do this to me, she wanted to protest. Hwa Young recognized the fundamental immaturity of the sentiment. She'd comprehensively torched her chance at an easy, uncomplicated life when she led the squad here.

Her words emerged as a dry recitation, reluctant at first, then gaining in steadiness. She pretended she was answering a question in a classroom, and the only stakes were exam scores that no one would remember in a year. "Normally I hear *Winter's Axiom* talking to me," she said. Eun and Bae nodded, which gave her the courage to keep speaking. "This battle, it was like a lightning storm. There was pain, then the neural link shut down completely. I couldn't hear my lancer. I could only view the battlefield through the physical displays, as opposed to the mental map the lancer normally provides. I had to pilot on manual, which is clumsier."

As Hwa Young spoke, she returned to the moment her mental map collapsed into blackness. It filled her with terror, even after the fact. She heard nothing from *Winter's Axiom,* just an overlay of jittery static. Every so often a whisper emerged from the static, like shapes half-seen in the snow, tantalizingly familiar—

"You see," Eun said, implacable. "My commander took injury because our effectiveness was compromised." Everyone reacted to that "my," Aera with a cold, slow blink, Hwa Young by flinching, Bae with a humorless smile. "Remove the scribers. We won't risk that again."

Zeng raised his head. His eyes blazed with an unaccustomed intensity. "Please reconsider." His voice was soft, pleading.

Hwa Young shook her head, disgusted. Did he care so much about his research, his personal pride, despite the failure? How else to interpret his expression? Hwa Young shifted her weight in case action was called for.

No wonder Eun looked like he was on the verge of breaking up with Zeng, if he hadn't done so already. Hwa Young didn't look forward to interpersonal drama while trapped in the hothouse environment of a starship. At the same time, just as he had her back, she had his. She didn't blame Eun for his reaction in the slightest.

"Don't," Bae breathed. "Not here." He reached out to restrain her. His fingertips burned against the skin of Hwa Young's wrist like a star of ice and embers, light as the touch was.

She was ashamed of losing her cool. Ashamed that Bae had seen it.

"It's not up for negotiation," Eun said, biting off each syllable.

Zeng's face crumpled. Hwa Young caught herself shaking her head, made herself stop. She might regard Zeng with contempt for his misplaced priorities, but they were trapped on the same ship for the time being. It made more sense to let him salvage what dignity he could, rather than making her feelings clear.

Commander Aera regarded Eun for a long moment. Her gaze slanted toward Hwa Young, rather than Zeng. Hwa Young lifted her chin fractionally: not defiance, but indicating that she sided with Eun, as much as it pained her.

I'm sorry, Hwa Young thought in anguish, as though Aera could divine her thoughts. *I'll make it up to you later. I'll find a way.*

Aera pursed her lips, then sighed and broke eye contact.

Whatever she'd originally meant to express went unsaid. Instead: "Very well. The researcher will remove the scribers."

Falcon Fleet docked at Dragon Mountain. Hwa Young paid little heed to the negotiations for resupply, repairs, exchange of information, the coordination of the auxiliaries, and the disposition of the evacuees. Throughout their journey, the auxiliaries had come and gone, come and gone, like bumblebees ranging from the hive. Logistical matters, which she wasn't involved with. The latest batch of evacuees, she gathered, was being transferred to Ekphora Fleet, one of those specifically devoted to such humanitarian operations.

Hwa Young refused to accompany Eun and Bae because of an irrational fear of running into Commander Aera, who was, at last report, overseeing operations. "C'mon," Eun said, "I hear they have live concerts. Fresh fruit. You could buy a *real paper notebook!*"

"No thanks," she said, "but you two have fun." She couldn't imagine having *fun* when she still hadn't heard back from Geum.

Bae was watching, his expression inscrutable. Hwa Young told herself this was appropriate professionalism. Bae wouldn't be so crass as to express affection, or other complicated feelings, in front of a superior. *If* it was a question of affection, which she didn't know for sure.

"Your loss," Eun said. He laid a hand on her shoulder and gave it a squeeze. "You ever want to talk—"

"*Go,*" Hwa Young said, then realized how ungracious she

sounded. The smile she put on felt like a mask from a horror play, but it satisfied Eun. He nodded and gestured for Bae to follow him, leaving Hwa Young to her brooding.

Dragon Mountain's primary starport was as vast as a city and composed of rotating cylinders. According to the friendly informational broadcast, it had been built during the era of mock gravity generated by centrifugal effects. Hwa Young absorbed the regulations that governed leave on-station, which included keeping her badge ready in case of emergency recall, and otherwise kept to herself. She'd found a meditation garden, free to the public, an excellent place to lurk.

The second time Hwa Young set out for the garden while off-duty, it took her several minutes to realize that someone had fallen in to her side. She hadn't realized she was that preoccupied. What if it had been an attacker?

The other person unnerved her more than an attacker would have. Hwa Young knew what to do in a fight. She had a whole set of combat moves she was itching to try on the next unlucky person to engage her in hand-to-hand; longed for a target to take out her frustration on.

A friendly face, on the other hand—

"Bonjou, Hwajin!" It was Rose-Merline, her eyes warmer than ever. Today she had leaf-shaped beads braided into her hair instead of the usual prisms. With a boldness that took Hwa Young by surprise, she caught Hwa Young's hand with both of hers and pressed it. "I was so relieved when all of you returned safely."

"'Safely,'" Hwa Young echoed hollowly.

"Your commander will be fine," Rose-Merline said, mistaking the cause of Hwa Young's lack of enthusiasm.

She remembered what Aera had said about clanner medical technology—an offshoot of the advances that created clones like herself. A madcap image flashed in her mind's eye: a garden of Hwa Youngs and Aeras, waiting to be harvested from the vine. She'd once been so proud of being Aera's heart-daughter. Had the Imperials' disdain of cloning as a practice rubbed off on her, even as her comrades delicately avoided the topic?

Rose-Merline shifted her weight, her expression abashed. "Your commander put me up to this. Zie said you needed company and refused to spend time with your squad. I was the first person zie had talked to who had free time *and* social skills. I don't like lying to people, so . . ." She shuffled her feet again. "But I really would like to hang out, and we could just . . . not tell zir."

Was Ye Jun *matchmaking* on top of the hints zie had already dropped in her direction? She should have been outraged, but instead Hwa Young started to laugh. Ye Jun had run out of hobbies. "It's not you," she said, gasping. "But sure. Sure. I'll come find you sometime. Just—not right now."

Among other things, Ye Jun might want her to interrogate Rose-Merline about the connection between life support and the ever-present plants, but was that what Hwa Young herself wanted out of a conversation? She needed time to think her approach over, find a way to chat that wouldn't be unfair to the ensign.

Rose-Merline bit her lip, then nodded. "Later, then."

This was the start of a series of friendly overtures from clanners after the battle, as though she'd been responsible for the so-called victory. (Ye Jun couldn't have strong-armed *all* of them into this, right?) Hwa Young found gifts on her bunk: bouquets of starblooms, knotted cords with suggestive carved charms, even a scroll in a language she couldn't read and didn't recognize, although the beauty of the calligraphy with its sweeping curves and dots and swirls needed no translation. An effusion of welcome, now that she'd proven herself to them.

One time the gift was a packet of shrimp crackers from the Empire. The exact brand that was Geum's favorite. A coincidence, Hwa Young told herself. It was a popular brand, easily obtained even in the haphazard flow of black market trade. There wasn't any way—any reasonable way—a clanner could have known. It was a gift, left for her in a spirit of goodwill, and not a taunt.

Hwa Young looked down. She'd crushed the packet in her hands without realizing it. Tossed it out, thinking instead of the last precious snack in her care package from Geum. Hwa Young didn't like sesame honey cookies because the seeds got stuck in her teeth, but that didn't matter. As long as she didn't eat the cookies, maybe—maybe—the *Maehwa* would be fine and Geum would be alive.

Instead, she'd cultivated a low-level communications officer in Falcon Command, Cai. She had offered him a bribe, had been humbled by the steady, sympathetic way he looked at her and said that he was happy to loop her in, given how worried she must be about old friends, no bribes needed. Every day she asked him if there was word of the *Maehwa*'s status.

No word, Cai said each time, no word. This time too.

Hwa Young was tired of the cabin, tired of the gifts. She could have sought Rose-Merline out, but Ye Jun's deviousness still troubled her; needless to say, she avoided Ye Jun for the same reason, and Eun because anything Eun knew, the commander knew.

That left Bae. Hwa Young was avoiding Bae for completely

different reasons. Who would have thought that being on friendly terms with Bae would be *more* complicated than having him as the forever barb in her life?

Today she visited Dragon Mountain's meditation garden again. She might as well take advantage of it while the fleet underwent repairs.

One could use the garden for purposes that didn't have anything to do with meditation. The bladder plants that clung to the walls, the sweet grasses, the bright flowers that turned the unappealing color of jaundice when one crushed their fallen petals—none of them cared if their human guests huddled in their shade and contemplated the unjustness of the universe.

Even in her worst moods, Hwa Young balked at destroying anything in this remote corner of the garden, and not because of station fines. She had a favorite spot up in the branches of a construct meant to represent a tree. It would have passed if not for the fact that it was made of cast bronze and had dragon scales.

The "tree" stood amid starblooms and vines that screened her presence. She was thinking like a hunter . . . a sniper. No one came here—the tree was unpopular because the lights flickered in a spooky manner. People pursuing meditation, and the occasional couples or moresomes seeking romance, preferred other spots.

Her foul mood made her clumsy. For once she didn't care. She incurred bruises climbing the tree, banged herself up.

Bae wouldn't have bruised himself, Hwa Young thought.

The wig tugged at her scalp, an unwanted weight. Taking it off would be unthinkable, so she didn't. Word would get back to Aera.

She lurked in the fake tree's branches for four hours. Her

back and shoulders screamed. Pain was good: it reminded her that Geum was in danger. It was tempting to think of Rose-Merline's open smile, to wonder what it might be like to kiss her. Rose-Merline's persistence was flattering rather than unwelcome. But Hwa Young would only be doing it for the distraction, rather than genuine interest, and that didn't seem fair to Rose-Merline.

Or Bae. Part of her longed to run her hands over his shoulders and chest, explore what she found there, make herself impossible to look away from; another part wondered if this brashness would repel him. Maybe he didn't return her interest. The simple solution, which she had not nerved herself up to do, was to come out and ask. Bae had never been shy about making his opinion known.

None of this, however diverting, addressed the real reason for her terrible mood. Who cared about dating when people might be dead? When a particular person might be dead?

Geum. Please be all right.

Normally it didn't take her this long to recover from the physical strain of piloting. Zeng's scriber had altered the experience and made it more harrowing. Days had passed and her entire body still ached. She endured a constant headache, even though she'd taken painkillers and hydrated the way Eun nagged her to.

Winter's Axiom remained distant, which fed her self-pity. She didn't want to tell Ye Jun or Eun about it, not yet. The connection would repair itself over time. She clung to the thought like a lifeline.

Blearily, Hwa Young stared at the vines. Nova afterimages and nightmare silhouettes danced across her mind's eye. Seong Su's doomed lancer, the spherical hell-flare of an explosion dwindling into the aether's variegated night. Her fingers opened and closed on empty air, as though she could claw his ghost back to join her.

The other benefit of this spot: she could hear anyone approaching.

The anyone was Bae. His steps weren't loud, but they weren't quiet, either. He wasn't attempting to sneak up on her.

Bae stopped beneath the tree and tilted his head back to fix her with a cynical stare. Whatever they'd done in sick bay, his face had healed cleanly, and he looked as flawless as ever. No trace remained of the bruises. "You look like you went two rounds with a tiger and are losing the third."

Only then did she notice he was carrying a bag. Her awareness of her surroundings was going to pieces. "I didn't invite you here."

"You missed mess again."

Oh, Bae was going to be *that* way about it. "I didn't realize you were gunning for Eun's position," she retorted. Bad enough that Eun was a mother hen. She'd dodged him earlier today by volunteering for an extra shift at ops.

"Shut up and get down here."

Hwa Young's mouth dropped open.

This was one hundred percent pure unadulterated Bae. In fact, this was a replay of the first words he'd deigned to say to Hwa Young back when she'd shown up at the boarding school as a ward of the state. She'd been so *naïve*. Thinking the other students would be friends with an orphan who'd made it in on a scholarship.

The spot under the tree had looked so enticing after a morning in which all the other students shoved her when the teacher wasn't looking, or talked over her when she tried to speak. In her early days, Hwa Young would have flown into a rage, gotten into a fight. She'd learned better. Mother Aera had taught her to pick her battles.

Only people who picked their battles got to pilot lancers for the Empress.

Now she was clashing with Bae under a tree again.

Bae was still glaring at her with the icy hauteur that was his trademark. "Get down here and pull yourself together. You're a disgrace."

The early days hadn't left her after all. Hwa Young's temper snapped. She clambered down, scraping her elbows in the process. Landed in front of Bae with a thud, unreasonably angry that Bae was taller, had always been taller. "Maybe *you* didn't have any friends on that ship, but *I* did!"

Too late she remembered that Bae had already lost *his* best friend.

Bae radiated contempt, although his expression didn't flicker. He might have been carved from alabaster and polished with cloth-of-diamond. "There are four of us left."

Despite the exquisite poise that Hwa Young had hated and admired since childhood, Bae's voice broke on *four*.

Four pilots, four lancers, and yet we are legion, Winter's Axiom whispered.

Hwa Young was too intent on Bae to pay attention to it, despite the fact that it had kept ominously silent since Zeng's meddling. There had been no funeral service for Bae's friend Ha Yoon after *Winter's Axiom* killed her. None for anyone lost on Carnelian. There hadn't been *time* to mourn Seong Su's death in battle. They couldn't ask the clanners to perform some after-the-fact rite for the "enemy."

"Four," Hwa Young echoed, scarcely a whisper. Bae's perfection taunted her. Hwa Young was sure she looked a mess. What would she see if she consulted a mirror? Sunken eyes and hollow cheeks? The disheveled wig?

"That's not counting the people we lost getting here," Bae went on, relentless. "The casualties on Serpentine. Instructor Kim, who died getting us to safety—do you think about her anymore?" A drawn-out silence. "Ha Yoon, who was always—she knew everything about me. She was always there for me, and I couldn't save her."

Hwa Young had no rebuttal. Everyone in school had known about Bae and Ha Yoon's friendship, but Hwa Young had never thought it went beyond a shared interest in fashion, gossip, and lording it over their social inferiors.

"You think you're the only one suffering? Guess what. We *all* left our homes. We were supposed to be fighting to save lives, aid the clanners, help border communities resettle somewhere safer. Now we're fighting the Empress and her elites. Think of the commander. Ye Jun is at war with zir *mother*. Zie doesn't hide like a sulky toddler when there's work to be done."

Hwa Young's head came up. She had a threadbare memory: Commander Ye Jun released from sick bay, fully recovered. It would have been a miracle in New Joseon, but it was everyday medical treatment here. "What did I miss?"

"Just a training session and the debriefing afterward," Bae said, biting off each word as though he wanted to crack it open. "No big deal."

"You could have paged me."

"We *did* page you."

Hwa Young checked her badge. "Oh no," she breathed. It was

powered off. She hadn't done it on purpose. It must have happened when she'd banged herself up against the tree.

Once she reset the badge, it reported that Commander Ye Jun, Eun, and Bae had *all* paged her. Plus a chat request from Zeng, of all people. Was he hoping that she'd patch up his relationship with Eun? Whatever it was, it couldn't be important, not compared to this.

Bae's lip curled, watching her.

"It's not the same for me," Hwa Young said. She was speaking calmly, reasonably, as though calm and reason could sway someone like Bae. "You don't come from the clans. I never belonged in the Empire and now I don't belong here either. There's nowhere to go!"

A moment later she heard her voice echoing from the garden's far corners. Why did it sound so loud when she'd been speaking at a normal level? Why did her voice hurt as though a beast had savaged its way out of her throat?

"So the answer is running away? Hiding?"

Hwa Young didn't know who threw the first punch. She didn't care. Here was a fight against an enemy close enough to touch, one she could defeat. A chance to bleed off her anger and frustration.

They'd trained under the same teachers for six years of school. They'd sparred under Eun on the *Maehwa*. She knew Bae's speed and agility, the way he moved like a dancer and struck like a spear. Hwa Young had never defeated him in hand-to-hand; she had consoled herself that at least she was the better shot.

Right now, her reactions clouded by exhaustion and anger, she was more outmatched than ever.

Hwa Young predicted the blow that felled her. It didn't help. She couldn't dodge fast enough, or block it, or redirect it. The vicious strike, precisely judged, came short of breaking her elbow. When Hwa Young staggered, Bae flowed into a cleanly executed throw, leverage so perfect that he didn't *need* his greater strength to fling her several feet away. The heat of his body, the tightness of his grip, pierced her deeper than any bullet.

She landed on her back, the breath knocked out of her. All she could think about was how much her tailbone hurt. It beat dealing with her humiliation—or admitting that Bae was right.

Bae looked down his nose at her. "When you didn't answer the commander's call and no one could find you," he said, only the barest contempt coloring his voice, "I thought you'd done something irrevocable. That you were gone for good. I've ransacked the station looking for you. Next time I won't bother."

14

HWA YOUNG

Two hours and sixteen minutes later, Commander Ye Jun called Hwa Young to zir office. She didn't have to ask what the summons was about. Was mortified that she'd gotten herself in trouble the day Ye Jun was released from sick bay.

The sight of Ye Jun's face lingered with her from their last call: the way small translucent green tendrils, their pale leaves fluttering in time with the vein throbbing in zir temple, clung to zir face. "Clanner medicine," Ye Jun said, quirking an eyebrow at her in query.

She knew then that zie wasn't *completely* furious with her, although she still wasn't looking forward to the dressing-down. "Not any medicine I'm familiar with," Hwa Young admitted during the call. "We weren't on the cutting edge where I lived. There was an itinerant medic who made the local circuit . . ." The memory came back to her, along with the sharp sting of astringent in her nostrils, the enticing herbs she'd gotten in trouble for trying to ingest and which, she had been informed sternly, would have left her in a coma. "I'm not sure what we would have done for something more serious than broken bones or a hunting accident."

"It stands to reason that they'd have more advanced medicine on a carrier," Ye Jun said, although zie didn't sound entirely convinced, and she didn't think it was a trick of the comms system. "I admit I was concerned when 'advanced medicine' consisted of being attached to genetically engineered parasitic plants."

Hwa Young made a face. "But it worked?"

"It worked," zie confirmed. "After another couple days, I should even be able to remove my vegetal adornments."

She laughed obligingly. "I don't know, sir. You might start a fashion trend."

"Quite. In any case, I need to talk to you privately in person. I expect you here on the hour."

"Of course, sir." Hwa Young wondered what the commander wanted to tell her that zie wished to keep secret from the rest of the ship, or more accurately, the other clanners.

Hwa Young stopped by Rose-Merline's cabin on the way, calculating that she could just about make it to the meeting on time. She prayed to the moon and stars and storms that Rose-Merline was present, because the alternative involved talking to Bae and she wasn't ready to face him yet.

Rose-Merline emerged with her hair in disarray, silver-gold pollen clinging to her clothes and fingertips. "What is it this—" Her cranky expression fell away when she saw Hwa Young at the door. "Hey! Did I miss a message?" Then: "Hwajin, what happened? Did someone rough you up?"

"No, it's not, I—can I come in?" Hwa Young waited anxiously for Rose-Merline's nod before slipping in and closing the door behind herself. "I got into a stupid fight with someone, and I have to report to Commander Ye Jun. I was hoping you had some makeup so I can hide the worst of the bruises." At least there wasn't too much swelling.

Rose-Merline pursed her lips. "I can probably blend something to approximate your skin tone." She disappeared into her bathroom, then emerged with a makeup kit. "Let me do this, it'll be faster."

Hwa Young fought the urge to fidget under Rose-Merline's light, expert touch; fought her own hectic wish that this were more than a five-minute interlude. Already she regretted bringing Rose-Merline into this at all. It felt like taking advantage of the ensign's interest.

"So who was it?" Rose-Merline asked, leaning in, her slitted eyes fierce and dark. "If it was that creep Tora, he's going to find out what happens when I douse him in quadruple-strength liquid fertilizer."

"You too?" Hwa Young asked, dismayed. She'd thought she might be imagining things.

"Please. Everyone can see the way he looks at you. You're not the first one either."

Hwa Young was mindful that she had a deadline, although she was enjoying Rose-Merline's ministrations more than she wanted to admit. *Why am I doing this? To get back at Bae?* That felt crummy too. Besides, *this* incident hadn't been Tora's fault. "Tora sucks," she said, compelled to honesty, "but it wasn't him. I picked a fight with Bae."

Rose-Merline's hand slipped on the makeup brush. She swore under her breath, then dabbed at Hwa Young's cheek with renewed care. "Bae," she said with forced cheer.

She had to know. "Are you and he—?"

Rose-Merline glanced at her sidelong, beneath lowered eyelashes. "I'm not the one he's interested in." She tilted her head; a speculative gleam appeared in her eye. "Unless that person were amenable to an arrangement that involved more than two people . . ."

Hwa Young thought at first that Rose-Merline was referring to Ha Yoon. But Ha Yoon was dead. Unless *Bae* had been talking about Ha Yoon, which seemed unlikely, there was no way Rose-Merline could know about her.

Me. She's referring to me.

Hwa Young opened her mouth to protest, *That's absurd.* She stopped herself just in time. Tried to think of an answer. Her thoughts swirled with confusion, with a refrain of *too good to be true.*

She told herself that Rose-Merline was naturally friendly. That wasn't a crime. Or, to be more cynical, Rose-Merline was looking for new blood after running through any dating prospects on *Falcon Actual* before the lancer squad's arrival. If Tora was anything to go by, she couldn't blame Rose-Merline.

Besides, asking Bae about a mutual dating arrangement immediately after a fight? Hwa Young didn't want a second beatdown hard on the heels on the first. "We'll see" was the only answer she was able to dredge up, aware how weak it sounded. She attempted to soften her response with a smile.

Rose-Merline's mouth crimped. "Duty first, I assume."

Hwa Young would rather have lingered than gone to her reprimand, but Rose-Merline was right. "Duty first," she agreed. Greatly daring, she lifted a hand and pressed her fingertips against Rose-Merline's cheek, as light as a butterfly landing.

Rose-Merline leaned into the touch. Then Hwa Young drew back. "I have to go."

Without taking the time to inspect the makeup job in the mirror that Rose-Merline offered, Hwa Young dashed through *Falcon Actual* to the commander's office. Ye Jun would have timed, to the second, how long it took to traverse the distance involved.

"I'm here, Commander," Hwa Young called out. She vacillated between knocking on the door and hitting the doorbell, then compromised by doing both. The story of her life.

The commander didn't respond, nor did the system acknowledge her. Was this a test? A mark of disfavor?

Zie wouldn't play a stupid status game, Hwa Young thought. Not a *stupid* one, anyway. The commander always had a reason, even if it only made sense after the fact. She remembered Ye Jun lurking out of sight while the psychologist on the *Maehwa* "assessed" her for a suitable military occupational specialty. Ye Jun had wanted to see if she would measure up as a potential lancer pilot . . . and today she'd let zir down.

Eun would know . . . but Eun was unlikely to tattle on their mutual CO, even if he'd come around to calling her something more dignified than *Menace Girl.*

Fifteen minutes later, Hwa Young started to sweat. Mind games were one thing. But the commander had saved her life in combat. Had rescued her from a dismal fate scrubbing decks or cleaning toilets or greasing gun mounts, and vaulted her to the rank of lancer pilot.

I cannot hear Bastard, *Winter's Axiom* said suddenly.

Hwa Young nearly jumped out of her boots. She'd learned that the other lancers talked to *their* pilots. But talking to each other?

"I'm on it," Hwa Young said aloud. She could mull over lancer relationships later.

Again she asked the system for the commander's location.

This time it gave conflicting answers simultaneously, the same voice twinned: "Commander Ye Jun is in zir office" and "Commander Ye Jun is in Magnolia Docking Bay."

Unless Ye Jun also had a clone, zie couldn't be in two places at once. She doubted zie was in the office. Which left—

Hwa Young sprinted toward the nearest lift. She'd memorized *Falcon Actual*'s layout her first week, poring over glaringly incomplete maps. (Someone had inscribed *Use your imagination, asshole* in the gigantic blank space that anyone could deduce contained the ship's engine core.) This included roving the halls during time designated for sleep or recreation, creating a mental map. Sleep didn't do the dead any good. Their lives might depend on her knowledge of the ship.

What was the commander doing at Magnolia, anyway?

She reached the lift. Tensed and untensed her muscles while waiting for it to arrive, performed breathing exercises that she rushed through, negating their value. Wondered if Rose-Merline would be willing to trade massages. (Was Hwa Young herself good at massages? Geum had dodged the question.)

There is an attacker in Magnolia, Winter's Axiom added, with a sangfroid that contrasted with her own agitation.

That much she could have deduced for herself, based on Ye Jun's failure to respond. The question was—who?

Hwa Young swore and banged the lift doors. She'd seen someone unjam the doors that way three days ago. Falcon Fleet had the same issues with janky equipment and maintenance that

Eleventh Fleet did. Ten thousand years in the future, someone would be banging on some "advanced" machine to persuade it to do its job.

She could go the long way, through the shafts designed as backup in case the lifts failed. But time was of the essence. The lift would arrive any moment now. The instant she took off at a dead run, the way her luck went.

The lift chimed to announce its arrival. The doors opened three centimeters, then stopped with a screech.

Hwa Young swore. If this were the *Maehwa*, she'd call Geum and ask if zie could override the doors. But this wasn't the *Maehwa* and Geum was—

Geum isn't dead Geum isn't dead Geum isn't dead.

Three centimeters allowed her to shove her fingers into the gap, although she was convinced the doors would slam and she'd lose her hands, at least until the clanners could regenerate them.

Hwa Young was strong for her size. The doors were (she'd been told, during some orientation in prehistory) designed to be opened manually in the rare case of computer failure. "Rare" failures were more like "twice a week."

Seong Su could have muscled his way past the doors . . . if he were alive. She choked back a sob, which turned into hiccups. What was *wrong* with her? She wasted precious seconds getting her breathing under control, then tried again.

Hwa Young snatched her fingers back a scant moment before the doors slammed shut.

Her gut told her this was an attack, not a malfunction. She needed to notify someone. If she was wrong, she could endure the mockery. At the same time . . . if this was sabotage, she didn't want to alert the whole ship and tip off the saboteur by accident. So calling Falcon Command was out.

Hwa Young called Commander Aera directly as she set off at a bone-jolting sprint. She gasped out her query.

"Repeat that, Pilot Hwajin," a bored voice said.

Oh no. Her call had been rerouted. Hwa Young recognized the low alto of Aera's aide, Subcommander Roshan. They hadn't interacted much. Hwa Young had the hazy impression that Roshan only cared about one thing, paperwork properly filed, and that Hwa Young herself inconveniently failed to fit into some neat checkbox. "I need to reach Commander Aera."

"She's off-duty. I'll take a message."

Trying not to snarl, Hwa Young recounted Commander Ye Jun's summons, the fact that she couldn't *find* zir, elided the part about *Winter's Axiom* talking to her so she wouldn't alarm Roshan with lancer pilot eccentricities, and ended with the lift's troubling behavior.

She closed with, "Please patch me through to Commander Aera right now, it's urgent," feigning the mixture of politeness and regal expectation she had learned from Bae, despite the fact that they'd just fought. "I'd appreciate it very much, sir."

A brief pause, during which Hwa Young wondered if she'd laid it on too thick.

Then the subcommander said, with a snicker Hwa Young didn't understand, "Fine, fine, it's on your head. Far be it for me to stand in the way of a heart-mother and her heart-daughter reconnecting."

This provoked a fresh wellspring of guilt. Hwa Young emitted a strained *Thank you* as the static indicated that her call had been transferred.

Farseer *lies in darkness,* Winter's Axiom added, filling her mind with an intensifying storm of icicle intent. *Kill the enemy. Kill the enemy. Kill the enemy.*

Am I too late? she wondered, in an agony of helplessness. How could she fight an enemy when she didn't know who they were, where they were, what they *wanted*? Especially since there were so many options? Random hostile clanners . . . random hostile Imperial agents . . . random bandits or mercenaries . . .

She reached for the lancer's perceptions, seeking clarity. The lancer did not answer her directly. Once more she was lost in a blizzard, trapped in an infinity of white stretching out on all sides. She did not know where, in this winter, to find her lancer.

Commander Aera's voice came over the comms, drawing her out of the snowstorm. "Pilot. What's your report?" She sounded . . . cranky? Distracted? Breathless, as though she'd been exercising and Hwa Young had interrupted her favorite workout?

Hwa Young repeated what she'd said to Subcommander Roshan, agonizing about the additional time it took.

"I see," Commander Aera said. This time she did a better job of covering her annoyance. "Are you sure it isn't a computer glitch?"

Hwa Young was so busy contemplating ways to kill everyone on *Falcon Actual* with the power of her mind (except the other pilots and Rose-Merline, that went without saying) that she almost missed the way Aera's question ended in a breathless surprised laugh. And after that, a low murmuring voice that—

Wait a second—

That didn't sound like Commander Aera taking a nap or reading a book or doing an exercise routine or . . . Hwa Young had no idea what Aera did for fun these days.

She recognized the playfulness in the other voice now, and its significance. It reminded her of the way Rose-Merline had flirted with her. Where had she heard that voice, that particular husky timbre, before?

"Pilot Hwajin? Are you there?" The commander ruined the effect with another gasp-laugh, then a hissed sotto voce "*Stop that*, you have to go."

Her heart-mother was in *bed* with someone.

Hwa Young didn't realize she'd squawked until she heard the not-Aera laughter and a stifled chuckle from Aera.

Commander Aera recovered and heaved a sigh that took Hwa Young straight back to her childhood, also not where she wanted to be, especially right now. "We'll talk about this later, Hwajin. I'll put in a maintenance request. I'm sure Commander Ye Jun got held up with some administrative matter."

Thanks for nothing. Hwa Young forced herself to smile even though she was in danger of splintering her teeth and no one could see her anyway. Which was good, because her expression would have fooled no one.

Hwa Young signed off before she could hear any more breathing or laughter or—she tried to stop thinking about other noises she might overhear. This sent her horrible imagination into overdrive. Aera and her lover kissing, possibly involving their tongues, or—

The unwelcome visuals accompanied Hwa Young all the way down the maintenance shaft, the fastest remaining way to Magnolia, despite her best effort to focus on the task of placing her hands and feet on the ladder.

She didn't know why she'd expected Aera to wall herself off

from human contact after the rest of the family perished. As opposed to moving in with a complete stranger she hadn't bothered introducing to—

Aera is your commander. Hwa Young wasn't clear how protocol applied to family in the same chain of command, other than that the clanner military found it unremarkable.

Winter's Axiom, she thought at her lancer, *where are the other pilots?* She called them as well, to no avail.

The wig slipped and the long strands curtained her vision. Hwa Young hissed and yanked it off. She flung it against the side of the shaft and watched it fall with its locks fluttering in all directions. It resembled a giant mutant spider descending.

Her eyes smarted. Geum went by Spider.

Hwa Young reached level seven and hoisted herself through the entryway. By reflex, she thanked the Empress that the gravity hadn't cut out. Something creaked and she flung herself away from the opening, landing hard on the deck.

Her mouth tasted like old socks. She had either a dehydration headache or a stress headache or the unwanted orphan child of both. (Hwa Young had strong feelings about unwanted orphan children.) If her heart raced any faster, it would rocket out of her chest.

Hwa Young gulped air so she wouldn't pass out. *Falcon Actual's* bulkheads surrounded her. If they started closing in on her like those claustrophobic horror games that Geum enjoyed so much—

The thumping noises reached her moments before Hwa Young burst into Magnolia. No sign of Commander Ye Jun, none of Eun, nor Bae either. She wasn't sure which absence frightened her the most.

There were explosives attached to one of the lancers: *Farseer*. She knew it despite its blank features. A suited figure was scurrying away.

She should have drawn her gun. But she hesitated to do so, even as she pumped her legs harder. Didn't want to shoot someone in the back, especially if they could be captured and interrogated. Instead, she gathered herself to tackle the figure.

She was midleap when the explosives went off.

15

HWA YOUNG

The explosion knocked Hwa Young back several meters. The exposed surfaces of her skin erupted in agony, especially when she hoisted herself up, as though moving threatened to tear her open. Twisting and squeezing her eyes shut had preserved her vision. She hadn't screamed; that saved her from swallowing superheated air. She did not want to see what she looked like; didn't care. Broiled or not, she had a target.

The hunt, the hunt, the hunt, Winter's Axiom said, its crescendo of raptor intent obscured by the image of an everywhere blizzard. Her connection with the lancer numbed the burns and allowed her to function.

Hwa Young found her sidearm in her hand, although she had no memory of drawing it.

The saboteur had cleared the blast radius and was running. Hwa Young had an adrenaline-blurred impression of a figure wrapped in reflective clothes. She shouted after them, intending to say something so clever it stopped them in their tracks. All that emerged was a wordless shriek.

She could have sighted and fired. Her specialty was the rifle, not handguns, but she could hit the larger target of center mass, assuming there wasn't body armor beneath that reflective suit. Even now, though, she wanted to take them alive for questioning.

Hwa Young ran, redoubling her efforts, and prepared to leap at the saboteur again—

Violet blaster fire sizzled ahead of her. Hwa Young flung herself to the deck, stifling a cry at the hard landing. Spikes of agony radiated throughout her burnt skin. She curled up, sobbing.

The blaster hadn't hit her. She hadn't been the target.

A heavy thud followed as the saboteur fell too. The sound reverberated throughout Magnolia.

Moments later, dazed, Hwa Young stared at her gun hand. She was still holding on to her weapon. Her training hadn't deserted her, even when she wanted to peel off her skin and emerge newly born, an incandescent, fully healed butterfly.

The harsh rasp of her own breathing, the conflagration of pain, alerted Hwa Young that she was alive. She could still carry out her mission. Especially if the saboteur was also—

I want hazard pay, Hwa Young thought. She dragged herself upright like a possessed marionette.

Her gaze snagged on the fallen silver heap. It didn't move. The entire head was a scorched bulb, no longer resembling anything human. The stench of singed hair and charred meat drifted to her nostrils.

Hwa Young gagged. When she fought in a lancer, the enemy

was distant. She rarely saw faces, or encountered smells other than her own. Even then, the lancer's filters countered the worst of the sweat and blood.

She looked up. Commander Aera stood there, a mirror-ghost of ambivalent intent, her own handgun still trained on the saboteur's body. For a dizzying moment, Hwa Young wondered if she'd fallen out of her body; if that slender figure was the real Hwa Young and she was a wandering delusion, an exiled ghost.

However, Aera's hair, black as tree roots, lacked the broad white streak that *Winter's Axiom* had bequeathed Hwa Young.

Hwa Young switched her gaze to the saboteur's target. *Farseer*, whispered a voice that might have been her own, or might have belonged to *Winter's Axiom*. At the moment she had trouble drawing the boundary between them.

Out of the corner of her eye, she spotted her own lancer shimmering slowly from neutral gray to the white of snow beneath moonlight in response to her presence.

Farseer had a hole in its armor. It was no longer spaceworthy. Hwa Young hoped that the damage wasn't deep, but even a casual glance suggested otherwise.

"You shot the saboteur," Hwa Young croaked as anger flared in the pit of her belly. Good: she could warm herself by it. "Do you have any way of getting answers out of a corpse?"

"Even corpses speak," Commander Aera said, dispassionate. "We can look at the physical evidence for clues." Her eyes flickered as she considered Hwa Young's absent wig, but she didn't remark on it. She strode forward, then bent to strip the body. "Pilot, you need to go to Medical for those burns. They've got to hurt. I can take care of matters here."

"I'll help you." There wasn't any tactful way to express Hwa

Young's nasty suspicion that Aera might have offed the saboteur on purpose, although she couldn't imagine what Aera stood to gain from doing such a thing. The fact that she could entertain such a notion pained her. But she owed it to the squad—to *Bae*—to find out the truth.

When Aera hesitated, Hwa Young added, "It's just a little pain. Delaying treatment a few minutes won't matter, especially when medical care is so excellent here."

Aera should have been immune to the naked attempt at flattery. Instead, she looked Hwa Young up and down, clearly torn between practical necessity and, well, *hovering:* not the assessing eye of a superior officer wondering if her charge was fit to fight, but the anguish of a mother. As much as Hwa Young needed to be taken seriously, her competence to serve acknowledged, Aera's concern gratified the long-dormant part of her that yearned to be a child again, tucked into bed and soothed with honey cookies and a song.

"Fine."

Prodding a naked corpse with her heart-mother, complete with its unavoidable dangly bits, took the prize for most mortifying interaction. At the same time, Hwa Young didn't want to be sent to sick bay and shut out of subsequent developments, or the ability to monitor Aera's investigation. If she stayed, she'd learn about any clues the saboteur had left behind at the same time the commander did.

Besides, while the saboteur's *face* was gone, she noted a large, pale scar on the inside of the right wrist. The place where Zeng's heart-brother Tora had had the tiger tattoo he wouldn't shut up about. An old scar, she would have said—except clanner medical technology accelerated healing.

She kept *that* observation to herself, chilled anew by the

possibility that Aera had killed one of her own crew, even under provocation.

It must be a coincidence. Lots of people have scars. We're all soldiers.

"How common is that type of armor?" Hwa Young added, nauseated by the way the corpse flopped as her heart-mother flipped it over. Hwa Young had gone over every square centimeter of the silvery suit. No ID, no cheap souvenirs (or expensive ones), no good-luck charms or smelly herbal concoctions.

Aera shrugged. "Salvager's suit, a standard model. This one is in disrepair. The saboteur could have purchased it anywhere in the Moonstorm."

The one thing Hwa Young turned up was a needle-shaped dagger, well-balanced and made of a material that resembled glass. Hwa Young assumed the saboteur had selected it because it wouldn't show up on security scans. She was tempted to pocket it, but with her luck it carried toxins or creepy diseases that turned one's eyes inside out, so she toed it over to Aera.

The dagger was a dead end. It had no maker's marks. Hwa Young had seen nothing like it in New Joseon or the Moonstorm.

"I'll make some inquiries on the station," Aera said. "I don't recognize it either, but my contacts might."

Is she lying? Hwa Young wondered. The answer had come too quickly, too easily.

No. She was imagining things. Aera must have dealt with many such investigations. Hwa Young's paranoia derived from tightly wound nerves. She needed to step back and stop flinching at shadows.

My heart-mother wouldn't lie to me. Not like that. She'd tell me if she knew something.

So why did the doubts linger?

Hwa Young returned her attention to the suit, and turned it inside out. She fingered the silken lining, and her eyes narrowed. Clanner suits used a different, coarser material.

"Commander," she said, "this is Imperial-made." She explained her reasoning.

"An Imperial agent," Aera agreed, frowning. "Someone must have screwed up with the disguise."

Hwa Young thought of Dragon Mountain. Thought of all the people who called the station home, or who were passing through, none of whom she knew anything about. "New Joseon must have sent someone ahead of us to sneak aboard once we docked. Must have figured out where we were going. Or they already had an agent in place, who did this opportunistically?"

"Yes," Aera said, her voice deadly soft, "that is the question, isn't it."

The insinuation went over Hwa Young's head. Then her shoulders pulled back as the implications sank in. "You think *I* set this up? And got an explosion to the face for my trouble?"

Decking her superior officer *and* decking her mom were two separate bad ideas that combined into a glorious fantasy of catharsis. Instead, Hwa Young glared at the face that was hers and not hers.

"I am not questioning *your* integrity," Aera said with a vehemence that made Hwa Young squirm, because that was how *she* sounded when she wanted someone to believe her. "You are mine and I am yours. But Hwajin, you're not the only one who defected from the Empire."

Hwa Young stilled at the questioning lilt on *defected*. Anyone else would have missed it. But *she* knew, and her heart-mother knew she knew.

Is she trying to turn me against the rest of the squad?

Or was she overreacting again? She hadn't slept well. She'd just been attacked. She had burns.

It's nothing.

Nothing nothing nothing, Winter's Axiom echoed.

"Do you have *evidence*?" Hwa Young demanded, wishing she didn't have to ask. Her face hurt. She wanted to peel it off and fling it to the deck, but that wouldn't help.

Commander Aera grimaced at the corpse, then shook her head. "If you see anything of concern, though, you can always discuss it with me. I know Eun's trust . . . has been damaged. He hasn't spent any time with Zeng lately."

Hwa Young dipped her head, not trusting herself to speak. It bothered her that Aera was tracking their personal relationships, even though it made sense, in case they impinged on unit effectiveness. Ye Jun would do the same.

Hadn't Commander Ye Jun fought loyally and well on the clanners' behalf? Zie had done everything they asked of zir. They all had.

She had. If Aera had let her rescue Geum *before* the *Maehwa*'s shields failed—

"Fine," Hwa Young said.

Farseer, came her lancer's voice. *Farseer.*

Hwa Young blanched. She'd been so distracted by the fight, by the body, by the pain. "I should check on Bae."

She'd almost stopped noticing the overcooked meat smell, including the one from her own body. Did the commander smell it too, or had she become inured to it? Hwa Young wondered if she was on the way of becoming that jaded, an awful prospect.

"Sick bay," Aera countered. "I'll escort you there."

This was the last thing Hwa Young wanted, although the expression of concern warmed her. Direct insubordination would get her nowhere, so she said, "I can get there by myself," and started walking.

She wondered if Aera would insist on accompanying her like she was a toddler. Instead, Aera merely called after her, "I'll take care of cleanup."

If she was relieved to be treated like a responsible soldier, why did she feel a twinge of disappointment?

It's been six years. Things are bound to be awkward.

Hwa Young thought back to the mysterious laughter of Commander Aera's probably-a-lover and shuddered. She remained convinced that she'd heard that voice before; perhaps the identification would come to her later. Paradoxically, it was a welcome distraction from everything that had happened afterward.

The pain became brighter, sharper, worse than anything she'd previously experienced. A litany of the things that could go wrong with burns rattled through her head as though someone had flung a grenade of misgivings into her skull. Infection. System shock. Sepsis. Scars. Skin grafts.

If they can clone people, they can fix scars. Besides, maybe Geum will think I look dashing?

"Bastard to Winter, do you read? I repeat, Bastard to Winter."

Hwa Young hissed in relief at the commander's voice over the comms. Noted zie had chosen the old callsigns, not the new ones: Bastard, not Vagrant; Winter, not Axiom or Axe. She responded in kind. "Winter here. Saboteur attacked *Farseer*. Where are you, sir?"

Give me an order. Give me something I can shoot.

"I'm with Hellion." Declining to give details beyond that, which told her zie considered the line insecure. "Get to Farseer."

Which meant Bae wasn't with Ye Jun and Eun. "On my way," she said.

She couldn't risk the lift, not after her previous experience. This meant another grueling jaunt through the shafts.

When Hwa Young reached the correct level, she pelted through the halls toward the cabin, in an agony of dread.

It's nothing. Bae's fine. He'll make a remark about how you interrupted his beauty sleep.

Nothing nothing nothing, Winter's Axiom whispered.

Not now! she thought at it.

Hwa Young skidded to a halt and almost crashed into the doors. Her shoulders weren't singed, but she was going to sport a splendid collection of bruises. *I don't think Rose-Merline has this much concealer,* she thought inanely, as though anyone was going to be looking at her *shoulders.*

The door opened for her.

Please be okay.

Bae lay curled up on the deck, face and hands smeared with blood, lips drawn back on a silent scream.

16

GEUM

Eight days later, the *Maehwa* was spaceworthy . . . if one rounded up.

The sole reason Geum could keep track of time was zir neural implant. Zie tried not to think about batteries or replacements. In principle, the implant drew its power from the user's body. In practice, everyone Geum knew had dealt with an inconvenient power failure at one point or another. Easily fixed when one wasn't trapped on a damaged starship.

In the past several days, Geum had woken drenched in sweat from dreams in which zie was immobilized. The implant sent silicate tendrils spidering through zir body, leaching zir ability to blink or call for help, a crystal parasite. Yet the ship's dire straits, and the unending repair work, were such that Geum always regretted the return to reality. More than once, it had occurred to Geum that total paralysis might be the only way zie achieved any rest.

Today Geum was mired in an emergency meeting, which was not the kind of rest zie had envisioned. Things must be dire for Chief to call them to a *meeting* instead of simply telling them what to do and where to find the spare tubes of sealant.

Chief's eyes were sunken. His head resembled a taxidermy skull. Geum looked around the table at the other technicians, including some junior marines reassigned as extra hands. Some people sported burns, cuts, scrapes. Kwan was missing an eye but had insisted on taking tasks that didn't rely on depth perception.

The meeting took place in a conference room that Chief had once insisted that they keep spotless. Now its corners were cluttered with haphazardly stacked crates and toolboxes, plus canisters of sealant, grease, paint, all the things Hyo Su called "space gunk." The area smelled of disinfectant, which beat thinking about whatever the disinfectant was covering up.

Geum had assumed responsibility for bringing snacks, because it made Hyo Su happy, and *someone* should be happy. Food made *everyone* happy, or at least, less hangry. One of the marines, Gang Su, helped zir in exchange for an extra helping of rice crackers. Together, they'd scrounged everything from expired choco pies (a contradiction in terms: choco pies would survive the heat death of the universe) to gimchi about to go rancid.

Best of all, they'd found energy bars laced with combat drugs. Not the kind that made one aggressive but the ones that kept one awake. Medical had told them, "Eat at your own risk." No one cared about risk at this point.

"We have a new priority," Chief said, coughing. He did that a lot these days, lung damage from smoke inhalation. No one dared to suggest that he stop by sick bay.

Everyone at the table fell deathly silent.

"Priority one is the air cycling system."

Geum's head came up. Hyo Su's eyes went round. Gang Su's hand froze on its way to another rice cracker.

"I thought you said—"That was Spade. He swallowed dryly at Chief's glare. "I thought you said the hull breaches were sealed."

"The breaches *are* sealed." Chief's emphasis made it clear that this wasn't the cause for celebration they'd assumed two days ago. "What Admiral Chin has not revealed to the crew is that the navigational systems are out."

Spade blanched. One of the marines emitted an incredulous low whistle. Geum stifled a gasp. Several of the older technicians rapped the table three times in rapid succession, superstition to ward off the unthinkable.

People feared the obvious deaths in space: aether poisoning. Life support failure. Explosions. Beyond explosions, gamma-ray bursts, powerful enough to wipe out entire systems; no escaping one of those.

There was one they rarely discussed: navigational failure. People dreaded the prospect of being lost, unable to find their way to a friendly spaceport, or even an unfriendly one. Refrained from mentioning it out of superstition, as though that would ward off the possibility.

Hyo Su recovered her composure first. "Out how? If it's just the sensor arrays, we can fix those—"

Chief was white-lipped. "Someone deleted the master maps."

The silence this time could have smothered a stadium.

Nothing was ever completely silent on a starship unless it had died, a thought that Geum didn't want to linger on. Instead, they heard the ship itself, muttering to itself in the language of machines. Clanging and creaking, the susurration of circulating air, the faint thready hiss of the filters they'd so diligently restored. Absurd cheerful snatches of a dance tune that had stopped being popular five years ago, someone singing along off-key and behind the beat.

Geum sucked in zir breath, then cracked the not-silence open: "The rest of the fleet?"

"The *fleet's* maps."

In the hush that followed, the ship's accustomed percussion resumed. More ominous this time, like drummers from chthonic depths. Thumping from pipes, pumps, the slosh of effluvia and hydraulics. Footsteps and the ghost echoes of voices. Sound traveled strangely in ships. Geum had taken comfort in this, considering zirself a friend to machines; not anymore.

"Sir," Geum said, mouth dry, "why hide this from the crew?"

Was this related to the "shield malfunction"?

Chief glared at zir.

Ah. I've hit a nerve.

"The admiral expresses her confidence that we will deal with this before—" Chief caught himself.

"Crew deserves to know," one of the other technicians said, oblivious to the slip. "It's our necks too!"

"Need to know only," Chief snapped. Sweat dampened his hair, what remained of it, and trickled down the side of his nose.

Geum could guarantee that someone in this room would "anonymously" tip off the rest of the crew and everyone would know by the shift's end. The only reason Geum hadn't done it already was that zie didn't need more trouble. Chief wouldn't be *surprised* when it happened, but he was too blunt, too honest, to set them up to leak the information *deliberately*.

"What about the Empress's maps? The captain and lieutenant?" Geum said.

"They're affected as well." Chief's glare intensified, a clear signal to shut up already.

Geum did not shut up. "Do you think the responsible party is still on the ship?"

Come on, Chief. Everyone's thinking it. Might as well bring it out into the open.

Geum meant the *Maehwa* specifically. Zie couldn't think of any way to wipe navigation throughout the *entire fleet* without top-level security clearance plus physical accesses present only on the flagship. Geum did not, strictly speaking, have the security clearance to be aware of this, although anyone with half a brain could have guessed it.

What kind of saboteur would take out *navigation*?

Unless—

"That's not for you to worry about," Chief snapped, which was as good as a yes. "We still have to stabilize the hull repairs. We'll swap some teams to computer duty, on the off chance that—anyway. Listen up."

Chief gave out assignments. Everyone stared at him with eyes gnawed hollow by anxiety. The marine Gang Su was the only exception, shoveling rice crackers into his mouth during every lull, and Geum had already figured him for a stress eater. Zie could relate. The crunching noise might have been the detonation of bombs.

"And me, sir?" Geum ventured, displeased that zie had been assigned to more space goop, even if it meant sharing duty with Hyo Su. "I could help with the computer stuff."

Chief rolled his eyes. "Spider, I know you think that playing videogames during meetings—don't think I didn't notice—makes you some kind of hotshot hacker, but let's be serious. Dismissed."

⊙⊙

Geum spent the next eight hours of zir shift working with Spade and Hyo Su fixing breaches to the temporary hull seals. Spade authorized a single break so that Hyo Su could replace the battery for Geum's neural implant. Right on schedule, it had picked a terrible time to need servicing. Under normal use, it should have been good for another two *years,* and never mind that Geum pushed the boundaries of "normal use" on a regular basis.

This would be romantic under other circumstances, Geum reflected, holding still while Hyo Su accessed the minuscule port in the side of zir head, so well-concealed most people never thought about theirs. Hyo Su's face scrunched up in the cutest fashion as she did the job. It took superhuman restraint to keep from flirting with her, but Geum wanted a short-circuit in zir skull the way zie wanted a dinner laced with tapeworms.

"The breaches have breaches," Hyo Su grumbled. "This is not the glamorous high-tech job they promised in the recruitment holos."

"Yeah," Geum said, "the holos smelled less bad."

Spade muttered to himself, paying them no heed. His entire face sagged in dismay each time he paused to catch his breath. Had his hair turned gray overnight? Was that even a thing?

Geum pondered the available clues as to the cause of the nav failure while zie worked. The number of likely suspects was small.

The Empress? Why would she endanger herself in such a

fashion? Geum couldn't rule out the possibility that this was some bizarre political maneuver. Still, zie dismissed this as unlikely.

Admiral Chin? Geum had looked up her record once, including all the classified citations; had a copy of it in a private partition. She'd been a spacer for over two *decades*. Spacers had strong feelings about star charts. Admiral Chin wouldn't consider this type of sabotage, except in her nightmares.

Geum sweated while zie contemplated the last two possibilities, in the process almost losing zir grip on a power drill. Wouldn't *that* be an ignominious way to lose an extremity? *Focus.*

How could anyone focus when the fleet was lost? CIC retained information based on whatever logs pertained to their previous movements. But distances in space were vast. The minutest change in angle, the slightest shift of a vector, could throw a ship catastrophically off course. Aether storms and currents compounded the problem, causing entire fleets to drift if their forces weren't compensated for. Dead reckoning methods faltered when the stars themselves admitted no predictable positions, not in the Moonstorm.

The clanners manage, but how?

Geum bet the clanners didn't eschew maps entirely, whatever form they took.

Assuming the *Maehwa* didn't have shitty security, a big assumption, the last two possible culprits were the Empress's lancer pilots: Captain Ga Ram and Lieutenant Mi Cha.

Geum admired the captain's regal bearing and respected Mi Cha's assertiveness, perhaps because it reminded zir of Hwa Young. This did not mean zie knew enough to speculate *usefully* about their goals or motives. Court intrigues where people backstabbed childhood friends made for great entertainment in dramas and manhwa, but Geum didn't want to get caught in the middle of the real deal.

Thinking about either as a possible traitor was treasonous, an irony that was not lost on Geum. Even if zie obtained hard evidence against one or the other (or both), what could zie do?

"Geum, pay attention to where you're pointing that drill." Spade's words emerged in a weary rasp, a safety reminder rather than anger. "I know you're tired, but losing a body part is even more tiring."

"Spoken like one who knows," Geum quipped.

"Who needs legs anyway?" Hyo Su said, and they all shared a chuckle.

After the shift, Geum endured another inadequate shower. Everyone had grown used to the stench: sweat, grease, disinfectant that stung the nostrils. Geum scarcely remembered what the sweeter, cleaner air of Forsythia City smelled like.

"Wanna snuggle?" Hyo Su asked after her own shower, waggling her eyebrows. "I don't think anyone is paying attention to regs." She flopped onto her bunk.

Geum hated to turn her down, but . . . priorities. "I have to run an errand. Later?"

Hyo Su was already snoring. Geum shook zir head, grinning. Too bad zie couldn't join her, even if all they'd end up doing was drooling onto the same pillow in an undignified manner.

What did we do to you? Geum asked the unknown saboteur, smile fading. *What kind of monster strands an entire fleet in space? Aren't you going to die with us?*

That was the key. That was how zie could catch the saboteur. No one could be so deranged—zie hoped—as to strand themselves along with the entirety of the fleet. This implied that the saboteur had left themselves a way out. *That* was where Geum should start zir search.

Unfortunately, Geum already had a reputation as a meddler. The saboteur might not know about zir specifically, but everyone else on the ship did. Which meant that Geum needed an alibi while zie conducted zir investigations, preferably the biggest, most obnoxious one available. Zie had a candidate in mind already.

Geum took a calculated risk: zie messaged Mi Cha. *Want me to show you around the ship?*

Zie couldn't think of an excuse to talk to Captain Ga Ram. Zir connection to Mi Cha was tenuous. But zie had to take the risk.

Mi Cha didn't respond. Geum waited, biting zir nails. Good thing zie had picked out all the grime. Zie had read the chemical hazard profiles for some of the substances zie had handled recently and did not want to die of convulsions.

Then Geum frowned at the approaching sensation of heaviness. Another gravity fluctuation?

Someone pounded on the door. "Come out," said a demanding voice: Mi Cha.

Geum emerged and smiled shakily at Mi Cha, who cocked a hip in zir direction and smiled her viper smile. Zie hadn't expected Mi Cha to show up with a companion in a space suit. *The copilot?* zie wondered.

The companion removed the helmet.

Geum's mouth fell open. It was the Empress, her hair mussed by the helmet, her eyes sparkling. Hastily, Geum bowed, hoping no one had noticed the hesitation.

Unlike everyone else on the *Maehwa*, including Mi Cha, the Empress stuck out because she looked radiantly *clean*. Geum harbored disloyal thoughts of sneaking onto her yacht and using her shower.

"Never be predictable," Mi Cha said with an offhandedness that Geum found both alluring and terrifying. "Don't gulp air like a carp, it's unseemly. C'mon, what were you going to show us?"

Geum had planned ahead. This was too important to mess up. Mi Cha would already have familiarized herself with the ship's layout. But she wouldn't know the nuances of the *relationships* among its crew. In theory, the ship kept personnel records; in practice, they were sporadically updated, with many lacunae. And information was power.

Zie had not accounted for the Empress's presence. A change of plans: "It's a surprise."

Not the snail races, then. Nobody would thank Geum for bringing the Empress to witness the not-entirely-regulation betting and black market trade that accompanied the meets. (Why snail racing? No one had given Geum a satisfactory answer.)

Geum settled instead for a tour of the crew's *other* meeting places, not the obvious ones like the mess or the gym. The docking bays that housed no lancers, or ones that had no pilots. Cargo holds, marked with symbols swiped from a videogame that had been popular a decade ago. Corridors less frequently used on *official* business.

Geum's heart almost calcified when Mi Cha demanded, "Are you always this twitchy?"

Ugh, why did she have to be so observant? Geum had hoped that the series of rapid-fire commands zie was sending the computer during their jaunt through the starship would pass as harmless fidgeting. "Sorry," Geum said, deciding there was no point in pretending not to be nervous, as opposed to offering a plausible lie. "I wasn't supposed to take that extra dose of stims during my shift, and, well . . ."

A calculated risk, admitting to this: this was technically a violation of regs, although Chief looked the other way as long as one exercised discretion.

This almost got the hoped-for response. Mi Cha rolled her eyes. "Look," she said, "everyone's done that at one time or another, but you have to be smart about it."

Geum breathed a quiet sigh of relief as Mi Cha launched into a suspiciously specific lecture on dosage schedules and ways to mitigate the worst side effect of a terrifying list of drugs, some of which even Geum had never heard of. Mission accomplished, at least as far as Mi Cha was concerned. But Geum remained aware that the Empress might be paying attention, so zie had better be careful.

The Empress did not speak when others were present, a wise decision. The helmet already looked suspicious as hell. No one aboard the ship could fail to recognize her voice, unless her talents included acting.

Inwardly, Geum fumed. At Mi Cha for bringing the Empress. At the Empress for coming along, even if the flagship didn't belong to her the way everything in New Joseon did. At Admiral Chin and Chief, for entrusting the technicians with a terrible secret.

At the unknown saboteur for doing this.

What would kill them first? Starvation? Life support failure? Something else?

Geum disguised zir anger behind smiles and banter, one hand casually draped over the slate even as zie tapped commands, routed around roadblocks, wormed more deeply into the

Maehwa's system and the abscesses where the navigational maps used to be. *I'm going to find out who did this if it kills me.*

"That's the spot where people pair up when they want random partners," Geum said at one bulkhead, pointing at the minute scratches. "Those are the people to talk to if you have a craving for plum wine," zie added as the three of them passed off-duty crew members huddled around a holographic jigsaw puzzle, a peaceable hobby. An *ordinary* one.

Geum had worried about boring Mi Cha and the Empress with the banality of shipboard life. Mi Cha's expression suggested that she was thinking, *This is all you've got? No gladiatorial combat or butcher shops?*

The Empress, though—the *Empress* was fascinated. She lingered everywhere they stopped, watching the crew with avid eyes, half extrovert and half vulture. At one point, in an empty corridor, she said to Mi Cha in a warm, confiding voice, "Get me some of those jigsaw puzzles."

What was her life like? Geum wondered. Did the Imperial family grow up without jigsaw puzzles or shrimp crackers? Did they crave experiences that people like Geum took for granted?

"Thank you," the Empress said when the tour came to an end: a high honor. She eyed Geum speculatively, and then Mi Cha escorted her away.

Geum dared not sag against the bulkheads, despite the relief that washed through zir. Didn't reveal anything but a bright smile to any watching cameras until zie returned to the cabin. All zie had to do—*all*—was await the computer's report after all the investigations zie had instructed it to carry out.

Hyo Su's bed stood empty, the blanket crumpled across it. Neither she nor Geum bothered making their beds anymore. Hyo

Su had left a *brand-new* bottle of sparkly nail polish in Geum's favorite color (orange) and a note on Geum's pillow: *Thought you'd like this. You owe me.*

I definitely owe you, Geum thought. Zie daydreamed about asking her out . . . but zie was leaving soon. As much as zie liked the thought of Hwa Young rescuing them *both* . . . Perhaps zie could casually drop a hint or two, suss out Hyo Su's feelings on the matter. Zie doubted Hwa Young would raise any objections. What were friends for, if not rescuing friends and their crushes from decrepit starships?

The computer made its laborious knocking signals, jolting Geum out of zir frivolous thoughts. It did, in fact, have something to report. Something that Geum didn't want to share—yet.

One of the Empress's pilots had found backdoor access into the *Maehwa*'s computer system, including the master maps— through, of all things, an otherwise routine request to reconcile the inventory of the Empress's yacht with the *Maehwa*'s own cargo manifest. Geum noted in passing that the yacht claimed a shortage of batteries as well as a surprising quantity of seaweed-flavored crispy snacks. Not even the good stuff, but the junky kind loaded with artificial flavors.

The cyberattack's surgical precision gave Geum the chills. Whoever was responsible hadn't wasted time screwing around, hadn't resorted to trial and error. They had known exactly what to do and how to do it.

All the same, Geum didn't dare accuse either Ga Ram or Mi Cha without hard evidence—evidence zie hadn't yet obtained.

The saboteur had been clever, but not clever enough. The inventory update looked innocent enough, as recorded by the master system. Thanks to complicated boring safety regulations, however, there was a backup log of all accesses to the ship's manifest on a separate computer, which could not be altered once written to.

Here we go—

Geum blinked, wondering if zie had imagined that the lights had flickered. There was a lot of that lately. Zie shivered violently, suddenly aware of zir clammy palms, the sweat soaking zir shirt. The trancelike concentration zie maintained when hacking shattered, flinging Geum back into the meat of zir body. It was as though all the worry and tension of the past few days had slammed into Geum all at once, at a time when water rationing meant the best solution for body odor was increasingly rancid deodorant.

But Geum had succeeded. Here, in the backup log, zie found clear evidence that the yet-unidentified saboteur had routed a copy of the star charts through the inventory "update"—and to their neural implant.

Someone in the fleet—on this *ship*—was walking around with the only copy of the star maps. Someone who now held them all hostage if the fleet ever wanted to reach its destination—or any destination at all.

17

HWA YOUNG

Hwa Young prided herself on taking action when necessary. Sometimes also when it wasn't, as all her teachers and commanding officers noted. She would rather attack than hide. When she did school herself to stillness, it was in service of an ambush or a hunt. Hadn't she proven herself effective over and over?

Action abandoned her now. For precious moments, as time hazed around her, Hwa Young stared at Bae. Unwillingly memorized his appearance: shoulders drawn back taut as a bowstring, the gaping mouth, the eyes squeezed shut. Huddled in on himself with no trace of his usual superior attitude.

Blood streaked his face. Blood oozed even now from beneath his eyelids.

Hwa Young unfroze. "Bae!" she cried.

All of them had sustained damage to their lancers before. Hwa

Young had taken a shot to her lancer's head in one engagement, back when they'd fought for New Joseon. It hadn't incapacitated her like this.

This made no sense, unless—

Empty empty empty, Winter's Axiom said more urgently.

Had Zeng's scriber screwed up the neural link, even after being uninstalled? Or had the explosion messed up some critical component in *Farseer*?

"It's me," Hwa Young croaked as she cradled Bae's head. "It's me."

He didn't react to her presence.

Time to call for help. "Winter to Bastard. I've located Farseer. He needs medical assistance." She detailed Bae's state, cursing the way her voice wavered. She didn't want the commander to think she couldn't be relied on. Not when zie depended on her.

Not when Bae depended on her.

Bae spoke, so hushed she almost didn't hear him. "Empty empty empty." A parody of himself: the refined accent, the hollow words, his voice scratched rough.

Empty empty empty, Winter's Axiom repeated.

Hwa Young didn't need to feel any more freaked out. Did her eyes sting because of the burns, or because she was about to cry? Crying wouldn't help Bae. She refused to cry.

That didn't stop the hot splash of tears hitting the deck as she twisted her head just in time to avoid dripping on Bae.

The comms link jittered, followed by a high-pitched electronic squeal that caused Hwa Young to grind her teeth. All she needed to improve the day: dental problems.

Commander Ye Jun replied after an agonizing pause. Static obscured zir words. "Get Bae to sick bay."

Had she heard zir correctly? "To sick bay, confirm?" Zie had switched to Bae's name, rather than his callsign. An acknowledgment that Bae was not functionally a pilot at the moment.

Hwa Young's heart, too, went to static. She'd always relied on Bae to be irritatingly competent. Even—especially—when they'd been rivals. Having Bae out of commission was like watching a moon plummet from the sky.

"Confirmed." Zie cut the connection.

Orders were orders.

Only three of them remained, Ye Jun and Eun and herself.

Don't think like that. Bae will be fine. This is temporary.

Bae did not look or sound like his affliction was temporary.

Hwa Young called ahead. Ye Jun hadn't forbidden it. "Sick bay, this is Pilot Hwa—Pilot Hwajin." She could deal with her conflicted feelings about the name some other time. Right now, she needed the medics to be as kindly disposed to Bae as possible. If playing the good clanner was what it took . . . "Pilot Bae needs help."

The deep, unhurried voice that responded would have soothed Hwa Young if she'd been capable of letting go of her death-grip anxiety. "Medical. What is the nature of your emergency? Do you require a responder?"

"He's having some kind of seizure and he doesn't recognize me," Hwa Young said raggedly. First responder training hadn't covered anything like *this*. "I'll bring him in myself. Uh—if you could contact Researcher Zeng, he might have some insight. His scriber device might have been involved. I think it's related to some short-circuit in Bae's link to his lancer."

There. She'd said it. She didn't like being so blunt, but what mattered was aiding Bae.

Medical's breath huffed out. "If you think *that's* the issue, go directly to Zeng's laboratory. It's closer anyway. I'll dispatch a medic."

"Wait—"

The connection closed.

What would the medic do, anyway? Tranquilizers? A sedative? A bunch of creepy vines like the ones Medical had inflicted on Ye Jun? Bae would hate that. And Hwa Young would hate watching it.

"Time to go," Hwa Young said.

Bae curled in on himself like a threatened shrimp.

Hwa Young was more accustomed to comparing Bae to royalty or an exquisite statue carved of ice and alabaster for display at the kind of museum only high-ranking people could access, not an overwhelmed crustacean. The one thing Bae had in common with a statue right now: his weight. He might have a slender build, but he was still taller than Hwa Young, and he'd put on muscle in the past two months.

"Bae," Hwa Young said, keeping her voice calm and matter-of-fact, as though she spoke to a spooked cat. Her only experience with cats back in Forsythia City involved getting scratched for her trouble, so this was an apt analogy. "Bae, stand up. That's all you have to do." She was lying. "Stand up."

Bae did so, slowly. His eyes focused on her face. No recognition lit them.

He doesn't recognize me because of the burns, Hwa Young told herself, squelching her hurt feelings.

Hwa Young had only caught blurred glances of her reflection in the bulkheads on the way here. She desperately wanted to avoid checking the extent of the damage.

"Come with me," Hwa Young said. Surely Bae would recognize her voice? Hadn't they been through everything important together?

Yes, came the answer from *Winter's Axiom,* as though she'd addressed it instead. *We've always been together.*

What about Geum? came another troubled whisper. *What if Geum is—*

She couldn't do anything about that. Right now she had to take care of Bae.

Bae rose, unsteady. His clumsiness hit Hwa Young like a slap. So many things about Bae that she'd taken as laws of the universe: *Bae is number one. Bae is the most beautiful person in school. Bae is the most graceful.*

Except even laws of the universe might prove mutable . . . like gravity.

New Joseon claimed the clanners had to be subdued for their own good. That they couldn't sustain their own gravity, which the Empress would graciously provide by folding them into her realm. Hwa Young had seen no evidence of this during her months on *Falcon Actual.* If anything, gravity was *more* reliable here. That bothered her.

It's been nothing but anomalies and problems since we joined Falcon Fleet.

Hwa Young guided Bae toward the door, shoving her own terror into a box labeled *deal with this after Bae is better.*

Beneath the terror—a heart-flare of anger. She wasn't sure who she was mad at. Commander Aera, for failing to prevent the sabotage? Herself, for growing complacent?

She frowned as a new thought struck her: Magnolia had been empty. No guards or technicians.

That's not so strange. Most of the crew was on shore leave. Still, that was lax security. She should complain to Aera.

Aera had insinuated that someone else had been involved with the sabotage. Not Hwa Young herself; certainly not Bae.

Eun? Never. Hwa Young clung to the memory of her first sight of Eun with his orange eyes, *Hellion* resplendent in flame-colored armor. How harshly he'd spoken to her and called her *Menace Girl*.

She'd hated him, but that was before she learned how many comrades he'd lost, or heard him crying their names in his sleep. (Did she do that too?) Eun, who watched over everyone and expressed his worry through snarls and grumbles. She'd learned to rely on him.

But what if—

What if he'd talked himself into disregarding clues? Not out of ill intent, but because sentiment overcame him. Even Eun had cracks in his armor: his romance with Zeng, however short-lived. No one could blame Eun for seeking companionship, given the opportunity.

Every pilot knew they had a limited shelf life, and turncoats more so.

What if she was at fault for not being paranoid enough? For not keeping an eye on Eun? She was seized by a sudden image of Eun and Zeng embracing, and more, in *Hellion*'s cockpit. Or Eun simply inviting Zeng and Tora up there, thinking it a harmless way to show off his lancer.

If Zeng's creepy heart-brother Tora had been the saboteur, had he gone after *Farseer* because it *wasn't* Eun's lancer? Or had there been some other motivation? While the lancers looked identical in their neutral state, the squad always landed in the same order these days: *Bastard, Hellion, Farseer, Winter's Axiom.* It didn't take a genius to notice that.

Mother Aera, Hwa Young thought with a clarity like a lens of ice. None of this had occurred to her before Aera made the oh-so-casual suggestion that another pilot might be involved. That couldn't be an accident. No way was Aera so incompetent that she threw around accusations without considering the potential impact on morale. Which meant—

Hwa Young recoiled from the implications. *This is my fault. She's mad that I didn't try hard enough to fit in. To be a clanner.*

To be her heart-daughter.

It might have been because she showed up without the wig that Aera had given her. The commander was human enough to hold a petty grudge and lash out. That was all.

Thinking about her heart-mother brought a different answer into focus. The voice she'd overheard when calling Aera about the sabotage. That had been Tora's voice.

Hwa Young was increasingly certain she hadn't been imagining things. The scar on the dead saboteur's wrist, exactly where Tora's tiger tattoo had been—someone must have burned it off to prevent definite identification. It couldn't be a coincidence.

The saboteur. What had the saboteur wanted? She tried not to think about his name. The name made him a person, despite Tora's creepy staring, the tedious boasts about the tiger hunt that his tattoo had commemorated. Had he desired glory, fame, an extra helping of fried rice? Being a saboteur didn't seem like a job that brought *public* accolades.

Maybe he'd become an Imperial agent in exchange for a kiss from the Empress, like in the dramas? Did people do that? Hwa Young flushed, selfishly glad that Bae wasn't paying attention. It was an impious thought, especially since the Empress was Commander Ye Jun's *mother*, but everyone had heard stories about the Empress and her rotating banquet of consorts.

Hwa Young grimaced, pierced by guilt that she'd gotten distracted when Bae was in such bad shape.

Bae put one foot before the other as though each step involved solving a calculus problem. Bae, who'd always moved like wind and wings, who could have been a dancer. It was like watching someone else puppet his body.

"You can do it," Hwa Young said, then clamped her lips together. Was she talking to *Bae* like he was a toddler? "Bae. You're going to let *me* beat you to the lift?"

That wasn't right either. Why was she so bad with people?

Bae's eyes flickered, although she wasn't sure if that was coincidence. But he kept walking, gradually growing steadier, more coordinated, more like himself, so she continued to speak. Maybe it didn't matter *what* she said, just the sound of her voice.

A clanner jogged toward them: Rose-Merline.

"Hey, Axe—" Rose-Merline began to say. Then she recoiled as she approached and got a good look at Bae. "Wh-what . . . what happened?"

"Injured" was all Hwa Young could think to say.

"No wonder you need a hand." Rose-Merline's voice shook. Worried. "A friend in Medical tipped me off that . . . I thought it was advanced first aid, n-not something this bad. Can I . . . can I help?"

Can I trust her?

Trust had to start somewhere, even now.

"Yes, thank you," Hwa Young said, attempting to smile. "This isn't the three-way date I envisioned."

It was a terrible excuse for a joke. Nevertheless, Rose-Merline squeezed Hwa Young's hand in brief acknowledgment before taking up a position on Bae's other side.

Together, the three of them passed through the halls and to the lab. Hwa Young hadn't visited it since she caught Eun and Zeng making out there. Offering them privacy. More accurately, avoiding the possibility of an embarrassing interaction.

Hwa Young trailed misgivings after her like a dark-winged flock. *If* she was right and Tora had been the saboteur, did that imply Zeng was involved too? Was it safe to leave Bae in his care?

At least Bae had regained most of his coordination, although the drying streaks of blood on his face gave him a ghoulish aspect. Nor did he respond when Hwa Young or Rose-Merline addressed him. Hwa Young told herself that staying upright might be taking all his concentration. She hoped that was all it was, and not permanent trauma.

Someone had called ahead to alert Zeng. He bowed to Hwa Young and Rose-Merline with his accustomed courtesy when they arrived. Today Zeng wore a plainer outfit, no jewelry anywhere in sight. Hwa Young couldn't help sniffing the air: no cologne. It shouldn't have mattered, but the lack of foppishness reassured her that he'd take Bae's affliction seriously.

"The medic arrived first," Zeng said, gesturing. The woman nodded an acknowledgment, then stepped forward to help support Bae.

Working together, they conveyed Bae to the pallet that had been set up for him. Someone had brought a planter full of starblooms, a gesture that touched Hwa Young. It perfumed the lab's antechamber, a place where people might meet or talk. Doors beyond hinted at a vaster space devoted to Zeng's research.

"There are tests I can run here that aren't available to Medical," Zeng said. He gave an explanation, which Hwa Young memorized without understanding. Large parts of it didn't make sense, but then, she wasn't a scientist or engineer or doctor.

"All right," Hwa Young said afterward. She smoothed Bae's hair from his forehead, beyond caring what anyone thought.

Commander Ye Jun picked up immediately when she called zir. "Bae's with Researcher Zeng now, not Medical," she said. She explained the circumstances. "Do you want me to have him transferred to Medical?"

One of Ye Jun's soft pauses followed. Hwa Young was at a loss as to how to interpret it.

Her anguish got the better of her. "I can stay here. Keep watch."

That provoked an immediate response. "I say no, Pilot." Ye Jun didn't speak any more loudly, but the note of authority was unambiguous. "The unit is shorthanded, but we'll be worse off if you wear yourself down to bone. Get some rest. Take some time off. Pet a therapy fern or make bad bets on racing lizards if that's what it takes. I doubt you'll sleep, but—"

"Sir, I can't just—"

"*Pilot.* I've given you an order. I will need you at your best, which is not what I will get if you stay up without sleeping for five days and nights hovering at Bae's side. I have matters in hand. *Go.*"

Put like that, what could she do? Hwa Young cast one last agonized glance toward Bae. The medic had already wiped clean his face, eased mysterious vines over his arms and shoulders, like a verdant cloak. He did seem to be breathing more easily, the lines of pain smoothed away.

"As you say, sir," Hwa Young said, aware that she was radiating reluctance. What she wanted wasn't *rest*. She wanted *release*—in action, in aggression, in—

"You must be so stressed," Rose-Merline said as the two of them exited the lab together. "I know how much you care about him—"

Action . . . aggression . . . or ardor.

Hwa Young hooked her arm around Rose-Merline's waist, drew her in, kissed her. The commander wanted her to "rest"? What did that leave except losing herself in headlong sensation?

The question was, would Rose-Merline welcome the overture, or rebuff her?

Rose-Merline's eyes widened. She didn't resist, but she held herself still, not yet committing herself. "Is this the right time—"

"Yes," Hwa Young whispered. Heat bloomed throughout her as Rose-Merline returned the kiss. She threw herself into it, exploring Rose-Merline's summer softness, the eager welcoming curves of her. A chance to forget about everything else, just for an hour.

18

HWA YOUNG

"What are *you* getting out of this?" Hwa Young asked Rose-Merline three days later. Neither of them had discussed Bae since the day of his injury, except briefly, when Commander Ye Jun forwarded Zeng's progress reports annotated with zir own terse comments. Each time, they said the same thing: Bae was stable but unconscious.

Time had ceased to hold any significance. Minutes elongated like taffy; hours compressed and shattered. At the moment, Hwa Young and Rose-Merline were checking on every starbloom planter (so it seemed) on the fifth level before heading to a café on Dragon Mountain that served novelties like honeyed fried locusts (more crunch than flavor), salted plum soda (delicious), and truffle potato crisps (also delicious, although Hwa Young wasn't sure what a potato was).

Rose-Merline didn't look up as she adjusted the flow of . . .

Hwa Young hadn't followed the explanation, which sounded like half mysticism and half paleochemistry. The shimmering particulates that swirled through the suspension that fed the planter looked less like water, or adulterated water, and more like . . . aether? Hwa Young's gaze shifted back to Rose-Merline's white-knuckled fingers. She'd only meant to give Rose-Merline an opening to talk about herself after the belated realization that she was taking Rose-Merline's attention for granted, and that was shitty of her. Instead, Hwa Young had hit a nerve, although she wasn't sure how.

Rose-Merline's hands flexed, and then she said: "I hear life in New Joseon is hedged about with rules. Prayers to the Empress, the clothes you wear, how you name your pets. But it's not as if clanner fleets don't have rules of their own."

There aren't any rules about pet names, Hwa Young almost said. That was beside the point. After all, Imperials believed equally absurd things about clanner traditions. "It must be nice to see new faces, then," Hwa Young offered hesitantly, although she suspected Rose-Merline was alluding to another matter entirely.

Rose-Merline's laugh had a hysterical edge that took Hwa Young off-guard.

What did I say?

"They say that lancers choose their pilots during a religious ceremony," Rose-Merline said after a moment. With her head tilted forward as she examined the leaves for rot or blight, her braids obscured her eyes; her expression might have been any one of several, ambivalent in its chiaroscuro. "You don't have to tell me about it," she added hastily while Hwa Young was still debating how much "religious" applied to an experience that had involved both desire and death, transcendence and tragedy. "But have you—have you ever thought about being something else? *Doing* something else?"

Hwa Young had thought they were negotiating awkward but normal relationship parameters. Instead, Rose-Merline had taken the conversation in an unexpected direction. *Being something else* didn't sound like it referred to *What's your favorite snack?* or *Who do you want to take the lead when we smooch, or do you like mixing it up?*

Hwa Young bit back the automatic answer, the easy answer, and said instead, "When I was small I wanted to go where my heart-mother went, do what my heart-mother did. Piloting a lancer only came after our—after our family died." Ah, that must be it: "Did your family push you into becoming a cryptobotanist, Rose-Merline?" And, when Rose-Merline's ragged breath was her only answer, "What did you want to be instead?"

Rose-Merline straightened and dusted off imaginary specks on her slacks. "Let's get some snacks. The starblooms are healthy."

The non sequitur told Hwa Young everything she needed to know.

Hwa Young attempted to escape into sleep afterward, with mixed results. Her old nightmares returned. They started innocuously enough. In the dreams she remembered the gravitational lensing that split the images of stars and distant galaxies into kaleidoscopic multiples, forming deceptively pretty rainbows. The unlight of the black hole as it formed.

She admired the black hole, or rather, its effects on objects outside the event horizon. Admired the fire-flower explosions in the battle presented for her delectation. Knew she and her lancer could instigate as many as they wanted. Look, there were targets:

bright specks moving across her field of vision, seeds of fire and tempest.

Hwa Young fired. Fired. Fired. Fired.

Her aim was true. *Their* aim was true, hers and the lancer's. The projectiles sang to their targets. Four explosions, one by one by one by one. From her vantage point, they defined a perfect diamond.

Four explosions: four Imperial ships.

The dream shifted. Four Imperial *lancers*. Not ships. She'd killed lancers.

In the darkness she heard Seong Su's anguished shout. Eun. Commander Ye Jun.

Bae—

She'd slaughtered her comrades. For a display of predatory valor; for a spectacle of fire.

We are together, Winter's Axiom said.

Hwa Young roused in her own bunk, blinking back the hot rush of tears. Had she cried out in her sleep, the way Eun did sometimes? The glacial shell she'd formerly taken comfort in, which served as shield and shelter, now constricted her, like a trap. *It was a dream,* she told herself desperately.

She drew a shaky breath and heaved herself out of bed. They had a mission today. Something else to focus on, thankfully.

Commander Ye Jun drew Hwa Young aside while Eun was showering and she was awaiting her turn.

"Sir?" she asked, puzzled by Ye Jun's stern expression. A flicker of Ye Jun's fingers caught her eye as zie launched into a tirade.

Ah. The lecture involved obsolete safety protocols specific to the lancer units, and therefore, in principle, more difficult (or more boring) to any eavesdroppers. It bored *her,* an impressive feat. Fortunately, she had deduced that she needn't pay any attention to the *spoken* words. She stared sullenly at the deck (this wasn't difficult) and nodded and mumbled, "Yes, sir," periodically.

Instead, Ye Jun was using the lecture as cover for the real conversation, which took place using New Joseon's military sign language. Hwa Young wished zie had clued her in to the likely location of any cameras, but maybe it would appear too suspicious if she made a point of occluding its view of zir hand. One thing was clear: neither of them had a future as actors.

Ye Jun signed, "I need to make you aware of some context. Eun already knows."

She confined herself to a nod, on the grounds that she should keep her "acting" to a minimum, in case of voyeurs.

"You will have wondered why I left the crownworld. A major problem with Imperial heirs, especially when more than one exists, is the certainty of infighting and the problem of securing the succession."

Hwa Young wished she had practiced more than the functional minimum of vocabulary. An oversight on her part, when a malfunction in space might mean that sign language was the most efficient way to communicate. As it stood, all she could manage for a query was, approximately, "Why tell me this now?"

Ye Jun continued zir lecture while signing the real conversation to her. "Captain Ga Ram chose to contact you, and chose *not* to contact me, not without reason. I would not have accepted any overture to parley. If zie approaches you again, this is context you need to assess any offer zie makes."

She bit her lip, willing Ye Jun to answer the rest of the question: Why *now*? Why not earlier, when she'd turned up with the cake box and its purloined crown? Or any point in the vanished past?

When Ye Jun resumed signing, zir expression held an unaccustomed bitter cast. "We were close once. Ga Ram was the only one of the Empress's legitimate children who showed me any kindness. And yet—Ga Ram has a reputation for honor, but honor doesn't travel in straight paths when it comes to palace intrigue. Zie told me plainly that if I'd stayed on the crownworld, zie would be obliged to kill me."

Hwa Young understood this level of family and political infighting—at an intellectual level, not a visceral one. Geum had enjoyed watching historical dramas that featured Imperial intrigue. "You wanted to avoid spoiling the succession?" she asked.

Ye Jun's history made a twisted sense now that she had this added information: remove zirself from the capital, serving with a disfavored fleet that no one would consider an alternate power base, or a threat to the highest-ranking lancer pilot.

She'd imagined that growing up as one of the Empress's brood, even a bastard, had involved a parade of smiling servants feeding one sliced persimmons by hand, and leisurely poetry-writing competitions, maybe the occasional swooning admirer. Her self-indulgent imaginings hadn't included casual threats of *fratricide* while people fought over who succeeded to the throne, or secured positions of power.

Ye Jun grimaced in response to her reaction. "The Empress favored me. Sentimental reasons, or political, to block the maneuvers of certain noble families; it doesn't matter. But my illegitimacy was a bigger problem for the traditionalists in court. My sire was of unacceptably low rank to be declared a consort. A commoner might rise to lancer pilot, but never to official consort."

She'd never asked herself why the Empress had produced

an illegitimate child, given that she must have the Empire's best doctors at her command and access to whatever contraceptives she desired.

"She offered to deal with the problem. Make me her heir."

Hwa Young blinked at the commander, puzzled by the shadows in them. The tight muscles along zir jaw, the tension she felt in zir body. She didn't think that zie was referring to some legal loophole.

"She was going to eliminate all of her trueborn children on my behalf. All my siblings, including Captain Ga Ram, who trained me. 'Securing the succession,' she called it." Ye Jun's lips drew up in a wince. "I declined and shipped out the next week."

Hwa Young's jaw dropped.

Ye Jun's next words were unusually emphatic. "Ga Ram didn't care about losing zir life, but zie wasn't going to see our *siblings* gunned down for my sake. Never forget, any time you deal with Captain Ga Ram, that zie will observe every courtesy—and just as meticulously plan your death if honor demands it. Stay sharp out there."

Ye Jun released her then. Hwa Young smiled automatically, despite her shaken composure. Her mind recoiled from what zie had revealed about the Empress's ruthlessness, and Ga Ram's. She couldn't imagine coming from a family like that.

If anything, this convinced her that Ga Ram had been sincere. Why else would zie take the jaw-droppingly treasonous step of *stealing the crown* and smuggling it to the disgraced bastard? She didn't know Ga Ram on a personal level the way Ye Jun did. On the other hand, Ye Jun's experiences with the captain of the guard might be coloring zir view in the opposite direction.

Hwa Young thought then of Mother Aera, *Commander* Aera.

Aera would never turn on family like that, whatever the provocation.

I'm yours and you're mine. Hwa Young repeated the phrase in her head, wishing she didn't sound so desperate to believe.

Eun emerged then. His gaze slid from Ye Jun to Hwa Young and back again before he began dressing. He knew what they'd really been discussing.

They all knew, now, except Bae.

Hwa Young showed up bright and early for the mission briefing. She brought flower cakes as an appeasing gesture, mainly because she heard Geum's bright voice in her head: *People love baked goods! It doesn't matter if you didn't bake them. They're just hungry.*

Do I think baked goods are going to distract Aera or Ye Jun? Hwa Young asked herself as she removed the box from the wrapping cloth and arranged the cakes on a plate. She dithered over the proper arrangement. There were *five* cakes, and only four of them, with Bae incapacitated.

Her hand fell slack to the table at the memory of Bae's battered face and the streaks of blood under his eyes. Ye Jun continued to forward Zeng's progress reports to Hwa Young, none of them revealing anything new: stable condition, not yet conscious. Aware that she was not, technically, owed any such courtesy, Hwa Young did her best (not very) to keep from spilling her worry in public.

She hoped as well that the flower cakes would distract people from the grotesque mask that covered her face, the gloves, both steeped in an ointment that was supposed to accelerate healing from her burns. The ointment resembled snail slime, because it *was* harvested from genetically engineered snails. Never ask doctors where medicines came from, was her new philosophy. She would have preferred the bizarre, parasitic-looking vines they'd inflicted earlier on Ye Jun to snail slime.

Hwa Young hadn't wanted to bother with mask or gloves. Ordinary medical treatment was good enough. Who cared about a few battle scars?

A message from Aera had changed her mind: *Please*, it had said, a rare plea. *I don't want you to suffer unnecessarily.* Keeping Aera happy was important, wasn't it? No matter how much she was starting to question her heart-mother's methods.

"Where'd you get the eats?"

It was Eun. His voice was rough, but he gave her a friendly nod. Thankfully, he didn't comment on her appearance. He'd seen worse in the line of duty.

"Black market," Hwa Young said, reflecting that the crinkling noises the mask made whenever she spoke or moved her face would take some getting used to. As for the black market, it was a constant of shipboard economics. If aliens kidnapped her and conveyed her to the next galaxy over, *they* would have a black market. What would they trade in? Action figures? Antiques? Iridescent beetles preserved in amber?

"Could've brought wine," Eun muttered. "I suppose that's harder to source."

Hwa Young had never seen Eun drunk and didn't want to start. After rearranging the buns one last time, she took a seat. Eun claimed the one next to her.

Commanders Ye Jun and Aera entered shortly afterward, already in the midst of conversation. "My requests for a forensic report on the saboteur's remains went unanswered," Ye Jun was saying.

Interesting. Zie could have asked Aera privately. Or had zie done so already? Was this an attempt to put additional pressure on Aera by talking to her in front of them?

Neither commander sat. Eun, sensitive to Ye Jun's moods, frowned. *That* worried Hwa Young.

Why did I think our lives would become easier *after we switched sides?* Hwa Young thought wryly. A logic failure on her part.

"Medical's still working on it," Commander Aera said, each syllable crisp and unemotional. "I checked on Bae. He's been sedated for his own protection as he regains function, but he's recovering."

Zeng's report hadn't mentioned *that*. On purpose, or was this a new development? Hwa Young hesitated, then said, "Is the sedation necessary?"

"I know you're worried for him," Aera said. Her gaze lingered on Hwa Young's bandaged face; a furrow appeared between her brows. "We're doing our best for him. That I promise, Hwajin." Her fingertips twitched as though she was about to reach out for Hwa Young's hands, but the distance was too great.

Empty empty empty, Winter's Axiom murmured. It projected the familiar forlorn image of a winter plain, a whiteout blizzard, death in all directions. From moment to moment, the silhouette of a young woman flickered in and out, curves and a commotion of shadows, long hair obscuring her face, accompanied by other ghosts. Then the image faded.

Hwa Young nodded, not trusting herself to speak. The next time she had a free moment, she planned to stop by Zeng's lab and ask to visit Bae again. The guards had turned her away earlier, saying he was in the middle of treatment. Not wishing to interfere, she had gone away, despite the worry gnawing her heart.

This time, she planned to insist on being let in. The reports, however assiduous, didn't satisfy her. She wanted to see Bae with her own two eyes, as opposed to a list of bloodless vital statistics.

Commander Ye Jun hadn't authorized visits, strictly speaking, but zie hadn't explicitly forbidden them either. She wasn't going to come in and ask, on the grounds that this was one time she preferred to ask forgiveness rather than permission. She could only endure so much enforced rest, even with Rose-Merline, before she exploded.

"In any case," Commander Aera said, "the claim that the Empress has taken the field with Eleventh Fleet, *if* true, is quite interesting. Possibly we could turn this to our advantage."

Ye Jun nodded, zir face as smooth and inexpressive as unembellished celadon. "I suspect the report is accurate. The Empress or Emperor has not abandoned the crownworld in some centuries. But your analysts are aware of the relevant history, and the Empress's habits."

The commander's voice roughened on *habits*. What wasn't zie saying?

"I have the analysts' reports, yes."

Hwa Young's vision blurred. "Do the analysts think she came after us because we destroyed First Fleet? Revenge? Or because we deserted?"

Hwa Young should have cared more about the fate of the Empress, their adversary. The person she wanted to know about, however, was Geum.

Commander Aera brought up a holographic map, which

indicated the distances involved and the travel times. Less predictable in the Moonstorm, but well established within New Joseon. A journey of three months from the crownworld to the present location, give or take a few weeks. Assuming the Empress hadn't made any detours.

"Eleventh Fleet undoubtedly knows we're at Dragon Mountain for repairs," Aera said. "They'll ambush us on the way out if they're in any condition for it. Or worse, threaten the station."

"How much longer on the repairs?" Ye Jun asked.

"Another five days. Some delay on sourcing hard-to-find materials. You know how it is." Aera leaned forward. "But I have a particular request for you, Commander."

Hwa Young stiffened. Out of the corner of her eye she saw that Eun, sensitive to Ye Jun's sudden tension, was ready to explode into action.

We're so on edge.

Edge, edge, edge, Winter's Axiom intoned, blurring into her own voice until she could no longer differentiate the two.

Aera and Ye Jun faced off, not like allies, but like fighters squaring up, assessing each other. Hwa Young's gut churned. She'd survived too many sparring matches not to recognize the body language, even if she didn't—yet—understand what the stakes were.

Ye Jun didn't speak. Aera's words hung in the silence.

Hwa Young wondered if she was hallucinating the whole meeting. If, in reality, she lay next to Bae on some dismal cot, hooked up to a perplexing machine while it fed her sedatives through an importunate vine snaking up her nose.

When Ye Jun did break the silence, Eun shifted his weight

forward. A small motion, but Hwa Young was watching for it. Not an attack, but the preparatory movement if an attack became necessary.

What does he know that I don't?

Aera's eyes flickered. She'd seen it too. But she looked directly into Ye Jun's eyes, her mouth curving. "We're aware that you have come into possession of New Joseon's crown. Admiral Mae, in consultation with the clan council, would like you to claim the throne."

Hwa Young became aware that she'd recoiled as though presented with a saber-toothed viper. No one looked in her direction.

She'd understood Falcon Fleet's goal as self-defense. To prevent New Joseon from devouring them. Had never considered that the clanners might consider the best defense to be a counterattack, or that they, in their turn, might aspire to claim the Empire's territory for themselves.

This isn't what I wanted when I joined you! she wanted to shout at Aera.

Ye Jun lifted zir chin abruptly, catching Hwa Young's attention before she could say something regrettable, and smiled at Aera. It wasn't the genial smile Hwa Young had become used to, with its subtext of *Don't cross me; I watch out for my pilots.* This expression was brighter, consciously charming: a politician's smile. She'd seen it over and over in New Joseon, the arrogant self-assurance.

Seen it on *Bae's* face, back when, and on that of Bae's mom. On the Empress's face in the holos.

If it hadn't been for Ye Jun's earlier admission, the anecdote about zir history with Captain Ga Ram, Hwa Young's faith in the commander would have wavered. She had taken the warning about Ga Ram at face value. She should have remembered Ye Jun's capacity for deviousness.

Ye Jun's real intent had been to prepare Hwa Young for this moment. A message given in advance that zie had no designs on the Imperial throne; that she could continue to trust zir. She knew it as surely as she knew the freezing temperature of water.

"I know what's in it for *me*," Ye Jun said, as if this were a normal policy discussion. "What's in it for *you*?"

Eun's weight had shifted back. No longer poised to spring at a threat. Hwa Young relaxed her muscles one by one, following his lead, even if she didn't understand where Ye Jun was going with this. Now that she had unriddled the purpose of zir recent revelation, she didn't buy for one second that zie was tempted, whatever impression zie wanted to give *Aera*.

This set the squad up—set *her* up—as Aera's adversaries. She'd figure out how she felt about that later.

Commander Aera said, "Don't play at naïveté, Commander. I should think it's obvious. You're in line to the throne, and the Empire is in disarray. Why not claim it?"

"Claim it on your behalf, you mean." Ye Jun's smile revealed the merest glint of teeth. "You want a figurehead."

"How long have you planned this?" Hwa Young demanded, partly because this was the role Ye Jun would want her to play . . . and partly because she needed to know.

Hangeul didn't mark nouns or pronouns for number, unlike some of the other languages spoken in Falcon Fleet; it didn't distinguish between singular and plural. "You" could refer to Commander Ye Jun or Commander Aera or clanner leadership, any or all of them. Hwa Young wasn't sure which one she was referring to. It wasn't an ambiguity she wanted to work in her favor.

Ye Jun might not plan to benefit from this, but it had clearly come as no surprise. She would have appreciated an earlier warning. Something she'd have to take up with zir later.

Commander Aera's eyes flickered. "We have to use all available resources." So calm. So *reasonable*.

Hwa Young did not feel that anything about this situation was reasonable. Nor did she care for the platitude, which sounded like the ones she'd memorized on New Joseon. The kind of thing COs told their soldiers before sending them into a hideous no-win situation.

She trusted Ye Jun to be straight with her about their missions. Her own heart-mother—not so much. And that *sucked*.

"What is your end game?" Hwa Young pressed.

"The strategy is fourfold," Commander Aera said, with the relentless patience that Hwa Young knew and chafed at. "First: to remove the Empress. Second: to obtain the singularity bomb. Third: to use the threat of the bomb to destabilize New Joseon to the point where it no longer poses a threat to the Moonstorm. If the Imperials think we're bluffing, we will inevitably have to prove them wrong. We will need to use the bomb at least once to convince them the threat is real. Fourth: to consolidate New Joseon under a friendly power." She raised an eyebrow in Ye Jun's direction.

The nausea in Hwa Young's gut came from revulsion, not unstable gravity. She couldn't tell the difference anymore. Perhaps there was a lesson in that.

"'Use the bomb at least once.' 'Friendly power,'" Hwa Young repeated with a sense of unreality, because she couldn't bear to voice the details behind her objection. It made sense that the clanners wanted to obtain the singularity bomb so they wouldn't be left behind militarily. Yet the idea of *more* people with their hands on a technology that destroyed worlds, and the cold-blooded intention to make use of it—her hands shook beneath the table.

Commander Aera's lips pulled back from her teeth. Hwa Young wasn't the only one losing patience. "What did you think it meant when you called out the Empress's tyranny, Pilot? That you were going to go out on mission after mission using random pirates as your personal punching bags, without any long-term strategy?"

Hwa Young inhaled sharply. *That's not fair,* she almost snarled.

Half a second later, the words struck Hwa Young like a serrated knife. Her own protest clogged her throat. Commander Aera was right.

Hwa Young had sought solace in her missions and the assurance that she'd eventually see Geum again. The day-to-day, moment-by-moment challenge of flying her lancer. Walls of ice and shields of snow around her own heartsickness. She'd let the routines numb her pain over Seong Su's death and her work as a soldier.

She'd also numbed away the fact that she was killing *people,* whichever side she was on. She'd balked at shooting the saboteur. Forced Aera to do it for her. If she'd been faster, more ruthless—if she'd embraced the killer's instincts that *Winter's Axiom* offered—maybe Bae wouldn't be incapacitated.

"Hwajin."

Hwa Young's head jerked up, and she met her heart-mother's gaze before remembering they weren't equals. She'd spaced out in front of Aera, Ye Jun, *and* Eun.

The only consolation was that Bae hadn't witnessed this too.

Aera spoke again. "What did *you* think the big picture was?"

Hwa Young straightened, squared her shoulders. "Freedom. Driving New Joseon back from your borders."

Protecting the clanners' families, but that one she wouldn't say out loud. Not to Aera, who had lost the same people she had.

"Specifics. What does that *mean*?"

She would not look to Ye Jun and Eun for an answer, but Ye Jun spoke anyway. "The commander is referring," zie said, "to concrete objectives. It's one thing to say you want to expel the Empire. But what is the scope of the mission? How do you accomplish it? Is it one and done, or do you have to keep committing to it year after year?"

Commander Aera nodded, her eyes blazing.

Ye Jun is manipulating her. The realization hit her like a wave of thunder. Hwa Young struggled to keep her face impassive.

Why hadn't she seen it earlier? Having figured out what Commander Aera wanted—must have wanted the second a member of the Imperial family, however illegitimate, came into her hands—zie was maneuvering by using her desires as leverage. Ye Jun must have worked toward this from the moment they joined Falcon Fleet. Hwa Young had been too absorbed in her own single-minded concerns to grasp it before; Ye Jun hadn't clued her in, even by implication, until recently. As much as that smarted, she acknowledged the correctness of zir judgment, or at least, zir assessment of her nonexistent ability to act.

Aera, in her turn, couldn't be unaware that Ye Jun had an agenda of zir own. A dangerous game, in both directions.

In fact, Aera had done the same to Hwa Young. What had she been *thinking*? *Of course* Aera had strung her along with promises. What possible incentive would Aera have to exfiltrate

Geum, when Geum was so much more useful trapped on the *Maehwa* feeding the clanners information and acting as their agent?

Fight smart. Understand the enemy and fight smart.

She'd allowed the messiness of her relationship with Aera to cloud her thinking and her ability to fight smart.

As a child, Hwa Young hadn't tracked clanner politics, or anything beyond the daily squabbles with her cousins and siblings, the joy of running through the hills with starblooms caught in her hair, dreaming of far-travelers and stories of treasure glimmering on forsaken moons. Carnelian's destruction had snapped her life into focus. She was a bullet pointed toward a single target.

Achieving her childhood goal hadn't brought her the joy she'd wanted.

Winter's Axiom said, *We are the knife in the shadows and the deaths at night. We are now and forever.*

We are now and forever, Hwa Young agreed, but the words carved her hollow rather than consoling her. Memory of Geum's smile haunted her. *Together forever,* she'd said over and over as she passed on Aera's lies, demanding more and more in exchange for a rescue that Aera had never planned on carrying out.

She was going to have to take matters into her own hands, and deal with Aera's reaction afterward.

Returning to the clanners—returning to Mother Aera—didn't feel like coming home. She was supposed to be welcome. She was supposed to belong. Everything was supposed to align.

It would have been so easy to lash out at Aera, but Hwa Young had done this to herself with her overblown expectations.

All she had left were the other pilots, Rose-Merline, Geum.

Hwa Young met Ye Jun's eyes, reassured by zir slight answering smile, then tilted her head toward Eun, willing them to understand her: *I wasn't ready before, but I am now. I'll follow your lead.*

"It sounds like you have a plan," Ye Jun said to Aera.

"First things first," Aera said with a nod at Hwa Young. "Your friend Geum is alive."

Hwa Young sagged in relief. Then she remembered where she was and why, and corrected her posture. "How did you—is zie all right?"

"We have eyes on Eleventh Fleet," Aera said, with the lack of specificity that Hwa Young had become resigned to, "and listeners too. Signal analysis indicates that Technician An Geum has, shall we say, resumed zir hacker habits."

Aera gestured at the map. "The mission's chances of success increase, Pilot Hwajin, if you are able to exploit Geum's friendship to guide us within Eleventh Fleet's defense perimeter so we can verify whether the Empress is in fact present."

Hwa Young almost choked on bile. Why had she imagined that Aera would give her good news for its own sake? Aera only cared about her friend as a *tactical asset.*

She's a clanner tactician. Second only to Admiral Mae in Falcon Fleet. It's her job *to care about tactical assets.*

Hwa Young's role in this stung, but she nodded her understanding. Her voice would expose her feelings, so she didn't speak. She was grateful for the mask, however ugly, that made it impossible for anyone to read her expressions.

Hwa Young admitted a reluctant admiration for Aera's focus and the sheer grim willingness to do whatever it took to protect the clanners from New Joseon. To prevent another disaster like the one that had destroyed Carnelian six years ago. A focus Hwa Young had once possessed, back when she'd aimed herself toward the goal of obtaining a lancer. Except she'd lost friends, and her resolve had faltered. Aera's resolve had not . . . did not.

All the while, Hwa Young examined Aera's face, which had no healing mask to obscure it: the underlying bones, the planes of her face. The two of them didn't look anything alike at present. Perhaps they never would again.

19

HWA YOUNG

We're going to capture the singularity bomb plans.

The words snaked through Hwa Young's thoughts again and again in the time leading up to the mission.

Eleventh Fleet possesses those plans, Commander Aera had said, hard and certain. *If the Empress is with them, there is no way she would fail to bring a copy of the plans with her. Your job is to disable the flagship without destroying it. Our marines will board and handle the rest.*

The scouts' reports claimed that the *Maehwa* had survived the previous battle. A testament to Chief's ability.

Despite Hwa Young's best intentions, she'd allowed the guards at Zeng's lab to turn her back *again*. "Midprocedure," they had said. "A bad time."

"All right," she challenged them, "when's a *good* time?"

They told her when to come back. The timing would be tight, given the preparations she had to make for the upcoming mission, but she was determined to make it work. She would bull her way past guards and gates—whatever it took.

Hwa Young had spent her sleep shifts in Rose-Merline's arms. Sometimes Hwa Young spilled her concerns about Bae, or alluded to her unhappiness with Aera. Rose-Merline listened attentively. At other times, Rose-Merline sang funny songs or offered makeup tips so obviously terrible that even Hwa Young could tell, and they laughed together.

"What is *your* story?" Hwa Young asked. "Why are *you* at war? Is it revenge against New Joseon?" Rose-Merline had alluded to family pressure, but Hwa Young didn't want to come out and ask. The story might be too painful to share.

"My family had reservations," Rose-Merline admitted, which surprised Hwa Young. "War only feeds the buzzards, as my aunt says. But our family has a tradition of service on ships like this one, we care a lot about our monopoly on cutting-edge cryptobotany, and if there's one thing all my relatives agree on, it's tradition."

Hwa Young had no background in anything related to plants other than basic foraging and herbalism. Ye Jun's comments on "cultivating" Rose-Merline returned to her, filling her with diffuse foreboding. Why did Ye Jun care so much about extracting information about the ensign's job? "What does 'cutting-edge' mean when it comes to botany, anyway? Higher crop yields?"

Rose-Merline pursed her lips. "It's complicated."

She wasn't sure whether that meant *These chemical formulas will bore you and I'd rather do something fun* or *It's top-secret,* but she could take a hint.

Naturally, this meant that she hopped to a different uncomfortable topic: "Hey. What *are* your feelings toward Bae, anyway?"

Rose-Merline propped herself up on one elbow. "Jealous? Or do you think *I* should be jealous?"

Hwa Young flushed. It had been an unfair question, but she couldn't avoid it forever, either. "My feelings aren't a secret," she said haltingly.

They weren't a secret to anyone in the entire fleet by now. That would have given her pause once; she had stopped caring about other people's disapproval, even Commander Ye Jun's, when she discovered Bae curled up and bleeding from the eyes and nose. Any messiness around fraternization with a fellow pilot could wait until Bae was cleared for duty.

Rose-Merline ran a fingertip over Hwa Young's brow ridge, down the nose, and ending on her upper lip. "How would he feel about this—about us? That's the real question, isn't it?"

"I should have asked first," Hwa Young said wretchedly. "But I never knew if he was interested in me—in anyone." Escaping into her relationship with Rose-Merline, whatever name they gave it, had been so easy at first. A respite from everything in her life going sideways at once.

"Shh," Rose-Merline said, leaning in for one kiss, then another. "We'll talk to him when he's better. We'll figure it out, all of us."

It was a beautiful respite, and one Hwa Young was loath to give up. It didn't *solve* any of the crises hanging over her head. Yet she wanted so badly to believe—for someone to reassure her that everything would work out.

Afterward, Hwa Young murmured, "I should get going," into Rose-Merline's glorious head of curls. It tickled: she liked that.

"You should," Rose-Merline agreed. Her kiss implied the opposite. "Still—" She drew out a fragrant sachet and fastened it around Hwa Young's neck. "I made this for you. Keep it on you always."

"Starblooms?" Hwa Young asked, startled and pleased.

Rose-Merline smiled secretively. "For luck. So you never get lost in the Moonstorm. Go, go."

So you never get lost in the Moonstorm. That was a sentiment she could get behind.

After dressing and making sure her collar wasn't inside out, Hwa Young stopped by Zeng's lab ten minutes early. This time the guards admitted her, although Bae had been removed to a private area. She chafed at the guards' hostility, but protecting Bae and the lab was a smart precaution.

All the same, if someone didn't let her see Bae soon . . .

"It's good of you to stop by," Zeng said after offering her tea and cookies, which she declined. One of the guards sauntered in like a stray dog, eyeing the cookies hopefully. Zeng dutifully let him have them instead.

Zeng was much more likable when he wasn't polished to a high sheen. Whatever the reason, his cheeks were hollow, his eyes haggard. He kept glancing at the cookie-munching guard with the air of an overwhelmed babysitter. The guard chewed more loudly in response. Stress was getting to all of them.

More than stress, in Zeng's case, if she was right about the saboteur's identity. She'd tried asking indirect questions, trying to ascertain if Tora was lurking elsewhere on the ship. Subterfuge wasn't her strength, though, and asking more directly would have aroused suspicion.

"How are you and your brother doing?" she asked with attempted casualness while the guard demolished the cookies.

Aha: Zeng winced, and the shadows in his eyes deepened.

"Oh, you know," he said in a transparently false attempt at nonchalance. "We had a fight. The stupidest thing. He kept borrowing my socks and then not washing them afterward. He's off sulking."

The explanation was so ridiculous Hwa Young almost believed it.

What am I going to say to Commander Ye Jun? Eun's ex-boyfriend was twitchy and the cover story involved dirty socks? She needed more convincing evidence.

"When Bae comes to, give him this for me?" Hwa Young asked, pulling the small wooden box from her pocket. It wasn't much, and that embarrassed her. She'd gotten it secondhand from someone who claimed they'd bought it on a stopover last year: it contained a comb carved of star-whale bone.

Yes. He'll appreciate that.

Hwa Young blinked, bemused that *Winter's Axiom* had an opinion.

The box's humbleness might keep Zeng from divining its primary purpose. The wood was of terrible quality, made of splintery layers poorly glued, for all the appeal of the painted bird motifs. This had enabled her to wedge a jury-rigged bug into one of the sides. She *hoped* Zeng would respect her overt gift-giving intention enough to keep the box, however shoddy, rather than recycling it immediately. All she had to do was check in periodically on the bug's transmissions, which were routed to *Winter's Axiom*, for any incriminating chatter.

Zeng accepted the box with a tremulous smile. "Certainly, Pilot."

Once she reached the docking bay, Hwa Young scrutinized

her surroundings with disquiet. She'd arrived half an hour early, partly out of apprehension, partly so she could run system checks. Twenty-seven minutes left, and no indication that the others, too, were going to show up early.

There were scorch marks from the explosion, some of which the deckhands had painted over. The incomplete job gave that section a piebald appearance, like the black-and-white cats she had sometimes encountered sauntering through the streets of Forsythia City.

She'd thought herself inured to combat scars and marks of damage. She had her own. The healing mask clung to her face, squelching every time she grimaced or smiled or spoke.

"Change it every eight hours," the medic had instructed her. "I don't care if you're with a *friend* and you're in the middle of"—he used a term Hwa Young didn't recognize and had deliberately not looked up—"or taming a space dragon with a space net or going back in time to feed the first Empress to a space tiger. Change the dressing."

I'll do it, Hwa Young thought. Not because of the medic's colorful examples, but because she didn't want to give Commander Ye Jun any reason to ground her.

As for her appearance—who would be more bothered if she emerged with a ruined face? Bae? Hwa Young herself? Her heart-mother?

She dismissed the matter. Either her face would heal or it wouldn't. Her focus was drifting, because she was trying to avoid thinking about her mission. She quickened her stride and emerged into the docking bay.

The tapestries and engravings, the starbloom planters, still contrasted with the industrial appearance of Imperial starships' interiors. The deckhands had been aggrieved about damage to some of the planters. Hwa Young spotted Rose-Merline talking to one of them, thought of waving, but didn't want to interrupt. Hwa Young had gotten accustomed to the lancers standing in a setting they'd never been intended for.

But there were three lancers, not four. Which she would have noticed right away if she hadn't been distracted by the sight of her girlfriend, or whatever Rose-Merline was to her.

The missing lancer was *Farseer*.

"Where's the fourth?" Hwa Young demanded of the nearest technician, a sour-faced woman.

The technician, fussing over an intership shuttle with half its side disassembled, didn't look up. "Fourth what?"

The technician's lack of interest, and failure to resemble Geum in either manner or fashion sense, steadied Hwa Young. For all she knew, the shuttle repair was urgent too. "The fourth lancer," she said, trying not to overenunciate. "The one that was damaged by sabotage." The technician must have heard the scuttlebutt.

She assumed correctly. "Moved it to Researcher Zeng's lab for additional repairs," the technician said, still bored. "Pass me that wrench? The number eight?"

Hwa Young did so. "What's special about the lab? Why couldn't the repairs be done here?" She reviewed the ship's blueprints in her head: they'd have had to haul it out of the docking bay and maneuver it to the lab's level *outside* the ship using waldoes. Physically possible, if logistically awkward.

How hadn't she known?

Be reasonable, Hwa Young thought. *Don't catastrophize.* She would have known if someone had moved *Winter's Axiom* without consulting her. Wasn't that her real fear?

Except she was afraid for Bae. Bae, who was in no condition to approve or disapprove of anything done to his lancer. That wasn't catastrophizing—not when sabotage had already occurred.

The technician finally looked up. "You pilots are a tight lot, aren't you?"

Hwa Young narrowed her eyes at the woman. What was that supposed to imply?

"Special equipment for special repairs that someone signed off on. Not the basic stuff." Her voice lowered, unexpectedly sympathetic. "Better security, since that's a going concern. The only reason *your* three weren't sequestered for safety, too, was that you need to access them to fight, yeah? But you didn't hear that from me."

Hwa Young started to ask for specifics, but then she heard Eun's footsteps, the characteristic heavy tread. Terrible timing: Who had given the order?

Commander Aera is the only one who would have authorized this. Unless she didn't understand the command hierarchy on *Falcon Actual.* She clung to the hope, however dim, that this was the case.

"Yo," Eun said. "Where's *Farseer?*"

Should she ask him if he'd seen Zeng recently? Suggest that he lean on that connection in the hopes of information? But that would be a distraction from the mission. She'd bring it up after.

If only I'd moved on this earlier—even though she knew better than to expect privacy on any military ship. Hadn't she planted a bug herself? What if Zeng had found the bug? Instead of destroying it, he might use it to plant disinformation. The possibilities made her head hurt.

"The damaged unit was taken to the lab," the technician said, her voice muffled by the metal panels. "Does no one tell you people anything?"

"Clearly not," Eun said in his best Eun-is-simulating-tact tone.

Hwa Young opened her mouth, then closed it at Eun's tiny warning headshake. He was right. Better not to risk the technician reporting back to her superiors. Especially since she had *seemed* sympathetic. Hwa Young hated how the situation had her second-guessing every chance interaction.

The clanners had never possessed an advanced repair protocol for lancer units for the obvious reason. Previous repairs to shuttles and fighters had been run out of the docking bay. Still, an advanced lab might possess capabilities that couldn't be duplicated elsewhere.

"Saddle up," Eun said, his smile crooked. Like her, he was suited up except for the helmet tucked under one arm.

"Saddle what?"

"You've never heard of horses? Even my home station had a petting zoo with a pony. An ugly pony, but still."

Hwa Young was already striding toward *Winter's Axiom*. "I know about horses!" she called over her shoulder. "And elephants! I just didn't expect you to discuss riding gear."

The lift conveyed Hwa Young to the cockpit of *Winter's Axiom*. A murmur stirred in her soul, snowdrifts and white wings. She stared at her reflection in the mirror-sheen of the cockpit's window.

The mask made her resemble a ghoul from the horror stories

she'd heard in her childhood. New Joseon primly claimed not to produce works of horror, although this was a lie. They relabeled their horror "experimental art," which satisfied propriety and offered hours of entertainment for Geum, who had an appalling taste for splatter yet wimped out when it came to cutting meat.

Commander Ye Jun arrived last. Hwa Young sensed rather than saw zir, a bright, unbent figure like a polestar in her lancer's senses.

Hwa Young climbed into the cockpit. It snicked shut as she settled herself into the seat, perfectly molded to her form, comfort beyond comfort. In the past, her meditations had included an imagined cockpit, three parts careful study of propaganda posters and one part thinking of that one teacher two years ago who had an incredibly comfortable chair that zie let favorite students sit in. (Hwa Young had achieved "favorite" status once, and she had to share with Geum.) The real thing was better. She hadn't factored in the steadying mental link with *Winter's Axiom,* the rapture of their connection, when things went well.

Nothing—not the visualizations, nor the training Eun had given the pilot candidates—had prepared her for a bond with an apex predator.

"Lancer squad, prepare for launch," Commander Ye Jun said over the comms.

Pretend it's the same as always.

Except it wasn't. Three, not four. Lacking *Farseer* and its sensor suite, they'd be flying without advance warning of any threats. Ye Jun's *Bastard* could perform some of those functions, which overlapped with its command and control specialty, but its sensors didn't reach as far into the deep.

Practical considerations. Hwa Young had to stick to the

practical ones, because if she thought about the *personal* ones, she'd break down. Letting the squad down wasn't an option. Not with their numbers diminished like this.

Bae won't die. Neither will I. I'm getting Geum out of there this time and Aera is just going to have to suck it up.

Hwa Young didn't care if she had to bend the laws of the universe to make it happen. She'd do whatever it took.

"Vagrant to Falcon Command," Ye Jun said. "Request clearance to launch."

Hwa Young clutched the familiar words to her heart like a knotwork talisman. Repeated them inside her head as though they possessed the power to keep her safe.

Praying to the Empress hadn't worked out either. She shoved away the comparison.

"Falcon Command here," a gruff voice replied. "You're cleared to launch. We'll be monitoring the situation when able. Moon's own blessing."

"Axiom. Are you ready?"

"Always," Hwa Young said, straightening at Ye Jun's words. This time it was true. Better an escape into action than waiting in the cockpit like an unhatched chick.

"You'll take point, Axiom. Follow this path"—Ye Jun transmitted the waypoints that marked her route—"and stay in the scan shadow of the indicated asteroids to minimize risk of detection until I say otherwise."

"Roger that, Vagrant."

The bay's doors irised open. *Winter's Axiom* launched. She was ice and storm and the wings of winter. She yearned for *flight*, the sweet winds of aether, a fight she could sink her teeth into. An escape from the miserable events of the past few weeks.

Is that what I want, or is it what Winter's Axiom *wants for me?* Did it matter? She was here. She was flying. She gloried in the way acceleration pushed her back into the cushioned seat, the familiar compensation of the lancer's environmental systems.

They shot out into the darkness, candle-lit by a procession of stars. Hwa Young felt the resistance as though it struck her own skin when *Winter's Axiom* knifed through the buffeting aether winds. As though she soared through a sky whose weather was war song.

The other lancers followed in her wake. They formed the points of a triangle, maintaining formation with the ease of long practice and shifting distances when incoming battledrift or debris made it necessary. Hwa Young could have continued this forever, reveled in the journey together, except—

Hunting, Winter's Axiom reminded her. With its own mordant humor, it added, *Your comrades are not suitable prey, even if Hellion would make an excellent trophy.*

We don't taxidermy people! Hwa Young told it, wondering if it was joking or serious and trying to scrub the visual out of her head.

Remember this, Commander Aera had said during the briefing. *Don't worry about capturing the Empress. My people know what to do, and I have contingencies. Focus on disabling the flagship so we can recover the plans. If we can capture the flagship intact, even better.*

Hwa Young considered ways to prepare Geum for rescue *without* alerting Aera or any unstealthed clanners. Ways to phrase her message.

I'll make this right. I'm coming, Geum. Together forever.

"Vagrant to Axiom. We're peeling off, but we'll be within range if you need backup."

"Understood, Vagrant."

Hwa Young spotted Eleventh Fleet on visual. At this distance, it was indistinguishable from the background glitter-scatter of stars and moonlets, fast specks and slow specks. Only her link with the lancer told her what was a star and what was a moon or a ship.

She was taking an enormous risk, and she welcomed it. Every nerve sparked alight. She wanted to do this over and over, luxuriate in this transfiguration from ice into pyre and back again.

Eleventh Fleet would shoot her on sight. Admiral Chin had never liked her to begin with. Hwa Young had to lurk out of sight while making contact with Geum in such a way that zie could verify her identity.

Possible conversations played out in Hwa Young's head as she made the approach, sprinting from asteroid to asteroid, staying in the lee of ancient shipwrecks so as to remain undetected.

Commander Aera would never approve of this. Ye Jun might not either.

I should have asked zir—

No. Commit to fire. Now or never. Act first, apologize later. That was the path left to her.

Together forever.

Hwa Young settled in behind the ruins of a ship, destroyed or wrecked in some previous battle. She prepared to bounce her transmission off an asteroid to prevent anyone from pinpointing her location. By the time the *Maehwa* calculated her point of origin, she'd be gone.

She sent a message specifically addressed to Geum's game server. *Geum. It's Hwa Young. I'm coming for you. Thanks for the snacks. Together forever.*

Now it was up to Geum.

20

GEUM

Geum had learned several things about human nature in zir increasingly less fabulous time in New Joseon. People never paid attention to what was going on under their noses if they had a more interesting alternative. Sometimes it made sense to carry out secret activities in a public place while pretending to be doing something innocuous, as with zir recent "walk" with Mi Cha and the Empress. In the past, zie had screwed around hacking while in the rec room "watching" a replay of a table tennis match from two years ago.

Zie had graduated to hacking in the midst of a meeting between the Empress, Captain Ga Ram, Lieutenant Mi Cha and her taciturn copilot, and Admiral Chin. To say this was awkward was an understatement. Still, the stratospherically high-ranking people present were so busy sniping at each other that Geum, the one fabulous if ordinary person, could fly under the radar.

The furnishings in the yacht's conference room included

everything from high cabinets with pristine glass doors and shelves, mysteriously empty, to something that Geum had first mistaken for a favorite blanket, tossed carelessly over an unused armchair. The latter turned out, on closer inspection, to be a priceless ancient painting of dancers amid peonies, the colors faded, on aged silk.

Geum would have found this an exciting opportunity, as opposed to an incipient ulcer, if it hadn't been for the stakes. The knowledge that *someone* in this room was a traitor—someone who knew how to get them all *un*-lost after stranding them in the Moonstorm—dampened the fun factor.

As far as Geum knew, Admiral Chin had taken move orders directly from the Empress, who declined to explain herself. Geum had overheard a terse exchange between Mi Cha, obviously relishing another opportunity to bully the admiral: "No," Mi Cha had been saying, "we are *not* releasing the Empress's master atlas to you. Do you think I don't know you'd run off and join the insurrectionist fleets if you had half a chance?" Geum had reluctantly crept away partly into the admiral's response, which began with a long-suffering sigh. Securing the cooperation of an entire fleet by *blackmailing* its admiral seemed like an inherently limiting life choice but fortunately one far above Geum's pay grade.

The Empress had summoned everyone to her yacht. She'd served them platters of *fresh fruit,* including peeled tangerines drizzled with citron syrup and apples sliced with some of the peel still attached so they resembled little rabbits. In fact, she'd carved the apples in front of them, smiling self-deprecatingly.

The Empress showing off everyday skills like *peeling fruit* charmed Geum. Not even world-class fruit-carving skills (zie had watched a cooking show where people carved lifelike roses out of white radishes), but the kinds of simple apple bunnies that Geum's younger dad had taught zir when zie was eight.

Geum had figured out the truth: the Empress didn't have any of her staff or servants. Everyone on the *Maehwa* knew by now. For all Geum knew, she was a newbie cook, having picked up the skill by watching tutorials to pass the time, or bleed off stress, during her voyage.

"Majesty, I don't think," Ga Ram was saying, "that negotiations with Ninth Fleet are going to tilt in your favor. Especially since that prick Admiral Gu's idea of a civilized conversation is to shoot everything in a nine-parsec radius and let the ghosts fend for themselves."

Captain Ga Ram had a quiet, dignified way of speaking. On the other hand, Ga Ram's habit of gazing sideways and off into space, as though it was embarrassing that zie had to bring such small considerations to the Empress's attention, irritated Geum intensely, and zie wasn't even involved in the conversation. If the Empress's slight grimaces were anything to go by, she shared Geum's feelings.

"What talks will do is buy time," the Empress returned. She was eating fruit with her fingers and licking her fingertips clean, unlike everyone else with their chopsticks. "Gu has a very high opinion of her own cleverness. If she thinks she's pulling some twisty fox-faced trick on me, it'll give me the margin I need to secure an alternate base of operations."

"Gu isn't stupid," Ga Ram said, tapping the side of the fruit platter to punctuate zir words. "She'll know that's what you're doing."

Geum had taken a single piece of fruit. The chopsticks and platters made zir nervous. They were bronzeware in the old style, meticulously hand-forged. At least they wouldn't break if zie dropped them.

The gathering reminded Geum of zir fathers, and the catered family dinners that involved fancy tableware. "Fancy," for Geum's family, had meant *overtly* fancy, plates with ostentatious glazed patterns of clouds and celestial attendants, or chopsticks with needle-fine designs in abalone inlay. The *Empress's* tableware, on the other hand, had *no* ornamentation, not even a maker's mark; presumably one was supposed to be refined enough to identify it on sight. The nakedness of their form revealed their quality, with no embellishment to distract from the craftsmanship.

Admiral Chin exhaled through her nose, a contemptuous snort. She'd spoken little but implied much through the subtle play of expressions. Geum's opinion of her was rising, however reluctantly.

"Your opinion of Gu is well-known, Admiral," Mi Cha said with a huff of her own.

The royal gossip sites would kill for my seat with the Empire's elites, Geum thought with a flash of wry humor. Zie had every intention of passing on the nonclassified juicy details next time zie saw Hyo Su, who would eat up every word.

The Empire's elites in exile. This included people who thought nothing of sacrificing entire *loyal* fleets for their power plays. An uncomfortable thought. Other ramifications blossomed in Geum's mind like an out-of-control fungal infection.

If the Empress was here . . . who was running the Empire?

Maybe multiple powers were fighting for the honor while Eleventh Fleet squandered its time in the Moonstorm, ignorant of recent developments in the distant core worlds. Without the Empress to keep the admirals, nobles, and planetary governors in line, what would prevent New Joseon from falling apart—or succumbing to some clanner sneak attack?

Geum had obtained, downloaded, and installed a new and improved hacker toolset, which had been lurking in the Empress's operating system. Possibly it was a honeypot meant to lure in people like Geum, but zie was sure zie had bypassed the security measures. An Empress whose education had focused on strategy and administration and how to tie up her ceremonial robes, who was learning Cooking 101, and who had an empire to reconquer couldn't *also* be an expert hacker, could she?

Because Geum had priorities, zie had configured the toolkit's interface as a portal to an updated stash for the *Maehwa*'s not-entirely-legal manhwa comics archive. No one in present company would dig too deep even if they caught zir scrolling through cracktastic fan commentary about a reincarnated Hong Gildong and his space dog. (The running joke was that the "dog" was a giant acid-breathing space mantis.)

I'm doing this for a good reason. Geum repeated the phrase over and over.

There—

Geum would have loved to poke around the Empress's personal files, but lingering risked getting caught. Geum didn't want to land back in the brig, or be shot in the head, before Hwa Young showed up. So zie yanked as much of a data dump as zie dared, peering at random files as the file transfer took place.

Inventory of forces, said one file name, alongside some pretentious quote from the *Handbook of Good Governance* by the First Empress. Geum couldn't read the quote because it was in an archaic form of the language, although zie recognized the title due to the screamingly ancient hanja logographs. Probably the bit that said *The first priority is keeping track of your resources, from the smallest grain of millet to the largest fortress.*

That's odd, Geum thought, examining the file size. Did the Empress keep everything in plain text? (Backward compatibility in file formats? Something zie rarely fretted about, despite New Joseon's centuries of history.) Maybe this was a list of links or passwords and the actual information was hidden elsewhere, in which case Geum had some entertaining sleuthing to look forward to. A welcome distraction from the question of sabotage and high treason.

Zie did not have entertaining sleuthing after all.

INVENTORY OF FORCES

myself (the most important one)

Nice to know the Empress had a healthy ego. Who wanted an *insecure* ruler?

Ga Ram and *Paradox*
Mi Cha and *Summer Thorn*
Eleventh Fleet
The plans

Forces from the core worlds cannot be trusted at this time.

Geum sucked zir cheeks in, aghast. Did this mean what zie thought it did—that the Empress was here with two lancers and the clothes on her back? That she'd scrounged up Eleventh Fleet because they were available and she had no one else? That there weren't other fleets carrying out her operations elsewhere or lurking protectively at a distance?

And *the plans*—that must refer to the singularity bomb. If the Empress didn't have her own fleet, let alone control of any star systems with their worlds, what on heaven and earth did she intend to do with them?

The screen froze at the same time that Geum's neural implant interjected a flicker across zir field of vision.

"Oh no you don't," Geum muttered.

"Oh no you don't, what?"

Geum looked up, startled. Zir cheeks flamed. The Empress, the two lancer pilots, *and* Admiral Chin stared at zir. The copilot had faded into the background and looked bored, her usual act. The others, previously arguing in heated voices about crane's wing tactics—whatever *that* meant—regarded Geum with sharp interest.

"Uh, tech problem," Geum said, still embarrassed, even if the Empress looked grateful for a break. "I was looking at spoilers for one of my favorite manhwa. Sorry."

Mi Cha snorted. Ga Ram, on the other hand, looked sidelong at Geum.

The captain is suspicious.

Did that mean Ga Ram was the saboteur? Or did this indicate ordinary levels of small-minded yet regrettably accurate suspicion?

A message scrolled across the middle of a touching full-page panel in which Hong Gildong taught the space dog to play fetch with . . . a fragmentation grenade? That sure looked like a grenade.

Geum. It's Hwa Young. I'm coming for you. Thanks for the snacks. Together forever.

Geum's heart flipped.

Ga Ram's eyes had narrowed the instant the message arrived, although the captain wasn't looking at Geum. This reassured Geum for the briefest moment. Then Geum followed the captain's sight line.

The captain hadn't been gazing off into space. Not exactly. Instead, zir gaze went directly to a cabinet whose glass doors were polished to a high sheen. It made for an excellent mirror, perfectly angled to capture Geum's activities.

Ga Ram had watched everything Geum was doing, seen everything that crossed Geum's screen—in the betraying reflection.

Great. I'm going to get Hwa Young killed because I made an amateur's mistake.

Another flicker crossed Geum's field of vision. Geum flinched: the neural implant wasn't supposed to trigger visuals without zir express permission.

Wait a second. This had happened before. Not just today, but when zie had discovered the saboteur's tracks.

The flicker was followed by a message, afterimages forming words:

YOU HAVE THE FLEET'S STAR MAPS, AMONG OTHER THINGS.

Geum blanched and checked zir neural implant. Whether it was Captain Ga Ram—Geum's top suspect—or Mi Cha who had engineered this, the message spoke true: zir files included the star maps.

Geum's own overconfidence had allowed the saboteur to plant a worm in zir implant. There would be others lurking in the *Maehwa*'s systems. Geum had to assume that Ga Ram had used them to discover that Geum and Hwa Young had been in contact this whole time.

On the other hand—the instant Ga Ram ratted Geum out, Geum was dead. Instead, the captain of the guard was going in for . . . blackmail? Which implied, intriguingly, that the captain wasn't entirely acting out of pure undiluted loyalty to New Joseon either.

There had to be a way out to turn the situation to Geum's advantage.

Revealing the blackmail was appealingly simple. Unfortunately, that would get Geum accused of being the saboteur zirself, thanks to the incriminating maps. Nor could zie take extra precautions, then quietly restore the maps: zie had no way of verifying their accuracy.

How much time could zie buy for zirself and Hwa Young?

"Uh, Majesty . . ."

The Empress looked up: she'd been rearranging the remaining tangerine slices. "Yes, Geum?"

Geum held the slate up. "I—I got a message. A message from the traitor Hwa Young." The word "traitor" almost clogged zir throat. "It . . . it could be fake, Majesty. But I don't think it is. I gave Hwa Young some snacks before she turned traitor. She must think we're still friends."

It was only a matter of time before the Empress and her lackeys found out about the message. By revealing the communiqué zirself, Geum had a narrow opportunity to establish credibility—and manipulate them into sparing Geum and Hwa Young. If zie got them focused on the *tablet,* they'd be distracted from conducting a separate audit of zir *implant* with the star maps.

The quality of the others' scrutiny changed. Everyone, from the Empress to Admiral Chin, sized Geum up like dogs presented with a stinky treat.

"I don't... it could be a trick," Geum said, starting to stammer. "But should I ignore this? In case it's a sick prank? Or investigate it, or what? Maybe if you lured her in, she'd have information about the clanners."

Please don't look too closely at the interface please don't look too closely. Not for the first time, Geum wished Hwa Young were here. She was the one with the gift (curse?) of coming up with a plan of action under pressure.

The Empress stopped fussing with the tangerines. "Plug it in," she said. "Hard connection." She removed a panel, revealing the ports in the side of the table.

Everything on the slate was compromised, encryption or no encryption. Geum had counted on that. With luck, the Empress would regard Geum's files, including the large pirated collection of foreign holos, as small-time petty hacking, ultimately harmless, and assume Geum wasn't hiding something more incriminating elsewhere.

The Empress provided the cables. Geum was familiar with old-fashioned connector cables but had never used this type aboard the *Maehwa*.

"Security bypass," the Empress explained in an undertone.

Admiral Chin called CIC. "I'm forwarding a signal," she said. She used her own slate, presumably connected to the yacht's computers as well. "Trace its origins."

Geum sweated. *I hope you're prepared, Hwa Young.*

"Of course, sir," CIC replied over the comms.

Mi Cha got up and began to pace. "Too bad this girl of yours isn't still on our side," she said to Geum. "I like her style."

Geum grinned nervously. *You have no idea.* What would happen if Mi Cha and Hwa Young met? Would they become instant friends or annihilate each other?

Several minutes passed. Then CIC spoke again. "Traced to Asteroid Na-17349. Almost certainly bounced off a rock in the area. I'm following the signal but it's unlikely the source is still there if they have any common sense."

Another pause. Mi Cha's footsteps filled the tense hush. Geum wished she would sit down. By way of contrast, Ga Ram sat still and calm, with exquisite poise.

CIC again: "Detected graviton traces, not ours. Probably a lancer."

Admiral Chin glanced at the Empress, who nodded. The admiral snarled, "One lancer or *more than one?*"

Geum hadn't thought of that. What if Hwa Young had brought her comrades? Zie slanted a glance at the Empress, who wore an interested smile. She gave no sign that she was worried about a confrontation with her bastard Ye Jun.

"It's unclear, sir," CIC said.

Admiral Chin eyed Geum. "Can you respond to Hwa Young?"

Geum retrieved the slate and booted out to the terminal. "Yes, sir. Wh-what do you want me to say?"

"Keep her talking. Find out what she wants. Talk to her about her videogame collection or her food allergies or her favorite ammunition. Whatever it takes to keep her on the line so we can trace her location."

Normally people offered Geum money to *shut up* about

videogames. But this gave Geum an excuse to talk to Hwa Young, as much as it disconcerted zir to receive permission from the admiral to do so.

Hey, Geum typed. *It's Spider. Had any chance to stick it to Bae on* Dragon Dumpster Battler 3*? I haven't watched her play that in ages.*

If this was Hwa Young, she'd know that Bae was too stuck-up to waste time on videogames, let alone ones with "dumpster" in the title. Bae had spent all her time studying with tutors who'd been lured away from professorships by extravagant pay. She'd shopped for cutting-edge fashion accessories like those darling cloud-and-raindrop ear cuffs, sucked up to the teachers, and lorded it over everyone who got in her way. Geum would never forget how, in a sign of the universe's unfairness, *Bae* had been the first to bond with a lancer.

If this was Hwa Young, she would—Geum hoped—pick up on the warning.

Hwa Young didn't reply for some time. Geum chewed on zir nails, aware of how immature this made zir look, and unable to stop. Zie had given up on nail polish, even the pretty orange one that Hyo Su had given zir. Spitting out the foul taste of the grime under zir nails was also contraindicated in present company.

Answer, Geum willed Hwa Young. Knowing the way aether jinxed communications in space didn't ameliorate the tension.

Was the message a recording, droning on and on to sow confusion and distract them from a deep strike elsewhere? Had Hwa Young crashed into a stray moonlet while avoiding detection? Geum couldn't imagine someone as hypercompetent as Hwa Young crashing, unless it was part of a cunning plan.

At last the answer appeared: *Yeah, Bae and I play it all the time. We still haven't beaten your high score. He got injured recently but I hope he'll be better soon.*

She'd gotten the warning. At least, Geum assumed that Hwa Young referring to Bae as a *he*, not a *she*, signaled that Hwa Young knew something was fishy.

At the same time, a spike drove into Geum's heart at how casually Hwa Young expressed concern for *Bae,* made-up or not. Would it kill her to ask how her best friend Geum was doing? After all zie had gone through—was going through—on her behalf?

"Your orders?" Geum croaked, afraid to check the Empress's expression, Ga Ram's, Mi Cha's, the admiral's. One sharp word and zie would melt down.

I can't screw this up. I can't get Hwa Young killed.

Hwa Young might be deficient in the tact department, but Geum had known that for a long time. Had found it endearing once upon a time, when it meant that Hwa Young relied on Geum to talk them both out of any trouble. Geum felt differently now.

It'll be better when we're together again.

"You have them," Admiral Chin said. The unaccustomed note in her voice couldn't be pity, could it? "Keep her talking. We're still pinpointing her location."

"You're going to shoot her," Geum said after a second. What was the point of all this if Hwa Young didn't make it? And if the Empress and friends had taken care of Hwa Young, and they had no more need of Geum, was zie next?

In the quiet that followed, the Empress picked up one of the tangerines and offered it to Geum, her eyes soft. Ga Ram's expression, watching this, was unreadable.

Geum accepted it and ate the tangerine segment without tasting it or the syrup.

"I know she was your friend, Technician," the admiral said. "But whatever that person was to you in days past, she's gone."

Keep it together, Geum. You can't give up the game this close to reunion.

Geum would settle for a hug, never mind getting off the *Maehwa*. That could wait for a better opportunity.

"*Think*, Technician. If we destroy her now, she dies cleanly in battle. Well and fine, but we only remove a single asset. A single lancer unit. Where are the rest of the lancers? Where are the clanners? What we need is *information*—for a decisive strike."

The admiral's words steadied Geum. It gave zir something to focus on other than the fear gnawing zir open from within.

Geum could work with that. Make this conversation real, but not too real. Zie thought for a second, then typed: *Listen, if you come in, I might be able to slip you something to convince your CO for real.*

The answer came more quickly this time. Less time to think? Something Hwa Young had prepared to answer? A sign that *Winter's Axiom* had moved closer, so there was less distance for the signal to travel?

Geum hoped in the Empress's name that the *Maehwa*'s shields were up and steady. Zie had no intention of getting *this close* to rescue only to die. If the shield malfunction repeated itself—

Hwa Young said, *I know. I'm sorry there have been so many delays.*

"Stay on task, Technician," Admiral Chin said.

Geum swallowed. Everyone was watching. Even Captain Ga Ram had zir hands pressed tightly together.

Admiral Chin's tone resembled that of the one picky calligraphy teacher who cared more about stroke order than actual spelling. Geum choked back a laugh. *Stay on task. Right.*

Geum typed, *Sure—but why are you here? It's dangerous for you.*

"Very good," Mi Cha murmured. "Get her to lower her guard, think you're worried for her."

Don't sound so surprised that I had a good idea, Geum thought sourly. This time zie typed: *The longer we do this, the likelier it is we'll get caught. So make it quick.*

If Geum closed zir eyes and let the world spin them away, it was almost like high school. Hwa Young provided a problem. (A lot of problems, to be honest.) Geum provided a solution. A perfect symbiotic relationship.

I need confirmation that the Empress is with Eleventh Fleet.

"What do I do now?" Geum asked raggedly. That was one thing zie hadn't dared tell Hwa Young earlier. Her superiors must have obtained the intel from other sources.

The Empress and the admiral exchanged glances, a question asked and answered in silence. The Empress nodded.

"Tell her yes," Admiral Chin said. "But change the subject. Offer her the complete blueprints to the singularity bomb. We're going to give them to her."

Geum could read between the lines. "Not the right ones."

"Of course not. Arrange for a dead drop. We want her to take back something physical. Something mostly correct, that will pass a first inspection. We just need a little time."

Something physical. "A bug," Geum said. "You already had fake plans ready."

Another exchange of glances, while Mi Cha paced and Ga Ram's face remained impassive and remote. "I believe in being prepared," the Empress said.

Geum typed numbly.

Thank you, Hwa Young said. *You doing all right?*

She couldn't come out and express her concern more explicitly. Not with eavesdroppers.

Geum thought about it. But zie couldn't think of anything else to add. Not with everyone watching. Both Ga Ram and Mi Cha could break zir in half with a finger.

Everything's good, Geum said, as much as zie hated saying it. *Just show up on time, okay?*

Of course, Hwa Young said, and signed off.

Admiral Chin nodded, her face relaxing into a genuine smile. "Well done, Technician. We'll snare that turncoat yet."

Together forever, Geum added, and signed off.

Soon, zie promised zirself and Hwa Young. *Soon.*

21

HWA YOUNG

Hwa Young drifted serenely in space as she waited for Geum's promised capsule: the dead drop. She'd turned gravity down to half strength and was enjoying the peaceful floating feeling. Surrounded by aether and darkness and starlit glory, she pretended it was just her and *Winter's Axiom*. All she had to do was wait.

The odds that Geum had liberated the real plans, as opposed to a fake, were maybe ten percent—but that ten percent justified the risk. The plans were too important for her to pass up the opportunity. Commander Ye Jun had agreed.

She'd marked the patrol patterns of Eleventh Fleet earlier. She had some time before any scouts headed her way.

Geum's alive. Geum's alive. It's going to be okay.

As disappointing as it was that Geum had warned her off a rescue, she'd talked to zir. She looked forward to hearing about zir feats when they got together again.

Soon.

In the past, she'd timed her breaths to poetry praising the Empress in her All-Wisdom. She'd discarded that and replaced it with clanner songs. Rose-Merline had taught her one in one of her languages, Kreyòl; had patiently helped her with pronunciation, explained what each word meant, how the grammar worked. Hwa Young remembered other songs that Elder Paik and Mother Aera had sung to her in childhood, mostly in Hangeul.

A different tune earwormed her now. Where had she first heard it?

Then it came to her. One of the battle themes from a retro puzzle-and-dungeon game, a favorite of Geum's. They'd played it together, snuggled side by side while munching on sesame snacks. Hwa Young didn't see the attraction of fighting big-eyed dancing chickens by matching up different colored marbles to trigger attacks, but she'd gone along to keep Geum happy. A small price to pay when she had only one friend.

Together forever.

"There it is!" she said aloud, because the silence that had been her friend for so long, the voiceless waiting of a sniper, felt like a jailer. She'd spotted the promised capsule. She didn't know what trickery Geum had had to pull, what risks zie had taken. But she was going to make it count.

Destroy the threat! Winter's Axiom insisted suddenly, flooding her mind with aggression.

Hwa Young couldn't see anything except the capsule's trajectory, drifting in her direction. The effect was more extreme than her usual battle-focus tunnel vision, where everything narrowed to her and her target. It was as if nothing existed but the "threat" and the imperative to obliterate it.

Don't be ridiculous, Hwa Young protested, alarmed by the lancer's baffling antagonism. Sometimes she wondered how much the lancers understood of human factions and politics. After all this time trying to reprogram its interface to display accurate IFF tags, was it now ready to destroy anything that came from Eleventh Fleet regardless of context?

Had Geum been tricked into sending something that would hurt her? She didn't think that was possible. Zie would have checked and warned her.

Destroy the threat.

"No," Hwa Young said, her jaw clenched.

Winter's Axiom moved—*against her will.* The sniper rifle tracked the incoming capsule, leading the target with a machine's accuracy. Hwa Young's experience told her that the shot would go true to its target.

"What the hell?" Hwa Young yelled. Her voice reverberated painfully in the cockpit's confined space. "Stand down!"

The rifle shuddered . . . then froze.

They weren't out of danger. Hwa Young forced the lancer's map in her head wider, zooming out so she could "see" Eleventh Fleet lurking in the distance. Some of the scouts nosed in her direction on their patrol sweep.

If the scouts approached any more closely, they'd spot her. She didn't want to trigger a premature battle between the clanner and Imperial fleets, both wounded, neither with an obvious advantage: the worst kind of fight.

Dread choked her at the prospect of fighting the *Maehwa* while Geum remained on it. She didn't want to be put in that position, especially if the shields were still unreliable.

"Retrieval, dammit," Hwa Young snarled.

They had Eleventh Fleet scouts incoming, she needed to retrieve the capsule, and her lancer refused to cooperate. Hwa Young had an unpleasant insight into what it felt like to be *her* commanding officer, given her track record for "independent action" (charitable phrasing, Ye Jun) or "going off the scorching rails" (less charitable, Eun).

I intervened at Abalone Observatory for a good reason, Hwa Young told herself. Whereas she couldn't discern any reason for her lancer's obstinacy now.

She reached out over the link, and found only icicle conviction: *Threat. Destroy the threat.* The lancer made no more jokes (if they'd been jokes) about trophies and bones. Its sole concern had narrowed to pinpoint destruction.

It's not! Hwa Young insisted, shivering uncontrollably. She'd never previously suffered temperature issues in her lancer, short of cracked armor. *Stand down! We have our orders. Our mission.* Would it respond to that? Acknowledge the primacy of the squad and its objectives? *Work with me, dammit.*

What if her own lancer, which she'd sacrificed everything for, turned on her?

Winter's Axiom yielded after harrowing moments of standoff. There was no softness. It felt instead like snow, the kind that stung one's skin and pierced one with barbs of diamantine light. *Winter's Axiom* gave way because it had no choice, not because it agreed with her, and that upset her.

Hwa Young took over the controls. At least she didn't have to pilot on manual.

The lancer became once more an extension of her own body, its limbs moving like her own, its levitators propelling her smoothly through the aether currents. The swirls and eddies tickled, phantom sensations caressing her skin, both refreshing and risky. Her face ached, and the smell of the mask had turned cloying; the suit's filters were failing to cope. But she couldn't change it right now, despite the medic's admonitions. She had priorities.

With a delicacy of touch that would have been impossible using manual controls, Hwa Young matched course with the capsule. Pale blue light from her lancer glinted off the shiny metal surface: the minimum illumination needed to do her job, too dim for the scouts to detect at their current distance.

The lancer reached out and grasped the capsule without crushing it. Normally Hwa Young wouldn't fret about her control, but with *Winter's Axiom* behaving erratically, she had newfound doubts. Sweat drenched her back and dripped down her neck and spine. Her suit clung unpleasantly to her skin, as though she were enveloped by a hungry parasite.

Hwa Young opened the cockpit. The lancer's massive hand brought the capsule up to her eye level. The hand closed into a fist. It hadn't crushed the capsule—yet. But it could with the merest application of pressure, and before she could react. An implicit threat.

For the first time since she'd bonded with *Winter's Axiom*, Hwa Young thought, *My own lancer could flatten me. No one's here to intervene.* One blink, one wrong movement, and she'd be paste.

She stared at the fist, which dwarfed her. When had this happened? She hadn't willed *Winter's Axiom* to form a fist. Just to grasp the capsule delicately, like a petal, with a heart's worth of bruising.

Give me the capsule.

Hwa Young didn't always think explicit verbal commands at *Winter's Axiom,* at least for routine motions. The point of the neural link was that thought became action in a much more intuitive fashion, especially during combat.

What if she didn't live to deliver the capsule? Commander Ye Jun would be stuck retrieving it, and maybe her carcass as well.

She'd seen too much of space, the way its immensity defied human compass. Like many spacers, she'd accreted a horror of dying by drifting into infinity, instead of a cleaner death in battle, even if the "cleaner" part was as mythical as snakes. As for proper funerals, no one had gotten one on the *Maehwa* while she'd served aboard it. She didn't expect one from Falcon Fleet either.

Winter's Axiom might be no *Avalanche,* but that was in relative terms. When it came to squishing small, fragile human beings, there was no practical difference. Having *any* lancer pummel a human would result in gruesome meat goo.

If you're going to do it, do it now and get it over with, Hwa Young thought, straightening in defiance. If this had been a human confrontation, she would have stared the interloper in the eye in a blatant challenge. Here, the scale was so radically different that this was impossible even if she hadn't been *inside* the cockpit.

At least *Winter's Axiom* hadn't ejected her. Unless it was saving that for its next move.

The lancer's response was puzzled and faintly hurt, not an emotion she associated with it. *I am doing this to protect you. You are mine to protect. We should destroy the threat so you are not hurt.*

Not *us. You.*

The capsule didn't pose a *physical* threat to a lancer. Hwa

Young wasn't aware of a bomb this size that could damage it. Geum wasn't a demolitions expert, or hadn't been when she'd last spent time with zir.

Geum would have warned me.

It's a threat, Winter's Axiom repeated. *Destroy the threat. I will not have you hurt.*

Its protectiveness would have gladdened her if not for the inconvenient timing.

Is there a bug? she asked. Something *Farseer* or *Bastard* would have been in a better position to ascertain. She doubted Eleventh Fleet would employ anything obvious; had assumed there would be at least one, which her superiors would locate and dispose of, or use to feed false intelligence to the other side. But she had to make the call: Trust Geum, or trust her lancer?

Hwa Young didn't want to antagonize *Winter's Axiom*. A sentience she shared her *mind* with. Perhaps the solution was not to butt heads with it, but to persuade it to go along with her. She wanted a long and fruitful partnership, after all.

Listen to me. Hwa Young willed the lancer to open itself to her. To understand that she was doing this for both of them, in service of a larger strategy, just as it cared about protecting her. To understand that she wasn't overriding its judgment out of whimsy or willfulness.

In response, *Winter's Axiom* pulled her into its inner world, its winterscape. Hwa Young saw herself as a small figure, straight-backed, identifiable by the brilliant white streak in her black hair (cut short, she noticed, no wig), and a New Joseon uniform in navy blue. Light came from everywhere and nowhere, beneath a sky of turbulent grays and luminous bruised violets and moons crowding close in chaotic orbits, over glittering snow. Cold, if she was human enough to be troubled by mere matters of temperature.

Hwa Young didn't see the lancer as such. North, south, east, west. Up and down. Where was it?

Then she understood. She'd been looking in the wrong place all along, expecting a human or machine avatar as though she'd entered one of Geum's videogames. The lancer's representation was the *entire winter landscape,* vaster than vast. It was right there in its name. She'd missed the obvious all this time.

I've known Geum since we were kids, Hwa Young told *Winter's Axiom,* schooling herself to patience.

We are one and always, Winter's Axiom affirmed. *What I want is what you want.*

Geum is my friend. Zie wouldn't knowingly put us in harm's way. In response to the lancer's immediate, chilly skepticism, Hwa Young added, *I can warn my commander there might be a bug.*

Commander Aera had pulled that trick on them when they'd been on opposite sides. The clanners would be alert to the possibility. The caution was justified, given the hostilities.

The winter softened. Hwa Young had no other word for it. The white of the fallen snow and the clouds became less glaring, less stark. The wind that whipped through her hair dwindled to a murmur. Even the moons had a diffuse glow, more distant, less of an implicit threat of collision.

In the outside world, the lancer's hand gently came forward, bringing the capsule within Hwa Young's reach. "Thank you," Hwa Young said, grimacing as the healing mask's gels sloshed in response to the movements of her mouth and jaw. Her voice sounded hollow inside her helmet. She echoed the words over the link to *Winter's Axiom*, reinforcing her expression of gratitude.

The hand withdrew. The cockpit closed in anticipation of her wishes, resuming the smooth partnership she'd taken for granted in the past. She would always wonder, from now on, how much she could ask of *Winter's Axiom*, how far she could bend it to her will.

Hwa Young unclenched her fingers from around the capsule, grateful for the suit's gloves. The capsule was bigger than she'd anticipated. Size was relative: a speck from a lancer's viewpoint could be the size of her torso, as in this case. The item felt surprisingly light, in part because she was still at half gravity within the cockpit to save on reserves, although she knew that handling high-mass objects could prove tricky because of the inertia involved.

She slumped in relief. Her argument with *Winter's Axiom* had resulted in tensed-up muscles everywhere, as though bracing for a blow. The suit struggled to neutralize the sourness of her sweat, the unavoidable odors coming from the mask. She imagined putrid vines and their tendrils worming their way past the healing surface skin and burrowing into subcutaneous fat, leaves growing out of her face until nothing remained of her but a vegetative façade.

Internal atmosphere normalized, Winter's Axiom said, its version of a peace offering.

She smiled and offered it her gratitude, even if she kept her helmet on. More than anything she wanted to remove the helmet, but she'd better not. Especially after almost dying in her first battle against the clanners and having to be rescued by Commander Ye Jun. She'd learned her lesson.

Hwa Young examined the capsule, then opened it, in the interests of thoroughness. There was a note on the inside, affixed with a tumultuously glittery masking tape. *THINKING OF YOU.* No signature, but she'd know Geum's exuberant handwriting anywhere. Her eyes welled with tears. Nothing else in the capsule looked suspicious either. She liberated the note, figuring that was harmless enough, since she didn't want to trigger another argument with Commander Aera about friends and priorities.

Hwa Young tipped her head back, exhaled long and slow. *I'll bring you something wonderful next time we see each other, Geum.*

Hwa Young secured the capsule in the copilot's seat. "Thank you," she repeated.

She could stand to remember that *Winter's Axiom* had a sentience of its own, however alien. That it appreciated the occasional "please" or "thank you" the way a human would. She'd have to keep that in mind, think of other tokens of gratitude that it would appreciate, although she drew the line at building it an ossuary.

Time to toggle on the comms. "Axiom to Falcon Command," Hwa Young said. "Objective acquired. There may be eyes on me." No point in being more specific, even over an encrypted channel. One never knew, according to Aera and Ye Jun, when the cryptographers on either side were going to make a breakthrough. "Calling to request rendezvous. I repeat, this is Axiom to Falcon Command..."

Don't borrow trouble. But the nagging worry persisted. Her gut clenched. What she needed right now: cramps.

"Axiom to Falcon Command." Hwa Young repeated the call. She could have played a recording, but she didn't want to leave one running. Besides, it mattered that it was her reaching out and not a recording, that someone would reply, that the reply would come from a person and not a machine with a ghost's voice.

Finally the answer reached her: "Falcon Command to Axiom. Proceed according to the following path."

Not just coordinates, for what good they did, but a transmission with a marked path and designated waypoints. Someday she'd figure out how *anyone* navigated amid the Moonstorm's unstable features, where the Empire's techniques of celestial navigation failed. For now, it was enough to return to Falcon Fleet.

Hwa Young's lips pulled back in a grin. "Roger that, Falcon Command."

Time to bring her prize home.

22

HWA YOUNG

Hwa Young fantasized about burrowing into her bunk after returning with the capsule and handing it off. Instead, she took comfort in the note, which she'd shoved inside the lid of a canteen, a precious memento of Geum. She'd also retrieved the last snack from the care package, just because. Once she delivered the capsule, she could enjoy it. It was the right time for it.

Soon, Geum. Soon.

She would have felt easier retrieving the capsule with the rest of the squad for company. Had known better than to ask, after all the missions she'd flown. She wasn't green anymore: bringing the others along would have put Eleventh Fleet on high alert, the last thing her superiors wanted. The last thing *she* wanted.

Instead, the other three had lurked far out of Eleventh Fleet's scan range. They, too, must have found the separation agonizing, knowing that they might not be able to respond quickly enough if she ran into trouble. She'd called in, assured them she was safe—but it was war, and no amount of *safe* lasted forever.

Falcon Actual awaited her. The other lancers had already landed. Hwa Young took comfort in the bland gray shapes, the painted emblems: the upside-down antler crown of Ye Jun's *Bastard*, the flame of Eun's *Hellion*.

Hwa Young guided *Winter's Axiom* in, grateful that she and her lancer were back on speaking terms.

Winter's Axiom settled on the deck: one of her better landings, although no one was evaluating her. She exited the cockpit and descended via the lift, cradling the capsule. Falling from the lancer's lift and breaking her neck would be a stupid way to go.

Hwa Young longed for a shower. She reeked. Story of her life. The incongruous fragrance of starblooms that swirled through the air, that wafted up from under her shirt where she'd tucked Rose-Merline's charm, came as a comfort.

Commander Ye Jun smiled at her, the smallest quirk of the lips, but the reassurance touched her.

Eun was scowling. Still, he gave Hwa Young a sharp nod of acknowledgment. "Good job out there," he said.

Hwa Young blinked, taken aback. Behind the grumpy expression she saw what he would not say aloud: that he had been afraid for her. Perhaps they were all afraid for each other. "I was taught by the best," she said, because that was the closest either of them could come to acknowledging the sentiment.

He laughed wryly. "You don't need to tell *me* that."

Commander Aera stepped forward. "You haven't changed the healing mask, Pilot," she said, chiding.

Hwa Young caught her shoulders creeping upward defensively,

as though she had been caught sneaking an extra honey cookie, then forced them to relax. "I wanted to report in first."

The commander wasn't wrong. The mask itched. The smell had gone bitter and pungent. Maybe everyone else could smell it too. Hwa Young wasn't sure how much was the concern of a heart-mother and how much was the purview of a commanding officer. Still, the expression of concern ignited an answering warmth in her heart.

I've been too paranoid about Aera. Her past suspicions regarding the saboteur melted away in the glow of knowing that her heart-mother cared about her. Someday—not now, but someday—Hwa Young could confess her fevered imaginings. They'd laugh about it together.

"You got my warning, sir?" Hwa Young asked.

"I did," Aera said. "I appreciate your diligence. If there's a virus in the files, or a bug in the physical apparatus, or anything of that nature, we'll find it."

Hwa Young nodded. A tide of ambivalence engulfed her. If only she'd *told* Geum how much she appreciated zir hacker skills. She could use a computer or a neural interface, but when zie started talking about anything advanced, it went over her head.

She hadn't shown *Winter's Axiom* enough appreciation, and look how she'd paid for it. While she wasn't sure that the lancer's recalcitrance had been based on recognizably human emotional responses, Geum was very definitely human. How many times had she relied on Geum to save her tail, secure in the knowledge that zie would always be there for her? Accepted the thoughtful care packages, the invitations to play videogames?

Together forever, Hwa Young thought. Soon she'd be able to tell Geum how grateful she was. Apologize for her lack of social graces. They could laugh about that, too. She needed to prepare the *best* welcoming gift for Geum.

Commander Aera made a gesture, and an ensign scuttled toward her. "You there. Take this to Intelligence for analysis."

"Sir." The ensign looked deeply unhappy about having attracted Aera's attention.

It's nothing, Hwa Young told herself, despite her unease at the ensign's air of fear. *You're imagining things again. Let it go.*

Aera turned back to Hwa Young. "Pilot, get that mask changed, and go rest. You've earned it." Her eyes softened. "Perhaps we could catch up afterward? Have tea together? I sourced some honey crisps that are almost like the ones you loved so much during festivals."

Hwa Young started to protest that she felt fine. But the backwash of adrenaline, not just from the mission but from her quarrel with *Winter's Axiom,* wore off, leaving her weak-kneed and wobbly. Limping away would make Aera question her fitness for duty. Nor did she want to rebuff her heart-mother's overture, even implicitly, whatever doubts she might have entertained about Aera's intentions in the past. "Understood. And yes—yes, I'd like that."

Aera strode away to snap orders to some technicians.

Ye Jun said, after Aera was out of earshot, "Get some rest, all right?"

Hwa Young wasn't going to let the commander leave it at that. "What about Bae? How is he?"

The commander eyed her sidelong. "I would like you to check on Bae. He's been asking after you." As zie spoke, Ye Jun signed, "I'm too closely watched, but you might have better luck."

Hwa Young almost broke into a sprint without asking to be

dismissed. She vibrated with the desire to *do something*. "You were with him?"

"Not as such. But I received word from Ensign Rose-Merline. She stopped by on your behalf, thought you'd want to know. We had an interesting chat." Ye Jun smiled crookedly. "I told her I wanted to know about anyone who'd caught your attention. As I said, having a friendly *cryptobotanist* under my nose . . ."

Hwa Young flushed, wondering about the odd bemused undertone. Did Ye Jun hope she and Rose-Merline would start a fernery together? A side business in bunjae or bonsai to raise funds for glow-in-the-dark lancer ornaments? She wished the commander would come out and *say* what zir interest was, because she doubted it had anything to do with dynastic planning.

"Understood, sir," she said. She might not be carrying germs, but she didn't want to stink up Zeng's lab. Everyone on the ship would lecture her if she didn't change the healing mask as Commander Aera had instructed.

"Dismissed."

Don't sprint. Don't sprint. If only she could teleport through the walls as easily as an electron, newly energized, leaping to some ambitious higher atomic orbit.

Urgency warred with decorum. Decorum won. What if *this* was the day that Bae woke and was able to return to duty? He might rouse the moment she walked in. She wanted her appearance to meet Bae's exacting standards, even if the mask made her resemble a slime monster and she'd never replaced the wig.

So she headed for the pilots' cabin and took a sonic shower. For once she didn't resent the hum that used to set her teeth on edge. It got her clean; that was what mattered. She would have welcomed Bae waking long enough to make a joke about her low-class choice of "perfume."

To fortify herself before setting out, Hwa Young smoothed Geum's note and read it again, as though she could take nourishment from the glitter tape she'd carefully unpeeled, vitamins of luminosity and cheer. Geum would be weirded out, given zir long-running enmity toward Bae.

When we're together again, I can explain.

Hwa Young's stomach grumbled. *What the hell.* She pulled out the last snack from Geum's earlier care package, the one before their separation that had exploded in confetti.

The snack wouldn't have occasioned comment back on Serpentine. However, Hwa Young had learned how difficult it was to vary one's diet on a starship with resupply problems. Geum had missed zir calling as a quartermaster or black marketeer. Zie had sourced a packet of limited edition white-chocolate-dipped biscuits topped with cherry blossom sugar sprinkles. Hwa Young would once have found the concept (a) excessively pink and (b) horrifying. She liked sweets, but *pink*?

Yet Geum had picked the biscuits out for her, likely at some trouble. In her turn, she'd saved them for last, not wanting to lose her last memento from her best friend.

I have a new memento now.

"Here's to a new start," Hwa Young said aloud, not caring if anyone was listening. Then she opened the package neatly, smiling dubiously at the glittering pink sprinkles, and tried one of the biscuits. It really did taste like candied petals.

She saved the rest to offer to Bae. Her experience of being an invalid was that food with flavor was one of the world's greatest gifts. Whether Bae appreciated flavor in the form of pink, petal-flavored crystals remained to be seen.

The expired healing mask clung unpleasantly to her skin. Her face stung when she peeled it off. A quick check in the mirror suggested that the skin was healing, although the uneven pink looked ghastly, in stark contrast to the biscuits. No flowers or leaves sprouted from her skin. Geum's taste for horror must have rubbed off on her: she was almost disappointed. She eyed her reflection, unable to make herself meet her mirror-self's gaze head-on.

I don't look like Aera with this on. Was that good or bad?

Hwa Young applied the new mask with mirthless diligence. Pulled on her uniform, checked her collar, and rubbed out a scuff on her boots as if she expected an inspection. She fussed with her hair before the realization struck her: *I'm primping*.

She flushed and stopped. Thank goodness for the mask, because the new pink skin would make blushing more obvious than ever. She made herself tuck the comb away and leave the cabin.

In Hwa Young's imagination, she swept confidently into the lab and arrowed to Bae's bed. In real life, the walk winded her. She kept in good shape—they all did—but quarreling with *Winter's Axiom*, plus the stresses of recent events, had drained her.

Halfway there, a wave of dizziness overtook her. She caught herself against the nearest bulkhead. *I have to do this.* She pulled herself upright and kept going, panting with the effort.

A guard intercepted her at the entrance. "Pilot Hwajin," she said, with an inexplicable wariness. The same guard who'd begged for Zeng's cookies, but with a woman's long hair today—a wig, probably.

"I'm here to check in on Bae," Hwa Young said, and remembered to add, "please."

"I'm not sure he's doing well. Maybe you want to come back later?" There was a definite plea in the woman's voice. Odd.

That stiffened her resolve. "No, I need to see him now." She'd allowed the guards to put her off too many times as it stood.

The guard hesitated. "I don't think that's the best—"

The doors opened, and the guard gnawed on her lower lip.

"Send her in," Zeng called from within.

Hwa Young strode past the guard. She looked past Zeng, who had come forward to greet her. No sign of Bae or his pallet. "What—"

Zeng shook his head sharply, then glanced significantly at the guard. His warning was comically obvious. The guard grinned nervously. *She* didn't look happy to be part of this charade, either, whatever it signified.

What's going on? Despite her impatience and increasing alarm, Hwa Young waited until the doors had swept closed, leaving the guard on the other side. "Bae. Now," she ground out.

"Come with me," Zeng said. His voice was soft and strained, nervous. His elaborate clothes and hairdo contrasted with the lines at the corners of his eyes. Nor did Hwa Young recognize today's cologne, with its funereal notes of cedar and incense smoke.

Hwa Young nodded, lips clamped tight, because snarling wouldn't help.

Here, as everywhere, starblooms scented the air. Suddenly, Hwa Young longed for the sweetness of maehwa blossoms, plum-sweet. She wondered if she'd ever smell them again.

They'd relocated Bae to a different room within the laboratory section. Hwa Young almost didn't recognize the pallet or the figure lying upon it, cradled among translucent, fat-leaved vines and their pulsing flowers.

Clanner healing, Hwa Young remembered. Better than the alleged snail slime that suffused her mask, right? The flowers should have reminded her, pleasantly, of starblooms growing wild on Carnelian, the cultivated gardens on Serpentine . . . of Rose-Merline and her mysterious cryptobotanical duties. Hwa Young recoiled, then scolded herself for the reaction.

Someone had dressed Bae in a flimsy shift. He'd kicked off an equally flimsy blanket, which lay half-fallen to the deck. Any breath of disturbance and it would complete its journey.

She squinted, trying to assess his condition. Had he lost muscle mass? Was he too thin? Or was she simply unaccustomed to his new physique? The entangling vines made it difficult to tell.

Determined to prove that she could overcome her Imperial prejudices about clanner biotechnology, Hwa Young reached toward Bae. Before Zeng could stop her, she stroked one of the stems, wondering why she'd never seen a vine of this type before. A stinging sensation greeted her fingertips, followed by numbness. The glancing contact sent a pleasant wave of lassitude through her body. But it could have been her imagination, or more exhaustion.

Zeng caught her hand a moment too late. "Don't," he said. He was smiling, but the smile, too, was strained. "They're sensitive to touch, and they adapt to environmental feedback. This one was specifically modified for Bae."

Nice use of a passive construction. Who did the modifying, I wonder?

As Zeng spoke, he nodded toward a corner of the room.

Great. Someone who sucks at acting as much as I do. That didn't look suspicious at all. Hwa Young swept the room with her gaze, not lingering on that corner. If there was a camera or other bug, it would be too small for her to spot it anyway. "I want to talk to Bae alone."

"You didn't answer my message requests."

She froze. "Message requests?" She reached for her neural implant before remembering that it did her no good here. Checked the log through her badge access.

Nothing.

Zeng stared at her, his mouth working. Then: "I thought that Eun had told you not to respond."

She could guess. "You tried Eun, and he didn't respond either."

"I thought he was angry." Zeng's mouth crimped. "I can't . . . I can't say I blame him." He hesitated, as though there was more he wanted to say.

"Must have been a glitch," Hwa Young said weakly.

She didn't believe that for one second. Eun *might* have been too pissed to answer, but she hadn't received the messages in the first place. And she hadn't thought to message Zeng herself. If she had, would *those* have gone through?

"Say . . . do you want some tea first?"

Hwa Young almost said no. *Tea? Why would I care about tea right now?* But Zeng desperately wanted to communicate something to her. It might be in her best interests—*Bae's* best interests— for her to figure out what it was. She gave him a stiff nod.

We both need remedial spy lessons.

Zeng disappeared, then returned with tea on a tray for both of them.

Hwa Young lifted her cup—cold, which suggested the tea

was too—and spotted a slip of paper beneath it. An absurd subterfuge.

PILOT COMMS ARE MONITORED ABOARD SHIP, said the paper, in tiny florid calligraphy of a style she didn't recognize.

Didn't that include her as well? That made no sense. She turned the paper over in response to a small, encouraging noise from Zeng.

I SPOOFED AERA'S CREDENTIALS TO TALK TO YOU.

Hwa Young's head rose and she stared at him. She mouthed, *Why didn't you find me* earlier? While she couldn't disassemble him into his constituent atoms with a stare, she was going to *learn.*

"Actually, you're right," Zeng said with forced cheer. He grabbed a lab notebook and scribbled in it. "You should have some time with Bae alone, what was I thinking?"

It took Hwa Young several tries to read Zeng's crabbed handwriting:

THE TREATMENT DID HEAL BAE—AT FIRST. SWITCHED TO SEDATION THE LAST COUPLE DAYS BEFORE TAPERING OFF THE DOSE. BAE SHOULD ROUSE SOON. DIDN'T WANT TO DISTRACT YOU FROM MISSION.

And, not that it excused anything: *HAD ORDERS.*

Hwa Young heard herself snarling. Finger by finger she relaxed the hands that had clenched on the table's edge, as though she could claw back the last several days, rescue Bae *before* this happened.

She grabbed the pencil. *WHY?*

Zeng choked back a sob. She had no room in her for pity or

mercy, and she stabbed him with her stare. If he didn't give her a satisfactory answer, she'd escalate to the pencil.

After several moments, he whispered, "My heart-brother Tora's gone. Permanently. It wasn't the socks."

Hwa Young took this as oblique confirmation that the saboteur had been Tora after all. Did Zeng blame Aera for dealing with the matter? Aera's combat reflexes were unfortunate, and Hwa Young had objected at the time, but in the heat of the moment—

"Go," Zeng said. He passed out of the room, taking the tea tray with him, shoulders bowed.

Hwa Young hoped he'd have the sense to dispose of the incriminating notes. A researcher must possess a handy source of acid or fire. She pasted on the polite smile she'd learned to perform during her years in New Joseon before remembering that the mask obscured any facial contortions.

She knelt at the side of the pallet, still shaking in rage, willing herself to calm down so she didn't alarm Bae. How "soon" was "should rouse soon"?

"Bae," Hwa Young said, softly at first. She didn't want Zeng to overhear her, which was ridiculous because he had let her in. More loudly: "Bae."

Bae had always possessed enviable elegant features. The yangban nobles in New Joseon all bred for aesthetics. Bae came from one of the most powerful clans on Serpentine. Back then he'd never let anyone forget that. Being a clone was all very well, but wouldn't it be nice to be a clone of someone *devastatingly beautiful*?

Devastatingly beautiful only protected one's looks so much.

His face had healed, as Zeng had promised, leaving no marks or scars, but Bae's visage was still: the unnatural repose of an ice sculpture, or porcelain lying unused under a layer of dust. His cheeks were hollow, throwing the fine bones of his face into sharp relief. Beautiful in the way of entropy, the beauty of the shrouded dead.

Hwa Young cupped Bae's chin, something she would never have dared to do while he was awake. "Bae, please. Talk to me."

Bae's eyelids fluttered open. Hwa Young was struck by how long and thick his eyelashes were, the dark sweep of them. His eyes were brown, not the luminous starlit violet they became when he was connected to *Farseer*. His clouded expression worried her, as though he couldn't focus on her, or wasn't aware of her presence.

"Researcher Zeng said you'd recovered." Physically, anyway. Hwa Young paused. What would anchor Bae in the present? "I just flew a mission. It was a success—"

The pupils of Bae's eyes contracted to pinpoints. "*Farseer.*"

Hwa Young had to lean close to catch the word. The threadiness of Bae's voice started a pang in her chest. "We've missed you," she said. "Rose-Merline asked after you too. Uh—she's an ensign. My girlfriend."

This was the worst possible time to mention her relationship with Rose-Merline, but Hwa Young couldn't stop herself. Couldn't think of the right thing to say, or even the wrong ones.

I missed you.

"You're awake," she added.

Bae's head lolled sideways. His eyes squeezed shut.

Hwa Young wriggled the fingers she'd touched the vine with earlier. The numbness remained.

Zeng had left disposable laboratory gloves on a nearby bench, prominently visible. *Thanks for the hint.* Hwa Young pulled them on as a precaution.

In retrospect, she wished that she'd quizzed Zeng about the vines' effects—and aftereffects. Would removing them hurt Bae? The thought of condemning him to unnecessary pain made her wither inside.

Experimentally, she yanked on one. It came free, wriggling like a demon snake from the stories. But Bae didn't seem to be harmed: a good sign.

After a deep breath, she ripped the rest of the vines off Bae. They resisted her. She crushed them with hysterical ferocity now that she had a *target* for her fury, shaking again, hands squeezing spasmodically. She'd always been strong. Right now she was fueled by grief and rage and—

This isn't about me. It's about Bae.

How much time did she have? Zeng was covering for her, but that didn't mean she shouldn't hurry.

The vines struggled harder. Hwa Young's hands convulsed into fists. She tore the last vines clear of Bae's skin. Astringent-smelling green pulp dripped from her gloves.

How long had Bae been entangled in the vines? If she'd known earlier that Zeng was trying to reach her—that he had information about Bae—

Who prevented his messages from reaching me, or Eun, or Commander Ye Jun?

More importantly, *why* had the clanners sedated Bae?

There was one answer that made sense. Hwa Young wasn't ready to face it. She focused first on rescuing Bae, all the while aware, sick at heart, that sooner or later she'd have to confront the dreadful truth.

Bae's porcelain-pale skin was streaked with viscous green slime. Hwa Young grabbed some wipes, also considerately placed in easy reach, and scrubbed at the slime. She might forgive Zeng for his part in this after all. *Wake up,* she wished Bae.

If it took a week for whatever drug to leave his system, that would complicate the logistics of getting him out of here. She had no intention of leaving him unattended while she summoned help.

Paranoia overtook her. If they'd done this to Bae under the guise of "medicine," what was in her *mask*? Especially since both Aera and the medic had been so insistent on it?

Had Rose-Merline known? Did her job involve designing or nurturing plants that incapacitated people? If she'd been involved—if Hwa Young had let her own feelings trick her like this—

Hwa Young yanked the mask off and flung it to the deck. A gasp escaped her at the resurgence of pain. Hwa Young clamped her lips tight: she didn't want to *ingest* the "bioengineered snail slime."

She stomped on the mask. It squelched satisfyingly beneath her heels. If she had decorative burn scars for the rest of her life, so be it.

A slithering sound came from the deck. The vines were *regenerating*. Their tendrils quested in Bae's direction as though they sensed him. If not for the gross green stains on the sheets and blankets, plus the puddles of slime on the deck, she wouldn't have been able to tell they'd taken any damage.

Why did it surprise her? If vines could heal *people,* why shouldn't they be able to heal *themselves*?

"*Farseer*'s gone," Bae murmured through a choked-back sob. While his voice was husky with poorly masked emotion, he enunciated clearly, with no trace of slurring. The detached part of Hwa Young that cared about logistics and planning noted this: a promising prognosis, suggesting that with the vines removed, he might recover more quickly than she'd dared hope.

Hwa Young looked at Bae, really looked. What she had mistaken for hazy unfocus in his eyes was something else: loss. An attempt to escape unbearable pain.

"There's nothing," Bae said. "I reach out and there's nothing on the other side." He lifted a hand, trembling at first, then with increasing steadiness. His fingers hooked into claws. "It's empty. *Farseer* should be there and it's empty."

23

HWA YOUNG

"No, no, no," Hwa Young choked out, her throat closing in horror. *Farseer* couldn't be—gone. Destroyed. She tried to imagine what would become of her if something happened to *Winter's Axiom;* couldn't.

Hwa Young grabbed Bae's wrists and forced them down until his hands relaxed. "That can't be right," she said, more to soothe Bae than out of any real conviction. "I'll retrieve *Farseer*. I'll fix this."

Hwa Young debated whether to spend more time cleaning up or battling the horrible vines. This was like getting trapped in one of Geum's games, except with a videogame, one didn't have to smell dripping slime. She compromised by removing the gloves, then cramming them and the wipes into the disposal. It wasn't as if she could cover her tracks.

Hwa Young took Bae's limp hand in her own and pressed a

kiss to it, feeling disloyal to Rose-Merline as she did so. Maybe later she'd find out if the three of them could be together. Right now, she had to deal with the problem of Bae's lancer.

"I'll fix this," Hwa Young swore again, as if repeating the words could make them come true. Once more she squeezed Bae's hand.

If this had been a regular storage facility, Hwa Young would have started a fire as a distraction. But in a laboratory that might house unknown chemicals? She didn't want to set off an explosion or fill the place with toxic fumes or release killer mutant vines.

Before that last mission, the technician had claimed *Farseer* was here. She didn't know if damaged lancers could explode thanks to nearby fire. Bae would never forgive her if she found out empirically. Hell, she'd never forgive herself.

Hwa Young narrowed her eyes at the doors that led farther into the laboratory. The maps had obfuscated that information, a reasonable security precaution. She should have asked *Eun* if he'd ever seen the rest of the area.

How could she force the doors? A quick scan of the area revealed no convenient blowtorches or laser cutters. She vented her frustrations on the door, slamming it with her hand.

The door opened so suddenly she fell through and banged her knee on the deck.

Well, that was too easy. No wonder technicians run around hitting machines to "fix" them.

Hwa Young looked up. She'd landed inside a workshop full of equipment, half the size of a docking bay. She had envisioned a glorified tool shed. This immense space, however, could have accommodated four lancers, and that wasn't counting the space already occupied by machines: matter printers, milling machines, and lathes, which she knew about thanks to Geum, and others that remained mysterious to her.

No vines, at least. She was never again going to be able to look at a vine without wanting to defoliate it.

The workshop contained an unfamiliar lancer, which dominated the space. But where was *Farseer*?

Hwa Young shivered violently, as though someone had driven icicle needles into her skin, rather than the sheltering chill she associated with *Winter's Axiom*.

The unfamiliar lancer stood in its inert state, like an incomplete statue. The whole unit repelled her. It made her skin feel like it had been invaded by biting worms. She'd never previously reacted so intensely, so negatively, to a lancer.

Besides the crawling sensation, the lancer's gray surface was mazed by a shifting blotchy texture, rather than polished smoothness. Its appearance reminded Hwa Young of the galloping acne she'd suffered when she turned thirteen.

Hwa Young had never witnessed a lancer's manufacture. Their construction was a state secret, taking place at special factories whose location no student would be trusted with. Even Geum hadn't unearthed that intel for Commander Aera.

Maybe the blotchiness was normal. Maybe *Winter's Axiom* had once looked like this, *felt* like this, before the final polishing steps in its creation. An image of an industrious team of technicians swarming over every square centimeter with jeweler's rouge and different grades of emery paper presented itself to her. She emitted a hysterical noise, which she choked back.

Above all, she wanted to destroy the *thing*. Couldn't stop regarding it as a *thing*.

It is not like us, Winter's Axiom agreed. She didn't know whether that made her feel better or worse.

The second lancer—

Hwa Young inhaled in shock when she recognized the second lancer. Or more precisely, a former lancer, now disassembled. *Vivisection,* as Zeng called it.

A memory rose before her: the first time Mother Aera called her into the kitchen to help skin and dress a moon-rabbit for dinner. The mess of red and white, the neatly peeled-back integument and glistening membranes and spongy marrow and blood, didn't have anything in common with the moon-rabbits she had glimpsed diffusely through her window, with their nervous movements and shimmering shapes; or, for that matter, with the silky softness of their white fur under her fingers, the few times she'd lured one close enough to touch before they hopped away.

Only after she'd helped butcher several more moon-rabbits, with Aera or another adult supervising, did she see how the anatomy jigsawed into the creatures that her family hunted. From there she thought about how people, too, disintegrated into jigsaw pieces. She stayed up at night when the star-showers came and gentle light flickered through the rutilated quartz windows, plucking at her forearms until she reached the boundaries of pain and wondering what she would see if her skin were transparent.

Then she'd learned what dead people looked like, inside and out, not something she could *un*learn.

"That's *Farseer*," Hwa Young said thinly.

It was, her lancer said.

Past tense.

She gagged. This time the revulsion wasn't because of the mutilated lancer's alienness. She imagined the same happening to *her* lancer. It could have been *Winter's Axiom*. What would it do to her to have that bond amputated, leaving nothing but a residue of remembered ice and glory?

If *looking* at the remnants of a lancer that wasn't her own affected her like this, how had Bae survived?

Hwa Young stalked back out. Zeng hunched over his tea as though he read portents of interference in the ripples. She didn't realize until the squeak emerged from his mouth, the shattering of the dropped teacup, that she'd seized him by the shoulders and hauled him up. "You. You are going to fix this," she hissed.

"I had orders," Zeng gasped, his eyes wide and panicky. "The Empire has used lancers to erode our borders, they said. Falcon Command said we needed our own to survive. That was what you offered us when you defected, wasn't it? Lancer technology?"

Hwa Young's grip tightened. Zeng stifled a sob. "'They said'? *Who* said?"

"Aera. It was Aera. She was the one who sent Tora to—to do what he did. He thought he'd be boasting of the deed in her bed. Earn her favor. And then she—then she—"

Hwa Young thought, distantly, *Eun will never forgive me if I strangle Zeng.* And: *If Eun was going to do it, he'd want to do it himself.*

Zeng had come clean. Tried to contact her. *Helped* her once she arrived. It didn't sound like he was acting out of raging loyalty to Aera; quite the opposite.

Who had acted out of raging loyalty to Aera all this time? Cozied up to her? Refused to see that the heart-mother she'd clung to in childhood was no longer someone she could rely on?

The last time she'd felt this sick, Hwa Young had been bent over the toilet all night because she'd eaten the wrong mushroom.

Tora's shitty life choices weren't Zeng's fault. He was trying to make amends for his heart-brother.

It was her turn now—to make amends for her heart-mother, and what she'd stood by and allowed her heart-mother to do.

She relaxed her fingers one by one, far from calm, but newly focused.

That was what she'd offered the clanners at Carnelian: lancer technology. The exact argument she'd made to Admiral Mae in exchange for asylum.

"I didn't think you'd *vivisect* one of our lancers," Hwa Young said, forcing the words past the knot in her throat, because the alternative was screaming, or choking on a miasma of her own self-hatred.

"I tried to warn you," Zeng said miserably. "But I didn't try hard enough. Originally Aera was willing to look for an alternative, with the scribers I developed. Remember? Because if she could keep four working lancers while still getting the data to manufacture new ones, why not? But I couldn't figure out how to ameliorate the feedback loop that interfered with the neural link. Eun insisted that I uninstall all the scribers. And that left us with one option: taking a lancer apart to find out how it worked."

His voice steadied as he spoke. He'd slipped back into his profession and reduced everything to an engineering problem.

What had she expected the clanners to do in their quest for better weapons? Especially when their existence was at stake? None of the research bases Geum had guided them to provided complete blueprints. She hadn't brought data cores purloined from a secret manufactory. She hadn't kidnapped an engineer with the expertise; hadn't managed to bring Geum with her. Besides, the only one aboard the *Maehwa* who might have possessed the relevant information was Chief, and maybe not even him.

Instead, she had delivered lancers to the clanners. Four of them.

Hwa Young worked through the logic. It unspooled against her will like an incandescent live wire, sparking cacophonies of guilt as it went. If she'd brought *one* lancer, the clanners might have hesitated to take it apart and risk destroying it for uncertain gain. They might have waited longer.

Follow the logic.

Would Aera have intervened if it meant destroying her heart-daughter's lancer? Hwa Young wanted to believe it, but the thought lacked conviction. She'd witnessed Aera's ruthlessness. Had even admired it, after a fashion. Aera had persuaded or ordered Tora to sabotage *Farseer,* then killed him so he wouldn't tell tales.

Aera had never reported back on any forensic analysis, including genetic samples, despite Ye Jun's prodding. When Hwa Young called Aera that one time, she'd heard Tora's voice in the background. The creepy way Tora had always stared at Hwa Young made a certain twisted sense if he'd been involved with her heart-mother.

Aera wouldn't have hesitated to sacrifice the *other* lancers. Hwa Young had overlooked this because of her ties to Ye Jun and Eun and Bae. But loyalty wasn't *transitive* like the property she'd memorized in the math classes of yesteryear.

Hwa Young shoved Zeng away. She hadn't meant to be so rough, but she had too much anger; had no other way to let it dissipate.

He caught his balance and stepped back. His cheeks were

flushed, his eyes hectically bright. He made a small crumpled noise.

The new priority: warning Commander Ye Jun. Zie must have anticipated this, but if so, why hadn't zie warned her or Bae? The eavesdroppers that Zeng had alluded to?

Ye Jun prepared for everything, calculated every angle. If zie hadn't pulled them out of danger earlier, there must be a reason. Even if it was the dreary but all-too-real issue of food and supplies. Still, she needed to know the details.

Hwa Young called Ye Jun's lancer directly, betting that zie was connected to its comms and monitoring everything that came in over that channel. Not entirely safe, but *safer* than going through ship's comms.

"Winter to Bastard." Winter, not Axiom or Axe; Bastard, not Vagrant. She didn't wait for confirmation, instead detailing her findings as succinctly as she could. Ye Jun needed to know about the saboteur's true identity and Aera's cover-up, as well as Bae's status.

Zeng was fussing with some computer terminal. She ignored him, willing Commander Ye Jun to respond.

"Bastard to . . . received . . . report immediat . . . repeat, rendezvous . . ."

Commander Ye Jun's voice, like a guttering light in the darkness. She almost wept when it cut out. "Commander!" she cried.

"It's not you," Zeng said without looking up. "Falcon Command has noticed. They don't entirely understand lancer systems, but they're jamming the signal. You'd better get out of—"

Alerted by Zeng's words and the cool breath of air against the back of her neck, Hwa Young whirled, cursing. She balanced her weight over her toes so she could advance or retreat on a second's notice. How many times had Eun lectured her on staying alert? He could upbraid her for her lack of situational awareness later—if she survived.

Commander Aera had silhouetted herself in the doorway, making an easy target of herself in a supreme display of confidence. "I'm sorry, Hwajin," she said. "I didn't want you to find out this way."

24

HWA YOUNG

Hwa Young glowered at Aera, sizing her up. "You mean you didn't want me to find out ever." Arguing with Aera was a great diversion. The alternative was dwelling on the barbs-in-the-heart confirmation that Aera had deliberately hidden all of this from her.

Why hadn't Hwa Young seen this coming? If only she hadn't dismissed Zeng's messages. If only she'd checked on Bae earlier, or asked Rose-Merline to do so, or warned the others. If only, if only, a thousand times if only.

She hadn't seen it because she hadn't wanted to.

Commander Aera shrugged, one shoulder higher than the other in the exact gesture that Hwa Young knew as *Oh well, doesn't matter*. Still, she wasn't as collected as she initially appeared. Her eyes widened. Uncharacteristically, her voice wavered: "Hwajin, your *face*—"

Hwa Young exploited the hesitation. Her kick caught Aera

on the side of the head. Aera's head snapped sideways. She fell with a thump.

Hwa Young's heart contracted. *Did I hurt her?* Why was she wrestling with herself? The *point* was to hurt Aera.

This was the reality she'd signed up for when she became a lancer pilot. She'd been so engrossed by the prospect of freedom and flight and power that she'd lost sight of a lancer's purpose as a war machine, and herself as a soldier. Hilarious considering she'd first encountered lancers during the destruction of her home moon in a military action.

She stepped over Aera's fallen form without checking for a pulse—she couldn't bring herself to do it, as though finding Aera dead would kill *her*, too—then retraced her path toward Bae. As she did so, she reached out to *Winter's Axiom*. *We need to contact Bastard and Hellion.*

It was too late for *Farseer*, but she could retrieve Bae and take him to the others. Then they could figure out their next move.

Bastard will ready the hunt, the lancer agreed, so serenely that Hwa Young choked back a grim laugh. At least one of them was unperturbed.

She'd aspired to be ice inside and out, an endeavor notable for how consistently she fell short. Had she been doing it wrong the whole time? She and *Winter's Axiom* were stronger as *opposites* complementing each other: she was fire, it was ice.

The wintry landscape overtook her mind. It was as though she strode through a blizzard, through pelting hail and past caverns of ice, winds blowing through the unexamined spaces in her soul . . . herself trailing sparks of fire and renewed purpose. She had difficulty distinguishing external reality from the winterscape; wanted to vanish into the manifestation, except she needed to remain connected to the outside world so she could help Bae.

Abruptly, Hwa Young realized she wasn't alone. "I'm in a hurry," she snapped, before the significance penetrated. *She wasn't alone*—in the lancer's winterscape.

"We're not friends," the figure within the winterscape said pertly: a ghost of ice-curves, almost as beautiful as Bae, keeping pace with Hwa Young. The wind lifted her long, rippling hair, revealing her face: Ha Yoon, who had only become a lancer pilot candidate because her best friend Bae pushed her into it. Who'd died as a result—because *Winter's Axiom* judged her unworthy, and killed her.

"I'm s-s-sorry," Hwa Young stammered after a moment's stunned silence, "Ha Yoon? You're *alive*?"

The pitying sneer Hwa Young received in response was so perfectly Ha Yoon that Hwa Young wouldn't have been surprised to land back in high school, bent over a slate committing trigonometric identities to memory, burningly aware of the zit on her nose as Bae and Ha Yoon laughed at her. These days Hwa Young would give anything for a *zit* to be her most pressing problem.

Ha Yoon inspected an imaginary speck on one fingernail. All her fingernails were much longer than she'd kept them in high school, like a bird of prey's talons. Come to think of it, she'd last sported the same short haircut that Hwa Young did, thanks to the latest crownworld fashion, rather than her current long, wild tresses. Her skin, always perfectly moisturized and free of scars or blemishes, was no longer the fashionable faintly tawny pallor with a hint of rose, but the lambent white of first frost under moonlight.

"I'm a *ghost*," Ha Yoon said, confirming what Hwa Young had just realized.

Hwa Young had rarely conceived of Ha Yoon as a person in herself, as opposed to a meanness-amplifying human appendage to Bae. Even so, she remembered Bae's admission that his friendship with Ha Yoon had involved more than lording it over their classmates; that Ha Yoon had known and accepted him in ways that no one else had guessed at the time. That, plus Ha Yoon's matter-of-factness and utter lack of self-pity, made Hwa Young nod at her with grudging respect.

At the same time, the six years she'd suffered from Bae and Ha Yoon's bullying hadn't evaporated entirely, ghost or no ghost. "If we're not friends," Hwa Young said, giving way to the welling-up of old hurt, "why are you here?" She regretted her sharp tone immediately. This wasn't the time to reignite a rivalry with a *ghost*. Especially a ghost trapped in *her lancer*, with an unknown amount of influence over it, and who had presumably not wanted that fate.

Besides, if Hwa Young had patched matters up with Bae, why did Ha Yoon deserve any less?

"You're helping Bae, aren't you?" Ha Yoon asked pointedly. "*I'm* here to make sure you don't screw it up."

"Thanks for the vote of confidence." Yet Ha Yoon's protectiveness warmed her. They had a shared goal. The implications caught up with Hwa Young. Ye Jun had admitted, long ago, that *Winter's Axiom* had killed other pilot candidates in the past. If Ha Yoon survived as a spirit within *Winter's Axiom*—"If you're here, what about the other—"

"Get moving."

Way to avoid the subject, but Hwa Young didn't disagree. She had many feelings about having Ha Yoon haunting her lancer, most of them ambivalent. But Ha Yoon was correct about priorities. They could argue later.

Commander Ye Jun, Hwa Young thought desperately, casting about in the winter landscape for some hint of Bastard, guidance to tell her where to go after she secured Bae. All she found were shadows and intimations: comma-shaped jades scattered half-buried in the snow, elusive footprints, distant flashes of gold. The gold-and-green that she associated with Ye Jun's lancer, never anything direct. Hwa Young had a flash of insight: her inner world and Ye Jun's were too fundamentally different for a direct interface.

She could have sworn her exchange with Ha Yoon had taken longer. When she returned to Bae's bedside, however, a quick glance at the wall clock suggested that less than a minute had elapsed.

Falcon Actual's security awaited her there.

Hwa Young reflexively blamed Zeng. Then she saw that two guards had shoved him up against some apparatus while he struggled ineffectually. It was likelier that Commander Aera had brought backup, or some silent alert had triggered when Hwa Young knocked her out. Why had she thought her problems would *end* when she clocked the fleet's second-in-command?

Hwa Young counted the rest. Six guards, their handguns unholstered. Why hadn't they sent more? Unless they'd counted on Aera to talk her down, or they thought people in a larger squad would get in each other's way?

"I'm taking Bae," Hwa Young snarled, "and leaving with him."

The one in the lead sneered. "That's not—"

She smiled at him: not her own smile, and not Commander Aera's either. Her mouth moved. Dimly, she recognized it as Commander Ye Jun's affable-but-dangerous *Try me* expression.

The winter landscape shifted. It was replaced by bright shifting graphs of gold thread and jeweled vertices, a computational visualization of alliances and analyses: Ye Jun's world. Zie was offering guidance. Where to go, what to do.

How to get out of this fix and rescue Bae, despite the fact that she was outnumbered and outgunned.

It's up to you now, Winter, Ye Jun said. The gold-and-jewel graphs withdrew.

The guards had guns. Clanner guns, with bullets, rather than the energy weapons that Imperials preferred. *That* should have clued her in that Aera was up to something during *Farseer*'s sabotage: the fact that she'd barbecued Tora's head with an Imperial energy weapon. Hwa Young had been too rattled to notice the discrepancy.

The guards leveled their guns at her.

Hwa Young allowed herself a moment's pity.

They fired.

Hwa Young *reached* for her link to *Winter's Axiom* with a strength born of desperation. The lancer responded with a burst from its gravity lance.

Kinetic bullets were fast, but gravity was faster.

Nausea overwhelmed Hwa Young, and she reeled.

The bullets *swerved* around her and ricocheted off something behind her. She heard breaking glass.

Sorry about the lab equipment, Zeng!

Hwa Young didn't give the guards time to figure out what had happened. One was puking; the others, judging by their expressions, had suffered the same spike of nausea. She barreled into one and snatched their gun, shot another en passant.

A shape rose up, moving with the wind-swiftness she recognized from countless sparring matches and missions flown together, a dancer's grace. Hwa Young held her fire. Bae flung a horrendous, hypertrophied mass of vines at the guards, splashing them with the slime for good measure.

Zeng wasn't kidding about accelerated healing, Hwa Young conceded. That, or creepy clanner vine-based sedatives wore off faster, with fewer side effects, than the shitty Imperial ones.

One guard's shout of dismay resulted in vines being stuffed into his mouth, like the world's most unappetizing instantiation of *Eat your vegetables.* His cry dwindled into a gurgle, and his eyes rolled up in his head before he slumped. The rest of the soldiers crashed to the deck in short order. Hwa Young had never heard such a satisfying sound before. She wished she could record it to replay whenever she needed a mood boost.

She met Bae's eyes. Only Bae could have projected dignity while clad in a stained medical tunic. Hwa Young caught herself admiring the restrained musculature of his shoulders, the curve of his neck.

Simultaneously, Bae looked like shit: bloodshot eyes, stringy hair, a murky greenish tint to his skin. Hwa Young had the irrational desire to push him into a bed, tuck blankets around him, and make him take a month-long nap.

In the confusion, Zeng had freed himself. A syringe gleamed in his hand, empty, a green liquid dripping from the needle; his attackers lay on the deck, twitching. Hwa Young made a note not to piss him off. "You two need to go," he said. "I'll—I'll cover for you." His mouth wavered, then firmed into a smile. "Give Eun my love."

"You can't stay here," Hwa Young protested. "They're going to— You won't be safe." She wasn't going to be able to say goodbye to Rose-Merline, either. Clanner leadership wouldn't look kindly on Rose-Merline: guilt by association. Unless Rose-Merline had been in on this with Aera all along. Hwa Young didn't think she could endure yet another betrayal, for all that she hadn't known the ensign for very long.

Hwa Young gulped. "Tell Rose-Merline—" The words dried up. What was there to say?

"I don't believe she was involved with any of this," Zeng said, intuiting her concern. "There's no love lost between Rose-Merline and Commander Aera, or any of Falcon Fleet's leadership."

She nodded her gratitude, too overwhelmed to find the right words. "I've got to get to Magnolia." Where the three remaining lancers were. "Come with me."

"I can take care of myself," Zeng said. "I have some tricks of my own, and I'm more *useful* here." He smiled thinly, and he resembled his heart-brother for the first time, feral and dangerous. "Aera should have realized that antagonizing her chief weapons engineer was a bad tactical decision. I'll tell Rose-Merline to meet you at Magnolia. Go!"

"Come on," Hwa Young said to Bae, suppressing her misgivings. Under other circumstances, she would have crushed Bae in a hug. Explained what the situation was with Rose-Merline. But this was the wrong time. Also, slime.

"You're telling me," Bae rasped.

They set out together. Bae didn't look back. Perhaps he couldn't bear to.

Bae walked under his own power. He'd almost completely regained his coordination, although every so often he slowed as though unsure of his balance. Hwa Young suppressed the urge to hover, but she was totally hovering, and trying not to chafe.

Bae murmured, "Moments of vertigo. If I could lean on you . . ."

Wordlessly, Hwa Young moved to Bae's side. They were both pilots. They were together.

First we get Bae out of here. Then I retrieve Geum. No more delays.

The wintry landscape had become so all-encompassing that Hwa Young no longer perceived *Falcon Actual* except through oblique glimpses. The ship might have been a ghost. Winter above them and winter below, the winds skirling past them, hunting horns in the distance.

Ha Yoon paced at Hwa Young's other side. "Does Bae know you're here?" Hwa Young asked her.

"I'm sorry?" Bae asked, looking at Hwa Young strangely.

Her face heated. "Nothing."

The images of snow and sleet shattered into metal and shadows. Hwa Young cried out at the disruption, torn between reaching for her sidearm and continuing to support Bae. Bae resolved the matter before she came to a decision by diving away from her.

Two clanners rushed them. Her fist took the first clanner full in the face. She barely registered the crunch of bone shattering. Bae took down the other one. Hwa Young had always been fast, but this time she was propelled by rage and desperation. She didn't know how long they could fuel her, but she was going to find out.

"I'm surprised there weren't more," Bae remarked, glancing contemptuously at the other clanner's fallen form. "I'd expect a general alert, unless I missed it?"

Hwa Young *reached* for her lancer again. The antler crown, *Bastard*'s symbol, cast a long shadow over the snow. "Commander Ye Jun is doing something," she said, secure in the knowledge that zie was handling matters. "Interfering with the comms, maybe."

Bae accepted this. "That would explain the clanners' lack of coordination. We'd better hurry so zir efforts don't go to waste."

They continued to the rendezvous that Ye Jun had communicated to Hwa Young earlier.

The first four crew members they ran into, traveling as a group, didn't know what hit them. Hwa Young was so hair-triggered that she smashed the blade edge of her hand with terrible accuracy against the weakest point of the clanner's skull without registering their face, then flowed directly into a vicious kick that slammed the other to the deck. She had a blurred impression of salient details: height, approximate mass, muscle tone, alertness, stance. The second one had reach shorter than her own, with stubby arms flung up in a belated and fruitless defense.

Only after they dropped, one spilling a nauseatingly sweet energy drink, did it occur to her that the clanners had been unlucky enough to run into her and Bae by accident, rather than being members of a search party.

Bae had taken down the other two. Hwa Young hadn't watched; had known he would get the job done and guard her flank the way she guarded his. "They would have raised the alarm," Bae said, dispassionate in the face of Hwa Young's momentary dismay. "Let's keep moving."

Each time they encountered crew members, she and Bae dealt with them in a similar manner, continuing to work together with an efficiency she would once have found unbelievable. She felt bad about the people they attacked, some of whom must be dead, in the distant way she'd feel bad cutting trail in pristine wilderness, regrettable but necessary.

Hwa Young had launched herself toward the latest hostile when Bae grabbed her arm. He could have used more force, but didn't. The simple fact of his intercession stayed her hand.

"Stop!" Bae hissed redundantly.

Hwa Young struggled to make sense of the sound. She'd sunk so deeply into the *fight* mindset of fight-flight-freeze that she had stopped thinking in words. She blinked at the hostiles.

The killing haze receded, as though winter had melted away. Before her stood Commander Ye Jun, haggard but clear-eyed, and Eun. Not hostiles. Her comrades.

And one more. Ensign Rose-Merline stood behind them, her lips compressed.

"Rose-Merline," Hwa Young breathed. "What—"

A wisp of starbloom fragrance drifted to her nostrils: the sachet that Rose-Merline had given her, and which she was still wearing tucked beneath her shirt.

Rose-Merline's face brightened as she took in Hwa Young's appearance, sweat and mess and all: so it wasn't Hwa Young she was mad at. "We'll discuss this later. They filled me in." She moved to support Bae's other side, and she and Hwa Young exchanged wry smiles. Bae raised an eyebrow, then accepted the aid.

"We can talk on the way," Ye Jun said. "Hellion, take point."

"Sir." Eun shouldered his way to the front and began walking with a longer stride than usual.

A pain that Hwa Young hadn't been conscious of eased in her chest. They were together again. All of them.

No one commented on Ye Jun's use of Eun's callsign. They all knew what it signified. *Falcon Actual* was now enemy territory.

If so, why had they only run into sporadic resistance?

"Sir, where will we go?" Hwa Young asked. If they had left New Joseon, and found no welcome among the clanners, what was left? Returning to a base like Dragon Mountain, assuming they could find it again, and begging for patrons?

"There are merits to big-picture thinking, Winter," Ye Jun

said. "Nevertheless, before long-term survival considerations, we need to deal with the immediate problem of getting off this ship with our lancers." Zir glance slid toward Bae. "Extracting your lancer is not operationally possible at this time."

Bae laughed harshly. "What lancer?" he said. "You don't need to cushion the truth, sir."

"Perhaps not. Nevertheless, I decided not to pull us out earlier, and you have suffered as a result." Ye Jun's smile conveyed a grim compassion. "We needed information about clanner navigation techniques in the Moonstorm. Having obtained it, we are able to leave."

The squad couldn't wander in exile through the Moonstorm. The Empire already wanted them dead. The clans weren't unified, but Falcon Fleet's enmity did them no favors. They needed allies and supplies.

As long as they were embedded in Falcon Fleet, they could rely on the clanners for transport and, more crucially, *navigation*. It seemed Ye Jun had finally obtained the mysterious navigational techniques that allowed Falcon Fleet to travel in a region of space where celestial bodies did not retain fixed positions—and which would enable the squad to plot a course to *somewhere* instead of *nowhere* in the staggering vastness of space.

Zie inclined zir head to Rose-Merline. "If you're willing to come with us—"

Rose-Merline lifted her chin. "I've been willing," she said with a fervor that shook Hwa Young, "from the moment you arrived."

"I understand the chain of command," Bae said at the same time.

"You and Rose-Merline will have to ride with Winter," Ye Jun added.

Hwa Young braced for a protest, fighting down her own ambivalence. She'd never had passengers—not living ones. And there was only one copilot seat, so it would be crowded. But Bae only returned a clipped "Of course, sir." Rose-Merline nodded agreement.

They reached the corridor opening into the docking bay. "I should have known it was too quiet," Eun said, sour as always, at what awaited them.

They were outnumbered. Hwa Young's first impression was that every marine on the flagship had gathered in the docking bay. Unfortunately, the squad hadn't had a choice. They couldn't leave without the lancers. The clanners had counted on that.

Wisely, Admiral Mae did not stand in a position that gave them a clear sight line or Hwa Young would have shot zir. Mae was well-screened by zir guards, scarcely visible except for the brilliant glitter of the medals on zir uniform. "Stand down, pilots," the admiral said. Firm, but not apologetic. "We can reach an accommodation."

Admiral Mae's lack of remorse infuriated Hwa Young. She opened her mouth. Commander Ye Jun shook zir head. Zir good hand moved in the Imperial military sign language, behind the cover of Eun's bulk.

"I don't believe there's any possibility of a mutually beneficial arrangement anymore," Ye Jun said.

Hwa Young startled at the arrogance zie projected, through both tone and perfect posture. It reminded her of the Empress's public bulletins.

"Ah, your true colors show," Admiral Mae responded, cynical. And: "Ensign Rose-Merline. I cannot permit you to leave."

Why had Ye Jun cared so much about a *botanist*?

Why did the *admiral* care so much about a *botanist*?

Unless the ubiquitous flowers weren't decorative. Unless they weren't just a religious quirk. Unless they were *very very important*.

Rose-Merline hadn't introduced herself as a botanist, but a *crypto*botanist. When she gave Hwa Young the starbloom sachet, she'd said, *So you never get lost in the Moonstorm.*

Navigation. The starblooms make navigation possible somehow. An incredible thought, except the clanners relied on biotechnology for medicine. Why not navigation too? That *was what Commander Ye Jun wanted.* Ye Jun, who had played matchmaker with an ulterior motive.

Hwa Young forced herself to pay attention to Ye Jun's signed message: "Connect to lancers. Blast our way out."

Eun and Bae had seen it too. They shared tight nods.

In the past, Hwa Young had suffered periods of disconnection from *Winter's Axiom*. At times she entertained doubts about their partnership and its recent defiance; about the fact that it was haunted by the ghost of Ha Yoon, which implied that other ghosts were archived in there. At other times, she wondered about her ability to cling to her sanity while working with it.

But now, the only way out was to surrender herself completely and embrace her connection with *Winter's Axiom*. The truth was, she was ready. She *wanted* this.

Hwa Young flung open the doors of her mind. The docking bay evanesced into a winter storm as she took upon the lancer's sense of self. Dimly, she was aware of herself/Hwa Young, a small figure standing amid other small figures, the human shells that contained the pilots. She herself had a giant's height, caparisoned in metal, her armor blazing white and blue and silver, ready to ride the aether to battle and beyond.

Carefully, she reached down, aware that the pilot's human shell was fragile and easily crushed. There were others, hostiles. She didn't need to be cautious with *them*. She lifted the pilot and placed the pilot upon her shoulder armor; didn't have the necessary finesse to take the pilot into her cockpit without causing damage. The pilot would have to handle that. Next she included the pilot's two companions, even more fragile, and was pleased: a hunting pair and their partner, the proper way of things.

The others activated next to her. *Hellion* flared orange as its artillery powered up. *Bastard*'s transformation was more subtle: it remained gray, largely formless, yet its jamming capabilities activated, jinxing *Falcon Actual*'s computer systems to discourage pursuit. Any time it bought them was welcome. While she didn't acknowledge a master, she knew to follow *Bastard*'s leadership as a courtesy to the pilot.

Hellion fired a missile at the docking bay's doors. Metal crumpled and exploded outward, creating an opening through which they could fly free. Screams followed, then a tumult among the hostiles, like swarming ants, as atmosphere vented through the breach and aether swept in. She paid them no heed.

The three lancers soared into space—and into the path of an enemy lancer.

25

HWA YOUNG

Hwa Young landed back in her body so forcefully that she was surprised her bones didn't jar loose from the prison of her flesh. Dazed, she gawked at the borderless horizon and coruscating swirls of aether, which lashed her like high winds during a storm. She was standing—what was she standing on? No starship she knew, Imperial or clanner, would display this extreme hull curvature.

Then the *colors* of the surface, wintry blue and white and silver, registered. She was standing on *Winter's Axiom*. Specifically, one of the pauldrons. Her lancer's shoulder armor wasn't anyone's idea of secure footing, or a safe place to stand during a firefight.

She lifted her gaze. The buffeting force didn't simply come from the natural gales created by the aether currents. *Winter's Axiom* propelled itself through the tempest without her conscious control, fleeing—fleeing what?

There was an enemy. There was an enemy, and she didn't know where it had gone. Out of her line of sight, apparently. It could be anywhere, or even blocked by the helmet and shoulders of her own lancer.

The memory of their escape returned to her. Hwa Young craned her head in an attempt to spot the pursuit before remembering that she could connect to the lancer's own perceptions, even if they no longer enjoyed the benefit of *Farseer*'s sensor suite. Her effort to do so only dizzied her further, however. The pearly colors, the everywhere luminescence, distracted her, drawing her into a world of hypnotic mystery, and her focus dissolved.

"Winter!"

She almost didn't hear it. What grabbed her attention wasn't her callsign, but the frantic urgency in a voice that rarely expressed such sentiments. *Bae's* voice, not cool and haughty, but rough with worry.

Hwa Young swayed, tottering closer to the edge of her lancer's pauldron. Laughter spilled from between her teeth. She recognized early symptoms of aether sickness—which often killed precisely because it destroyed one's judgment and perception—yet she couldn't stop laughing.

"If only saying *Snap out of it* ever worked," Bae muttered. He grabbed one of Hwa Young's arms, Rose-Merline the other. The two of them coaxed her back from the pauldron's edge.

Hwa Young looked wide-eyed into the visage of eternity, embroidered with stars, darkness coming unhemmed in all directions, and laughed some more.

"We can't do this without you," Bae said. Even in her current state, Hwa Young registered the undertone of panic in his voice. "We need to get into the lancer before—"

"Keep it simple," Rose-Merline whispered. "Don't explain. Just tell her what she needs to do."

Bae nodded, regrouped. "Winter. We need to get into the lancer. *Your* lancer."

He was right. Difficult as it was to think clearly, Hwa Young recognized that she and *Winter's Axiom* should be together. Why Bae and Rose-Merline were here, she couldn't figure out, but that didn't matter.

Open, she wished *Winter's Axiom.*

Welcome to the hunt, all of you, the lancer replied. *We are legion.*

The entire curved slope of its shoulder vibrated ominously as the cockpit slid open. Hwa Young flung one arm outward, not sure whether it was to steady herself or to fly into the aether like a migrating bird, never to return. Bae, blanching, caught her wrist. Coaxed again, urging her upward toward the cockpit.

The metal armor, polished to a high sheen, made for treacherous footing. The lancer, responding to Hwa Young's need, roughened the texture to give their feet extra purchase beyond the stickiness of the magnetic boots. She couldn't tell whether it was holding still, for some value of "still," or drifting at a constant velocity. There was no difference from a physics standpoint, although her inner ear, which could not decide which was up or down or sideways, complained.

"Just a little farther," Bae said. The giddy edge to his voice suggested he was starting to be affected by the aether too.

Rose-Merline, unencumbered, clambered in first, taking the copilot's seat. "You're going to have to sit *on* me, sorry," she called to Bae. "But this way you can reach the controls."

A bolt of dark sizzling plasma rocketed over Hwa Young and Bae just before they reached the cockpit. Aether blew hot against Hwa Young's half-healed, sensitive skin. She choked back a scream.

They were under attack. The enemy lancer was close enough to fire. Built and piloted by the clanners—and Hwa Young was the one who'd delivered the technology to them.

She had to reconnect to *Winter's Axiom* so she could use its sensors to locate—and hunt down—the enemy. A pittance of penance for her error in judgment.

Hwa Young's fingers closed over the edge of the cockpit. She hauled herself into the pilot's seat. Had enough presence of mind, barely, to offer Bae a hand.

Bae scrambled into the copilot's seat, doing his damnedest not to squash Rose-Merline in the process. She made a stifled "Oof" as he sat, but no more. Hwa Young heard him gasping, or laughing, or both, as the cockpit snicked shut over the three of them. It did not feel like a trap but a homecoming to a castle, one she could always take with her, and which was an extension of her own mind. She wished she could luxuriate in the feeling.

There is a counteragent to aether sickness in the medical kit, Winter's Axiom reminded her. *Hurry. An enemy lancer is an opponent worthy of us.* And, slyly: *I prefer your bones intact.*

Hwa Young moved her muscles one by one, arm then hand then fingers, despite the temptation to gape at the gyring patterns of color and shadow that danced across the cockpit window.

"Pass it here," Bae said. His head was flung back: she'd never seen such an unguarded grin on his face. That sobered her enough to open the kit.

Hwa Young drew on *Winter's Axiom* to steady herself against the aether sickness. She opened up the kit, took one of the counteragent tabs, then passed two over, one for Bae, one for Rose-Merline.

The clanners' tabs worked more quickly and effectively than the Imperial ones. She tried not to think about their origin: Did they contain microscopic seed capsules or fungal tendrils waiting to take root in her belly? Whether due to the tabs themselves or her morbid imaginings, her head cleared with a sharpness like a slap. Hwa Young was staggered by her own rashness in relying on clanner medications, except they had no choice.

"Strap in," Hwa Young said. Her own harness fitted itself over her, offering her safety against the maneuvers to come.

She consulted *Winter's Axiom:* no luck. The probability cloud that indicated the enemy lancer's position was so large, so diffuse, that she might as well have planned to fire into an all-encompassing fog. Not knowing where it was lurking set all her nerves jangling. Losing *Farseer* sucked for Bae, that went without saying, but it also hampered the squad's ability to detect—and fight—their opponents.

"On it." Bae huffed in pain.

"This wasn't how I planned to get to know you," Rose-Merline murmured to Bae, a hint of mischief in her voice.

Hwa Young listened for the click of their buckles. "All set?" She didn't want the other two to be knocked around the cockpit.

"Set," Bae said.

It was time to fight.

Geum. You're next.

Four people would strain the cockpit's capacity, unless she stashed Geum in the back, but they'd figure something out.

Hwa Young didn't know where they'd go that the clanners couldn't track them. With any luck, Ye Jun had a plan for that. They might be hunted for the rest of their lives—but they'd be together.

She'd retrieve Geum. Eun would reunite with Zeng.

Together forever.

"Bastard to Winter, do you read? Over."

"Winter here," Hwa Young said. How long had Ye Jun been calling for her? "What's the plan?"

"First order of business is taking out the enemy lancer." Ye Jun spoke rapidly, but without panic. "It's the most maneuverable of their units, and the immediate threat to us. Second will be disabling their flagship. We want to damage them so we can get away, while minimizing casualties."

"I don't think 'minimizing casualties' is on *their* mind," Eun growled.

Zeng is still on that ship, Hwa Young thought. If Zeng had anticipated the battle—found a way off *Falcon Actual*—

"Nevertheless," Ye Jun said, "there are limits to what we do in war. For moral reasons."

Hwa Young shut her eyes for a moment as the memory of Carnelian and the singularity bomb returned to her. They'd killed people then. Her childhood dream festered beneath a heap of unlucky corpses.

"Hellion to Bastard. Hostile lancer is gaining on us."

He was right. Its pilot, whoever it was, couldn't have had much opportunity to practice. Hwa Young chafed at the easy display of expertise, remembering the challenges of her early training, before she developed her present rapport with *Winter's Axiom*.

The hostile lancer had a gracile build, with sleek, elegant curves and implied agility. Its speed, displayed in sudden zigzagging bursts of acceleration that made it a difficult target, suggested a correspondingly lighter mass. Its armor sported a darker, more ominous version of *Winter's Axiom*'s color scheme: sunken black with highlights in sullen, stormy blue rather than ice blue, dull steel rather than bright silver. Conflicting emotions warred inside Hwa Young. Should she be flattered or outraged?

Bae blinked away tears, fruitlessly. "It looks like *Farseer*," he whispered. One rolled down his cheek, leaving behind a glistening trail.

Bae's statement wasn't entirely accurate. Rather, the enemy lancer had *Farseer*'s chassis, yet parodied the colors of *Winter's Axiom*—and it bore a lancer-sized rifle like *Winter's Axiom*.

It's smaller than ours, her lancer noted smugly, almost causing Hwa Young to squawk in laughter.

A chord of fear reverberated through Hwa Young. Not all of it belonged to her. Perhaps none of it did. Snippets and fragments of Bae's thoughts swirled through her mind like a stormcell of misgivings: memories of an all-encompassing awareness of his surroundings, much more detailed than the overview than *Winter's Axiom* granted her on its own.

The hell? Hwa Young was more bewildered than angry. *What are you doing in my head?*

But if Bae had any control over the phenomenon, or awareness of *her* thoughts, he showed no sign of it. Instead, *Winter's Axiom* said enigmatically, *It is proper.*

Who was *in* the other lancer? Had the clanners discovered how to fly one without the guidance of a human pilot? Knowing the pilot and their tendencies would help her prepare to fight it.

"Hellion, target *Falcon Actual*'s main guns. You'll have to go through point defense first."

"On it, sir, and you can teach me the order of the alphabet while you're at it."

Hwa Young smiled at Eun's quip. It wasn't that the ragged quality of his voice didn't matter. They had a job to do. He wouldn't have welcomed anyone's fussing.

Commander Ye Jun wasn't done. "Winter, that leaves you to deal with the hostile lancer. I will be monitoring the situation, but understand, you will not have backup for this fight."

That gave her pause. But if zie wanted it that way, zie must have good reason for it.

Another wave of despair, not hers: Bae. "If only—" He bit his lip, head held high but with an unaccustomed rigidity, as though he was holding himself together through sheer stubbornness.

Rose-Merline hesitated, then squeezed his shoulder in silent acknowledgment.

Hwa Young knew what they were both thinking: if only they could help.

"I'm not alone," she told Ye Jun. Her lips pulled back in a fierce grin. "I've got Farseer and Rose-Merline."

And Ha Yoon, and the ghosts of the other people *Winter's Axiom* had devoured, whom she planned on acquainting herself with after they survived this fight.

Bae inhaled sharply, as though Hwa Young had landed a blow. She spared him a glance, mouthing, *Are you all right?*

"Do it," he said, his tone colorless.

This was Hwa Young's first time guiding *Winter's Axiom* with a copilot's help, and it was happening in the midst of combat. She had the discomfiting sensation of all her thoughts echoing in a vast cavern, of contending with someone else for control of the lancer—and the source of the conflict didn't come this time from *Winter's Axiom* itself, but from Bae.

Anger flared in her, followed by chagrin. Bae had lost his lancer in the most horrible way possible. He hadn't *chosen* this role.

Just as she could sense Bae's thoughts and emotions, he might sense hers. She needed to keep a lid on any petty grievances.

Bae formed an indistinct presence at first, slowly gaining clarity in the winterscape as though illuminated by an inexorable sunrise. A familiar shadow, slender and unselfconsciously elegant.

Hwa Young reminded herself of Bae's virtues. How his arrogance was backed by a willingness to do whatever it took to excel and the ability to lead. His quick wit, which she appreciated when she wasn't its target. His loyalty, once he decided someone had earned it.

This raised the question of how *her* virtues and flaws balanced each other. What did Bae see in this winterscape when he regarded *her*?

Hwa Young didn't get a chance to pose the question or ponder the answer. The enemy lancer fired a kinetic projectile at them. This time, they dodged, cutting into an adjacent current at an angle that reduced drag. Likewise, the internal sense of friction eased away. She and Bae were working in tandem, their purposes aligned. A synchrony she would never have believed possible a year ago, when Bae had been the bane of her existence.

It wasn't just the two of them. Lavender rose petals blew over the snow. Ha Yoon's shadow accompanied them at the winterscape's periphery, a ghost of possibilities past and future. More shadows stood beyond her, slowly growing more distinct, people whose names she'd never troubled to find out: she would have to remedy that if she survived.

We are Winter's Axiom, she thought, and heard the statement echoed a hundredfold: by Bae, by Rose-Merline, by Ha Yoon, by the crowd of the cannibalized dead. A connection deeper than any she had experienced before, as though they were bound by braids of need and knowledge.

Hwa Young screamed a battle cry as her lancer's rifle grew larger and longer, manifesting additional mass by siphoning it from the very aether around them. The longer barrel and its rifling gave the projectile greater accuracy at extended range, both of which she was going to need. She expected it to change her experience of recoil, which might require additional acclimation.

While piloting, she could twist and shoot independently of her movement vector. Something she'd done in the past, with varied results, as in the battle with *Paradox*. This became tough when avoiding the debris and battledrift endemic to the Moonstorm.

In the winterscape she shared with *Winter's Axiom,* the debris transformed into snow, the aether into winter winds, moons into vast projectiles of ice. She was vaster than the shadows between stars, eclipsing the sky. Lifting her rifle, she prepared to fire on the enemy lancer.

Proper aim required proper focus. The lancer's targeting system had automatic stabilization to compensate for human fallibility, but when the system itself responded to the pilot's intent—

She had lock-on. Lost it when a shard of rock hurtled out of the nowhere darkness and she had to fling them out of its path.

Plated armor protected her lancer, but an object that moved sufficiently fast could still puncture it.

"Give me manual control," Bae said. "If I pilot, it'll free up your concentration for the shot."

Hwa Young didn't recognize his voice at first, echoed through the chaotic ice crystals of the phantom winter: a half octave lower, huskier. But the refined accent she'd once found so aggravating remained the same, even if the curious note of deference was new.

"You're on," Hwa Young said, grateful for the offer.

Without her willing it, a communications channel opened. The enemy lancer spoke: "This doesn't have to end with your death," said a horribly familiar voice.

Commander Aera. Her heart-mother. An image of her face appeared in the enemy cockpit, black relieved only by sinister, unforgiving dark blue and tarnished silver. Like Hwa Young, she'd been marked by the lancer she claimed, which had claimed her in turn. Her eyes shone the same corroded silver displayed by the lancer. As for her hair, hers had turned white with a black streak, the inverse of Hwa Young's.

"The hell?" Bae demanded. "How is that woman on this channel?"

Hastily, Hwa Young double-checked. They were receiving the transmission, even though she hadn't cleared it. At least they weren't transmitting—that she knew of.

"The lancer," Hwa Young said hollowly. "I should have realized. The clanners *copied your lancer*. All our comms are compromised, if they reverse engineered everything down to the operating system and the encryption/decryption protocols . . ."

No wonder Ye Jun had told her she was on her own. Zie must have anticipated this.

"I had hoped, when you returned to us, that you would fight by my side," Commander Aera said. "That you understood where you belonged. But it seems your years in New Joseon have tainted you beyond all hope of salvage. The clans' survival is more important than one heart-daughter."

Hwa Young couldn't think of anything to say to this. If only she had Geum's glibness, or Bae's self-assurance, or Ye Jun's gift for calculation. Instead, roaring static filled her mind.

She toggled the channel open without thinking, despite Bae's hiss of warning. "I'm done with you and your *strategies*," she said icily. "I have my squad, and I should never have given you the singularity bomb plans!"

"Yes, the plans," Aera said as if she hadn't noticed the outburst. Her voice warmed to a purr. "Always pieces and fragments and fakes. Still, we're close to a breakthrough. Ekphora Fleet's on their way. If you worked with us again and *committed* to the winning side—got your hacker friend to steal the *real* plans from the Empress—"

With effort, she held on to her temper. She needed more information. "Ekphora Fleet? On their way *where*?"

"The crownworld," Aera said. "A deep strike. You see, Hwajin, there's no point going back to the Empire. It's about to be decapitated."

Her face hurt. "You'd sacrifice *clanners* to create black holes?"

Aera's eyebrows shot up. "Of course not!" Before Hwa Young could exhale in relief, Aera added, "I thought you were paying closer attention. What did you think all those rescue missions were for? Why would we sacrifice our own people when we could round up Imperials and border people of questionable loyalty as fuel instead?"

Hwa Young was struck speechless.

"Winter," Bae said, sotto voce, "she's your *mother*. Use that."

"Are you with me or not?" Hwa Young shot back before her brain caught up to her mouth.

Bae's jaw tightened.

Aera raised a hand as if she could reach across the distance to caress Hwa Young's cheek.

"In your years away," she said, "how often did you think about me? Or the rest of our family? The way our household was obliterated by the Imperials? Was it that easy to cast your name off and throw me away?"

Hwa Young strove to keep her face from crumpling. She had no idea whether she succeeded. The hot wetness that streaked down her face suggested she hadn't.

"Hwa Young, your mother *sucks*," Rose-Merline muttered.

"Come back, Hwajin," Aera said. Her voice softened, as though Hwa Young were a child lost amid the reeds. "Come back, and we'll fight side by side. Lead the clans together. We can start over. Rebuild our family. We don't need the others."

Hwa Young throat closed on a sob.

Once she would have jumped at this opportunity. Her own lancer *and* her heart-mother, the fulfillment of her twinned desires. She could have everything she used to want.

All she had to do was help Aera massacre a world.

All she had to do was sell out the people she loved.

"No," she cried. "I'm Hwa Young of *Winter's Axiom*, and I'm done with you."

Next to her, Bae sagged and whispered a prayer, an obscenity, both at once. It hadn't occurred to her that he had been genuinely uncertain about her loyalties. Maybe Ye Jun and Eun had entertained unspoken doubts too.

No mercy remained in Aera's silver-dark eyes. "Very well, then. It's a pity." As a parting shot, she added: "I can always make a new heart-daughter."

Hwa Young fired, screaming.

26

HWA YOUNG

The shot raced directly toward the head of Aera's lancer. To Hwa Young's intense frustration, despite the close range and true aim, a contingent of ships from Falcon Fleet unstealthed in its vicinity. Between the momentary confusion and sudden mental static, she couldn't tell whether she'd hit her target.

Easier to think *her target* than *her heart-mother*.

Easier not to think about Aera's life or death, or worse, about the way her last words rang in Hwa Young's head like the tolling of a bell cast from bullets and distilled abandonment: *I can always make a new heart-daughter.*

Hwa Young didn't know whether she wanted Aera to be alive or dead, or to linger in an indeterminate limbo so she could be steeped in the worst of both worlds. What kind of daughter did it make her if she'd *killed* her heart-mother?

What kind of soldier did it make her if she'd failed?

Aera's lancer no longer showed up on scan. Hwa Young

couldn't tell whether she'd destroyed it—or if it had been picked up by a clanner ship. Or, dreadful thought, it had stealth of its own, in which case it might ambush them at any moment.

More contacts detected incoming, Winter's Axiom reported. *Imperial scouts. Reconnaissance for a larger force.*

Just what they needed: hostile clanners on one side, hostile Imperials on the other.

"They tracked us," Bae said. "There must be a bug or transmitter somewhere. They're coming straight for *us*, not Falcon Fleet's unstealthed ships, but they're out of scan range."

"That's impossible," Hwa Young protested, not because she disagreed with Bae's logic, but because she desperately needed not to have *one more thing* spiral into disaster. "If they'd had any such thing on *Winter's Axiom* all this time . . ."

Hwa Young's face froze; her lips numbed as the words died on her lips. *Winter's Axiom.* It came back to her with unwanted clarity as though needles engraved the moment on her eyes: *Winter's Axiom,* objecting that Geum's capsule was a threat. That they needed to destroy it. The way she'd overruled it, coaxed it to stand down, trustingly conveyed the capsule back to *Falcon Actual.*

"Geum's capsule," Hwa Young croaked.

"But you handed that over to Falcon Command."

"There was a note," she heard herself say in a hollow voice. "A note from Geum. I have it with me."

Geum had sold her out after all.

"Give it here," Bae said. "I'll destroy it." When Hwa Young balked: "I'm sure Geum would write you a *whole diary* if you asked! An encyclopedia with footnotes!"

She handed it over, eyes stinging. Couldn't watch. Sat cocooned in her own misery.

Hostiles, *Winter's Axiom* said sharply while Bae was in the midst of shredding the paper. *Be ready.*

Imperials swarmed her mind's eye, like a storm of red light. Diminished as the fleet was, it fielded enough ships to distract opponents with some units, attack with others, formations shifting and changing according to some strategy of Admiral Chin's devising.

"That's Eleventh Fleet," Bae said.

"It can't be," Hwa Young said, willing the IFF to change no matter how much the evidence pointed to Geum's complicity. But the display remained obdurate: Eleventh Fleet.

The Imperials could have faked the whole exchange after torturing or blackmailing Geum. If Geum was still alive, if she could get zir out and they could talk it out—

She was making excuses. Had to adapt to the situation as it was, not the way she wanted it to be.

The *Maehwa* hung well back for protection. It launched two lancers, *Paradox* and *Summer Thorn*.

"Focus, Winter," Bae snapped. Rose-Merline remained quiet, almost deathly still. She might be a botanist, but she understood the exigencies of combat.

Bae was right. She couldn't get distracted.

The good news: geometry worked in their favor. It was harder to "corner" someone in three spatial dimensions than in two, something Hwa Young had learned as a child when the household elders took her on a clan hunt. Not a real hunt with real (delicious) prey, but a ritual one involving hovercars, celebrating the settlers chasing and appeasing the first moons. It had been so easy for the prey to escape, even in a choreographed chase, when they could go *up* or *down* as well as *front* or *back* or *left* or *right*. Space offered more freedom of movement. They didn't have the bulk of a moon in the way.

The bad news: space was big, but the lancers were intended for short-range use, tethered to a fleet or transport.

"Winter to Bastard," Hwa Young said. "Instructions. Are we swinging by *Maehwa*?"

Ye Jun had been listening. "Negative, Winter. I've got eyes on Falcon Fleet. They're closing in on Eleventh Fleet."

"Please," she insisted, "we grab my friend Geum, then escape while they're fighting each other. If you cover me, I can message Geum and tell zir to be ready at docking bay six." She remembered Geum's assigned bay, remembered that she'd spent untold hours there. With any luck, the *Maehwa* wouldn't be in such dire straits that Geum had been called away to patch up damage elsewhere on the flagship. "It'll be easier for me to get to zir than for zir to leave zir assigned post in the midst of a battle."

She'd abandoned Geum for too long. One last chance to reunite with zir. She couldn't leave Geum behind again.

"I've picked up some of the comms chatter," Ye Jun countered. "Falcon Fleet's going after the Empress. We can't allow them to—"

Ye Jun interrupted her. "They're going after the Empress *and the blueprints*."

Her voice sharpened. After all this, her *commander* was preventing her from retrieving Geum? "Let them fight it out—"

"We can't take out *both* fleets," Bae said quietly. "Not under these conditions."

"No," Ye Jun agreed. "But neither can we allow Commander Aera or her allies to recover those plans. If we can delay the completion of the clanners' singularity bomb, we might buy time to warn the crownworld. Save innocent lives."

Hwa Young knew what zie was going to ask her to do. *Don't don't don't don't—*

"Hellion, you'll provide covering fire so Winter can safely get in position. Winter, you will target and fire on the *Maehwa*'s engine."

Delay the completion. What a pallid euphemism.

They didn't have the resources to destroy one fleet, let alone both. Even if they did, by some miracle of inspired tactics, destroy one side, the other would swoop in and kill them in turn. Nor did they have any credible way of simply swiping the plans from the Empress and *guaranteeing* that some backup copy didn't survive for the clanners to purloin. At the same time, it seemed unlikely, from a security standpoint, that the Empress would have distributed the plans to every ship in Eleventh Fleet.

That left Commander Ye Jun's proposal: destroying the *Maehwa* based on the calculation that this would deny the plans to the clanners with minimum loss of life.

"Geum," she croaked. Then hope sputtered to life: "But the flagship's shields—"

"Captain Ga Ram assured me the shields will go down. The rest is up to us."

Her breath hitched. She couldn't cry. She couldn't *not* cry.

Assured me the shields will go down. "Captain Ga Ram," she said. "Your half sibling." Would the resulting explosion kill Ye Jun's family too? Was that part of *acceptable losses*?

Ye Jun's voice was impersonal. "You can take it out on me later, soldier."

A singularity bomb had almost obliterated Carnelian. Hwa Young had been desperate to prevent the disaster. That had been a sparsely populated moon, as opposed to the massive crownworld, center of New Joseon's civilization. She didn't remember the crownworld's exact population. An estimate floated out of her memories of school: ten billion.

The entirety of Eleventh Fleet, at paper strength: one hundred ships, three thousand crew per ship. Three hundred thousand people. A *lot* of people.

But nowhere near as many as *ten billion*. Three hundred thousand wasn't even *one hundredth of a percent* of ten billion.

I'm so sorry, Geum.

She sent one last message, hoping beyond hope that Geum would receive it in time to act upon it.

GEUM. THE MAEHWA WILL BE DESTROYED. GET OUT. I'LL PICK YOU UP. TOGETHER FOREVER.

A lifeboat. A dragon. Jet-propelled roller skates. *Anything.*

"I understand the orders, sir," Hwa Young said.

Hellion spat missiles toward both Falcon Fleet and Eleventh Fleet.

Hwa Young maneuvered. Registered the bursts of fire as flowers in a damnation garden.

Bae and Rose-Merline were talking. Their voices blurred into static. Everything did.

Nothing remained but ice and iron and dead ideals.

She could see the *Maehwa* clearly. It dominated her vision. She wondered if she'd ever see anything else.

Hwa Young fired.

Time slowed. Time sped. The shields were down, as Ye Jun had promised. Nothing stopped her bullet.

Transfixed, she watched as the *Maehwa* exploded, consuming everything around it, along with her heart.

27

HWA YOUNG

Time slowed. Time sped. Bae was talking. Ye Jun too. She drifted numbly. Nothing mattered. She continued ignoring them, ignoring the strain in their voices, the worried looks.

Hwa Young used to think that a lancer would solve all her problems. That it would welcome her, and bring her welcome from others. That it had the power to prevent her from ever being hurt again, ever being vulnerable, ever losing the people she wanted to protect.

She had never considered the possibility that all the armor in the world, all the lances and bullets, could not protect her from her own decisions, or her own hand on the trigger.

After another eternity, she heard a voice. A signal.

"Spider to Winter, do you read? This is Spider. Please come in. I—I got out. Spider to Winter, do you read? My lifeboat—it got—" Zie didn't finish the sentence. "If you're out there—" Geum's voice sounded as though it was abraded down to bone. Like zie had been crying nonstop for hours.

Hwa Young opened the channel. Not even a supernova could have stopped her. "Geum? Geum!" She was sobbing in relief. "Tell me where you are. Guide me to you."

"Hwa Young," Geum said, still sounding awful. "I'm sending the coordinates by tight-beam—"

Yes. She saw it. A lifeboat, damaged. She had to hurry. Get to Geum at last.

"Bastard here." Ye Jun's voice was gentle. "We'll all go. We have your back."

Eun: "Easy for you to say. I'm the one who has to—"

"Hellion. *Not now.*"

It was easy at first, easy the way nothing had been since she turned coat. She flew toward Geum's lifeboat, giddy with joy.

She urged *Winter's Axiom* to greater speed. At first she found it difficult to care that she'd have to decelerate as she approached, match her velocity to facilitate the retrieval. *Efficiency* didn't matter, only getting to Geum as quickly as possible.

The ease with which they streaked through the aether woke in her a hysterical surge of delight. After all they'd endured, after what *she'd* endured, something would go right. She would keep her promise to Geum.

Unease pricked at her awareness, slowly at first. *Winter's Axiom* was being pulled off course, accelerating in ways that she hadn't directed it to, and *Hellion* and *Bastard* with it. She'd experienced this once before—

"Scorch it." Eun. "We were tricked."

"Yes." How could Ye Jun keep zir voice so calm? "I'm aware. That's *Paradox*'s telekinesis."

"It's not showing on scan," Eun hissed, "and I've never heard that—"

A starship blinked into existence before them. Hwa Young had never seen its like before: a gull-like yacht designed for both spaceflight and atmospheric flight, bristling with a terrifying number of gunports and missile racks. The Imperial design aesthetic, and yet the *stealth*—

The yacht's single docking bay opened to swallow them. *Paradox*'s telekinesis pulled the lifeboat in first, then the three lancers. Hwa Young could adjust her altitude so she didn't scrape up the deck upon landing, but any more control was denied her.

She was tempted to turtle up. Stay in the cockpit. Refuse to face what awaited them.

"Come on, Winter," Ye Jun said, still maintaining that terrible calm.

In a daze, Hwa Young exited the cockpit after Bae and Rose-Merline. Joined Ye Jun and Eun on the deck. Ye Jun's apparent equanimity was revealed as a cadaver's mask; Eun cursed in a steady monotone.

Two lancers already rested within: *Paradox* with its flashing blue and red, *Summer Thorn* venomous green and yellow.

The Empress awaited them, regal in a richly embroidered hanbok, flashing the radiant smile that everyone in New Joseon knew. Two lancer pilots flanked her. Hwa Young recognized *Paradox*'s Captain Ga Ram and *Summer Thorn*'s Mi Cha.

A woman with a truly unflattering haircut and drab clothes with the insignia of a lancer copilot stood diffidently next to Ga Ram and Mi Cha. It was to her that Ye Jun bowed. "Hello, Mother," zie said without warmth. "May I ask how you acquired stealth?"

"Oh, spoil my fun, why don't you," said the not-Empress in the extravagant hanbok.

The Empress arched an eyebrow at Ye Jun. *Now,* despite the haircut and unflattering garb, Hwa Young saw the resemblance. "The clanners aren't the only ones who dabble in industrial espionage," she said.

Then the lifeboat opened, and Geum emerged.

Hwa Young made a glad cry and started forward. Stopped and gagged as the stench hit her. *Where do I know that smell from—*

Geum raised zir head, impaling her with a bloodshot gaze. Geum's expression—that wasn't the welcome of a friend. *This isn't how it was supposed to go.*

Hwa Young sucked in her breath as she took in the details. She had last seen Geum in a technician's uniform, with faint grease stains, wrinkles, and splotches. She remembered Geum's smile and bright eyes, the way zie styled zir hair *just so.* How zie helped her look passable, even if glorious fashion was beyond her.

Geum no longer radiated sunshine and glitter. Zir cheeks were hollowed out, as though zie had embraced "more stressed than you" as an aesthetic. Zie was almost a head taller than Hwa Young now. She hadn't been prepared for that.

Whatever Geum had been wearing, uniform or otherwise, it was drenched in gore and impossible to identify. Zie stank of corpses. Of *someone's* corpse.

"Hello, Hwa Young," Geum said conversationally, with as much expression as a sheet of paper scraped raw. "Did you know I was the only one put in that lifeboat? A lot of good people didn't make it out. None of the other technicians made it out. But I did."

Geum didn't sound grateful to have survived.

"Geum, no," Hwa Young whispered.

"I didn't think you'd shoot the *Maehwa* while I might be on it," Geum added, "even with advance warning. You didn't message again to check that I'd gotten out. I'm lucky . . . lucky I was kept alive as bait. The Empress, at least, saw to my safety. There are benefits to being bait."

Hwa Young did not look to either side; no longer perceived anyone but Geum, in the purest tunnel vision she'd experienced in her life. An apt metaphor for the decisions, good and bad and abysmal, that had led her here.

"But you did it. You destroyed the *Maehwa*. I saw the lock-on and the bullet hitting and the engine going critical. *I know it was you.*"

"I had to . . . I . . ." Words ran dry. What was she going to tell Geum? That she'd had orders? Everyone knew how much she sucked at following orders. That she'd done this to prevent an attack on the crownworld—a world neither of them had ever visited?

"Hyo Su saved my life. You remember her? I suppose not. She died before the ship exploded, when shrapnel got through the shields. It cut her in half at the hips. She had no *legs*."

Hwa Young's throat closed in horror.

While Geum spoke, Ga Ram approached and locked a bracelet around Hwa Young's wrist, a restraint of some type. She didn't resist; was scarcely aware of her comrades being wrestled into submission.

Geum smiled viciously, the first emotion zie had displayed since exiting the lifeboat. "Together forever, Hwa Young. *Together forever.*"

SELECTED CHARACTERS

THE LANCER SQUAD

Bae. Callsign Glass; old callsign Farseer. Pilot of *Farseer*, the reconnaissance unit. (m)

Eun. Callsign Silence; old callsign Hellion. Pilot of *Hellion*, the artillery unit. (m)

Hwa Young (Hwajin). Callsign Axiom or Axe; old callsign Winter. Pilot of *Winter's Axiom*, the sniper. (f)

Ye Jun. Callsign Vagrant; old callsign Bastard. Pilot of *Bastard*, the command unit. A bastard child of New Joseon's Empress. (nb)

CLANNERS

Do as others do. Stay where others are. Unity is survival.

FALCON FLEET

ON THE FLAGSHIP *FALCON ACTUAL*:

Admiral **Mae**. (nb)

Commander **Aera,** Hwa Young's heart-mother and the admiral's second-in-command. (f)

Researcher **Zeng,** a cross-disciplinary scientist, and his heart-brother **Tora,** a soldier. (m)

Ensign **Rose-Merline,** cryptobotany, whatever the hell that means. (f)

THE EMPIRE OF NEW JOSEON

Trust the Empress. Move at her will. Act as her hands.

The **Empress** in her All-Wisdom. (f)

Captain of the Guard **Ga Ram.** Callsign Paradox. Pilot of *Paradox*, which has long-range telekinesis. The Empress's third-born, now her heir. (nb)

Lieutenant **Mi Cha.** Callsign Thorn. Pilot of *Summer Thorn*, which can temporarily disable computer systems. Common-born and salty about it. (f)

ELEVENTH FLEET

ON THE FLAGSHIP *MAEHWA:*

Admiral **Chin.** (f)

Chief. Everyone calls him Chief; that's it. (m)

Technician **An Geum,** known as Spider. Hwa Young's best friend. Zie has fabulous hacking skills and more fabulous nail polish. (nb)

Technician **Hyo Su,** one of Geum's friends. Maybe more than friend. (f)

ACKNOWLEDGMENTS

A black hole ate my homework!
—Arabelle Betzwieser, who demands to be credited ☺

Thanks to my editor, Hannah Hill, the folks at Delacorte Press, and my agent, Seth Fishman, for all their support, guidance, and patience.

Special thanks to Helen Keeble, Book Whisperer and Genius, for saving my giant robot bacon in the space of *ten minutes* by diagnosing a giant structural problem that I had been banging my head against for a month. Next time I will *ask earlier* and send appropriate bribes, delivered by special asshole goose courier!

Thanks to the following folks for cheerleading and assistance: Marie Brennan, Rachel Brown, China_shop, Chris Chinn, Pamela Dean, Dhampyresa, Eller, Stephanie Folse, David Gillon, Goss, Havocthecat, Isis, Zohar Jacobs, Ellen Million, niqaeli, Redsixwing, Ursula Whitcher, and Storme Winfield.

Thanks to my family for putting up with me during my giant robot struggles: Joseph Betzwieser, Arabelle Betzwieser, Yune Kyung Lee, and last but not least, my catten, Cloud, who helped *so much* by sitting between me and my keyboard for enforced writing breaks and, in time-honored catten tradition, chewing preferentially on my outlines/drafts.

Thanks to my husband (then boyfriend) for spoiling ALL OF BATTLETECH for me when we were dating in college. Hanse Davion! Aidan Pryde! Phelan Kell! Natasha Kerensky! Kai Allard-Liao! Katherine Steiner-Davion! The list could go on. I have spent the last couple decades on-and-off reading the tie-in books, occasionally playing the miniatures game, playing various iterations of the RPG, and (briefly) Mechwarrior: Living Legends as Maratai.

Husband-then-boyfriend may also have taken me to see anime for the first time. Having one's *very first exposure* to *Neon Genesis Evangelion* be the movies set directly after the TV series, without having seen the TV series, was sure a mind-altering event.

Thanks to my old friend Alex Winbow, who probably regrets his life choices, especially explaining the Schwarzschild radius, event horizon, and black hole physics in lay terms to me at lunch in middle school in Texas. Sorry not sorry. 😊

The "decay radiation" of black holes is known in our world as Hawking radiation, named after physicist Stephen Hawking. That said, the universe of the Lancers books runs on magic, not physics. If *you* are a gravitational astrophysicist (Hi, beloved Joe!), *I'm so sorry.*

If you would like to learn about some cutting-edge *real-world* gravitational physics, LIGO (Laser Interferometer Gravitational-Wave Observatory) has the deets (ligo.caltech.edu). Full disclosure: my husband works for LIGO as a staff scientist but is not responsible for anything to do with this book other than bringing me snacks while I was writing. ♡

ABOUT THE AUTHOR

YOON HA LEE is a Korean American who was born in Texas, went to high school in South Korea, and received a BA in mathematics from Cornell University. Yoon's previous books include the Hugo Award–nominated Machineries of Empire series and the *New York Times* bestseller *Dragon Pearl*. His hobbies are game design, composing, and destroying readers. He lives in Louisiana with his family and a flopsy catten and has not yet been eaten by gators.

YOONHALEE.COM